She woke with an involuntary scream. Wrapped in her last vision of the stunners firing ten thousand lightning bolts through her chest, she jerked awake but she couldn't force the scream out past her plastic gag. Slick walls of glass held endless banks of something slithering and grey. And the stench of unwholesome meat permeated the room.

Clamps and cables held her head but sliding her eyes to one side she could just make out Regenerator on another gurney. And Twiss was strapped down to her left. Wires led to probes sunk into his brain; a droplet of blood crusted one of the shaven patches on his skull.

It can't get any worse, she told herself.

But she knew it could. And it did.

ANNE GAY

Dancing on the Volcano

ORBIT

An *Orbit* Book

First published in Great Britain in 1993 by Orbit
This paperback edition published by Orbit in 1993

Copyright © Anne Gay 1993

A CIP catalogue record for this book
is available from the British Library

ISBN 1 85723 131 7

Printed in England by Clays Ltd, St Ives plc

Orbit
A Division of
Little, Brown and Company (UK) Limited
165 Great Dover Street
London SE1 4YA

CONTENTS

1 Black Ash 1
2 Ghost Waking 10
3 Life and Fear 22
4 Before the Sky 30
5 Dead End 39
6 Regenerator 48
7 Rebirth 58
8 Arms and the Randoms 70
9 Starwing 81
10 Harith 93
11 Naked Rain 105
12 Rainshadow 120
13 First Wave Attack 134
14 A Golden Rope 149
15 Blood of Harith 161
16 The Eye and the Storm 175
17 Living Knives 187
18 Point Counterpoint 203
19 Pre-emptive Strike 213
20 Tang Escapes 225
21 Axes and Acids 235
22 An X in the Desert 248
23 The Sea 260
24 Lal's Teacher 269
25 Sowing Teeth 278
26 Earth-Bites 289
27 The Weather-Man 298
28 A New Earth 309
29 A New Beginning 317
30 Underwheels 329
31 Beads and Bugs 343
32 Omega 351
33 The Electric Kiss of Death 361
34 Red Lal 376
35 Thought Pool Hollow 387
36 Fog-Fencing 403

To Johnny Hunter
the man with the lifeboat.

In friendship and with love.

1

BLACK ASH

The Watchtower

From the eyrie of the Watchtower high above the mass of Camelford Mountain, Irona watched the sleepers for mohocks and seditionists. She threw herself back in the seat, talking to the consoles.

'Nothing. There never is.'

Or hardly ever, not this late at night when the dawn was waiting just beneath the domesticated horizon. She yawned and tried not to look out of the windows of the Watchtower. Nothing happening in the Mountain.

Picking an outside Eye at random, Irona sent a control signal to it. She imagined the Eye, its globe sheened with will-o'-the-wisp moonlight, floating over the dark trees and ferns of the Park, but what she saw was only what the Eye picked up. Trees small as cauliflowers massing inky beneath her; a gibbet of rocks spiking up on the ridge against the opalescent sapphire of the Sky.

And beyond it a rose of fire blossomed in the croplands.

Irona screamed, slammed the alarms. The psychic indicators splurged their acid shock into the emptiness of the watchroom. An avalanche of sounds tumbled into the sharp-odoured air; it would have summoned help from the day-shift, but this was the last watch and Irona was alone on what should have been the quietest of shifts. And fear-ghosts jerked through their danse macabre to panic wardens into action.

But Irona didn't need all that. Whatever else she was, she was good at her job and everyone knew it. Already she was summoning the Arms from their subterranean base.

Irona jetted the Eye out over the rippling silver seas of wheat. It circled high above the ruby heart of the blaze, then

swooped down over the golden shooting thorns of flame.
The smoke made a smear of ugliness that rolled outwards
spreading its charcoal foliage over the pale threatened wheat.
Roaring, crackling, the fire-rose exulted in growth. Rising
like a phoenix, it rooted hunger and poverty in the death of
Camelford's food.

She sent the Eye plummetting. Its transmitted images
jagged into a plunging fall. Caught up in it, Irona felt herself
diving to her death but she forced her breathing to steady
and her moment of dizziness passed. The rush stayed. She
looked again at the screens. Her targets were in range.

The soot-smeared faces of the mohocks branded themselves on her brain. They yelled in shrill terror. And they
were only kids. (Some emotion twinged inside Irona but she
could not afford the time now to worry about what it was.
The loss of the wheat would be a disaster for Camelford; she
could not let it happen. She had work to do.)

Irona moved a finger. The console caught her signal and
translated it into action. At her command the Eye sent a
blue net of electricity lancing out at the vandals. Three of
them there were; they tried to run but there was nowhere
to hide from the shooting Eye and Irona's lightning forked
to noose them.

It jerked through their bodies. They fell thrashing to the
ground, then lay ominously still in the leaping firelight but
Irona knew they weren't dead – yet. Through the psychicator
she could still feel their unravelled neural circuits. They soon
would be dead, though, or as good as, with pain eating
through them, thorough and relentless as caterpillars. The
Synod dealt harshly with acts of anti-citizenship.

Now the monitors in the watchroom whined as the Arms
came rocketing above the curve of the hills. The Eye picked
up the three black sparks that raced across the smeary stars.
Irona saw them grow until they blotted out the moon, their
carapaces black and bulging with weapons. Not even Irona
knew how much of their body-armour was crysteel and how
much the result of gene manipulation. Someone up in Synod
knew, but it was knowledge denied to the wardens in the
Watchtower.

The speed of the Arms screamed the air apart around them; thunder clapped and the wheat flattened out under their path. Unstoppable, they bore down on the trio of youths.

Then, for an instant, Irona saw the Arms closer than she ever had before. Gilded by the flames, shadowed by the night, their faces showed beneath the crysteel visors. Inhuman implants – a third eye, nightmare tendrils that fingered the air for the hidden scents of fear – fleered between webs of tattoo. All three eyes wore coloured mascara.

And a lacquered maggot chewed in the cage of a cheek.

Then the Arms came to earth beside the small ink-blot silhouettes of the arsonists. Irona heard the thump of their landing, a sound as deep as an earthquake, and their jets smelled of sulphur.

One of the mohocks was half-conscious. He heard it too. There was a tear in his shaven scalp and a triangle of flesh flapped as he recoiled. He groaned and writhed backwards in fear, his body scything stalks of precious wheat, and the firelight polished his blood with the gleam of rubies.

But he couldn't escape. One Arm took two long strides, coming at him out of the wreathing smoke. She kicked him casually in the ribs. It sent him spinning through the air to crumple onto the soil.

He looks so young. Irona swallowed. *He should have stayed home in bed.*

A second Arm didn't even bother to watch. He knew the mohocks were no danger now. He picked up two of them and draped them over his shoulders.

The third Arm marched casually into the dancing saffron fire. The flames couldn't reach through her exoskeleton. They whirled outwards, trying to escape, but her boots trampled and her jets roared and the fire muted helplessly to dull red embers that died. Even the charred wheat was too cowed to hiss any more.

Igniting their jets, the Arms launched themselves into the peacock vault of the night. Dangling the mohocks casually by a wrist, an ankle, they soared upwards towards the hard cobalt dome that blurred Earth's stars. A victory roll a

thousand feet up in the air – Irona thought she heard a
ghastly scream as the Arms played catch with the vandals
– then the Arms were gone and the Eye turned its attention
to the ruined crop to make sure the fire would eat no more of
Camelford's supplies. Irona was sure she could smell smoke
even up in the Watchtower.

Now other Eyes, automatically called by the first, grouped
round to fly a search-pattern. In the Watchtower, the light-
and infra-red displays relayed only repetitive visions of the
damaged crops. It was only routine. There was no point in
searching for other mohocks. They would have seen what
had happened to the first three. Besides, almost nobody but
the tractor-talkers liked to walk around under the hard naked
Sky, least of all in the hectares of agoraphobia that was the
endless cropland where once villages had been.

But Irona's thoughts weren't on the boring tapestry of
wheat and char. She kept thinking of that poor, puny boy
with his scalp drooping and his red blood flowing down.
Irona didn't want to know his name. She wouldn't even look
at the data wriggling across the banks of displays: pictures
of the mohock and his friends, identity by body-mass, by
scent-signature, by oscillographs that matched their screams
to their prerecorded voice prints. Their history. Their emotional base. Their friends.

Their ex-friends, Irona thought sourly. *Why did they have
to do it?*

Even though she could no longer see the Arms, she knew
they were dragging their prey back to their underground lair.
Tomorrow – no, the day after – was the sabbath.

But on Moonday morning Irona knew the Synod would
find the mohocks guilty. Then kill their minds with screaming
worm-death.

A new thought: *And it's my fault.*

What if they find – her mind would not commit the betrayal
of saying the name – *him?*

The Warren

There was a man, and a good Cornishman at heart. The
trouble was, he was breaking Synod law and he hoped

no-one would know it. But the fear that hot-wired him wasn't just for himself. He wasn't yet twenty but he knew almost no-one else who was afraid. No-one else who failed to fit in. No-one else whom the Matriarch hadn't lulled in her sleepy embrace. The black-shelled Arms would never come for them.

But Twiss couldn't help it. He was caught between fire and flood. If only he could escape from the Admin, get beyond the reach of the Synod, to one of the new colony worlds say, he'd be all right. There'd be a point in living then. But Granfer was too old, and Twiss had failed the psychic index when he applied for one of the worlds he'd seen on a newscast. He was a prisoner in the Admin.

When the next night fell he stood at the open door of his grandfather's roomlet and looked into the dark.

'Good-night, Granfer,' he whispered to the drowsing old man. 'You'll be all right, I promise.'

It was a lie.

When the youth let himself out of the tiny apartment in the warren of Camelford Mountain, the old man opened his eyes. For days he had watched his grandson's pain growing and his own terror had grown alongside it, but they spoke of other things. Not of Twiss's frustration in the claustrophobia of his make-work job. Nor of boredom on boredom that ground bleakness into his soul. Never of a society that emasculated and defeminised and made an old fisherman redundant in his prime and never taught him the words to understand what he was feeling.

Twiss's pain was still there though: the anger and the frustration, hot as lava, waiting to burst out incandescent through the slightest little crack.

And Synod would know that Twiss was wrought with rage. If he didn't vent it soon, the watch would see the red of his ire and the Arms would come for him anyway. And for Granfer. Fear for the old man added a special kind of torment to Twiss's danger.

But Twiss was ready to explode. He needed a safety-valve. So tonight Granfer had played his part. He went early to bed in his windowless room, grousing about the aches in his old bones, and listened, lonely, as the door out into the row clicked shut.

'Take care of yourself, Twiss.' The old man's lips framed the words in the darkness but out of his dread of the omniscient Eyes he never made a sound.

The Watchtower

Irona had felt honoured at the call to Centre Shrine. She knew it was the highest cachet a simple warden like herself could achieve. She smiled with pleasure as she got up and turned off the contact-screen in her outside apartment. Saturnday was far advanced and though she had slept badly, the honour brushed away the cobwebs of her black dreams.

Irona bustled around. She didn't see how her dove-grey bodice accented her creamy skin and brought out the colour of her blue-green eyes, how the white of her cap made her hair a more striking blond. Her skirt swirled as she moved but she never noticed how its soft fall defined her rounded hips. The call and her eagerness to get ready had sponged out the stain of her pity for the mohocks.

She tried not to think of the secret sin she committed only in her heart. Nobody could know about that.

Knots of obedience flouncing down from the sash around her narrow waist, she stepped reverently towards Centre Shrine. It was no mass-inducing transmitter like those in the sleepers' levels below, blasting out a worthy message of citizenship to anyone who chanced by or who might choose to go and admire the gaudy symbols.

No, Centre Shrine was where the wardens themselves were allowed their closest access to Synod. It lay at the heart of the stone simplicity of the watchlevels, and it was a gem of perfect beauty. Maybe her parents knew she had been called. *Maybe*, ran a secret thought in the back of her mind, *maybe they're proud of me now*.

But maybe they didn't know. And maybe they just didn't give a damn.

Bowing her head, she went to meet her Matriarch. There was plenty of time before her next shift. A slim smile betrayed her pride as she entered the rose and gold harmony, while the perfumed warmth of the place wrapped her in a mother's love. Other matriarchs smiled serenely as she passed them. Attuned like any warden to subliminals, she felt none. Centre Shrine needed none. The truth was enough.

But when her Matriarch, Carandis, had let her settle on a sofa in a cosy parlour, Irona's happiness vanished.

Deep-bosomed and wide of jaw, Carandis may have been big-boned but she moved so gracefully that she seemed slim as Celtic queen. Her hair was brown; in the tactful lighting around her throne it gleamed with gold and auburn tints. The statuesque woman sank regally onto the seat and curled her hands over the armrests but she did not speak of love. For the first time Irona began to sense the personal power of the matriarchs. Carandis built up a silence that closed Irona inside a wall of apprehension.

'Irona Warden, in your heart of hearts you have sinned against Synod.'

Irona felt the strength ebb out of her muscles; her jaw relaxed, leaving her mouth stupidly agape. Fighting for self-control, she finally managed to say, 'N-no, Matriarch! I would never—'

From Carandis, on her tall seat that wasn't quite a throne, flowed out a glacial aura of disapprobation. Irona shivered as it shrouded her skin like a corpse in the Arctic. 'Don't lie to me, Irona, not here. Especially not here in Shrine.'

'But I haven't! I'm good at my job.'

'And don't,' Carandis dropped the words like glaciers falling into the sea, 'don't answer me back. Did you honestly think that Synod wouldn't know how the indices shrink when you are on watch? That no-one would see how few seditionists you tranquillise these days? You know fine well' – and the implication was that the Matriarch knew too – 'what it is you get up to when you should be watching over the sleepers below. Don't you care about them? About those poor benighted souls in your trust?'

Irona was bewildered. With the anger of innocence she said, 'Of – of course I do, Matriarch. How – I never let any sleepers get—' She couldn't go on. Because guilts she dared not name broke through her awareness like the bones of some badger slaughtered out in the Park.

Now the Matriarch allowed a hint of austere compassion to show for this misguided daughter of the watch. 'How have you failed in your duty? You must ask your conscience, Irona. This is not a dictatorship. You are not under my aegis alone.' Carandis closed her lips to trap further speech inside; her square-jawed face set sternly.

What is it she's not saying? Irona wondered, seeing the tiny play of the muscles in the irises of Carandis's eyes. Hard negative emotions pushed out from the Matriarch. Irona was not a warden for nothing but for a moment she doubted her empathic sense: *Jealousy, is it? Not of me, not when she's a matriarch, surely? Who, then? What is she frustrated about?*

Carandis's hesitation was so brief that Irona didn't have time to pin the thought down and the moment was lost. In a voice roughened by anger to such a slight degree that anyone not of warden status or above would never have noticed it, Carandis said, 'You are under the patronage of Matriarch Bernardina herself. You have the autonomy of free will. Use it.'

Her frosty blue eyes compelled Irona's gaze. (Irona thought of *him* and withered.) It was as if the Matriarch could read Irona's every shameful thought. 'Give me your hand, Irona.'

Irona stood and walked the two steps closer, feeling her knees shaking under her modest skirts. She held out her left hand, the hand of honesty that was closest to the heart, and Carandis's cool fingers brushed her skin. Yet in that gentle touch was a sudden sting that stabbed Irona and she inhaled sharply in pain.

Yet at once the sting was gone. There was just a tiny cold spot on the back of her hand, then that vanished too and she must have just imagined it.

'That's your punishment, Irona Warden, laid down personally' – Irona heard the saw of anger again and still didn't know why – 'by Matriarch Bernardina, the mother of us all, for you in her infinite wisdom. You will feel their hurt, their fear more sharply than they do. She says you must learn to care for them totally.'

How dare you! I've always cared!

But Carandis couldn't know what Irona thought or she would never have let her get away with such rebellion. She gave her an almost friendly squeeze, then signalled with her chin that Irona should sit down once more.

Irona obeyed, absently rubbing her hand.

The soft hyacinthine dome of the ceiling spread a glow from behind the Matriarch's carven chair. Rosy as dawn, it shed the light of forgiveness from Carandis over the twenty-year-old warden and it offered the unmistakable gift of a new day free of sin.

Tonight, Irona made herself the promise that she had made so often before, *I won't look for* him. *I won't even think about* him. *And if I do catch* him, *I'll call the Arms.*

2

GHOST WAKING

Camelford Park

Twiss felt the Sky above him. Even at night, with the tor spiking high above the hillside, the Sky was so close that it battered at his head with its hardness. It bleared the stars like a dirty window, swallowed the moon into a vague pearl as the sea-frets had once done – or at least that's what Granfer said. For Granfer still remembered riding storms that fought the cliffs of Port Isaac. Not now, though, because that was before they roofed the world in claustrophobic crysteel and a net of solid force. Now the only storms were cooked up as generators and his Granfer's trawler was a museum for puritanical tourists. And the hard Sky was shield and radiator for tired old Earth and the sea was a lap-dog for the Administration.

Twiss hated it.

The Park was silent around him: the one empty space in all this part of crowded Cornwall. Never mind the drowned wreck of Londover, the polluted ruins of the North. Here, outside the capital of the Admin, was peace. Twiss needed it, let it sink into his being as a darkling calm in his frayed nerves. For a few moments he could imagine there was freedom in the world, places where the wild was still wild. Nobody here in their strait-jackets of chastity and citizenship. Not a single bio-metal Eye hovered humming overhead with messages of death worming painfully through his brain. Synod knew where they all were but Twiss couldn't hear a single one. At least he could relax before—

A cough, harsh as a stag's, crept down the pre-dawn wind. For an instant Twiss ducked, thinking any sound was another Eye of the Admin or the vegetal spying of an Ear. A thrill of terror spiced the blood-paths of his mind – then he cursed silently. No time to think of Granfer now; Twiss pushed down the guilt he felt when he thought of the old man, scattered it from his fingertips that were cold with the rush of adrenalin despite the warmth of the furze-scented night. Fear made him come alive.

It would be all right. It would. Nothing would happen to the old man. No worms crawling through the tunnels of his ancient ears . . .

And Twiss thought no-one knew. No-one who counted, anyway. He thought no-one could see his emotions ripple across his sculpted face, charge the air with the hormones of his fear, his guilt. Synod was as hide-bound as the society it programmed. He thought no-one could trap him.

He coughed back, twice. Somewhere a real stag answered in challenge but Twiss didn't smell of musk and besides, the stag already had its summer harem. Soon Twiss could hear the small, counted herd tearing at the grass in the last hours before dawn.

Upwind an Ear that had nothing to do with flesh creaked as it pressed itself into the earth, but Twiss was far more worried about the all-but-silent Eyes. No way to detect them in the dark.

In a moment Sticker pushed through the bracken. His greasy hair was yellow in the moonlight. 'Got you this time, then,' he said, trying not to sound proud.

'No you didn't, then. Heard you bulling through they trees clear across the stream. You didn't need to cough. They could of heard you clear in the Sahara Communes.'

Sticker scratched his leg; his fingers rasped over the fabric of his muddy trousers. It was loud in the darkness and Twiss flinched. Synod had let it rain at sunset and moisture still clung shining on the knee-high fern. Fragments of moist earth pattered to the grass.

After a minute Sticker asked, 'How's the old boy?'

Twiss said gruffly, 'He be all right. You leave 'un out of it.'

A silence passed between them that they both tried to feel

was not awkward. Twiss tilted his head back and let the wind lift his dark hair. 'You ready?'

'What is it tonight then?'

'You'll see, boy. And don't make so much bloody noise this time.'

Twiss led off, angling down from the tor. Now it had started, the fear came back to him, his companion, his stimulation. It was the risk he needed to convince himself he hadn't died at birth. Nothing else in the compressed life of Camelford could do it. But he was sure he would beat them again, beat all of them that programmed the Ears and the Eyes. He'd done it often enough before. It would be all right.

All the same the breath came short in his lungs, dried in his throat, as he let it whisper in and out through his mouth. His heartbeat was as fast as the grasshoppers' rasp. He let his feet fall soft and slow so that the Ears set all around the park wouldn't sense the vibrations. He hoped.

It would be all right. It would.

He could still do this and make sure they didn't come for Granfer in the neat nine o'clock of morning.

The Watchtower

Irona didn't know what it was but she felt somehow different after her meeting with Carandis. Unloved. Unlovable. It was stronger after she left the embrace of Centre Shrine. She had had the feeling before, ever since she was a child, and worse after her parents were translated to Synod and left her behind. But usually she could cope with it. It must be that Carandis had let her feel the indifference of two million sleepers to her very existence. The dim corridors around her seemed very cold.

'Irona! Aren't you coming to the canteen before watch?'

She started. 'Oh, sorry, Jem. I didn't see you.'

Scylla linked her arm through Jem's, an immodesty they would never have dared to commit outside the stone impersonality of the Watchtower. It made Irona uncomfortable and she sought an excuse but couldn't find one. She dropped her head. 'Er, I'll give it a miss if you don't mind. I'll catch you later.'

The Warren

Irona slipped down below the Watchtower to the warren levels, making for a common shrine.

It was her favourite one. Only a couple of levels below the entrance to the Watchtower, it was in a little inside plaza between glass- and granite-fronted shops. In the artificial evening light, you could hardly see the stone roof that ceiled the plaza over. And it was quiet at this time of night, with cosy lamps glowing from the windows over the shops that had closed for the night. Homely cooking odours made her feel safe. There would be three or four other people – sleepers, yes, but that scarcely mattered in the shrine's atmosphere – with whom she could share the experience. It always made her feel good.

A man and a woman already knelt before the shrine. Kind, sonsy, dressed like good citizens in sombre blues and greys, they had brought a baby and a teenage daughter with them. The girl had a rapt look on her face.

Irona smiled for the first time that evening and sank to her knees within the aura. The shrine went on glowing, its form and colours designed to provoke subconscious responses in the human mind. There was the blue of purity spreading over her like a sheltering Sky, the warmth of kindness, the fresh green leaves of the cycle of life. And reaching inside her were subharmonics while a gentle music inspired her again to work even harder for the common good.

But the communion with other people didn't work tonight. Long before the shrine's cycle had finished the girl lost her raptness and the baby started crying. Never mind the warm woodland scents and the burble of a forest stream; tonight it was remote. It didn't touch anybody and Irona couldn't help wondering why. The petulance on the man's face was enough to curdle his wife's good humour. Instead of staying, they left.

Irona hoped that the shrine was a little out of order. Because if it wasn't, then it was something in her.

The Watchtower

In the marble and limestone pinnacle of Camelford Mountain, Irona signed on at midnight. The previous warden hadn't heard her come in to the Ear and Eye room. The first she knew of it was when Irona's breast brushed over Ellen's shoulder as Irona reached across to key in to the system. The accidental touch startled them both. Physical contact between family, that was strange enough. Between colleagues, it was unknown. It was anti-Admin.

Ellen covered her surprise with an elaborate yawn and scratched under her crumpled cap. Her heavy perfume grazed Irona's nostrils. Ellen slanted a sardonic glance upwards at the younger girl. 'You're early, Ro. On your own again or feeling keen tonight?'

Still vibrating with the shame of that touch – *Why did it have to be that harlot Ellen?* – Irona felt herself blush. 'Oh, keen, of course, what do you think?' She was aware of the mockery in Ellen's blowsy face; Irona heard herself babbling to cover the nakedness of her soul, felt herself running the knots-of-obedience on her belt through her fingers. 'Action-packed, that's what it's going to be. Just for a change. Four hundred sleepers suddenly changing into axe-murderers. That'd move the Mountain, wouldn't it?' Irona didn't want to talk about being on her own. 'What does the system say?'

'Nothing much. Tension-levels about average for late spring. A few isolated pockets of stress sprinkled about, mainly because of the air-conditioning having itself a bit of a thrombo, but there're plenty of teams on it. And Mairi gave some junk-heads in C-12 a quick blast of calmant around nineteen hundred hours but the Arms picked them up with no trouble. She was probably just being alarmist. Still, it kept her occupied for a bit. We haven't found any mohocks tonight yet. Nothing to bring us fame. Not like last night, hey? What's it like being the talk of the watch?'

Even as Ellen's unorthodox speech grated on her sensibilities, Irona cringed inside. She hadn't even contemplated the chance of jealousy.

But Ellen obviously was. Maybe she'd heard about Irona's call to Centre Shrine.

At least she doesn't know what Matriarch Carandis said to me. I hope.

It was almost a relief when Ellen started her usual game. Only tonight – *Is it something I've done?* – it was worse.

Sliding a glance full of mockery at Irona, Ellen accidentally-on-purpose trod on the hem of the girl's bloused-over shift. As Ellen had known it would, it pulled the sepia fabric loose from her knotted belt.

Irona gasped and quickly tugged her shift back into place so that it hid the gentle curves of her figure.

'Oh, so sorry,' said Ellen, but her face was lit by a lewd mischief. 'I didn't mean to betray you into immodesty. Especially not here in Admin. We keep that sort of behaviour for private times, don't we? It's much more fun that way.'

Irona stammered, 'I don't do that sort of thing anywhere.'

'Oh, but you should. Just think what you're missing out on! You're as bad as the sleepers, Ro. But I'm surprised that you'd fall for the sort of pap we feed them. Why, only last night I went to this party in the Upper Levels. Just a small party, you understand.' Ellen giggled in a parody of maidenly innocence that sat badly on the wrinkles of debauchery around her eyes. 'Actually, there was just me and some men.'

Two of them there'd been, by the sound of it, two at once, but Irona tried not to listen. She couldn't believe Ellen's graphic descriptions; she suspected that Ellen made it all up anyway. Surely nobody could really make themselves do that?

I wish I'd reported her, Irona thought, flushed with hot embarrassment. It wasn't the first time she'd wished it but when she had first been raised to warden-status, she had been too humble to report Ellen for her subtle immodesty. Since then, however, Ellen had pushed the game well beyond a joke but it was too late to say anything about it because for a year Irona had been her guilty accomplice by allowing Ellen to say such disgusting things in the first place. Somehow, though, she felt it much more keenly tonight.

In the meantime Irona pushed aside Ellen's clutter and perched on the panelling of the console, trying to concentrate on running the usual equipment checks, but the Admin planned well and built well – for itself. Hardly anything ever went wrong. Anything mechanical, that is.

One thing Irona didn't do, though, was scan the Park, not while anybody else was there.

She scanned the corridors of the warren, yes. The computer accounted for the body-heat of sleepers and wardens in the warren of Camelford Mountain – but it never scanned the Synod. They stayed inviolate in their perfection.

Due to a tiny glitch that Irona had slipped into the system under her signature, a few digits here or there didn't register. Nobody knew about it, not even Roger Watchwarden; it was her own programmed malfunction. That way they could never catch *him* – or at least, not on her watch. She didn't like having it in her name but the alternative was even worse – and Irona was gambling that there'd never be a mass waking in Camelford anyway. But the risk was worth it – for *him*. So she never scanned the Park when there was another officer in the command room, especially brass-blonde Ellen.

Ellen finally stood, yawning, raking at the pudge of her stomach with her long nails. 'You haven't been listening to a thing I say.'

Irona shrugged and slipped into the command seat. After Ellen had been sitting there it was always uncomfortable. 'Why would I, Ellen? Half of it seems like dreck and the other half is about as credible as a natural hailstorm, but if it keeps you amused . . .' She shrugged again, pretending she didn't care.

'Much you know.' Ellen picked up her scatter of things from the console and smiled nastily. 'We're going to watch a holo of it tonight. Why don't you bring a manfriend along? Oh, I forgot. You don't have one any more, do you?' Ellen drifted out of the E & E room, swaying her hips. Even their gyrations seemed a mockery to Irona.

A holo-disk winked abandoned on the console but Irona

didn't call Ellen back for it. *Serve her right*. But Irona was ashamed of her uncitizenlike thoughts.

What's on it? Surely she wouldn't have left that party one lying around, would she?

Curiosity? Self-preservation in the face of such naked hostility? Whatever it was, Irona resisted her conscience for barely a minute. Then she slipped the disk into the player – for about ten seconds. That was all her embarrassment would allow her. Ellen, her pale flab quivering, cavorting naked with two men that Irona tried not to recognise—

Sickened, Irona ejected the disk and slid it out of sight, breathing deeply to settle her stomach and calm her mind.

When the command room was empty even of Ellen's perfume, Irona dimmed the lights as much as she dared. It was stupid, she knew. All the same, it was somehow easier being furtive in the dark, when thick shadows hid the banks of empty consoles.

And she needed the darkness if she was going to scan the Park. Because she didn't know what she was going to find there. Who. And if her dread did have a cause for once, if she did find *him*, Irona herself would have to become the axe-murderer. The one who ordered the worm put in Twiss's brain.

Four hours 'til dawn. Fearfully, to get it over with, she called the floating microphone over to her. Whispered the code for the wood by the river, afraid that he would be there – or that, worse, he wouldn't, and she'd have the dread of searching and searching for him, hoping he wouldn't be out running risks tonight.

Irona swallowed, closed her eyes, feeling the strain building up around her lungs, squeezing her neck until the dull throb of a headache settled its weight inside her. Her eyes were hot and aching.

Let him not be there. Let him not even be out tonight. She took a deep breath to control her anxiety – and her longing. And the longing was how she knew she wouldn't find him tonight. If she wanted him – and she did, always – he'd be invisible in his apartment where she wouldn't follow him, not out where she could watch.

He won't be.
She hoped.

Irona didn't focus on her reflection – pale skin, soft blonde-brown curls on her forehead, round chin. Instead she scanned the screen from Eye to Eye down the corridors of the warren, seeing late revellers shushing each other in stealthy laughing groups. Secret tensions trembled just past the corners of vision. She jumped the sensors from Ear to Ear, listening to nightmares and whispers of half-baked sedition that made her feel bad enough. On the grid-map display sparks of anger-red and the magenta of depression flared and faded with their hormones; the psychic indicator was programmed to reflect disturbances into the watch-warden's mind and keep her alert. It did nothing for her equanimity.

Once a strange shrieking laughter made her jump. It echoed down a long row of semi-derelict houses in a lower level where mohocks flitted from shadow to shadow, their shaven skulls bouncing back the tired yellow of the lamps in the rows. But there were no victims out tonight. The Mountain was restless – and afraid.

She should have reported them. In the past she would have, but she couldn't do it now. Not after seeing those poor kids torn like rag dolls by the Arms. Responsibility knotted her throat into tensions that seemed like they were strangling her.

Carandis was right. I don't report many any more.
What if she gets the Arms to come for me?
Would my parents even know?

If she'd been Ellen, who always formed the seat of the command chair into a sort of phallus, she would have tuned in to the couples making love, a sort of legalised voyeuse. Irona was wise enough now to know that most of the watch did, out of a contempt for the citizens they called sleepers. There were even rumours of blackmail, but that couldn't be true. Not in the Administration, even though Mikel ran a black-market trade in pornography from the E & E room – or so they said.

But not Irona. Irona couldn't do that. Not now she'd

discovered Twiss. His wavy brown hair, the humour in his hazel eyes, the way the column of his throat pushed up from the neck of his shirt, the mischief in his laughter. He, a sleeper, had woken her up from her sexless, impersonal duty. It was better to marry than to burn – but Twiss didn't even know Irona and her shameful thoughts incandesced with the brimstone reek of hell. *A warden and a sleeper? Blasphemy.* Especially now the Matriarch Carandis had seen into her soul. So to see couples – not just sleepers, but real flesh and blood people – writhing as they strove for ecstasy, or merely to watch as they slept entwined when she had to sleep alone, was torture for her. Her hatred of Camelford was renewed, as so often now on watch. It stretched the skin tight on her face, burnt it dry and feverish. *Why did I have to wake up? Why can't I be like them any more?*

But it was her duty to spy. To be forever reminded of her sin.

Irona rumpled her fingers through the piled-up hair under her cap and stood the strain as long as she could, the strain of prying into sleepers' private lives. Then she forced herself to stand it a little longer, just a little more, watching the neutered cats stalking through an empty market-place in their hunt for tagged mice.

At last, though, she gave in to the frustration marching its phalanxes through her head. Twiss was an itch inside her skull where she couldn't scratch it. A legion of thoughts broke formation behind him, trampling the ordered surface of her life.

He was the only person in all Camelford who was even half-way awake really. *I'm certainly not*, she thought. *I might be a watcher but I'm just as much of a zero as any sleeper. He doesn't let them file him away into some tidy box, program him to duty and the empty pleasures of virtue.* Her thoughts became visual. She saw his youth, instinct with strength that was more than physical. And though he wasn't conventionally good-looking, when he smiled that wide smile of delight he encompassed her longing to wake from the prisoning sleep of her duties, to feel the same flooding joy.

Irona couldn't stop herself giving the command that screened the Park.

The Park

The night was alive with images of pain. Irona saw them, heard them, felt them. Tiny insects, frantic with life, beating their wings ragged as they failed to escape destiny. Worms slicking down the hedgehog's throat. A fieldmouse cowering in a crack beneath a tree-root, safe but dying of the fear exploding its fluttering heart.

Entropy rules, k.o., she told herself. The mouse would feed the oak, the hedgehog's dung would make the grass fill out into wild wheat to nurture the daughters and sons of the mouse. The world turned. *Life goes on.*

And the Ears hidden in the long grass shrilled to the footfalls of Twiss.

I've found him! Then: *Oh Synod! (Blasphemy!) I've found him. What have I done?*

The stallion flung up his moon-silvered head.

Twiss froze. Sticker, though, was caught on one foot. He overbalanced, one arm brushing a gorse-bush, and the crackle of dry branches set the stallion to flight. Even as Sticker wrenched free of the thorns in a mooncloud of pollen Twiss burst into a run.

All fear was gone. The night filled him. He stretched out his arms and the wind ran at him, cool as a river, strong as the pumping of his legs. It seemed to lift him so that every stride was an ecstasy of flight. It stung his eyes so that the mock stars sharpened in his tears. The primal joy of hunting stretched his senses to infinity. He was doing what he had been made to do. Sticker was far behind.

The stallion dodged an overhanging branch at the eaves of the wood and, as he jinked to one side, Twiss's outflung hand brushed the silken flank. It was a moment of life so pure that there was no thought, nothing but a night, solid with sensation that filled him to the brim and overflowed. There was no beginning and no end to Twiss and he leaped for the horse's mane. In that minute he believed he could do anything.

(In the watchroom joy swelled in Irona. Duty was forgotten; pleasure wiped it out. From the psychicator flowed the sap-green scent of his delight to swallow her, lift her to fresh crests of delicious sybarism.

It wasn't a physical habit but the long custom of her mental yearning that stretched out her hand to key another of her little modifications: a program that linked Twiss's emotions to her own. Copies of his hormones filled her with the contagion of his happiness. His boundless exhilaration burned in her, bright and eternal as a star. Rich juices ravished her senses, entranced her body, as her mind's limits burst with the orange tang of exaltation. Deep pangs of rapture thrilled through her loins, caught sensually at her breath. She hung for an eternity impaled on his enchantment. In that moment she could have lived forever, held more closely than she could ever have been in the shelter of his arms.)

It was a surprise when the stallion bunched his legs and jumped, bowling Twiss aside to leave him lying in the trampled grass beneath the trees.

Sticker came panting up. 'What are you doing, you idiot?' he hissed, and Twiss laughed, the sound loud as a beacon in the darkness.

'Ssh! You'll get us worm-wiped.'

Twiss sat and leaned his elbows on his knees. His teeth gleamed in a smile of memory. 'Don't think so, boy. If I can almost catch a stallion I don't think they can catch me.' He inhaled. 'I can still smell 'un. Big old feller, weren't he?'

Irona leaned back against the contour-seat, grinning with remembered ecstasy. *If I could just get him to the colony on Harith, we'd both be free of the Synod. And we could have that joy between us . . .*

Unknowing, Sticker grumbled on about hunting rabbit-meat which didn't have nothing to do with no dumb old horses.

And the touching of the horse triggered the alarm.

3

LIFE AND FEAR

The Watchtower

Warning tones cascaded through the watchroom, pungent as a rainbow of acids. A thousand lights glared ugly on the shadowed air, ineradicable smears of anxiety beading the walkway to the command seat. Blood-soaked nightmares spasmed against the normality of the desks, their outlines half-seen, wholly felt. Visceral purple and death-ochre, the livid terror-shapes tugged subliminally at Irona, unleashing nameless atavistic fears.

They broke her half-horrified admiration of Twiss. For an aeon of shock Irona couldn't move. Then her resurrected hands skimmed to the master-switches to cut that hideous shrill but it was too late. Though she hadn't cued it, the automatic alarm was already recorded. In the morning everyone would know.

What went wrong? What can I do?

Full of jangling panic, Irona shadow-palmed the switch that said malfunction.

Stillness broke heavy over her. It echoed against her eardrums, clubbing her with its abrupt fracture of her bliss, but the path of bruise-lights across the darkness didn't fade and the fetid green stenches of putrefaction still slurred their angular dirge. The psychic and visual alarms were doing what they were supposed to do. Irona was trembling, sweat-skinned.

Then footsteps grazed the silence and Ellen's voice said, 'What's up? Why haven't you called the Arms? That's an A.S.A. going on there, you deve!'

Startled, Irona swivelled the chair. The nightglow cacophany had drowned Ellen's entrance. Absurd guilts whirlpooled inside Irona.

'Ell! What are you doing here?' she babbled. 'I thought you'd gone.'

Ellen perched on the console, her ample buttocks spreading sideways. Slime-green lights limned her chins, outlined with cruelty one side of a smile. 'So it would seem. Good job I came back for my holo-disk, wasn't it? Otherwise you might have had to handle a waking on your own. We wouldn't want the Matriarch's pet to make any mistakes now, would we?'

From the corridor a drunken voice stammered, 'Can't you find it? Synod, Ellen, I don't want that lying ar—'

The silhouette of a man poked round the doorway; his shirt bagged open to the waist. Roger, the chief of watch. Irona could have died.

He stopped his blasphemy in mid-word when he saw the alarm-lights' flare. From the infra-red picture on the scan-screen Twiss's pleasure still glowed while Sticker chuntered his complaints.

Irona sank her head to rest on her hand. The skin of her forehead seemed to scald her chilly fingers. It was as if she had been interrupted in the middle of making love; her body didn't know how to respond. She was glad the semi-dark camouflaged her flush. Her thoughts were tumbling.

Roger sobered. He all but ran through the aching lights; they swept up and over his jouncing belly, cloud shadows on a mountain. Panic suffused his face. His anxiety summoned a floating microphone.

Before he could start the call to Arms, Irona said, 'Don't do that, Roger. I've got the disk.'

It took a second for the message to get through to him, then he batted away the microphone. Inertial power dragged his anger from the orb; it drifted through violet light like smoke.

'And?' Roger husked out the word.

'And I need time to think.'

Behind her, Ellen was rootling desperately through the clutter she'd left on the console.

'You won't find it, Ellen,' Irona said. Her voice wavered through a scale of uncertainty. 'D'you think I'd leave that loose? A porn epic starring the chief of watch? That would be irresponsible, wouldn't it?'

Ellen's frustration sent a nest of plastic cups and straws flying into strands of corpse-light. The microphone, confused, bobbed this way and that.

Angrily Ellen ordered daylight that bludgeoned Irona's hot eyes. At least the alarm-visions faded into paler spectres though their ghostly lines went on quivering along her nerves.

'Don't worry, Roger,' Ellen said in viperous tones. 'I'll get the bloody thing off her. She won't run any risks for some stupid sleeper. Especially now she's famous. Will you, Ro dear?' Suddenly Ellen's hands clawed into talons that sank into Irona's throat.

Orange fire flared around black suns in Irona's vision. Irona arched instinctively, her fingers digging for the nerve-spot between Ellen's knuckles. Her heel jabbed for Ellen's midriff; Ellen shoved it aside with a bony elbow. The command chair hissed pneumatically, trying to shape-shift to their writhing weight.

Roger said savagely, 'Stop that, Ellen. It's stupid. Violence is the resort of the incompetent.' (He didn't say that a recording of the Watchtower in a potential waking would be sent to the Synod after the sabbath but Irona knew it would. She prayed he wouldn't think of it yet.) Caught mindless in his guilt, Roger went on, 'We've got to reason with her.'

Ellen's hands uncurled spastically, leaving a lingering scratch under Irona's jaw. Blood seeped into the runnel of flesh. Irona felt pain thunder hot as summer lightning through the congestion in her head.

Roger forced reason into his voice. It was unaccustomed, dry and sickly as stale honey. Irona found it as nauseating as the lights that strobed on the darkling air. 'Irona-love, what's the problem? Why are you risking a mass waking like this? D'you want a promotion, or what?'

Irona could have laughed. She was so surprised she couldn't speak.

'I'll tell you what it is,' said Ellen. 'She's jealous. Skinny little goody-two-shoes here, she wants to blackmail her way in. I bet you that's what she's after. She thinks she's somebody now she's seen the Matriarch, she thinks she stands a chance, but none of the guys here would give her the time of day. She's watched the disk and now she's on heat. She wants us to pimp for her.'

Hatred polished Irona's eyes night-black. 'I wouldn't have any of you in a lucky-bag. Synod, Ellen, you think that because you want to screw your brains out so does everybody else.' The lewd violence of Irona's own words shocked her.

Over the aisle between the desks the alarm-lights, tired of being ignored, flickered manically, still pumping their decomposed glare at a frequency designed to induce panic. Acting at bio-harmonic speed they worked directly on the central nervous system; they would stop only when the call to Arms was activated.

Unless . . .

Roger was shouting now, twitching. 'Tell me what you want, you stupid cow! Just let me put the call out before the alarms drive us all insane then we'll talk about it. All right? All right?'

Irona gripped the arms of the command chair to stop herself giving in to the compulsion of the lights. Through tetanus-stiff jaws she uttered a strangled 'No'.

'Look, Ro,' yelled Roger, his voice tight as a noose with anxiety, 'just tell us, OK? There's a sleeper waking up and all you can do is waste time! Haven't you seen the riot-cubes? Don't you ever watch the newscasts? We could have a mass waking on our hands, two million sleepers waking up to the fact that they could kill us before breakfast.'

Roger grasped her hands, pleading. He stared at her, his face less than a handspan from hers; there was no room in him for any other emotion but the sheer panic in his eyes that tried to pierce Irona's denial. 'For Synod's sake, Irona, let me call the Arms! Please. Before he wakes the whole of Camelford! Because if we don't stop him we're all going to die.'

'Give me a day!' she pleaded. Retinal afterfires still burnt panic into Irona's bodyrhythms but she fought off the heat-waves sweeping out along her blood. 'You're watchwarden, aren't you, Roger? You can say it was just a mis-scan. He's only a boy after all.'

Roger ran a hand over his bald spot. Nerve-pulses twitched his fingers; a tic scrambled the lines around one side of his mouth. He pulled his shirt together in an attempt to re-establish order. 'How do you know what he might do? Today, frightening protected species in the Park. Tomorrow, hurting little boys? Maiming old ladies? He could start a wave of violence that'll rip Camelford wide open. Come on, Ro. We can't risk everyone's life for some deviant.'

'He wouldn't hurt a fly.'

'How do you know?'

And Irona couldn't tell him. *I could never admit I've been watching Twiss for almost a year. He'd never understand the beauty of Twiss's joy in a simple, pure act like touching a stallion. How can I let something like Roger trample that moment underfoot?* So all she did was stare back at her boss with a coolness she didn't feel.

His pale eyes sought help from Ellen who said, 'Don't look at me, Rog. I'm not watchwarden. It's nothing to do with me.'

'But it is, you stupid deve!'

(Irona dared not risk a verbal order; she surreptitiously passed the heat of her hand over the message-recorder. It began disking the room as she rolled her chair out of its line of vision.) Roger went on, 'If you hadn't suckered me into your filthy immorality I wouldn't be in this mess now.'

Rage drove Ellen to her feet, her face drawn into battle-lines. 'Who're you calling a deve? Whose flat is it in that disk? It sure as Synod isn't mine. I can't pull enough strings to blank the scanners in my place.'

Roger blanched. 'Who said the scanners are blanked in my apartment?'

Ellen clicked her tongue scornfully. 'Of course they are, you hypocrite! If they weren't you'd never have had us back there. That is the word, isn't it? Had us?'

'But you started it, Ell!. You and Mikel.'

(The emotion-scanners in the watchroom showed the solid reds of anger. Irona smiled thinly. She knew it was all going down on the disk. Roger Watchwarden was digging a grave for himself. *Maybe Twiss and I'll be safe after all . . .* It was the first time she had really linked herself with Twiss in her mind.

Ellen glared back at the warden's rancour-twisted face. 'So how come you didn't report us to the Synod, Rog? You're in more trouble than I am, sunshine, and if I go down I'll take you with me. See how you like the worms marching through your head.'

Roger shouted back, 'It's her, isn't it? That Irona.' (Casually, disguised in the pantomime of a shrug, Irona shadow-palmed the recorder's pause. She wanted nothing about herself on any recordings.) 'She's doing this to us and you're giving her more ammunition by the minute. Shut up, can't you, and let me think.'

Indignant, Ellen yelled, 'Me giving her ammunition! I like that!' But she did dam her poisonous tongue though her bitterness engorged her. Irona activated the disker once again – and as quickly blanked it when Roger said, 'All right, Irona. Tell me what you want.'

'I want you to edit tonight's scan so it doesn't show that boy.'

'How can I? He's a waker. For all you've broadcast that it was a glitch, that alarm's going to be in every automatic known to man. And even if I could chop the watch-scan, there's no way I could get at all the back-up systems. By the sabbath everyone in Synod will know anyway. And by Moonday they'll have you. And him.'

Irona knew she had lost but she was determined to go down fighting. She glared at Roger. 'Then you've got two days, haven't you? And I'm only asking for one. After that you can have your holo-disk.' Irona saw the folds around his eyes tighten in a crafty smile. 'Mind,' she added, 'there might be the odd back-up copy around, just to be on the safe side. I have to make sure that my immunity lasts as well.'

It was too much for Ellen. With one hand looping into Irona's hair and the other curved choking into her throat, the bulky woman dragged her from the seat. Roger made feeble flapping motions but he wanted Ellen to find the disk too and his gesture was a half-hearted token.

Irona hated Ellen's fat fingers groping her but the stupid

deve outreached and outpowered her. Irona was left with the cutting edge of logic. 'You'll never find it, Ell,' she croaked. 'You think I'm stupid enough to let you?'

Ellen shoved her sideways with such force that Irona cannoned into the command-chair. The primeval fear of falling spasmed through Irona's intestines as the chair canted dangerously but her drop carried her past it and the chair righted itself, the response-padding sucking resentfully back into its normal mode. And inside its gelatinous back-padding the blackmail disk stayed safe.

Her head ringing from the impact, Irona pushed herself up on one arm. 'Made you feel better, that, did it, Ellen? You want to think about the consequences of your actions.'

'Ha! You're a fine one to be saying that. Anybody would think you were trying to waken the sleepers. Heroine of the revolution, is that it? Down with the Admin and you to chair a new Synod?'

Irona talked across the river of Ellen's insults. 'I want you to delay passing on that scan to Matriarch Carandis for at least twenty-four hours. And I want you to sign off my watch all clear.'

Roger's voice rose to the pitch of despair. 'You can't have twenty-four hours. Just 'til watchwarden Allis takes over. You know that's all I can give you!'

Irona pulled herself painfully to her feet. 'Then I'll take that.' Under cover of her aching slump over the console, Irona extracted the new disk from the message-recorder's log and slid it into her decorous full sleeve. 'And don't mess it up, Rog, or we'll all be worm-food. All of us, hear me? I'm going to count my bruises.' She palmed the other disk. 'And Ellen, you'd better count them too before I go, because each one has your name on it. So have a little think about that.'

Then, with as much dignity as she could muster, Irona limped out through the ghost-lights of panic.

Below the highest room in the Watchtower, a junior matriarch fluffed nervously at her hair, polished one shoe on her opposite leg. Then, as silently as she could, she went up the steps and irised the trapdoor.

'This is an emergency,' she whispered to give herself confidence. 'Carandis told me to.' And the junior wondered why Carandis's anger had seemed to hold an edge of malicious glee. After all, the sinning warden was supposed to be one of Carandis's supervisees, wasn't she? The junior couldn't understand why she hadn't felt guilt in the Matriarch and wondered if her senses were inadequate to the job.

The petals of the trapdoor above her fanned aside and a strange, old-fashioned perfume drifted down. It only emphasised how out-of-place the junior felt in this rarified place. She was scared to intrude . . .

Her head came level with the floor. There was no-one there.

Her lips formed the words, 'This is ridiculous! I know she came up here. I saw her!'

Her gaze travelled across the smooth, blood-heat floor with its islands of priceless rugs. Eyes widening in astonishment at the windows open all around the circular room, she saw the Sky, hard and blue, closer than she had ever seen it before. Something circled outside; it was called a bird, wasn't it? A bee buzzed by a vase of pink scented flowers. There were shelves of old-fashioned books, antique cushions that didn't change contour.

Yet there was no sign of an occupant.

Unless . . .

The junior matriarch went closer to the only piece of furniture in the room. It wasn't a desk after all. It was a nutrient flotation chamber, and its dark-pannelled top was closed. A tiny green light winked to show it was being used.

She hesitated, peripherally aware that somehow Carandis was using her to hurt—

'No,' the junior told herself quietly. 'Carandis wouldn't do that.'

All the same she had to summon all her courage to press the contact-key, once.

4

BEFORE THE SKY

Camelford Park

'You sure they old Eyes ain't seen us?'

'Shut up, Sticker,' Twiss whispered.

It was good to bring down a rabbit with a stone on the dawn-dewed grass. Twiss felt the balance of strength and control in his arm, the smooth weight of the stone, the perfection of his swing. In his lungs the steadying breath tasted sweet as grass and he savoured it with one part of his mind, his senses heightened with the thrill of danger. He hurled the rock at exactly the right instant.

The rock curved dark against the paleness of the Sky then pale against the grey-green velvet of the grass. Twiss both watched it and became the moment. His breath still pent kept the missile on course; he only let it go to wince – and to whisper a repressed 'Yes!' of triumph – when the soft fawn-furred doe crumpled, the useless warning of her scut buried in the turf. The other rabbits scampered pointlessly to their burrows.

But now the real risk began. The myoelectronic transmitter inside the rabbit's jugular would gradually stop pulsing when the electricity of life faded: the watch would send Ears and Eyes to investigate.

Twiss smiled.

Sticker shambled hastily to the body and cut the tag out of her limp neck. Tearing at the clean fur with his knife until it was a bloody rag, he left the little metal stud in a piece of fox-dung where it too began to die.

Meantime Twiss carved the loins from their silvery membrane and stuffed the haunches into the lining of his coat. It was little enough to share between Granfer and Sticker but it was also a bright score against the Admin. From practice, it took only seconds. Still Twiss grinned. A heady vitality thrilled through him.

Then, watching for the Eye, both men raced silently for the sheltering anonymity of Camelford. One behind the other, to mix their dark trails against the pearled grass, they hurled themselves beneath the June-bright canopy of the trees. Twiss inhaled the sharpness of bracken fronds uncoiling tapestries of jade around his knees.

Hilarity bubbled under the skin of his face and he knew Sticker felt the same, but they hid it from one another in practice. Soon enough they came to E4, Simmery's Gate, where the dappled entrance to the Mountain stood in the sun's long shadows.

Twiss breathed in the last light of the dawning and scooped Sticker's cap from under a rowan. Then he reached his own hat down from the crotch of the tree and brushed the grey bark from its nap. Using each other as mirrors they combed and tidied themselves into the picture of modest citizens. Wide-legged striped trousers, sombre coats of brown and dull blue, though their wide collars were no longer as snowy as they had been. (Twiss wondered what snow was really like.) They even used twigs to scrape the clotting mud from their square-toed boots. Sticker walked quickly into the corridor's mouth.

'See you then,' whispered Twiss, pulling down a cluster of hard green rowanberries and idly tossing them at the wind.

'Ain't you coming in with me?'

'Nah, boy. You go on ahead.'

Made nervous by the discovering sun, Sticker shrugged a goodbye and went inside. Twiss stood watching him go, reluctant to leave behind the illicit joy of the night, but the shops in the lower terraces were beginning to rip the sounds of citizen music into his waking dream and Twiss felt the glow fading from his face. A modest housewife came out to flap washing on her terrace while her baby grizzled and she croaked a nursery-rhyme to it:

'Bye, baby-bunting,
Daddy's gone a-hunting

To get a baby rabbit-skin
To wrap my baby bunting in.

But Twiss doubted the child would ever know the softness of rabbit-fur and it made him grieve for the gentle life he had taken. Even the nostalgia, though, was a link with his night running and he tried to shadow the dull normality of Camelford over his face.

With the pretence of conformity came Twiss's habit of worrying about his Granfer. He threw the bunch of berries aside, missing their hardness in his fingers. Straight-faced, he ducked into Simmery's Gate, though its roof arched high above him. It was a pointless, unconscious gesture of submission to the tyranny of Camelford above and all around him, like the automatic bowing of his head to a blue-mantled shrine.

As quickly as he dared, Twiss slipped from rollway to elevator. Around him sprawled the everyday life of Camelford. He was armed with the immunity of habit and crossed the flowering boulevards with the same inattention he gave to the smoke of the factory quarters or the shouted lies of the market-stalls. Plain in their muted blues and greys and browns, the citizens of Camelford went about their orderly lives and Twiss walked through them.

He went round and round the spiralling ramps, trying not to look as though he wanted to break into a run. Down in the root of the Mountain he marched through a shaft of sun, mirrored down from outside. It disconcerted him and he broke stride. For just a second the reality of it all broke through his carefully-grown façade. A thousand shapes of window gleamed between lilacs or cracked plastic. Tens of thousands of homes, two million lives carried on around him and he wasn't part of it. For the first time in years he heard the throb of the generators beneath his feet.

Then a gang of boys from the end of his row frothed around him, throwing a stolen bag over their heads. Behind, red-faced with anger, a chubby boy followed. Twiss snatched the bag out of the air and swung it into the boy's grasp and the gang backed away from the naked emptiness of Twiss's face.

'Thank you, Twiss,' said the fat boy and his hero dredged up a smile from the distance where his mind dwelt.

At last – it was later than he had thought – he reached the inside flat he shared with the old man. He just hoped he could slip in before Granfer woke up and then – he could picture the broth of delight and anxiety on the beloved, wrinkled face – he would show the old man the meat. Pushing open the plastic door, he strode inside – and stopped. There, where she had no right to be, stood a woman. A girl. Flushed, her green-blue eyes fever-bright, she said—

The Watchtower

And Twiss woke up. But it hadn't been a dream, for he was lying on a cold clinical couch with only a sheet to cover his modesty, and wires trailed from dozens of parts of his skin.

Banks of monitors with disk-screens stared impersonally at him, showing graphs of marching lines and static fuzz. Even the white of his chest was studded with electrodes held in place by cherry-red tape, and his head was clamped motionless. Something sticky on his hairline tickled but he couldn't scratch it because his hands were trapped by yellow light. And his legs. Deep inside the sleepy part of him, anxieties began to rise like dinosaurs in a swamp. The girl was still there, though, inside the hospital-green surgery. Absently he noted the long lashes sweeping dark and graceful as reeds around the blue-green pools of her eyes. She wasn't conventionally pretty but her vividness was attractive. He was wondering faintly who she was.

She said, 'They call you Twiss, don't they?'

He was too astonished to answer.

Soft as a breeze on the aseptic air, she said, 'They've found you out, Twiss.' Her voice lingered over his name. 'They don't know about the rabbit yet but they will. Even when the Ears and Eyes don't see you directly they can reconstruct what happened from your footmarks, fingerprints, even the traces of your scent.'

His voice was thick with slumber. 'I don't believe it. And I didn't kill no rabbit anyway.'

'Then how do you know one was killed?'

He stared at her with wide-eyed defiance though he was still half-comatose. 'Who said one was? I never.'

She smiled softly, with great sadness. 'Twiss, you're a poor liar. And you smell.'

'What do you mean, I smell?'

'Don't be angry. I didn't mean it as an insult. It's just that all of us have our own personal identity-scent. Even I can smell your sweat, among the clinical smells. And the gorse-pollen in your hair and the grass-sap staining your fingers.' At the mention of his fingers, Twiss strained to move his hands but he couldn't. He didn't give up struggling, though, for all that thin loops of wire cast the golden glow of force-restrainers over his limbs. The fear-monsters were beginning to lift their heads above the waters of his subconscious.

Irona watched him with compassion while part of her admired the liquid hazel of his eyes. She went on, 'And if I can do that, don't you think Synod's machines can do it better? Because they can, I promise you that, Twiss, they can. The Ears and Eyes have hormone tracers too.'

'So I went out for a walk last night. What's wrong with that?'

'Nothing. Except they scanned you, Twiss. The Ears and the Eyes, you might not have seen them – well, you didn't, did you, or you'd never have done it? – but they recorded every move you made. You and Sticker both. They'll say you threatened one of their horses. It's eight now, and they'll be only a few hours behind me with the Arms.'

He writhed harder than ever, the veins cording his neck. Around his wrists and ankles the gold light grew more solid.

'Oh, stop it!' she shouted. 'This is one thing you can't get out of by brute force, or by running faster than any-one else.

'D'you think I didn't see your memory-replay just now? What d'you think those screens are for? I could tell you how you felt every step of the way.' But the enchantment of his communion with the stallion sprang moon-coloured and night-scented into her mind and she couldn't bring herself to defile that moment by talking of it. Instead she changed the subject.

'The whole of Camelford is a trap for you now. You think they can't send out an Eye to jolt your heart wherever you are? I've seen them do it.' Irona didn't say that she had been the one to send them. She closed her eyes against her mental picture of electricity jerking bodies into a physical shriek before they fell unconscious, but the images were strong and the last ones of all were of the agonising insanity of brainworms digesting a woman's ego.

'Well go on then!' Twiss yelled back. 'Get it over with.' A sweat of fear glazed his face as he arched his back in a futile attempt to free himself.

'Look, Twiss, stop thinking just of yourself for a moment, will you? What do you think they'll do to your grandfather? D'you think he'll like being in a home for the elderly, knowing you'll never come to see him again? That's if they don't worm his brain too. But I'll make you a bargain.'

Twiss slumped back against the crackling mattress. The strong planes of his face curved into lines of distaste. 'All right then,' he said. 'Tell me what you want to get me out of this. A true-food freak, are you? Get your rocks off dipping real blood off a plate? Or is it just a reward you're after? Blackmail?'

Irona felt her insides gripe at his view of her but it wasn't worth arguing about. *Let him think what he likes. It doesn't make it the truth.* All the same, it hurt.

Drawing a deep breath to calm herself, she said, 'The watchwardens think you're dangerous because they don't understand you—'

'And you do, I suppose?'

Ignoring his ironic interruption she went on, 'The watch are terrified you're planning some vast anarchy. They're scared you're going to tumble the order of Camelford Mountain and bring civil war to this part of the Admin. And when they dig out your background they're going to think that it's your grandfather's fault for unbalancing you with tales from before the Sky. You're both going to get it. And Sticker. So you've got to get out of here.'

She took another shaky breath, afraid to commit herself, but scared not to. 'And I've got to get out too. But I can't do it without you, and you can't do it without me.'

An expression of disdain stamped his face into ugly lines. 'You think I'd fall for that? Why on earth would Synod be scared of a couple of poachers – if we were poachers, that is.'

How could she tell him about the psychicators? The deep paranoia of the watch outnumbered ten thousand to one? Even if her deep conditioning had let her, she was too uncertain herself of Twiss's unpredictability to teach him more secrets than he needed. All she said was, 'Take it from me, Twiss. You must have heard about sleepers – I mean' – Irona heard her slip and covered it nervously – 'people from the lower levels who lose their memories and then just kind of disappear for a while and come back different? Wasn't there one down your row last year?'

'Ha! She was just some old tart they put in a home when she went ape. She was all right after that though.'

The conversation wasn't going at all how Irona had planned it. For some reason she'd thought he would metaphorically fall on her neck with gratitude. In his place, she would have.

But Twiss was swelling with contempt. 'Anyway, why should I go with you? How far d'you think we'd get? If they've got all this electronic monitor crap like you say, do you think Synod's just going to let us ride a ring out of the Admin to the Liga Mediterranea or somewhere? Be your age.'

'No, of course they wouldn't just let us. But I can fix it. And somewhere safer than that, too.'

'Oh yeah? What d'you need me for then?' He thought about it for a second more. 'What are you, some sort of deve?' A new, harsher expression marred his features, puckered the skin around his hazel eyes. 'You know something, sweetheart?' (The word was laced with arsenic.) 'You wouldn't turn me in anyway, would you?'

He knows! She felt like a child again, admiring some boy from afar and praying he never found out. But there was more this time. The Arms. Life and death. Panic nova'd in her heart but Irona forced herself to match his gaze. 'Oh no? Who do you think brought you up to the wardens' levels – sweetheart?'

Irona keyed hastily for alpha-waves and the electrodes piped sleep into Twiss's mind. The long, sinewy body stilled, despite its struggles; the sheet slithered to the floor with a rustle of paper. Embarrassed, Irona stooped to grab it and lay it over Twiss.

Of course, Mikel would choose that moment to come in. She tried not to think of him with Ellen and Roger, his sallow, skinny body—

'Hurry up, Ro!' he was saying, 'I don't like this.' Then he saw Irona arranging the sheet over Twiss's loins. He rolled his eyes in disgust. 'Is that all this is about? A bit of deve?'

'No, it isn't! How dare you?' Swiftly she blanked the monitors before Mikel saw what Twiss had really done. Killing – even a rabbit – was a far worse deviation than sex outside an approved contract.

'I dare because you're blackmailing me, Miss High-and-Mighty. So there's sweet f.a. you can do about it. But whatever it is, get a move on, will you? The Arms are bringing a couple or three wakers in. So you've got about five minutes to get your leg over.'

Fear renewed its assault on Irona as adrenalin rivered into her bloodstream. She could feel her heart slamming in her chest. But she stared him in the eye.

'Look, Mikel, can't you at least pump him up with a hypno so I can get him the hell out of here?'

He looked at her.

'Oh, for crying out loud, Mikel! Look, I'll do it, OK? Just give me a skin-patch, will you?'

Mikel handed her a thin circle of synthflesh loaded with chemicals. He said, 'Where are you taking him?'

She stopped, the metallic nub of the hypno-shooter poised over Twiss's pineal gland. 'Think I'd tell you? But you'd better help me get him moving because if the Arms get here first you're going to be in it as deep as I am.'

Mikel peeled back Twiss's eyelids as she aimed the electronic fires of the shooter onto the sleeping retinas. At the same time a skin-patch in the centre of Twiss's forehead roused him from his alpha-drugged catalepsy. Mikel nodded violently at Irona and she swiftly disconnected the alpha-electrodes and the various monitors.

'Twiss,' she said softly, 'you want to stand up. Won't it be nice standing up, Twiss?'

Doubly a sleeper, Twiss swivelled on the couch and slid his legs to the floor. Irona averted her gaze as she tucked the sheet around his muscular waist. 'There's a good boy. You like standing up, don't you, Twiss? That's right. Now, turn towards the door. We're going on a little adventure, Twiss, just you and me. You'll be glad to come with me to—'

She stopped. Her fellow warden looked up in alarm, then said, 'OK, I get the message.' He disappeared into a store-closet and she probed the computer for an empty room nearby.

Twiss was beginning to look around him in a vague sort of way, as though he had lost something.

'Ssh, ssh, Twiss, it's all right. We're going to Tau 7. You'll be happy there with me,' Irona said.

She put her hand under Twiss's elbow and felt an almost electrical fire pulse through her at the contact. Even in this state his personality had force. Mesmerised by its potency, she led him mechanically towards the door. 'Stop a minute, Twiss.'

Irona scooped up Twiss's clothes and thrust them into his arms. And led Twiss towards the maze of his future while she wondered if he still had one.

5

DEAD END

Irona propelled Twiss across the empty corridor. To her the environment was familiar, but not to Twiss. Even in his torpor something of the strangeness of the place got through to him and he moved with stiff unease. It was nothing to Irona's fear that the Arms might come for them at any moment.

Carved stalactites scaffolded an atmosphere of cold justice. It was nothing like the cosy community he came from, the warren below the watchlevels. Sparse lighting daggered shadows across the roughness of the granite, the glabrous pallor of the imported limestone. From somewhere came the echo of footsteps but Irona knew they could be hundreds of metres away. It didn't stop her casting a frightened glance round a pillar as she hauled Twiss behind its safety. Her head was throbbing so badly she thought it would explode. She wasn't even sure she'd hear the Arms' jets over the pounding in her ears.

Twiss stopped at the foot of a staircase as steep as a ladder. In a voice like a child's he said, 'Where is everybody?'

'Ssh! It doesn't matter. Just give me your clothes and get up there, will you?'

Twiss obeyed with all the alacrity of a broken machine. Using his hands as much as his feet, he climbed the stairs with a deliberation she found maddening. From time to time his head turned to observe a weird bulge in the walls or some sparkle in the shadowy rock.

Irona saw his toes splaying on the chill rounded edges of the stone. She wanted to shout, 'Hurry! Hurry!' at him but she kept the words inside herself, frightened that she might distract him and he would fall and the Arms would hear him and . . .

Down in the sleepers' levels she knew they had only ramps and elevators that could be no danger to the seething crowds. Here, webbed in the narrow top of the mountain, the edges weren't straight. Wardens weren't protected from their carelessness. They had to be alert to danger because at any moment the revolution might come, the sleepers might wake.

So she said nothing and Twiss continued to put one slow foot in front of the other, up the winding flight of stairs. With his clothes in her kilted-up skirts she still had a hand free and longed to shove him faster. But she didn't dare. So she followed Twiss's slow progress with tension tangling in her stomach and tightening her chest.

At last he reached the top and without so much as looking left or right he blundered through the archway and straight across level Tau. It was all right. They were lucky. No mighty black-shelled Arms heard them. No-one was in sight.

In seconds she had dragged him into the empty room. The automatic light came on, weak and waxen, gliding along cases of grey glass that gleamed unpleasantly along two sides of the room. When she saw what they were, Irona had to swallow the bile that clawed up into her throat.

'Here,' she said, panting with fright. 'Put your clothes on. And hurry!'

Ingrained modesty made Twiss dress without a word. Obviously the hypnoshot was beginning to wear off because he turned his back to her, no longer quite the child he had been. Irona tried not to watch him but looking at the oily grey heaving in the culture-tanks terrified her and she hesitated even to contemplate what might be in the vast refrigerator opposite the door. Instead she stared up at the ceiling or down at the grimy tiles, trying to plan out her next step, though awareness of Twiss's body streamed through her.

Am I a deve after all? she wondered. *Is Mikel right?*

Now she had had time to get used to the shock of panic, thought was beginning to reassert itself. Mikel. Mikel could easily sell her out so it would be stupid to spend too long here, though at least there were no body-heat scanners.

As far as she knew.

But the only way out was down. *I'll have to take Twiss through the sleeper levels in spite of the Ears and Eyes. What if Mikel's already sold us out? How long can I hold Roger and Ellen back?*

Oh, Synod! It's not even them on duty any more! Who else has found out?

A new anxiety spiked in her mind. *Granfer! What if he's reported Twiss missing? The Arms'd be all over the place anyway then. I should have left him a message. Only then he'd have been panicking and the psychicators would spot him . . . I'll have to get word to him somehow.*

The memory of the rabbit came back to her and she wondered if people had transmitter-tags as well. *Stop it! That's just paranoia!*

Then she wondered if there were psychicators in the watchlevels too.

She heard the sucking sound as Twiss ran his fingers over the pressure-seal of his coat. Irona turned.

'I think you're exaggerating the danger,' he said.

What? thought Irona, then almost laughed as she realised that for Twiss almost no time had elapsed since the conversation in the clinic.

She pointed to a dusty visiphone, trying to control her haste. *I've got to convince him or we'll be . . .* She glanced at the heaving greyness in the cases and stopped the thought before it rooted any deeper. Acting casually, she said, 'Have it your own way. Just call your Granfer, will you, to humour me? But don't stay on line too long. And don't say where you are.'

Twiss keyed the number, one tuft of his brown hair sticking up on his crown. His squared fingers were deft now. While he waited, Irona moved out of the machine's line of sight.

Granfer, his round head in a nimbus of wild white hair, shouted, 'Twiss, you bastard! It's half past eight! Where have you been? I've had your boss on the line. You haven't been in. I had to lie.'

'Well, um, you know, just round and about. I'm fine. Don't worry.'

'I'm not going to waste good worry on you, you stupid,

pathetic, great lump of a drunken bastard layabout. You've been out getting soaked again and I won't have it while you're under my roof. Just get yourself home, will you? I'm sick to death of people complaining about you. And that's another thing. I had some bloke come knocking seven bells out of the door saying as how you'd frightened his kids. It's about time you grew up. Be back in half an hour or I'll belt you into the middle of next week.'

The screen opaqued; the angry shouting cut off, leaving a vacuum in Tau 7. Twiss's expression hadn't changed throughout the tirade but a shadow veiled his eyes. She could feel his discomfort.

'He worries about me. He just doesn't like to show it.'

Irona listened to the indifference he put into his words. How much of it was real she didn't know, not without a psychicator. *Most of it, probably. He killed that rabbit, didn't he?* Wariness made her feel as though she were walking on egg-shells as she picked her next sentence with care.

'You can go back, you know, but the watch'll have you. The Arms will come and get you before the shift's half-way through and you'll be up before the Synod by Marsday. They really do use worms.'

'Garbage!'

Irona felt the sting of his contempt. 'Garbage, is it? Go and look in those cases then!'

Twiss raised his eyebrows and his mouth curved down in a sneer. He didn't look like he was going to move. Suddenly Irona couldn't think what she'd ever seen in him to risk her career for him, her whole life. This was her symbol of waking? Her bringer of joy? Then, arrogantly, Twiss strolled closer to the solid wall of glass cases.

And recoiled.

For the inside surface of the glass was powdered with a fleshy grey dust that didn't stay still. Drawn by an appalled fascination, Twiss bent to stare in past his reflection. And in the leucid matter were slithering threads of worms, short and faceless, darkened with a streak the colour of veins from the eyeless pit at their ends. The worms moved relentlessly, sliding their way up the sides of the tank on a drool of milky slime. The bottom of the tanks rolled with a slow animal motion that shifted to some purpose of its own, a purpose that was disconcertingly beyond human grasp.

And Twiss saw his own face with worms crawling over his mirrored eyes. He retched.

The sound made Irona hawk in sympathy but she swallowed her acid fear and said, 'They won't be looking for the two of us together. What do you say?'

'What about Sticker?'

'He's not a killer.'

'That's all you know!' Then Twiss realised that he had betrayed his friend and shook the last muzziness of alpha-sleep from his head. She could feel the violence rising in him. It pushed out of his body in an expanding wave of emotional turbulence and suddenly she was certain that the Admin must have psychic indicators here where their precious mind-worms might be at risk. Synod knew they were paranoid enough about a mass waking. Tension cinched tighter about her ribs but she didn't dare tell a mere sleeper. She was in enough trouble already.

Quickly, to calm him, she said, 'All right, Sticker too, if we can manage it.'

'And Granfer?'

'Oh, for Synod's sake! Yes, Granfer. And every other flaming soul in Camelford if it'll make you happy! Stop pushing your luck, will you? We'd better get out of here.'

'Where to?'

'Just out! You're broadcasting enough mayhem to set off every alarm they've got, but if you think I'm going to give my escape-route away you've got another thing coming. It'll only work once. Now, you wait outside. I've got to make a call. And take those bloody chunks of meat out of your pockets, will you? They're starting to smell.'

She watched Twiss pull the rabbit-haunches out. He looked around, not seeing anywhere he could hide them. Then he walked to the refrigerators and lifted the lid.

Horror jerked his arm; the rabbit fell and he wrenched himself backwards, dropping the lid. A stench of unfresh meat still drifted through the room like a miasmic dread when the lid crashed down.

Irona stared at his blenched face and decided not to ask him what was in there. Because she already feared the answer.

Irona called Roger and fretted at every second it took.

No answer.

Then she tried to call the Fixer.

No answer there, either.

Then, dizzy with anxiety, Irona led Twiss through the metal and stone coldness of the watch levels. The horror of that moment had faded from his features to be buried somewhere inside. He stayed close by her, whether from suspicion or insecurity she didn't know, but he looked no different from any of the wardens they saw. Just another man, taller than some, in dull blue suiting, dark boots and grubby collar, walking purposefully but without haste. They met hardly anybody she knew. And they didn't see any Arms, not even off-duty ones.

She kept stealing glances at Twiss's face, but without his smile to enliven it, he wasn't particularly attractive. None of the women gave him more than a cursory glance.

When they reached the unobtrusive door whose outside was marked 'Private', Irona said forcefully, 'Now don't blow it. Just keep calm and don't look as though you're in any particular hurry or you'll bring a whole flock of Eyes down on us.'

The Warren

Once the door swung shut behind them, Twiss's whole manner began to change. The opulence of level ZZ obviously didn't intimidate him – or else he tried to show that it didn't. He scarcely glanced at the swagged vines looping between separate houses, though nowhere lower in Camelford could sleepers see dwellings that weren't in terraced rows. There were even public windows shafting light down over the cheerful crowds. And the flower-starred green of the vines was heady with an outdoor fragrance that drew people from lower down, because most of them could never even dream of having an apartment where the windows didn't give onto a crowded row. Music tinkled in bright cafés and clashed with the sounds of a gilded carousel.

But Twiss strode fast downhill along the crushed opal of the path and never so much as looked at the children playing on the swings. He didn't glance at the chastely courting couples rapt in the romance of the place. Irona saw with fresh eyes the matrons dispensing disapproval at every furtive handclasp or whispering almost-embrace and wondered where it had started, all this control of feelings, but it didn't seem to register on Twiss. When they passed a sunlit shrine its emotion-projectors touched her heart with their appeal to good citizenship. It arrowed the sweet nostalgic guilts of childhood through her as it always did, made her want to be good. Almost she began to look for the Arms, to welcome the cleansing they would bring her.

Not Twiss, though. He barely touched his hat as he passed the shrine, heading directly down to the glowing sign that meant 'ramp'. Neither he nor Irona were in the mood to trust elevators that might trap them. Wordlessly they moved into the broad downsweeping spiral, passing level after level.

Irona stole a quick glance at him.

He was looking at her curiously. 'Why did you save me?' he asked.

'Because – because you woke me.'

Twiss seemed puzzled. 'Do I know you? I don't remember . . .'

Sleepers weren't supposed to know about the watch being kept on them in their comfortable cages. Irona was still warden enough to know that. She said archly, 'You mean you've forgotten?'

Twiss slid his hands swiftly across her shoulders and withdrew discreetly, yet the intimacy remained. 'How could I forget someone with a smile as sweet as yours?'

The murals beside the ramp were beginning to look grubby and faded, scuffed with the rebreathed fetor of the lower warrens.

But he's got no idea about the Arms, no idea at all . . .

She said, 'Let's find a phone. And an olfactory, while we're at it.'

They found the olfactory first. Twiss yawned and said, 'After you.'

She stepped inside and let the doors close around her.

She keyed for an instant declench. The walls darkened around her, shutting him out.

Soft as a breeze on a summer's night, the star-gemmed blackness enfolded her. Hundreds of tiny needles barely grazed her skin with their even pressure but they poured muscle-relaxants into her blood while moist rose-scented zephyrs cooled her burning head. Then gentle beads massaged the aches from her neck and rolled lovingly along her spine, and the chemicals that soothed her flesh gave her at least a superficial calm with their tang of cedar and orange for uplift. Sub-audibles whispered *You are wonderful. You are valuable. You deserve happiness.* Mind-melded patterns flashed stars of lifejoy direct into her subconscious. Even her legs stopped aching.

With a sigh she palmed the door. Brightness flooded in but at least it didn't scream in her eyes as it had before.

Yes, he was there. He was skimming through the news at a stand under some straggling potted palms. It was showing a pastel town by a summer sea, guarded by a volcano mantled in snow. Cedar and salt winds spoke of freedom. Harith. So what if the news from the colony was over twenty years old? The sea-breeze still flowed through his hair.

A fat woman was beside him, tutting to an equally fat man; they made Twiss turn to an item they wanted to experience. Irona pulled a face and went over to him.

It was the usual stuff about a riot in a hot place far away. They never showed wakings in Londover or Tiger Bay or anywhere in the Admin, not to the sleepers anyway, though from time to time Irona had heard wardens whispering rumours at shift-change. The news in the Admin was always good, heart-warming stuff.

Sunset images pulled her into the experience: a haze of sparkling red dust so real she could smell it. Veiled women and men in striped robes were stoning each other across a rocky rift. Beyond it, what had once been a desert was tamed with lines of intercropped orchards. But it was the Saharans who were red in tooth and claw. Jags of fire flamed out of the arched doorways pocking the sides of the gorge; black smoke rolled down from the sunny side to the human carrion-eaters waiting in the abyss.

The news-stand was good. Sharp waves of heat buffetted Irona even when she was metres away; heaven alone knew what it was like up where Twiss was standing. For a second she just stood drinking in the way his soft brown hair curled on the nape of his neck but the news-stand soon drew her in. The smell of charred flesh burnt her nostrils and as she watched, lines of projectiles wrote death on the sandstone walls. Explosions ripped the air and from the battalions of shuttered windows rose shrieks and babies' cries.

Irona felt the thrust of distaste and superiority, and knew a psychic transmitter was broadcasting it. *These sleepers haven't got a clue about it,* Irona thought. Then wondered if that was a result of the transmitter, too. She had to stop thinking about it because that way lay madness.

'They old Saharans ought to get theirselves a Synod like what we got,' the fat man said chattily to Irona, but his partner was less cheerful.

'Serves they right for being 'eathens.'

'Sorry, my dear,' Twiss said to Irona, and she was aware that he didn't even know her name, 'but while you were in the olfactory, I been thinking. I ought to get back to Granfer 'cos he'll be fretting. I'll be all right now.'

'You won't! They'll get you! The Arms—'

He took a couple of steps and was instantly submerged in the crowds. He called back, 'Not in the Admin. We don't have nothing like that. Synod won't let them. Thanks anyway. 'Bye.'

And he was gone.

6

REGENERATOR

Playing hide and seek with the Ears and Eyes, trusting that the scramblers she had left in the watchroom programs would blur her identity, she headed down towards the centre of the artificial Mountain to hunt out Twiss and force him to see reason. And hoped that no Arms with their tell-tale jiggers came to hunt her down in her turn.

But he wasn't at his work.

He wasn't at home – and neither was Granfer.

And when she plucked up the temerity to ask his neighbours in the market-place, they were all but comatose and the cloying scent of deep calmants lingered beneath the smells of cabbage and onion.

No, they hadn't seen Twiss or the loopy old man.

They hadn't seen Sticker.

In fact they were sleepily amazed at how late it had got when they weren't looking. They hadn't seen anything at all. Besides, the Arms were just a myth, weren't they? How could you have Arms without a body?

The only person Irona could save was herself.

For hour after hour Irona spiralled down the ramps to the factory levels hundreds of metres beneath the surface. Fear for Twiss and the knowledge of what he had cost her ached, but what really hurt was the way he had left her. Irona felt very alone.

At last she reached level A, where sunlight had never been. Turning left through the huge square hole of the entrance into the darkness beyond, she imagined she was being swallowed. Again she felt the juggernaut of Camelford bearing down on her, trying to keep her from the relative safety of her destination. Or what someone had once told her might be safety. Now she wasn't so sure and her footsteps began to lag.

Until an Eye started to follow her. *Don't be stupid! It's not after me. Roger and Ellen promised me I had until tomorrow. Only I'm not stupid enough to trust them, am I?*

But when she had tried to call them from the worm-room she could get no reply.

And the Eye was still there. Still shining faintly through its iridium surface, still telling the sleepers that they were safe because the Admin was watching over them. Only at this time of the evening there were no sleepers here. No-one but Irona – and the Eye.

Glancing just once over her shoulder to check it really was hovering along behind her, she had to force herself not to walk too fast because anything out of the unusual might attract the watchwarden's attention. It would be Greg on a Saturnight, wouldn't it? She thought it was Greg. He wasn't a deve. He was a man who got off on the exercise of power. Irona pictured him, alone up on night-watch, and hoped that tonight he'd be happier seeking comfort at the bottom of a bottle than watching the monitors for victims. But there was no telling what he might actually be doing. Guilt and insecurity combined to glaze her skin with hot sweat. If it was Greg, if he was watching, the psychicators would be having a field-day with her output of hormones.

Irona wouldn't look round again. She felt conspicuous enough down here as it was in the neon gloaming. The work-force had long since gone home; even the rollways had been switched off. Her footsteps came back to her, distorted, through the faint colours of factory signs.

However hard she hoped, the Eye in the twilight wouldn't go away. It wasn't just a figment of the fear scorching her imagination. She hoped desperately that it was just following her at random.

Trying to summon up professional detachment, she recognised the head-sized metal globe as almost the newest model of Eye and wondered immediately what was important enough down here for such high-grade equipment. It had sound and picture; it had a psychicator. It also had a grade-one stunner.

I must be glowing red as a fire, she thought. *Swirling guilt and fear and anger. A cocktail that'll kill me.* Stress cramped her exhausted limbs. She could feel the Arms casually batting her unconscious and dragging her off, carrying her by one carelessly-grasped ankle like those mohocks she had seen caught in the fields last night.

I shouldn't be thinking of this.

At once she tried to focus on the crab-apple trees outside the machine-sheds, but the trees themselves were sickly-looking things with leaves burnt brown at the edges by the acid from the steel-works. The odours of dirty steam and chemicals on the air reminded her of the power of the Admin and her guilt renewed itself. She resisted the impulse to look again to check that the Eye had a stunner. Of course it had. She could already feel its pain arcing across her heart like blue lightning.

Where is this damned hole?

Even in her year as watchwarden she had never actually seen the entrance to it. Which was why it was still here – if it really did exist. But it had to be around here somewhere.

Once I would have reported it. How far down have I sunk?

Another corner, another roofed-in row. Dozens of albino starlings were squabbling in the trees or screeling in anger at being dislodged from some favourite perch. In the fading purple light they were no more than silhouettes, ugly fruit in the branches over her head. She was afraid they would mess on her clothes but she felt safer here from the Eye that continued to bob along behind her. She wished someone else would walk past but it was too late for that. The only lights were in the towering blast-furnace that burned for days at a time. And the whole level was so much bigger than it had ever seemed on the monitors. So much further when you had to walk across it instead of scrolling along with the Eye.

Synod, I hope Greg's looking somewhere else!

Footsteps – *Arms!* But no. It was just some old security guard with her dog padding along beside her. A sign of the times. Once you wouldn't have needed human security in Camelford, but now gangs of mohocks stoned the electronic alarms or axed down the doors, so somebody had to keep repairing the bells. At any other time Irona would have been glad to see someone who could protect her from the vandals.

'Evening,' said the woman, suspiciously, in a West Country burr so strong she must have learnt it from a docudrama. Her hand was resting just inside the lip of her work-apron. Presumably she was holding a jolter, which did Irona's mind no good at all, but worse than that was the dog.

It came up to her, resting its wicked fangs on her shoulder. Its meaty breath iced her skin with nervous sweat and filled her mind involuntarily with the memory of the worm-room. Her eyes felt vulnerable to the beast's yellow teeth and to the metal-tipped claws that clicked as it edged closer to her. Irona felt her bladder weakening.

'Evening.' Irona's voice was hoarse.

'What be you doing 'ere?'

'I'm – um – making up a poem.' *Surely that's harmless enough?*

The woman raised her scraggy brows and stood aside, pulling the dog's leash a little. Reluctantly the massive beast backed off but its growl crawled through Irona's flesh and she felt that she was about to dissolve. She could hardly walk.

The woman laughed. 'Don't 'ee mind old Bess 'ere. She don't bite – 'less I tells her to.'

Irona put one hand on the fence, holding herself up on the dirty plastic as she pulled herself unsteadily along.

Oh, Synod, don't let her drop the lead. Don't let the dog pull her over. And please help me find that blasted entrance soon. Irona was surprised to find that her thought was less of an exclamation than a prayer.

The Eye seemed almost friendly in comparison – especially when it decided to follow the dog and its owner; its earlier persecution must have been just casual after all.

It was kilometres before Irona found what she was looking for, hours in which she heard footsteps following and saw shadows move as the artificial night deepened. But every time she turned round there was nobody in sight, despite the hollow feeling in her back that made her think someone was watching her.

Maybe the Arms were just playing with her.

Or maybe it was someone else altogether.

Away in the distance laughter howled; Irona gasped. Something scuttled on the oil-slicked roadway, just too far off for her to see what it was. A regular booming so deep she felt it rather than heard it tunnelled out another layer of anxiety in the electric web of her brain.

She turned another corner. At first she was uncertain, the light was so dim in the foul air, and she almost passed the first landmark without realising it. The sign on the front of an office block read FR. MES. S. and Irona hardly took it in, but then she realised that the dark teeth of the sign might make it into the name FRAMESAWS.

A little flutter of hope drew her to climb over the railings. Naked in the space between the buildings, she ran across inky grass and earthworms slithered down into their holes away from the vibrations of her passing. Skirting the wall under the harsh green lights of the sign, she reached the end of the building and stepped into shadows thicker than soot. Now she had to run her hand over the crysteel and stone to find her way.

I'm going to run into a spybeam, I know I am, she couldn't help thinking. *And if it's connected to the Watchtower they'll get me after all.* Unconsciously she slowed.

That manic laughter burst again across the darkness. It was definitely closer this time. She whirled around but she couldn't tell which direction it was coming from. Nor the clatter of many footsteps racing her way.

Fatigue fell away from her. She followed the wall again, her other hand groping out into the blackness. Something brushed her face and she would have screamed but down here it might have been a mutospider's web and the spider might get into her mouth. Irona could already feel its legs thrashing on her tongue and its hard body, crushed between her teeth, spurting its ugly blood behind her lips.

Her free hand collided hard with another wall. The

blow bent her nails back, broke them with a bright slash of pain.

Carefully this time, she felt the unseen thing. No, not a wall. A panel of cracked plastic. It didn't stand quite true; at one side the hatch was warped and air pushed out against her skin, hot and palpitating like some dragon's breath.

Behind her the footsteps broke their messy rhythm and yells pierced the night. There was a slur as someone fell, and derisive laughter coarse as a jay's.

Full-scale panic pumped up her heart until its frantic beating filled her chest. She wrenched at the plastic until it broke free at one hinge. The bottom edge scuffed the ground, making a graunching noise that was horribly loud.

'This way!' shouted a man's voice, high-pitched with excitement.

In her haste Irona couldn't free the panel entirely. Heedless, she bulled her way through the gap, tearing her clothes and her skin on the broken edges. Then, panting so hard she thought her throat would rupture, she yanked the thing back as hard as she could. Again that hideous, advertising shriek of plastic on stone, but she couldn't pull the hatch back into place and she gave up.

Irona stumbled down into a space that felt cavernous. Without the signlight from outside the dark was almost total. It was alive with the hot dry breath of some unseen presence whose nature she couldn't even guess at, though there was a deep womb-music that throbbed against her ears and vibrated up through the soles of her feet. Strange musky odours caught in her throat and dust skirled against her skin.

Synod, I hope I don't meet that! What in heaven can it be?

But Irona had no time to speculate on exactly what mutated monster was prowling down there in the dark. A shout from outside pierced the thick atmosphere of the lair. 'I reckons she went down yere. What's your jigger say?'

Someone answered, 'Dunno. It's gone crazy.' The sound of several slaps on plastic smacked the air. ''at's better. It's still not right, mind. I'm gonna take it back to that Toad and shove it so far down her's throat that she'll be layin' it like an egg.'

Another slap, this time of skin on skin, but it was right outside the hatchway. A woman's contralto voice shouted, 'Stop wasting time. I need that bitch, you hear me? Get after her.'

Somebody started tugging at the hatch; Irona heard a piece of it crack. A faint light stabbed in through the opening. She was paralysed.

Another fragment of sharp plastic split loose. A man yelped. 'Shit! That hurt.'

'Stop pissing about and get on with it. I need her.'

I've got to get away from the door! There must be somewhere I can hide. The pressure of their approach pushed Irona out into the frightening dense cavern and towards the heart-beat throb of the beast.

Well across from the doorway, something grabbed her ripped hem and pulled her up with a jerk. Irona's heart tripped and she tried desperately to yank herself free but the thing wouldn't let her go. Panic spun sheet lightning through her brain and the beast's breath baked the fear-sweat that prickled her skin.

Oh Synod! It's got me. No – her eyes picked out a nest of rusting pipes and half by touch she unsnagged her skirt. Edging round the tangle of abandoned ironmongery, she barked her shin, but she was adjusting to a ghostly luminance that seemed to have no source yet still left chasms of blackness where she had to test every step.

Outside reinforcements skidded to a breathless halt. *Don't let it be Arms!* she thought. The panel shivered to a harsh impact. Then a strange keening chant dried her mouth with a different flavour of terror.

'Kill the bastard, cut the invader. Kill the bastard, cut the invader. Whose is the ground? Deathangels!'

Behind her a hurtling body crashed the panel wide open.

Irona knew she was going to die. Time opened out into a nightmare infinity. She huddled into a pool of shadow, hearing her breathing, shaking to the beat of her heart.

The woman who had shoulder-charged the door got up from her sprawl. For a second she was limned green in the signlight. Her silhouette seemed ragged until Irona realised that the oiled jade was the woman's naked skin and the striations were some stygian paint.

The rest of the mohocks stooped to shove their way through the entrance. Shaven heads agleam, they spread wordlessly through the pit. Irona could hardly tell where they were; she saw only denser shadows dipping and skimming over the uneven floor. The silent shuffle of their feet was more terrifying than any words could have been.

Because Irona knew it meant they had tracked victims down before.

If I stay here they'll kill me. And the knowledge was textured with images from her briefings, things that the sleepers never saw because to see them by accident was to be brain-wormed. To have your memories eaten away and replaced with bland citizenship. To feel your mind die as you screamed, haemorrhaging your life into the worms' guts, their programmed DNA bonding you into a subhuman citizenship that was perfect in its emptiness.

For the Synod didn't want anybody knowing how it kept control throughout the territory of the Admin.

And I do. So that and Twiss make me doubly dangerous. But that's only death of the mind. Surely even I don't deserve the mohocks on top of it!

Irona shivered and ran. Giving herself to the phantasm of light, she dashed through the cavern, blundering into unseen things and trying to keep to the deepest shadows. The womb-music solidified around her; she was heading closer to the dragon. She heard her own footsteps and knew by a triumphant ululation behind her that the mohocks were close on her tail.

I can't see them so they can't see me.

The syllogism was very little comfort.

She cannoned into a crate – no, a wall, she realised, as its roughness snatched at her ripped clothes. But she shoved herself off it and plunged deeper into a tunnel, feeling its sides closing in on her. They looked insubstantial as clouds in the night sky but they were cruel and hard as she scraped her hand along the jagged surface to give her some guidance. Three deep scratches wavered under her touch, parallel to the floor of the tunnel. Her fingers sank into them and thin slime greased her hand.

What sort of beast-claws made that?

The slime burned the skin off her fingers one layer at a time, and its cloying muskiness rasped in her throat made raw by the hot shuddering air.

Now she panted onwards with the mohocks' steps echoing back from ahead. *It must be a dead end! I've run out of places to escape.* The leading mohocks were so close now that their footsteps struck with her own against the cadencing echoes.

Suddenly the wall bent back on itself as the tunnel sank sharply. Irona was too late to save herself. She crashed to the ground and something leaped over her prone body.

Stiletto claws scrabbled at her shoulders. With a feral scream the thing launched itself from her back. Abruptly the half-dark throbbing air was strung with flying bodies, beaded with animal howls.

Irona raised her ringing head. One creature landed full in the face of a mohock boy only a metre behind her. Its dark weight sent him sprawling, half his face clawed away. His shrieks speared her hearing. A wave of beasts broke over him in a comber of civet-stench and unearthly calls. The boy kept on screaming, over and over, begging for help.

Up at the bend in the tunnel, the mohocks clattered to a confused standstill. Irona saw them only as a milling medusa of shadows bound together by the boy's sobbing screams. The mohocks sounded scared.

'For Synod's sake!'

'What is it?'

'I'm getting the hell out of here!'

'Lardy! Are you all right? Lardy?' *Lardy must be the boy with the mashed face*, Irona realised.

The woman's contralto lashed out dark across the river of screams. 'You're going nowhere! Stand your ground.'

Lardy kept spilling his agony like acid on the air. The rest of the mohocks couldn't take it.

'Stand it yourself, Brunhilde!'

'I'm getting out!'

And over the maze of shrieks and beast-screams Irona heard them running away.

'Don't leave me!' Lardy yelled. 'Ow! Synod! Help me, Brunhilde! Help me!'

Irona saw the vast tiger-bulk of the woman take a tentative pace forward. Four or five of the creatures broke away from the screaming boy and slunk towards her. Brunhilde dredged some gadget out of her belt and threatened the creatures with it. Her whole arm was shaking as she stabbed at a button.

A high-pitched whistle drilled through Irona's head, descant to the womb-music. The predators cowered but then the shrill stuttered to silence. Menacing, they yowled and leapt at Brunhilde. Metre-long, knee-high, they sprang at her, jaws a-gape.

Brunhilde's nerve gave way. She ducked back and hurled the useless gadget at a beast's muzzle. The creature twisted in mid-air and fell, raking Brunhilde's thigh. For a second Irona saw the bright flash of a bone then it was drowned in welling blood.

Incredibly swift, Brunhilde pounced on the creature. Lifting it by the scruff of its neck, she slammed it against the wall. Its skull crunched. Then she whirled it into the pack and darted away, the creatures belling at her heels – but only those who had targeted her. The rest were still chewing at the fallen mohock.

Lardy had stopped screaming. Only slurping noises came from where his body lay under a seething mound of predators. The womb-music was soft as a lullaby in comparison.

Somebody prodded Irona gently in the buttocks. Her body jolted in a spasm of shock as sharp as electricity.

'Ssh, mistress. Ain't nobody going to hurt you now.'

Irona pushed herself shakily to her feet. Her knees felt as though they had independent suspension. Cowering, she faced her rescuer. Or her executioner.

'I be Regenerator. Hee-hee. Regenerator.' His voice was high and fast. 'Come you quickly before they cats finish or you'll be on the menu. 'Cos I'm going to' – he giggled again – 'regenerate you.'

7

REBIRTH

Regenerator's home was a cross between a magpie's nest and a rat-hole, and it was only marginally less dark than the crooked tunnel-junction where he had built his refuge. Three of the five walls were covered in flickering wallscreens that crackled with bursts of soundtrack between odd whines of static. Their colours shifted dizzily, glittering off chains of broken glass and odd shapes of chrome and iridium that dangled from the ceiling. A jigsaw of mirror-shards shattered black shadows on the ceiling and reflections of violet and orange crawled up the corners of the walls. The womb-music was so loud that Irona felt the pressure dancing on her ear-drums; the chains twirled erratically, sending prisms of red and green and indigo light spinning across her vision on chance-lit shafts of incense.

'The odour of sanctity, get it? Odour of sanctity, see? Incense.' Regenerator shot his words out at speed, glottal stops tangled with clipped vowels.

More the stench of unwashed humanity, Irona thought to herself. *Wonder how long it is since he cleaned this place out – or had a wash?* Underneath it was the depressing thought of how far she had sunk below the level of good citizenship.

'Come in, sit down, siddown, don't stand in the doorway, I can't get through.'

Irona stood on the threshold, wondering how to thread her way between the heaps of unidentified clutter she could dimly see on the floor. 'Where shall I sit?'

'Try the couch, see it? Over there opposite the news-stands. Sags a bit but it's always good for a meal. Entirely. Go in though or I can't shut the door and we'll be the meal. Not enough on they mohocks to feed a mess of cats, messy buggers.'

He put one hand on her back. Irona stepped down hastily away from him and Regenerator slammed a stainless steel door into place. It gonged and she thought every single item in the room reverberated; it hammered into her headache. Once the door was shut the heat and the writhing smoke intensified.

'Get in then, go on.' Carelessly striding across a slithering pile of pre-Sky magazines, Regenerator bounced his way around her and turned to look up at her. His every move was quick and jerky; his eyeballs moved continually, gleaming in odd colours as the chains spun their webs of light through the gloom. 'That's the couch there, see? Hee-hee.'

Striding to a heap that was taller than the others, he swept a stack of disks aside. They clashed as they toppled to the floor, revealing part of an ancient mattress. Dubious stains covered the ripped plastic and Regenerator quickly pulled a paper sheet over it that looked equally grubby to Irona's straining eyes.

She was too exhausted to object. She slumped onto it, hearing the paper rustle. A smell compounded of spice, mould and tired sweat puffed up around her in dust-motes that shimmered in the wild lights.

'That's right then. Go on, say you like it. You do, don't you? I salvaged it all myself. Entirely. Took me ages. They spy-Eyes – I don't like they, do you? Give me the creeps, ghosting around after innocent people that ain't done nothing wrong. And the cats, have to sort they out before I can set foot outside the door. Not like that upstairs, is it? Boring. Slow up there. Everybody's slow. Entirely. You're better off down here. Food's nicer when you have to catch it.'

He plumped down beside her. She almost gagged at the smell. Then he started talking again and she had to cover her mouth with her hand to avoid his foul breath. Gold and green and scarlet scintillations wavered over him because the chains all jangled again as he moved.

'Don't say much for a warden, do you? Different when I've got you down in my little hidey-hole, ain't it?'

It stopped Irona wondering what the food that he caught might be. With a vestige of cunning she summoned up a laugh. 'Me? A warden? No, not me, citizen. Wardens are just rumours, aren't they? I'm a poet.'

Regenerator twisted his thin face into a smile that pushed his cheeks up into little round knobs and dragged long lines down to his jaw. Light as blue as hyacinths tangled in the creases of his skin. It was disconcerting. Worse was how he winked and squeezed her knee conspiratorially. 'Poet? Not you. You're one of they watchwardens gone and got yourself into trouble. Think I didn't know? Think I haven't seen you before? Poet, my ass.' His gaze flickered continually to the ever-changing screens and back again to peer at her.

'Of course you haven't seen me before. I've never been down here before. I was just out for a walk. Looking for—'

'Bullshit. I saw some bullshit once, the genuine article—'

'You? You're not brave enough!' she said to give herself courage.

He just smiled and continued. 'Oh, I did. In that there Park they got outside. The crap you're shovelling me smells about the same. Entirely.'

Irona tensed her legs in the first movement of standing but Regenerator wasn't having it. Holding even more tightly to her knee, he said again, 'Bullshit. And look you at they screens. Quick, now. That little one, top right. See? Told you. Hee-hee.'

Amongst the kaleidoscope of dramas and news and the romanticised rural scenes of the harmony channel she saw something she'd never seen before. A corridor hung with paintings in gold frames and floored with a jewelled mosaic of flowers on a sapphire background. A woman in a swinging shoulder-cape was slinking along it, swaying her shoulders as though she were dancing. No ordinary citizen would ever be caught dead walking like that. And natural sunlight haloed her fluffy hair when she leaned out of a window.

The view was exactly the same from the Watchtower. Only seen from higher up. In the Synod.

A crepitating snow-storm blotted the picture out of existence. Pale light washed into Regenerator's rat-hole. Somewhere in a corner a news-stand spawned an odour of fish rotting in seaweed.

It can't be the Synod. Not really. 'Just a play,' Irona said shakily.

'Hee-hee. You know better than that, don't you, young Irona. 'Course you do. You ain't dumb, you're just stupid. Entirely. Think I can't see into the Watchtower from here? 'Course I can. Seen you, and that Ellen pulling your skin. Thousands of times I seen you.'

The pictures went on tilting and swooping in Regenerator's hidey-hole. They matched Irona's mind exactly. Her headache re-established itself with the tom-tom beat of the throbbing air. She didn't know what to think.

'Ha! Got you, then. And you think she's a deve. What about you and that Twiss-feller you watch?' Regenerator pointed to another screen, one that almost covered a narrow slanting wall. He said admiringly, 'Look at that, will you? One of the last-ever ground cars. Hear they wheels scorching the road? Class, that was. Bread and circus.'

Irona was bewildered. She clutched at Regenerator's last words. 'What?'

'Bread and circus, see? Hee-hee. They get you, Synod gets you, they gets you so's you none of you don't like to go outside under that nasty plastic Sky. So then you don't want private transport, see? And they give you, Synod does, food and shelter and entertainment and a couple of hours pushing little things, little symbols, round on scanners and make you think it's work. Then you gets the entertainment, see? Tells you here's the best place to be. Seen that old desert war, then? Hee-hee. Wouldn't want to be there then, would you? Wouldn't want to wake. 'Course not. Bread and circus. Hee-hee. How d'you know it's real, though?'

Outside cats began to yowl. A scene of dusk over ocean spilt a sheen of amethyst onto the clutter but there was no calm here. Irona jumped as a paw the size of her hand scrabbled through a corner where two steel plates didn't quite meet.

Regenerator laughed. 'Oh, you don't want to worry 'bout they old cats. Cat-proof this place is, see? Entirely. Hee-hee. Think I wouldn't make it cat-proof? 'Course I would. Ain't no old cats going to get in here. 'Specially none that's the size of they ones. Well, I can see the dogs. Makes sense, don't it, sort of, having watchdogs the size of Arms? Frighten they old mohocks silly. Well, it don't really, but at least it gives they a sort of challenge, see? But what they wants to go round messing with cats for, I don't know. Cats don't want to be trained. Should of kept 'em all little like they tagged ones upstairs.'

He shifted, cross-legged, to watch a ballerina pirouette across a screen before a back-drop of desert women stoning each other across a news-stand's night-lit gorge. The ballerina was a flash of white and dove-grey dancing untouched through fire-flares while tracer-bullets spanged against arpeggios. On another screen a schooner skimmed across a moon-kissed bay, and a man's voice whispered, 'I love you' while a scent of burnt almonds crisped in Irona's nostrils.

She said nothing. Her scratches and her burnt fingers were stinging fiercely. When she moved, her dress tugged at the scabs on her back. Aqua sparks marched across her hands.

Regenerator wriggled sideways to stare at her with his curiously colourless eyes. 'Your turn now, Irona.'

'Pardon me?'

'That's how conversation goes. I say something then you say something else. Conversation, see? Your turn. Entirely.' He looked at her, ludicrous expectation on his thin face. His lipless mouth curved in a faint smile.

'I – I'm thirsty.'

'Well I don't call that much of a conversation. Still, it's a start. Better than lies. See, you can't lie to me because I know everything. Hee-hee. Have to, don't I, with all they screens? Have to know.'

And Irona wondered why. And, worse, what it was he had to know.

The Watchtower

The junior matriarch all but broke her conditioning and ran down the steps from the trapdoor. She was clammy with sweat; her heart was beating double-time.

'And hurry up!' The words stabbed out at her just before the trapdoor irised shut.

It couldn't have been half an hour before the junior came back to the room in the pinnacle, the man she had been sent to summon – so secretly that she couldn't even call him – at her heels. Just being in the presence of his greatness made her tremble. The black-haired girl bowed him in and made her escape, hearing the tide of wrath breaking above her, thunder between the gods, as the trapdoor slammed shut over her head.

'So where is she then?' The woman in blue didn't shout but Elditch felt as though she had. Though her face was grey with stress and age, the character behind it still cowed him. 'Come on, where's Irona?'

'I don't know,' he said.

'Oh, for Synod's sake, man, stop cringing! You can't help being stupid. And I should be used to it after all these years. As for Carandis—' The woman dominated herself. Two or three calming breaths and she said with some remnant of civility, 'Sit down.'

Elditch did. He perched on the edge of a low chair, his hands between his knees, for all the world like a guilty child.

The woman in blue could have laughed – if he weren't so pathetic. 'Now, Elditch, tell me how you lost her.'

'I have done!'

'So tell me again.'

Elditch cleared his throat. 'We – er, the watch – had the computers cross-reference through all the Eye-sights since she went off-shift. They tracked her up to the Watchtower . . .'

The woman in blue snorted, a sound that ill became her age and dignity. 'Don't be so coy, man! Say it plain – you let her get right into your precious worm-room with that deve waker and then just waltz out again!'

'All right, yes! And we tracked her all the way through the double letters of the warren right down to the factory-level—'

'And you even had an Eye following her but you let her go! Synod, you make me sick!'

Anger jerked him to his feet. He paced to stare out of the window. Below, as far as the Eye could see, stretched rolling cropland where once deer had grazed on the moors. Nothing was squandered in the Admin. The human waste of Camelford was recycled to enrich the acid soil. Part of him was growing in those wheatstands now. To the south, a tidy rainshower cast a rainbow over an orchard.

The woman watched Elditch's jaw working as he strove to control his anger. A smile flitted across her withered face. 'Well?' she goaded.

'Then she disappeared. She was controlling her fear. You trained her well. You, not me,' he added nastily. 'The psychicator spotted some patches of potential violence that were much stronger and the Eye followed them . . .'

'And nobody was monitoring it?'

Élditch glared at her. 'It's impossible! There aren't enough wardens to watch every Eye all the time.' A moment of rebellion: he added, 'Particularly when one of the specials you selected becomes a waker.'

For a moment Elditch felt and quailed before her rage. He knew she meant him to and he still couldn't help it. But it burnt hard and bright as magnesium and died as suddenly. He let loose the breath he hadn't known he'd been holding.

'Well.' The Matriarch drummed her ringed fingers on her knee. Even such an idle act was given weight, if not by her office then by her rheumatism. 'You'll just have to find her again. She's important, Elditch. Important and dangerous. Wakers in the warrens are bad enough. But in the Watch . . . If Carandis can get to her first, she could destroy me. And if I go down, so do you. Find her.'

'But she's down in the tunnels! The disruption – nothing works down there.'

'That's your problem. Otherwise you might get to play a different game with your slimy little pets.'

Elditch raised his eyes to Bernardina's – and blenched.

The Warren

'Can't you hear they old cats, Irona? They likes the smell of blood. Tang. That's good. The tang of blood. Hee-hee.'

Between the cats and her hunger, Irona talked. At first she just rehashed old gossip, as a sort of down-payment on the food and drink she wanted. It didn't seem as if Regenerator would run to an olfactory. At least she couldn't see one in the murk.

But the little man's narrow shoulders drooped in sympathy or juddered to his endless breathy giggles as her stories grew less stilted. More personal. She began to ignore the background noises: the clinking chains, the manic screens, the hiss and thud of the dragon's womb-music, the occasional whines from the cats outside his shelter. Even the insane flickering of the coloured reflections.

'Mm,' he would say. Or 'You didn't! Aren't you brave. So what happened next?'

And Irona began to wrap herself in the romance of her life. She was so engrossed that she hardly noticed when he brought her a cup of instant tea; she just swigged it down and said, 'Cheers. You're right, I am a warden. Or rather, I was. Now I'm nothing, just a deve. And because of that idiot Twiss I can't go back.'

'Hang on a second.'

There seemed to be nothing left for her to hide. All of a sudden she felt curiously light. Free. Irona watched him lean forward – she flinched – and rummage under the mattress.

What have I got left to lose?

She said, 'Do you know the Fixer?'

Regenerator dredged out of hiding a fat half-round of cheese. He said nothing at all. Then jars of unidentified pickles with dried sauce crusting their necks. And finally what she thought must be biscuits. He broke off a wedge of cheese; it was hard work for his skinny fingers. Then, depositing it on piece of relatively clean cardboard, he bowed from the waist and handed it to her. Its clean, sharp smell made her mouth water.

'There, then, Irona the Waker. What do you think of that? Tit for tat. Fancy some pickle with it?' He didn't wait for an answer, just tipped a mound of spicy brown stuff onto her cardboard plate. A thin juice dribbled from it onto her lap.

'Whoops. Sorry about that. Never mind. No use crying over spilt chutney, eh? Hee-hee.'

Irona was too hungry to care. Even the limp crackers were good.

When she had taken the edge off her own appetite she tried again. 'Can you take me to the Fixer?'

Indifferent, cramming food into his mouth, he nodded. Regenerator stooped low over his own meal as though she might take it from him. He scooped up handfuls of pickles straight from the jar, licking his fingers and wiping his face on his sleeve. He didn't bother to touch the seals back onto the jars. Irona supposed he couldn't find them in the fulgurating twilight.

Finally she remembered to say thank you.

'You're welcome. Entirely.' He belched. 'Pardon me.' Cocking his little head on one side, Regenerator looked up at her. 'So what do you want the Fixer for?'

'I'll tell him when I see him.'

'Mm-hm. Meantime you're safe here. You know that.' He nodded several times and she found herself mirroring the movement. 'Entirely. You got they old cats, and you ain't got no jiggers that'll work down yere, not longer than a minute.' He screwed up his face in an expression of anxiety, worried that she might not believe him. When he was nervous, he spoke even faster. 'Like they screens, now. There they are, working happy as Larry one minute, and the next they looks like a Artic blizzard. The jiggers, they works on electric same as the screens. And it's so hot down yere that there ain't nobody going to find your body-heat. Nor your brain-waves nor nothing. You can be mad as hell down yere and ain't nobody going to care a flying – care a bit. Go on, try it.'

'Try what?'

'Try being angry. You should be angry. I would. Entirely.'

Modesty made Irona duck her head. Citizens just didn't get angry. From one of the jigsaw screens, pictures of a fairground at night cast pale gleams onto her face. She felt a failure, unable to experience even a hint of the rage Regenerator expected.

He tutted. 'That ain't it. It ain't natural, not being angry after all that.'

'But I'm not.'

'Oh yes you are. Try and find it.'

'Find what, for goodness' sake?'

'That's better.' He smiled, his mouth a yellow triangle of teeth. 'Find your anger.'

'I'm not angry, though.'

'Then what are you yelling for?'

She said less quietly, 'I'm not yelling!'

'You are.'

'I'm not. I am not yelling. Citizens don't get angry.'

'Hee-hee. You believe that crap, you'll believe anything. Ain't you seen enough of it on those there psychicators? I mean, it's your job, ain't it, anger? Where would you be without it?'

Somehow the dichotomy had never presented itself to Irona before. Momentarily she floundered for words. 'But – but anger's the exception!'

'More fool you if you believe that. Synod pickled you well, didn't it? Entirely.' He turned away triumphantly, creaking to his feet. Blood-red shards of light flamed across his chest then lost themselves in the density of darkness. An actor's agony exploded from a screen; Irona cringed, thinking of the sleepers she had sent to torture, the mohock with the triangle of scalp. And Twiss, whom she had tried to save.

'If you know everything,' she said, 'where's Twiss now?'

Regenerator was shuffling along a wall, groping into cupboards. His voice was so muffled that she could hardly hear what he was saying above the basso profundo of the dragon's heartbeat. 'Didn't say I knew it all at once though, did I? Anyway, what do you need Twiss for? He's got the brains of a kerbstone.'

Hearing her fantasy-figure insulted touched nerves too painful for her to talk about it. She could feel herself blushing in the darkness. 'He's not stupid. He might not be the world's brightest but he's got a sense of humour. He knows how to make people happy. And, and – if I could have persuaded him to take me with him, we could have got away to Harith.'

'So go on your own. The Fixer could do that no problem.'

'I can't!' Irona shouted, and immediately covered her

mouth with her hands as though she could stop the words winging outwards.

'So take me with you.'

'I can't,' she said again, 'you wouldn't do.' She gasped. 'Oh! I am sorry. I didn't mean to offend you.'

'Hee-hee. Bit hard offending me. Entirely hard. Why do you think I lives down yere? I been offended by experts.' Regenerator didn't wait for an answer. Instead he fumbled back through the distorted darkness and grabbed her burnt hand.

Frightened, she tried to pull away from him but Regenerator didn't let go. His wiry strength overmastered her. She toppled forward, skin twitching with fear. Her pulse polka'd in treble time to the womb-music. Scrabbling to find purchase with her feet on the slippery mattress, she lunged at his knees.

Regenerator tripped and fell over her. His body-reek choked her and she couldn't breathe. She rolled onto her side, trying to bring her knee up into his groin, but he crawled along her body, pinning her hip between his greasy thighs.

'Stop it, will you? Irona! I'm telling you. You got to trust me. All I want to do is fix they cuts. I ain't going to do nothing to hurt you. Promise promise. Ow! If you stops kicking me, I won't touch you no more.' His words spumed the darkness faster than bubbles in water.

Centimetre by centimetre, they disengaged, each watching the other for any sudden act of aggression. Irona backed away to kneel, compact but wary, with her shoulders to the smelly matting behind the couch.

'Deve!' she said bitterly.

'Entirely not. I only wanted to fix your hand. See? See?' He rootled through a heap of rags to find a small oblong case.

'What – what is it?'

'Little baby pocket olfactory. Some of the stuff's still left. I ain't going to harm you. Promise promise. Didn't my cats save you from they mohocks?'

'Tell me where the Fixer is then.'

But suddenly all the screens came on at once. Pictures clear and sharp shot glaring colours through Regenerator's bolt-hole. The slurred sound-tracks focussed in bright disharmony and the glittering chains chimed from the ceiling like elfin bells.

Regenerator quivered, his mouth sagging in fear. Tension stiffened his body until it seemed made all of bones. 'The randoms!'

'The what?'

But he didn't answer. Instead he darted to the narrowest wall, sliding over plastic, sending paper flapping up into the air. He began throwing things out of a cupboard, every movement carving panic on his frame. The scent of his sweat soured the air.

'What is it? Tell me!'

'The randoms, the randoms! Are you deaf? Can't you see they screens? Everything's working. Entirely. Even their jiggers. Especially their jiggers. We stay here and they'll trap us.'

'Who?' She plunged across the room to grab his arm. 'Tell me who! The randoms?'

'No, you daft bat. The Arms.'

8

ARMS AND THE RANDOMS

'Here!' he shouted. 'Take this. And this.' Regenerator didn't give Irona the opportunity to argue; he just crammed things into her arms. 'Careful careful. They'll break and then we've had it. Entirely. Goodbye head. Now come on. Quick.'

The screen-programmes, each perfect, clashed in intolerable discord. Regenerator ignored the musics and the dramas, waded across to the door.

Irona was beside herself, caught up in his obvious fright. 'You said we were safe! You said nothing could track us here!'

'That's when it's normal.' He shoved something under his belt, another package inside his shirt. 'But it ain't normal now. It's different. This is the randoms. Things are working properly. Synod alone knows why. Or how long for. We got to get out of here.'

Irona gave up. He thrust a bottle at her and she tied it to her belt, touching the incongruous knots of obedience. 'What about the cats?'

'Don't worry about they. At least they just eats you. I seen where the Arms takes you.'

So had she. Irona tacked across the rubble as he flung the door open and skittered into the shadowy tunnel. A giant cat fled past her knees, yowling with fright. Regenerator followed it.

Something flittered over her neck and her stomach contracted, but it was only one of the chains. It fell behind her, clinking against the rest. Irona followed his retreating footsteps and ran.

The objects in her arms began to glow. Their pale radiance shone out so that for the first time in this maze of twilight she could actually see where they were going.

And it sounded like they were heading straight for the dragon.

Somewhere behind them came the whistle of split air. Arms flying on their jet-packs. Irona knew it was stupid but she daren't look round; if she actually saw the Arms they'd have to be real and she wanted to kid herself that they weren't.

'Where are we going?' she hissed.

His answer floated back from his own pool of light. 'Generators.'

Irona's relief was ludicrous. *Generators! I knew that really. It's not a dragon. How stupid can you get?*

His lustres suddenly jinked off to the left and winked out of sight in a side-tunnel. Tangled in the throb of the generators and the wheezing of the air-conditioners – *Womb-music! What a fool!* – Regenerator's voice said, 'Stay there.'

'What?'

'Stay there! Synod, are you deaf?' His lights reappeared in front of her, paler and subtly different in colour. 'Right, come on then. Can't you hear they dogs?'

And waves of cats flowed by her, waves that were scummed with the small sinuosities of fleeing rats. They screeled as they ran but they didn't drown out the distant shriek of the jets nor the growling of engineered dogs. Rats skithered under her feet, seeming to know just where she was going to put each foot and getting to the exact spot to trip her as her bruised toes touched the ground. Pulling her skirts up between her legs, Irona hastened after Regenerator as best she could.

Again and again he disappeared off to the side, leaving her standing, afraid to be alone, and each time he came back into sight his radiance was fainter. Soon it was no better than the meagre ambient light. The cats had all flooded ahead of her; the rats sang in front. Behind came that sound of jet-packs cleaving the dry air, and just higher-pitched than the hiss and thud of the generators was the baying of the huge dogs.

Regenerator was jigging up and down with impatience. Blue sparks jumped from his heels. 'Come on! Catch up.'

She panted up to him, her legs trembling with weariness – and something besides. For where her hair escaped from her torn cap, it writhed and crackled around her with an unearthly life of its own. Turquoise rivulets of electricity streamed out along the path of the rising wind.

Regenerator said, 'Give us one of they lights. A long one.'

She handed him a tube of warm pink light. There was no battery, no power-source at all. It glowed through his hand so brightly that she saw the bones of his fingers dark inside the blood-red outlines of his flesh.

'It's the last one,' she said.

'Ain't far now, though. And this time I'll put it in the tunnel we're taking. All the others, they was just decoys. They'll think we gone the other way. Entirely.'

Neither of them spoke of the baying dogs.

Even as he spoke he was tugging her along. The dragon's breath howled past her, pasting her skirts against her legs so she could hardly totter into the gale. It snatched at her breath. The awful pounding compelled her heart-beat to an unnatural rhythm. Corrosive adrenalin bucketed along her blood-paths and tingled up the back of her neck.

Then Regenerator pulled her around a corner, and grit and dazzle streamed into her eyes. Tear-blinded, Irona could scarcely see the ranks of metal fans wheeling and wheeling to circulate the air.

But they were there. Sharp blades chopping endlessly round inside the metal ducts, they were black spinning bars between her and the bright safety of the generators.

'We're trapped!' she yelled, then had to yank him back to scream it in his ear. The noise beat at her hearing. For all they knew, the Arms and their hounds might be just around the bend behind them.

Regenerator shook his head. Shouting made his face even odder in the whirling shadows. 'We just goes through they old fans, see? They Arms, they can't do it. Too big. And the dogs'll be turned into little bitty meatblobs. We'll be fine.'

Irona finished the thought for him: *Entirely*. Only in her case, it was rank irony. The thing was impossible.

'Timing, see? And don't leave no arms and legs lying about. A dive and a somersault. You watch. Somersault.'

He did. Rolling forward, he kicked off with his feet just as one arm of a triple blade passed bottom centre of the duct. He tumbled head over heels and Regenerator was through to the other side, a silhouette crouching against the white light of the turbine room. His mouth distorted in a shout but she couldn't hear him.

Irona's body seemed to have no bones to hold it steady. Once, twice, she made false starts but chickened out at the last moment. The second time one of her cap-strings was chopped clean in half. If it hadn't have been for her terror of the Arms, she would have stayed where she was.

What the hell. *It's all trivia anyway*.

And half-hoping, half-fearing the blades would slice her out of existence and problems, she threw herself through the maelstrom fans.

Regenerator dragged her to her feet. He was leaping and capering, laughing ecstatically. 'We did it! We did it!'

Irona couldn't believe it. She wasn't dead after all, though Synod knew why not. Again she felt light as air, as though her body were splitting into millions of component atoms and infinity were dancing ecstasy inside her. She was laughing too.

And then, from between the mountainous generators, an Eye appeared. The Arms hadn't needed the dog-pack hunt at all. Deduction had been enough. They had come another way.

Vast and immune in their black carapaces, their dogs loping waist-high, the Arms marched out into plain sight and wove a spear of blue fire that shot burning through her chest. Her last thought was *It's not fair—*

The Watchtower

She woke with an involuntary scream. Wrapped in her last vision of the stunners firing ten thousand lightning bolts through her chest, she jerked awake but she couldn't force the scream out past her plastic gag. Slick walls of glass held endless banks of something slithering and grey. And the stench of unwholesome meat permeated the room.

Clamps and cables held her head but sliding her eyes to

one side she could just make out Regenerator on another gurney. And Twiss was strapped down to her left. Wires led to probes sunk into his brain; a droplet of blood crusted one of the shaven patches on his skull.

It can't get any worse, she told herself.

But she knew it could. And it did.

'The theory's quite simple.' The man was tall and patriarchal, his dark eyes commanding. Mind, they could have been any kind of eyes because not Irona nor Twiss nor Regenerator, strapped and gagged as they were, could have argued with his commands anyway. The man's name was Elditch, and Irona believed he was not the nominal but the actual head of the Synod. A man to be obeyed – but the matriarchs were there to temper his orders with mercy.

Elditch bounced up and down once or twice on his toes, radiating smugness. 'I'm sure you're well aware of it, Miss Warden, but these two sleepers probably aren't. So' – he bounced again – 'I'll tell you.

'Now, science found out long ago that a lot of information is stored in genomes. Genomes, of course, are – well, that is, genomes . . .'

He covered up his uncertainty by continuing, 'Let me put it in simple terms so that you sleepers can grasp it. If you teach a worm a way through a maze to a food supply, all well and good. It can't communicate what it's learnt, though, not directly.

'But if you chop that worm up and feed it to its companions, all of a sudden they'll know the way through the maze too. Then you can chop them up and spread what they've learnt to a whole new generation of worms, do you follow me? It's all to do with . . . er . . . PNA.'

Irona wanted to wring the self-satisfied Elditch's neck. *PNA, he calls it! Next he'll be trying to tell us he's an expert on kinetic diseases. What a moron!* But her silent levity was more like hysteria. Anything to keep her mind off what was coming next.

'Now,' Elditch said. His grey-streaked moustache twitched; Irona thought he might be smiling under it. He strolled casually across to the far wall where ominous glass panels glistened wetly. 'Just as humankind has learnt to manipulate species such as dogs to breed certain shapes and sizes and characteristics, in the same way, over the last several hundred years, we of the Synod have inculcated desirable personality types. We can build bodies to match, like our dear helpful Arms, but we wouldn't want too many aggressives, now would we?'

None of them could answer him so he answered himself. 'No, of course not. What we need are quiet, sociable, biddable folk who aren't going to be too greedy or too curious. After all, with the size of population just in little old Camelford Mountain, not to mention the rest of Admin territories, it wouldn't do to have lots of nasty selfish types stirring up trouble and rioting all the time, would it? We'd end up with something uncivilised like they have elsewhere. Not all the news-stands are faked, you know. But you won't know for long.'

Elditch leant casually against the glass cages. He caressed the panel possessively but something underneath it slithered and he couldn't help pulling his hand back. If Irona could have laughed, she would have.

'But you three,' – he shook his head regretfully, like a father who has just discovered his children stealing – 'and especially you, Irona, who should have known better . . .' He tutted and his red mouth closed tight on the sound. 'How could you repay us like this after all the love and trust we've showered on you?'

Words dammed up behind Irona's gag. *Love! Synod, when has anyone ever shown me any love? Not even my parents (two citizens, their faces twinned with their expressions of stern duty) or they wouldn't have left me behind. It's not just this last two years. Nineteen years I've spent alone, trying to live up to what everybody else expected of me and whatever I did, it was never enough. Love!* But the plastic skinning over her face and forcing its way down over her tongue stifled her until her throat swelled with frustration.

And she watched Elditch watching her thoughts on the screen and hated the nakedness of her mind, but still she couldn't help thinking what she did.

Elditch smiled patronisingly at her. 'A touch of the 'poor me's, is it? There, there. Still, that'll soon be a thing of the past for all of you. And, of course, Irona, you won't have your nice outside flat any more, but you won't mind that, will you? Because you'll be a sleeper too, like this silly anti-social boy you so misguidedly admire. A room in a row down on the single-letter levels will content you totally. And so it should.

'Because we have also discovered a way of storing human genetic information – specifically behaviour-patterns – in our dear little mutated worms. And in a minute we'll get a nice technician to drill a little hole behind your ear and slip some brain-worms into your heads.'

Twiss gave a strangled grunt, the only sign of his fierce struggles. On her other side Irona could hear Regenerator humming, a simple, pointless repetitive drone like a jingle you can't get out of your mind. Her own limbs stiffened; her stomach was so tight she could hardly move her ribs to breathe.

Elditch didn't care. Flicking dust from the front of his elaborately simple jacket, he sauntered over to peer down at Regenerator. 'Mind, some of you might not really notice a hole being drilled in your skull. You will notice the worms, though, I promise you that.'

He smiled. 'Because the worms are designed to eat through certain parts of your brains and leave their own little PNA messages of acceptable behaviour in their dung. And after a while the dung, of course, together with the worms themselves, will meld in your brains. Become part of you. Simple, see? Doing just what they're designed for. Teaching you what's right and wrong. Of course, it might hurt a bit, but you won't mind that, will you? After all, you've already hurt other parts of our society so it's only fair.'

'What about a trial?' screamed Irona. Or tried to. What came out from the gag down her throat was only the faintest of whimpers. Elditch glanced over at a monitor she couldn't see and said to the thought-imager, 'A trial? How silly. Of course you can't have a trial. We don't want the rest of Synod thinking we can't guard the guardians, now do we?'

The door hissed open, bringing just a touch of the clean cool astringent scent Irona associated with the watchlevels. Elditch smiled with a hint of malice – and something more. Irona could feel it but she couldn't understand it.

Elditch bounced on his toes again. 'Ah, here comes the excellent Maeve. Carry on, my dear.'

Maeve folded her hands neatly over the front of her matriarch's dress and bowed respectfully as Elditch swept out of Tau 7, but the minute he left she tutted and shook her head like a mother with a stubborn child. 'Poor dear, he doesn't like the next bit. Or at least, he doesn't like it from too near. But it has to be done. Doesn't it, Irona Warden?'

And Maeve didn't look at Irona's face either to see what was written there. Instead she gazed at the mute horror writhing across the thought-screen. And Irona seemed to feel the cold probes inserted in her brain though that was supposed to be impossible.

She did feel the drill, though. A cool spray forced the muscles in her neck and face and scalp to relax but it didn't take the pain away. Silent tears dripped tickling from the corners of her eyes and ran into the aseptic jelly that Maeve rubbed behind Irona's ears. And the drill itself sent almost imperceptible judderings through her head, peeling away a neat circle of skin, sealing the tiny blood-vessels, shoving through the thin flesh over her mastoid bone, stabbing agony into the bone itself. Every second that passed, Irona thought it couldn't hurt any more.

But it did. And it went on.

'I thought I'd do you first, dear, because you should have known what it was like,' Maeve said. Her smile was as serene as the symbolic blue of her matriarchal robes. Maeve flicked a glance at the monitor to read Irona's thoughts and her lips stretched just a little wider. 'No, dear, it's not strange at all. What loving mother doesn't punish her children when they're naughty? And you have been, haven't you, dear? Very, very naughty indeed. We could have had a full-scale insurrection on our hands while you lusted after this witless fool beside you. Now, you just lie there and suffer for a minute or

two until I finish you off, and I'll start setting your littl
friends up.'

Irona was too numbed even to turn her eyes towards Twis
but through the fog of pain her mind registered the sound
from beside her: the subdued rustle of Maeve's clothing, th
puff and hiss of the muscle relaxant, the impossibly high pitc
of the drill that shocked through her ears as Maeve began he
systematic torture of Twiss . . .

And there was nothing Irona could do. Nothing, not ever
speak. Even breathing was an effort: she felt her epiglotti
sagging over the airway to her lungs, heard her own bubblin;
breaths groaning through her uncontrolled larynx.

And all the time, beside her, her own shafting agony wa
being spiked into Twiss's brain *because I was too slow to sav
him. It's my fault. I should have stopped him long ago.*

But then this would have happened to him before.

Her open eyes couldn't even blink. Irona wondered wha
was showing on Twiss's screen, what were the colours an
shapes of his pain. She could hardly see for her own.

A flash of blue across the soft white of the ceiling, th
heaving grey of the glass cases. That was Maeve, going roun
Irona's gurney to work on Regenerator. Again that high whis
tling that seemed to pulse fire through her injured head.

Muffled, woozy, as though the words themselves wer
drunk, Maeve's voice phased in and out at Irona from vas
distances. 'There we are, then. All done. Now we've just go
to put a few worms through asepsis and wash out their littl
bowels. We don't want them giving you any nasty diseases
do we? We don't have many people die of this operation
Well, not too many.'

Irona tried not to give in to the terror Maeve wa
inculcating, but it was impossible with the cold metal tub
sucking reason out of her head. Fear sharpened the axe o
agony in the folds of her cortex.

Maeve's shoe-heels clicked efficiently over to one glass
wall. She opened a panel and Irona heard a soft, uniden
tifiable sound; the panel sprang shut again with a cris
snick. Again Irona saw that lying, loving blue of purit
fleet across her field of vision, then the Matriarch held u

a little vial of genetically-altered worms close before Irona's staring eyes.

'Here you are, dear. We just let the DNA-strands renew themselves as dear little worms inside your head. I'm going to share these out between you and your co-seditionists. That's what our society is all about, isn't it? Giving people what they need. Then making sure they don't take away from other people. Now, this is going to hurt. Quite a lot, I should think. I'll start with poor little Regenerator, but you've got lots of imagination, so I'll save you for last.'

Through the sound-swell of extreme torment, Irona thought she heard the slurp of worms being slicked down the syringe and into the tube. Maeve was right; she did have plenty of imagination, enough to hear physically the plunger excreting two or three wormlets into Regenerator's neural paths. Tears blinded her – *What's going on?* – but Irona couldn't blink them away.

Then she felt a breeze on her bare arm but she could see nothing. Whatever it was, it was behind her head. Perhaps Maeve had just been playing with her, and Irona was going to have those hideous alien worms in her, inside her. Now. She couldn't even swallow.

Logically it shouldn't have hurt any more than it already did, but when Maeve inserted a thin tube into the convolutions of grey matter that should have been safe inside Irona's skull, pain soared brightly into the black cosmos of her brain. It flew like a comet whose trail was starfire agony, and its razor-pinioned wings spread outwards in shining torment that exploded her mind from its nucleic core. Sharp metal tasted on her tongue – or was it in her eyes – and the steely scent of blood burned like bile in her throat.

I didn't mean it!

Acid light rasped her stomach, weighted down her lungs.

I didn't mean it! I don't want to die.

Hives of bee-stings jabbed swarming under her nails; sulphurous gases clogged her lungs with iron filings and cymballed in her bleeding ears.

Synod, I'll do anything! Anything you want me to. Only let it stop!

But it didn't. Ponderous and clawed as time, it crushed
her out from the present into a past and future that broke
her on their rack. Torture was her mother, her child, an
unbroken chain of descendants that lived in her forever in
exquisite hurt.

I. Ro. Na.

She was fractured. Smashed. Tiny ice-needle fragments.

And each of them went spinning out into different dimensions that wrenched her through guilt and heat and cold into
gaudy darkness, and the darkness flashed in the thunderstorm of her heartbeat.

Then it stopped. Not entirely; the hurt didn't go away,
but eventually she was again living in one body. From
somewhere beyond, splinters of sound dragged through the
infinite loneliness between her atoms. She could make no
sense of it. Nausea flowed back from her limbs to smoulder
in her stomach; pain still zigzagged its incandescence through
her head.

But at least she had a head.

She was damaged, but she existed.

Irona.

At first she believed it was her own thought, but then it
came again.

'Irona.'

And it came from outside her. It clanged loud as hammers
on an oil-drum, but it came from outside.

'Wake up, Irona.'

The blessedness of syllables! They didn't make sense and
they slipped inside her head with the cloying syrup of old
guilts, but they came over and over again. She was not a
galaxy alone.

There was something else, too. Something that rocked her
head until she wished it wouldn't, but it kept on happening
until she found the synapses that would open her eyes.

Her mother.

9

STARWING

'Mom?'

'Don't be ridiculous. I am Matriarch Bernardina and I insist you address me as such.'

'Wh-what?'

The woman with her mother's face rolled her eyes heavenwards in disapproval. It was a gesture Irona knew well. But the woman snapped, 'Matriarch Bernardina. Oh, for Admin's sake! Here, you!'

For a moment Irona was bereft. The moon of her mother's pallid face swam out of her vision and Irona had the most ludicrous urge to cry. But only for a moment. Then the white space over her head was filled with two faces, one blank of expression. The mother-figure's mouth said in what seemed like slow motion, 'Here, Maeve. You will enjoy giving this child another pain-killer. Go and get it. Yes, good, that's right. Now administer it.'

Something prickled cool and hissing damp against Irona's neck. It spread like a refreshing river through her system. Though the words still dopplered in Irona's hearing, they came more sharply now. 'Good girl, Maeve,' said the woman who wasn't Irona's mother. 'Well done. You liked that, didn't you?'

A grunt from Maeve.

A click of the tongue answered her.

How well Irona thought she knew that sound. But she was aware that she must be mistaken because now the pale woman said in syllables that began to have some burden of meaning, 'I am Matriarch Bernardina. Do you understand that, Irona Once-warden? The Matriarch Bernardina.'

There's something wrong! thought Irona as the mist began to roll heavily out of her brain. *Those eyebrows, the sharp*

little down-tug at the corners, the way their ends are wispy
didn't they used to be darker than that? And the skin's so tire
you can almost see through it. It never used to be like that.

Irona shook her head and wished that she hadn't. B
the twinge of headache took with it the last dazzling ra
of mind-fog. Still, though, underneath her awareness was
dreamlike memory of the face that had once kissed her.
was more vivid than the pallor she now saw marred with th
purple-red lips of an old woman.

'You can get up any moment now, Irona. Maeve will enjo
switching off your shackles, won't you, dear?'

Maeve sleepily grunted her assent once more.

The woman in the robes of shimmering celestial blu
nodded once, sharply, and said, 'You'll be all right now
Irona.' It sounded more like a command than sympath
'Now, Maeve, come and have a nice time disconnecting thes
two. You won't be interested in anything any of us has to sa
for a while.'

Sluggishly Maeve drifted over towards Regenerator, he
white uniform crackling as she began to move.

Irona wondered subvocally, *Why doesn't she disconne*
me first? It's not fair, but her childish feelings only coloure
her perceptions; they didn't actually form themselves into
coherent idea. She was still aware, though, of the chill met
tubes probing her brain. She wondered if the worms wer
there yet.

The Matriarch sat on the side of Irona's gurney, strokin
the girl's hand. 'Now, dear' – the word had a wire-edge
it – 'tell me what you thought you were going to accomplis
by running around after two sleepers. You must have know
they were dangerously close to waking.'

How can I say? (Images of a smile that shone bright as th
moon, strength exulting in her limbs as her mind touched
stallion's silken hot flank. And the corpse-lights of fear th
she had blackmailed Roger Watchwarden into covering up
and Twiss's rejection that burnt like an ulcer in her stomac
as she tried to escape with him the worm-death he wouldn
believe was coming.) How can I put feelings like that int
words?

Irona shook her head, dumbly, and a faint treacherous moisture dripped from her eye.

The Matriarch didn't seem to mind that Irona wouldn't answer. She merely stroked away, her dry old skin papery against Irona's, and asked, 'Well then, how did you propose to carry out this so-called escape from the Admin?'

The probes, the manacles, seemed sharper and more ineluctable. It was as if Irona could hear the worms' siren slithering close behind her ear – she flinched – and the matriarchal blue was no longer soothing but a deadly threat. She forced her mind away from the Fixer she'd planned to meet in the generator chamber because the old woman plunged a regard sharp as a dagger into Irona's eyes. Shadows of the past: she couldn't meet that gaze that stripped her of independent identity. 'I – I wasn't!' she lied, but Irona knew the old woman didn't believe her. She never had. Not even when she was telling the truth.

'And where, quite, did you intend him to send you?'

'We – I—' And Irona said nothing of the pictures wheeling in her mind complete with the perfume of cedar and the texture of a soft, teasing wind: *Harith, with its blue marbled oceans, the sea-plain backed by the green forests rising on the flanks of the dormant volcano. Nothing of the life her subconscious had dreamed up: a life far from the mother who had abandoned her (a spear of jade pain) and with lots of friends and – and – Twiss*.

But the stone-faced old Matriarch of Matriarchs said nothing of Irona's silence, either. Somehow that forbearance jarred with a feeling deep in Irona's psyche.

'And you, Irona. Just a moment. Keep still, will you!' And somehow Maeve was behind her, and so was the Matriarch. Seconds marched past then Bernardina said, 'Sit up – slowly, numbskull! Or you'll be feeling dizzy.'

That voice! To Irona it sounded just as peremptory some-how as it had done when she was a child. But no. Because this woman who looked and sounded and moved like her mother had a different name. Irona pushed herself up on one elbow and rolled to sit on the gurney. When she turned her head, half-expecting the probes to pull at her brain, the monitor behind her showed only blurs of rainbow static because the probes were lying naked on a metal tray.

But their ends were still wet.

She hadn't needed to say anything because her mother – because Matriarch Bernardina had seen it all.

And while Irona's mind was blank with despair, nakedness and wonderment, a hypno touched her pineal gland. Did she hear Bernardina her not-mother say, 'Harith? Hm. That might do after all.'

When her eyelids fluttered open, Irona slammed them closed to shut out the nightmare.

Only unfortunately it was still there however cautiously she peeked.

There was nothing. Endless, boundless nothing, black as all the fear of the dark that there had ever been. And she was floating over it, her gut already twisting in the anticipation of gravity. But far from falling, she seemed, somehow, to be rising. The fall would come next . . .

How could she be rising? And if there was nothing to judge it against, how could she tell she was rising?

Because there was something out there. A transparent room, pale and curved, with lines of cupboards limned in ghost-white shadow against the belly of darkness.

A reflection.

A reflection in crysteel.

For a split second reality dopplered. Grey slithering oils of worms that were the bleeding from the mind-rape of her mother drilling to get inside her head – only it wasn't her mother. It was Bernardina, the mother of them all.

Irona's hand leaped to grope behind her ear – and there was nothing. No hole, no scar. No brainworms gnawing—

Yet the thought of Twiss's smile was still a warmth in her mind. It was impossible. And reality shape-shifted—

A reflection of the sleeping-chamber of a ship that thrummed in the tesseract of hyperspace. And the fact that she was awake meant something. If only she wasn't feeling so muzzy perhaps she could work out what it was.

'Here, have this.'

She took the warm drink that someone gave her and sipped it through a straw. The sleepy taste left her mouth. Rubbing her eyes and yawning, Irona looked at her single companion.

It was a pleasant-faced, chubby girl, whose warm, golden-brown complexion seemed rich as chocolate against the sterility of the sleeping-chamber. She gave off a scent of perfumed soap and clean skin that was very human, a welcome contrast to the chemical odours of the chamber. 'Better now?' she enquired.

Irona nodded sleepily and stretched, luxuriating in the sense of well-being that began to glow inside her. 'Yes. Thank you.' Soft as silk, the safety-padding around her body held her in its comforting grip, but released her arms and shoulders when she wanted to sit up fully. The side of her bunk – the lid of her coffin – was fully retracted. Irona propped herself on one elbow.

'Who are you?' Irona asked, at the same time as the woman said, 'You're probably wondering who I am.'

They laughed.

'I'm Jaimindi. I'm the wake-up nurse. You're on the *Starwing*. It's a ship.' She looked at Irona and added, 'A space-ship. We're going to Harith. We're nearly there.'

'You mean you've been awake the whole trip?'

Jaimindi laughed again, for no reason that Irona could see, except sheer good humour. 'Ah-huh.'

'But you don't look old enough.'

'I'm not. I'm only five.'

This time it was Irona who laughed.

'Oh don't, Irona. I am five, really. Well, my personality is. They switched it off when I was a toddler to imprint my training, which took a while. But I'm the only medic this ship's got so I had to know my job, and I had to be young enough to stay awake and still be here when you lot got close to landing-time. It was all of eighteen years ago that we set off. I only got my memories back a while ago.'

'They've robbed you of years of your life! That's awful.'

'No it's not! Don't say that.' Jaimindi's liquid brown eyes

showed how hurt she was. 'Anyway, I've got memories of growing up in a training hospital and they feel like mine.

'The pilots are all ancient and you're the first person who's near my biological age that I've ever had to speak to. I've really been looking forward to it, ever since they imprinted my adult identity.' Jaimindi swallowed back her tears and changed the subject. 'Who else do you know? What about that Thebula with the carroty hair?'

'I'm sorry, Jaimindi. It's nothing against you. It's just that—' Irona stopped, not knowing what to say that wouldn't hurt the girl worse. Looking around for a subject to fill the uncomfortable silence, Irona asked, 'How did I get here? And how come no-one else is awake yet?'

'I suppose you applied for transfer to Harith like everybody else did and Synod approved your application.'

Gravity leaped inside Irona. *It was the Fixer. It must have been the Fixer . . . not Regen – another one . . . Worm-room? Where's Twiss?* And behind that urgency was her mother – or Bernardina? – a slimy grey slick. Only it wasn't real. They wanted her to believe it didn't matter . . . It was all slipping away from her, part of her life stolen—

The possibilities of truth coruscated through her mind. They burnt like sparks, blinding her inner vision, clouding her eyes.

Jaimindi didn't know. She said, 'Irona? Are you all right?'

And though Irona wasn't, she couldn't say so. She had to keep her mind hidden. Whose side was this nurse on?

Jaimindi carried on blithely, 'Good. I wanted to wake you up first. I've had plenty of time to go through all the info-discs and I thought you'd be the most fun.'

Me? Fun? and behind that, the slower thought, *The most fun?* warmed in Irona's personality. 'Well, thank you. That means a lot to me.'

They smiled at each other.

Irona tried to be casual. 'Are you going to wake anybody else up yet?'

'Not today. Today is going to be my day off.' And Jaimindi grinned mischievously.

*   *   *

Jaimindi set up the particle shower and then tactfully disappeared so that modesty could be preserved. The gentle stinging brought Irona more fully awake. Then she revelled in the attentions of the olfactory that Jaimindi had programmed for her. Peace and happiness filled her soul; vitality tingled in her body.

When she stepped gladly out of the olfactory, she saw that the wake-up nurse had laid out some clothing for her. Irona was glad to slip into a dove-grey skirt and bodice that felt familiar. As she knelt to lace her boots, she repeated the prayer that all good citizens taught their children when they learned to dress themselves: 'May these ties be in my mind as the love and duty that tie me to the Admin, mine to them and theirs to me.'

It was the same with the ribbons on her cap and her cord belt with its knots of obedience. A calming, comforting ritual, it was an ingrained habit that came automatically every time.

After that it didn't occur to Irona to wonder how she had got here. Or even to wonder why she wasn't wondering . . .

The lights dimmed momentarily and a soft chime filled the air. Irona was crossing the room to open up when Jaimindi put her head through to say, 'Are you ready yet?'

'Mm. Ready for what, though?'

'I thought you might like something to eat, perhaps, or to go and meet the crew.' Jaimindi was talking really fast, as though she were afraid that Irona wouldn't want to listen to her for very long. 'Or there's the library with all the disks about Harith – we'll be there in a couple of weeks now, Irona. Aren't you excited? I am. Or—'

Irona laughed gently. 'Slow down. You're making me breathless just hearing you. Let's have something to eat, shall we?'

Jaimindi made them both a snack in the big commissary next to the sleep-room; Irona helped. Both of them picked at the salad as they watched the protein-cakes start to sizzle in the pan. Even something as simple as that was fun with somebody else there, and the two girls giggled at childish puns in high good humour.

When Jaimindi served it up, though, she picked up her plate and the bread-basket, saying, 'Come on. I've never liked eating all by myself in this huge great barracks of a place. It makes – it always used to make me remember that I was on my own.'

The cabin was stuffed with personal touches. There were a family of fantastic animals in clear red and blue and green glass on one white shelf; a rag doll amongst the pillows on the bed. A vase of rainbow-painted feathers stood by the bed next to the computer remote. Little tapestries and oriental paintings were framed on the walls. It all smelt of perfume and Jaimindi's own clean, earthy perspiration.

Jaimindi plumped herself down and Irona sat across the table from her, looking at all the knick-knacks that were souvenirs of a life Jaimindi only thought she'd led. Irona didn't know whether or not to ask about them; she didn't want to upset her companion but at the same time she didn't want to look as though she weren't interested. What she did say as she took a bite was, 'Mm. You cook a mean protein-cake. I hadn't realised how hungry I was.'

'It's all down to the way I open the packet.'

They laughed. Then they picked who to wake up next.

'Mmm, I can see why,' Jaimindi said when Irona stopped the scanner at Twiss.

'Hands off, he's mine.'

'Well I'll have that other blond one over there then.'

'Sticker?' Irona thought of his childlike simplicity. 'You were made for each other.'

'Really?'

'How would I know? Try him and see. And wake that skinny little weird one up, Regenerator. He makes me laugh. And he saved my life.'

'Did he? Tell me about it.'

'Well I'll think about it.' Irona winked, covering over the embarrassment that came to her when she thought of just herself and Twiss with nobody to hide behind except Jaimindi. Flipping through the hundreds of profiles on the scanner, she wondered where to start.

Thebula? Red-headed, outrageous, an only child and an

orphan. ('Like me,' said Irona. 'Like both of us,' Jaimindi answered.)

'What about that Dilla?' They looked. A beauty with a chip on her shoulder, a nagging mother (they cross-referenced her and decided to leave her as long as possible) and a baby daughter. 'No,' Jaimindi said. 'She's always moaning, see?' Irona nodded. 'Her husband left her. Let's do the same.'

'How about this one?'

'What, that lad Spinon? He looks all right but he's about as intelligent as a slug, see? And not even a flicker of humour to brighten him up a bit. Help yourself, Jai, but be prepared to talk about floor-fibres from now until doomsday.'

Jai wasn't sure how to take Irona's levity; Irona wondered for a moment if she'd upset the girl until Jai said, 'Well, how about this one for you?'

Irona looked – and swatted her. Sinofer was a fine, solid man – thirty years older than she was. She said with wry irony, 'Mm, tasty. I'd ask him to contract marriage with me but his wife might not let him. Meantime let's start that Thebula-girl thawing out first, shall we? Wit and cynicism, hm? Looks like she'd be a laugh.'

The wake-up nurse never thought to ask Irona where she had learned to read psych-profiles.

For the next two weeks Irona and Jai had the time of their lives picking out their ideal society – and living in it. It was like a holiday with only the best of friends to talk to against the staggering fire-opal of hyperspace. The only thing Irona had to do was experience the data-disks about her new world, and that was a pleasure.

A pity, she thought, that the twenty years of sleep hadn't used their frosty grip to wither the brambles in her character. Because now that she didn't have to be responsible, any time alone clawed at her with questions she had never had to face: *Who am I? Now I'm not defined by duties and the Synod's expectations, who is Irona? What am I supposed to do with myself for the rest of my life? How am I supposed to use up all the hours and days and years?*

Jaimindi breezed along to call her out of her coffin retreat.

'Come on, Irona, stop slopping about. Let's go and see how Thebula's getting on in the gym.'

And Irona seized on activity and companionship to keep her away from her mental desert. Without the structure of Synod, she felt like a limpet hooked out of its shell.

As soon as she could get up the nerve to wake Twiss, as soon as there were enough other people to hide herself behind, she coded for his defrosting. Shielding her nervousness from Jai, she waited anxiously.

Twiss woke, his hazel eyes focussing after he had had the drink she handed him.

'You again! Where are we?'

'We're going to Harith,' she said, and he smiled. 'You, me, your Granfer, Regen – the lot of us. On a sleeper-ship on the way to the best colony the Admin's got.'

Twiss blinked. 'How . . .?'

'I fixed it.'

He didn't notice the white lie she needed to give him so that he would give her some respect. He wasn't angry any longer.

'Honest?'

'Yes, we're less than ten days from Harith. Honest!'

Squeezing her hand, he grinned with a charm that did strange things to her. 'You were right, Irona. You said you could pull it off and you did.' He gazed into her eyes with his piercing hazel ones. 'Where can we go to get a quiet drink around here?'

He didn't seem to have any memory of the worm-room at all. And though he didn't immediately become inseparable from her, Irona had sense enough to realise that this was reality, not fantasy. He might talk to everybody, but he still came back to her sooner or later with some new, amusing anecdote to make her chuckle. And she had friends of her own now, too, though Regenerator refused to be part of any group. He spent his time up in his bunk with the lid down, fiddling with the electronic gizmos he always had in his pockets. He told her he was making a portable screen. Irona told everyone but nobody believed her until it picked up a visual from the flight-deck's log.

Hour by hour, as the sight/sound/smell of the disks about

Harith entranced them all, excitement grew. The hard white snowcap of the volcano guarding their new home in the bay symbolised its exotic allure. The tang of snow and pines blended with the perfumes of citrus and salt water.

Sitting watching the pastel, wave-form houses up with Regenerator on the edge of his coffin, high above the cheerful crowd, Irona felt their joy rising in her true and strong and bright. Outside her link-up in the Watchtower, she had never experienced such force of emotion from other people. *Must be because I feel it inside too*, she thought. Her thoughts shied away from the worm-room and the hole behind her ear. She didn't even remember Carandis stinging her hand with something cold.

The alien sun dropped gems of gold on the crushed velvet sea. Happy expectation grew.

Until the starscape died.

There were no juniors in the Matriarch's sanctum. The only colour seemed to be the hard angry blue of the Sky.

Elditch swallowed and avoided Bernardina's eye. Just the two of them, they sat on a window seat. The plummetting view outside made Elditch nervous. He said, 'Do you think it'll do?'

Bernardina lounged back on her tapestried cushions. It was the most relaxed he had ever seen her. Even her lips were a better colour and her wrinkled skin had a healthier bloom when she looked in the mirror. He couldn't understand why.

'Oh, I think so, Elditch, at a pinch.'

'I can't see why she's so important.'

Bernardina poured him wine with her gnarled hands and he appreciated the rare honour. She sipped from her own goblet. 'Oh, she's not really.' The conviction amplified in her voice didn't blind Elditch to the truth, though he pretended it did. The Matriarch of Matriarchs went on, 'I just don't like wardens to hear of treason in their ranks.' Bernardina smiled to herself. Her pleasure at least was authentic. 'And I've used it to contain Carandis once and for all. She has nothing she can use on us now. I had to use your seal for the databanks, of course.'

That distracted Elditch, as she had meant it to.

'I hate it when you do that,' he said petulantly. 'It always makes me feel there's something going on behind my back.'

Bernardina shrugged expansively, her old hands encompassing the austerity of the room. 'And without the datafiles to prove a link between the waking warden and the others' – she nodded to herself, satisfied – 'Carandis will be well and truly going round in circles by now.'

Elditch felt his brows contract in puzzlement. 'I don't get it. Why save those two wakers with the girl? And that old fellow?'

'Save? My dear Elditch, I'm merely killing four birds with one stone. Rather a neat solution, don't you think? Their records sent off-planet with them, just a little edited version left. Carandis must be spitting mad but there's nothing she can use against us.'

Elditch didn't notice the force of that 'us'.

'But wakers? On Harith? They could be up to anything!'

The Matriarch of Matriarchs laughed. It startled Elditch, it had been so long since he had heard that sound. Bernardina admired her rings in the sunlight and said gloatingly, 'Forty years to get there and back? They'll be asleep for the first twenty anyway. Who cares what they're up to? They'll be safer out there than if they were brain-wormed.'

What she didn't say was safer for whom. Elditch assumed she meant only that Carandis was neutralised.

'Besides,' she told him, 'I did put a little something in their heads. Wherever they are, they'll always be mine. And anyway, when they get there, they'll either take care of – a certain little problem. Or it'll take care of them.'

Bernardina smiled.

10

HARITH

The sky was gone. No more soft, starstrung womb-night. Hard white walls squashed them inside the sleeper-ship.

'Don't panic.' Jaimindi had to shout to make her soft voice heard. 'They always blank the crysteel for landing. It's to stop everyone getting vertigo when we drop down through the atmosphere.' She added in an undertone to Irona, 'Mind, I'm surprised the captain didn't announce it.'

The hubbub continued, only slightly muted by Jai's news. Irona watched the sleepers – *No, I've got to stop thinking of them like that. We're all settlers now* – trying to suppress their panic at the sudden disappearance of the stars. With the instantly visible fourth wall of whiteness it was as though the room had shrunk. The half a thousand occupants all at once experienced a collective claustrophobia that bred barely-controlled terror.

'Go on, shoo,' called Jaimindi above the rising babble. 'Back to your coffins – I mean, beds. Use the foam to hold yourselves in. You too, Irona.'

The crowd was nervy; it swayed this way and that. People shouted for their friends, their family. Children yelled for their mothers. Still some vestige of citizenship pushed a hundred or so reluctantly to the ladders up the tiers of coffins. Others, already trapped up there, shoved to set foot on the steps to climb down. Echoing chaos reigned.

No-one wanted to go back to the helplessness of mere pre-packaged freight, especially when the ship jolted side-ways. It was only fractional, but enough to unsettle the balance-centres of the inner ear and induce a feeling of instability. One or two parents battled to get their offspring into the padding, but the children had caught the tension all around them. They screamed and fought to stay free. The noise began to spread like a contagion. Something blared over the ship's intercom but nobody could hear it clearly.

Jai looked totally out of her depth. Turning breathlessly to Irona, she put her lips close to her friend's ear and shouted over the hubbub, 'What can I do?'

No ghost-alarms nor acid sulphurous corpse-lights here to announce panic, but the effect on Irona was the same. If it had done nothing else, her training had taught her that riots meant death.

She glanced over at Twiss. He and Granfer were standing back to back. Sticker was a couple of yards away to give cover and divide any attack, his shoulders safe against a wall, his straggling hair greased back out of his eyes. Sinofer, a burly tractor-talker, had his arm round his plump, jolly wife Tebrina; their toddler Fessbar was screaming against her neck. Skinny Thebula was backed against another wall, her red hair rampant.

'Got any olfacts you can spray into the air?' Irona yelled back at Jai. 'Calmants, say?'

The ship began to bucket. Five hundred people groped for handholds or fell, tangling in other people's legs and bringing them down screaming from the ladders. Already there were split heads and the sharp crack of a broken bone. Scarlet splashes of blood screwed the tension tighter.

'You what?'

'Calmants, Jai! You must have some somewhere. Go and get some out of the olfactory and stick it in the air conditioning somehow.'

The wake-up nurse's face was a blank as she swayed against the ship's wild motion.

'Oh, come on!' yelled Irona. 'You've got to be able to put stuff into the air or you wouldn't have been able to keep the place sterile. Go on, go and get that sorted.' The ship lurched suddenly upwards. 'And hold on tight.'

The crowd was rapidly becoming a mob. Suddenly all the Watchtower talk of a mass waking came home to her. Suddenly she understood emotionally, where before it had only been a superficial logic thing, the need for Arms and calmants and the fear of the worms.

Elbowing, wriggling, she shoved her way through the noisy throng to Twiss. Behind her came a vast shout: it seemed that someone had tried the door through to the ship's corridor. It was locked. Above the density of panic came the captain's voice turned up loud as a thunderclap: 'There is no need for alarm. The doors will remain closed until after touch-down for your safety. Please fasten yourselves in.'

But half of the crowd had only seized on the word 'Alarm'. Already two men were trying to break down the door mechanism with chairs. A woman started trying to hot-wire the door circuit; she fused it and acrid smoke came out of the ruptured liquid crystals.

Someone yelled, 'They're trying to poison us!' as a fine choking dust clouded out of the fire-dampers set in the ceiling. An adolescent boy was having an attack of hysterics. Regenerator clambered monkey-like up to the highest sleep-pod, chittering to himself in a piercing torrent of undistinguishable words. A silver-black glint of metal sparked in his hands; Irona had no time to work out what he thought it was for. A coffin-lid the length of a man clattered down beneath his feet and onto the heads of the seething sleepers below. Someone groaned; someone collapsed under its weight. Hysterical wails filled the dusty air.

Irona reached Twiss. He was still in his back-to-back position.

'Don't just stand there!' she shouted at him. 'Calm them down! Tell them what's going on!'

He looked at her as though she were insane. Or irrelevant.

'You can do it, Twiss. Only you.' He began to take notice, his eyes focussing on Irona rather than beyond. She went on, 'Everyone talks to you. They look up to you. Tell them to stay still. Look, they're hurting each other. See, over there by the door. Stop them or they'll kill each other.'

The sealed exit was hardly visible now between smoke and jets of powder extinguisher. People were pushing to get away from it even as others at the back were stampeding for the doors. Those caught crushed in the middle were screaming, stumbling to their knees while the panicky mob eddied this way and that, blundering over the fallen.

'Go on, Twiss! Do it! Tell them to sit down before they murder each other.'

Twiss rescued a girl nearby just before she fell under the trampling feet. Young, crinkly-haired and cute, she clung to his neck, her legs clamped round his waist.

'Sit down!' he roared. 'Sit down. Hear me, Granfer? You sit down, you daft old bugger, and you, Sticker, you make 'em sit down.'

A few sleepers, happy that there was someone to take control, did as they were told. Irona, close by him, was alerted to the first few sprays of calmants adding to his power. The ring of people sitting at his feet grew.

Surprised at his own unsuspected force, Twiss bellowed his message again. Sticker staggered around the leaping deck pulling people to the floor. Emboldened, Twiss added, 'Come on now, let the fire-fighters do their work. If you want to live, sit down!'

On him, the calmants merely acted to strengthen his new-found feeling of potency. They reinforced the sleepers' security in being told what to do.

Irona didn't mind. All over the vast sleeping-chamber those already sitting were hauling their neighbours down beside them. The uproar was beginning to subside enough for the captain to be heard once more.

'. . . the newly-designated landing-site in approximately ten minutes.'

Now, in all the chamber, there were only three people still standing: Irona, Sticker, and Twiss. But Twiss stood tall and commanding, heroic with one arm protectively around the child, the natural focus for all eyes. His wavy blond-brown hair glowed like the evening sun against the white surroundings and something about his strong face drew the attention of women and men alike.

He knew nothing about the reasons for the change of landing-site. In fact, when a youth called out a question about it, Twiss stood helpless for a moment. Irona could have kicked herself for not staying near enough to him to tell him what to think.

Twiss, unhampered by knowledge but bolstered by calmants, merely said, 'Don't you worry about that. It's all right. Don't worry. Everything's all right.'

And the bald fact of his saying so made it right.

Irona could only be grateful. Wading between the seated bodies, she headed for the washrooms close by. Inside she grabbed a pocket olfactory, thrusting another one at Jaimindi who was huddling in the farthest corner, her skin a sickly grey.

'Jai, come on! We can't leave those kids bleeding to death.'

Jaimindi's eyes were white-rimmed, staring. 'All those people! I can't go out there, Ro.' She sketched a frightened gesture at the half a thousand sleepers beyond the washroom who were barely under control.

'You've got to.'

Jai clung tighter to a stanchion.

Irona advanced on her. 'I mean it, Jai. You've got to go out there or they'll be coming in to get you. Don't let them see that you're scared.' She held out her hand encouragingly. Her own fingers were chill enough with tension but Jai's were frozen.

'I can't face all of them at once!'

'You don't have to. You can only treat one at once.'

Somehow the syllogism worked.

When, hand in hand, they emerged from the washrooms, Irona led Jai to a child with a dramatic but superficial cut bleeding on the forehead. The wake-up nurse responded to her imprints. 'Oh, that does look nasty. Come on, let me make it better. That's right, little lovey. Jaimindi make it better for you.'

And Irona anaesthetised the broken arm. Its owner stopped whimpering and the tension-levels sank at once.

Twiss announced calmly to his sleepy audience, 'Just stay where you are while Irona and Jai fix you up.'

Nothing like stating the obvious, Irona thought, while she calmed the child and Jaimindi set the arm in inflatable splints.

Twiss reslung the child wriggling in his arms and patted her back clumsily. He smiled down at her, eyes aswim with narcotic peace. 'Everything's all right.'

By touch-down, everything was.

'Assemble on the baggage deck to reclaim your possessions.' Now the captain sounded perfectly calm. Audio only, his message boomed out through the sleepers. He went on, 'The purser will ensure that everyone receives his or her possessions in an orderly fashion. There may be a slight delay while the freight is unloaded. Please wait quietly. Disembarkation will take place as soon as possible.'

Irona, wishing she could get at Regen's pocket-screen to see what was going on, wondered whether her mental recall of the alarm in his tone had been just her imagination – until the captain added something that wiped such irrelevant speculation from her mind.

'Wake-up nurse Jaimindi Perel, report immediately to the flight-deck.'

Now what's all that about? Surely she'd be more useful here with the passengers?

But Jai was half-way across the dense crowd, Regen was ten levels high in his coffin, and there was no-one with whom Irona could discuss it.

Ahead, the doors leading to the gangway were peeling apart. Twiss strode naturally through to the front of the crowd, Sticker and Granfer unconsciously falling in to flank him in arrowhead formation. Twiss handed the child back to her mother, the flirtatious brunette Desselie, who was visibly grateful.

Too visibly. Something turned over uncomfortably in Irona's subconscious but it went back to sleep before she could identify it.

Desselie was crying with relief, not a wrinkle on her face, and she was staring intensely at Twiss. *Am I the only one who can see how uncomfortable she's making him?* wondered Irona, shuffling forward a couple of steps in the pointless urge not to be last.

But Twiss merely smiled slightly. Irona could tell it was

because he couldn't think what else to do, but she heard
a young couple in front of her say, 'Will you look at
that, now. His modesty!' and the answer, 'True nobility,
that is.'

Can't they see him blushing? Irona asked herself, taking
another step forward and casting a swift glance to check
that the little boy with the splinted arm was still safe with
his father.

Then Jaimindi wormed through to her and grabbed her
sleeve. She looked more apprehensive than usual.

'What is it, Jai?'

'It's that order from the captain. That's not supposed to
happen. I'm supposed to stay with the passengers.'

Irona suppressed her own curiosity to soothe her friend's
jitters. 'Don't be scared.' Another half-step forward. 'He's
probably just going to tell you why the landing-site's been
changed.'

'No he isn't, then. He could tell that to everybody all at
once over the intercom, couldn't he? He's going to tell me
off for the panic in here.'

'Well you tell him he should have warned everyone
about the crysteel opaquing before he did it. You tell
him how you used the calmants and organised the passengers.'

'But that was you!'

'Who cares? I'm not the one he's going to bawl out, if
that's what he is going to do. Besides, what difference does
it make? You treated the casualties, you put the calmants in
the air-conditioning. I didn't do anything.'

Shuffle-shuffle.

'But it was your idea.'

'It doesn't make a blind bit of difference where you got the
idea from, does it? It was still you who did it. Take credit
where it's due. But go on now, Jai, or he'll be slating you
for being late as well. Go on, off you go. I'll see you on
Harith.'

'But who'll look after the passengers? That's my job.'

'Tell him you delegated it to me. And King Twiss over
there.'

Jai didn't even acknowledge the irony. She scooted off, twisting her body to get more quickly through the throng converging on the doorway.

Expectation gave way to boredom in the muted gloom of the baggage deck. For a while every clang that reverberated through the hull caused a buzz of excitement. Everybody picked up their luggage and poised themselves to move out onto the surface of Harith for the first time.

But nothing happened. Gradually the weight of the carrisacs and boxes got too much for straining arms. Each time the cymbal-sounds crashed out, the lifting of luggage went on for a shorter interval as it gradually became clear even to the most hopeful that it didn't presage the opening of the hatch.

But the irregular thuds that set the walls gonging went on, and nothing else occurred except that the pall of tedium grew denser. Nobody bothered to move at all now, except to squat on their cases or lean more wearily against the corridor's sides. Conversation had died. She would have welcomed even Regenerator's cheerful inanities to break the silence but he was invisible somewhere at the back of the queue. There was no need for calmants now.

Irona watched Twiss, perched on one of the few seats ahead of her, mop the sweat from his face. She too found it hot and stuffy in the confined crowd. Again she wondered why the landing-site had been moved and what, if anything, it had to do with the delay.

After almost an hour the intercom chimed. Energy spread through her, so quickly that she knew it couldn't be a simple reaction. It had to be some olfactory stimulant. Adrenalin and some joybringer.

Jai. But Jai would be following orders . . .

Before ever the captain spoke a word Irona knew there was something going on. And it couldn't be good if the sleepers needed adrenalin-boosts to cope with it.

'When the doors open you are to proceed at once to the area beyond the markers on your left and before the perimeter fence. Do not attempt to leave the confines of the perimeter. Leave the ship in an orderly fashion and wait quietly for further orders. Keep well clear of the ship's exhausts. Good luck, everybody. Captain Dainty signing off.'

There was still no sign of Jai when the doors finally split to let in the dazzle of daylight. In some strange, unidentified quality it was not the same as the light back on Earth.

Irona squinted against the glare to make out Twiss's silhouette and followed him and his companions, using their wedge-shaped formation to break a way through the sweaty throng and out into the brightness.

Air! Sweet and chill and charged with ozone, it scythed through the fetor to revive her. She needed nothing now to alert her to the thrill of the new horizons opening up in her life. It was a moment she would never forget. As expectant as any them, she stepped eagerly onto the ramp.

A vast, uncitied land rolled away towards desert and distant hills capped with thunderheads that lowered black and purple. Nearer, the air was livid with the colours of sunlight after the storm. Raindrops sparkled – *Natural raindrops!* she realised excitedly – on the sweep of sparse vegetation, freeing a sharp, greasy odour from the plants, and a rainbow glimmered pale above the yellow of dunes off to her right.

Close behind Twiss – the people seemed to part for her – she bounced off the metal ramp and made her first footfall on Harith. The burgeoning future seemed to explode in a fountain of joy inside her. Each breath was intoxicating, the wholesome wind her friend, and the earth that was tussocky beneath her boots called to her of home. Here was where she belonged, and it was a wonderful feeling. She had never known anything like it. She couldn't even separate the enchantment of the strange sounds from the normal buzz of the crowd around her. It was all one in pleasure and promise.

I'll be different here! she thought, and the strange blue sky above her marked her covenant. For the sky was rich and soft, and no Admin marred it with a roof of prisoning crysteel.

It was harder to walk on the uneven ground than she had realised. The low plants had glassy tendrils clustered with spiky grey-green balls in place of leaves. Between their irregular growth the soil was dark with moisture but only a centimetre down it was pale and dry as dust where her feet scuffed it. By the time she had covered the half a kilometre of flag-strung pathway her ankles were aching. *I'll get used to it*, she promised herself, tripping on a hummock.

The wire-marked walkway widened abruptly into an oval twice as long as it was broad. Irona drifted to a halt but the pressure of people behind her drove her towards the far side of the enclosure. *Where's the volcano?* Irona thought at about the same time as Tebrina behind her asked her husband the same thing.

'It'll be behind the ship somewhere,' Sinofer said in his Kentish accent. 'We'll see it soon enough, don't fret. Probably be sick of the sight of it afore too long.' But the good-humoured way he said it showed he was just trying to mask his own excitement.

Twiss, just ahead of her, had come to a halt near the fence. Irona stood by him. It was hard to hold her emotions down; she couldn't help grinning in delight at her new world.

There was a faint buzzing that was soon drowned out by the murmur of the growing crowd. Too aware of Twiss to bother wondering what was causing the noise, Irona forgot about it in moments. She would have felt better with Regenerator to make her laugh but he wasn't in sight. Nor could she see Jaimindi.

She saw another wire fence some fifty metres beyond the first. It crested a fold in the ground and it seemed somehow to fade in and out of vision. Irona assumed it was the tiredness in her eyes because when she glanced down, the fuzzy green balls of ground-cover plants seemed to shift and shiver in the same way. Harith rippled disconcertingly.

From behind the ship rolled two huge balloon-wheeled tractors linked nose to tail. Strangely silent, they dragged behind them a convoy of shallow wagons loaded to the brim with crates and arcane agricultural machinery. Their motion caught Irona's gaze and gave her something to look at while the interminable waiting went on. The long train disappeared momentarily in a dip in the ground, then reappeared heading

off towards the mountains. At first she thought it was the First
Wave of Harithians unloading supplies for the new settlers
but the convoy trundled past the enclosure and kept on going.
Anxiety began to tighten her stomach.

Stop it! she told herself. *You're just being paranoid.*

All the same it was strange to see their goods shrinking
towards the horizon. The last she saw of it, the train was
trundling away fast into the foothills looking as small as a
child's abandoned toy.

They'll come back for us, she thought. *It'll be all right.*

Meantime the rest of the settlers filed noisily into the oval.
Irona still couldn't see Regenerator, but then, he wasn't tall
enough to stand out in a crowd. The boy whose arm she had
set gave her a tired wave and she waved back.

Then the ship's speakers chimed into deafening life. 'You
are now on Settlement Knoll. This is where you will make
your homes.'

A babble arose. 'This isn't my plot!'

'This don't look nothing like where they showed us on
the disks.'

'My bit were by the sea.'

'Where's that volcano at?'

'How come it's so dry?' In the hubbub she missed what the
captain said next.

What she did hear was, '. . . newly-designated site . . . to
you . . . Synod of Harith.'

So where's all our goods going? Irona thought in mounting
unease.

As if the captain had heard her, he announced, 'The
government of Harith has also taken its awaited supplies—'

'So what are we supposed to use?' Irona asked of no-one
in particular. Around her people began to ask the same thing
as a low roll of thunder predicted another storm. They were
caught in the open and unease began to spread through
the sleepers. As if in warning, the air began to darken.
Silken veils of rain began to hiss across the scrublands
towards them.

'—which will be redistributed . . . strict proportion . . .
work you do.'

A group closest to the landing-site started to break back to the ship but the unseen Captain Dainty's voice rose to a nervous pitch as he said, 'Keep well clear of the exhausts . . . lift-off . . . luck to you all . . . and goodbye.'

Almost invisible behind the rain, the ship rose long before anyone could get close to it. They were marooned in the empty wastes of Harith.

11

NAKED RAIN

Hours passed. There was no sign of the First Wavers.

'They are coming back for us, aren't they?' Jai asked.

Irona didn't think so, but it wouldn't help to say it.

Twiss was reassuring. 'Sure they are. They needed us enough to bring us here, didn't they? Besides, they wouldn't leave us out in this.'

The rain was still falling, plastering his hair darkly to his head.

Irona watched Granfer shiver. At least, because of his sailing before the Sky, he wasn't frightened of the water tumbling from above. 'We can make shelter out of what they've left us. OK?' Irona said in the quick huddled conference with Twiss, Granfer, Sticker and Jai.

'Sure, why not? What else is there?'

Lightning rocketed through the nightfall and dazzled again in reflections from the rain-pocked pools spreading across the scrubland. Not two seconds later thunder shook their bodies. Screams split the night as Second Wavers clung to one another or shrank or grovelled in the water-polished scrub. For the sleepers it was the first time any of them had experienced a storm as rain and wind stinging cold on their skin, not just a newscast thrill they could leave at any time.

'That – that was close,' Jai said after a shocked silence. Their ears were ringing from the shattering sound and she had to raise her shaking voice to be heard. 'Do you think – no.'

'Think what?' Twiss asked.

'I was going to say, do you think it's out to get us?' Jai rubbed nervous hands over her face, then pretended she was just wiping the rain from her eyes. 'But it's not out to get us. I'm just being paranoid. They haven't got shields here. It's just random.'

The words brought images of Regenerator and the randoms to Irona but she peered through the rain at the sleepers and said, 'Go on, Twiss. No point in waiting for the First Wavers.' She gestured at the cowering mass. 'Get them moving. The kids are freezing.'

Twiss straightened then ducked his head as he got a face full of blinding rain. 'Well I can't stand here fannying about all day. I'm not getting any drier. Let's go, let's go, let's go!'

Without ceremony he strode to the nearest sleeper. The man was kneeling in the mud, back bent to the rain, arms over his head. Twiss hauled him to his feet and the sleeper uncoiled spinelessly. He would have slumped again but Twiss shook him and yelled against the echoes of thunder that still rumbled from the mountains. 'Don't just sit there! Tip that stuff out of the packing cases. We can use them to get the children under shelter before they freeze to death. Go on, man!'

Almost the sleeper crumpled to the ground again but one glance at Twiss's face was enough to convince him: Twiss would hit him unless he obeyed. Soon, by example and fear, Twiss, Sticker and Granfer got enough people moving to make a difference. Others copied them though some stayed huddled in the mud.

Irona and Jai organised what cases to use and where to pile the different sorts of goods: food canisters, clothing, kitchenware and so on. Unfortunately there were so many people now that it was impossible, especially against the crashing thunder. In between the heaped-up bales, men and women were trampling bedclothes underfoot and stumbling over tins that rolled around in the dark. It was chaos.

'At least they're doing something!' Jai yelled to Irona as they passed.

'Well whoop-de-doodle-do.'

But Jaimindi's comforting presence had disappeared again into the night. 'Hey!' Irona shouted at a bedraggled woman 'Leave that one! And the next—'

But the woman couldn't hear her. Taut with impatience, Irona went and pulled the woman off the computer-cases. 'Not these! We can't let the computers get wet. Use those boxes, OK?' But where the rest of the powered goods had gone was anybody's guess. Irona just had to hope they were all right. And that the First Wave hadn't taken them all . . .

At last the makeshift camp was as ready as it was going to get that night. The packing cases provided shelter for the children, if for no-one else. The rest, as Twiss, prompted by Irona, told everyone, would have to make do with the plastic coverings the machines would have to do without. As far as she knew, only the computers were left under cover, but where the power-packs had gone was anybody's guess.

Shot with lightning, the dark clouds only grew darker. Heavy rain stung like sweets tossed at a carnival back in Camelford. Irona, busy helping Twiss to weight the last flapping sheets onto the impromptu roofs of cases, heard Sticker say, 'Why don't somebody turn that there rain off then?'

He couldn't have been the only sleeper to wonder that as the wet penetrated clothing until everyone was shivering. It was a relief when the last of the colonists huddled under the final lean-to.

After shelter the prime necessity was food. In the fitful darkness it was hard to make out which canisters contained edibles. Stabs of lightning lit the pictures on the cans only for a frustrating instant at a time. The fact that people had tossed them this way and that when they emptied the cases didn't help at all. Irona's arms ached with her efforts to sort the mud-slicked plastic cubes. It annoyed her that hardly anybody ventured beyond the shelters to help her, though Twiss, safe himself under cover, did send a few volunteers out to help her when he finally realised what she was doing. Out of irritation and a cock-eyed sense of martyrdom she hadn't bothered to ask him.

'Look!' called Jaimindi from somewhere among the mounds of supplies.

When she appeared in a stream of artificial light, Irona hugged her joyfully.

'A power-pack! Well done, Jai. That's great!'

It seemed to hearten the sleepers, too. Soon they were

chattering away in the warm glow of other lanterns, speculating as to when the First Wave colonists would come to rescue them and how much work they would have to do to earn a decent meal. It didn't seem to occur to any of them that the First Wave meant what they said: that this was now their land.

Plumping herself down next to Jai, Irona looked across at Twiss. He was lolling at ease on one arm, the lamp-glow warm on his pleasant face. Whatever he had just said had Granfer smiling wryly while Sticker guffawed.

Jai smiled wearily at her friend and handed her a steaming can of curry. Irona nodded her thanks but she was too tired to eat much. Still, the warmth of it spread through her and presently she felt strong enough to ask if anyone had seen Regenerator.

'No,' Twiss said. 'Granfer were just saying that we ain't seen nothing of him since he weaselled up they bunks. Maybe he were too scared to come off of the ship.'

'I don't think so.' Irona tried not to sound tetchy but it was hard hearing her friend maligned – especially when she had been wondering herself whether or not it were true. 'He might be jumpy sometimes but there's nothing wrong with his nerve when the chips are down. I daresay he'll turn up tomorrow.'

Twiss shrugged, not really interested. He hadn't quite got a handle on Regen. Yawning, he wriggled down and pillowed his head on one arm. The camp was almost quiet now though somewhere a mother was hushing her baby. Soon the lullaby engulfed them all in the blanket of night.

When Irona woke the first thing she saw was Regenerator. He was sitting cross-legged on the roof of a shelter opposite. Cool sunlight silhouetted him but there was no mistaking that gangling figure. Here and there were the quiet sounds of adults trying not to wake their neighbours or especially their children and on the freshly-washed breeze came that high-pitched hum Irona had heard yesterday. It was almost as though Regenerator had brought the song of electricity with him from his subterranean home.

What really uplifted Irona, though, was the high blue of the sky, reflected in silver on the standing water that the breeze rippled in the desert. And the sight of Twiss, innocent in sleep opposite her. Smiling to herself, she turned back to Regenerator and slipped out of the shelter.

Regenerator winked at her.

"Morning,' she said quietly.

'Certainly is. Entirely. How are you today?'

She stretched and groaned. 'Stiff as a board. Where did you get to?'

'Sneaked away, didn't I, on one of them there wagons.'

'You didn't!'

'I did. Proud of it too.'

Irona looked horrified. 'But they told us we hadn't got to go beyond the fence.'

'Oh come on! Who cares what they say? I didn't come all the way to Harith to be bossed about by a load of faceless folks I ain't never clapped eyes on. They're right about that fence, though.'

'How do you mean?'

'Got it wired up, ain't they? Closed all around you now, entirely. No way in or out. Touch it and you'll fry.'

'Surely not! Oh, Regenerator, you've got to be joking.'

'I ain't, though. Couldn't think why none of you lot hadn't found out. Then I thought what a lot of sheep you all were upstairs in the Mountain. Talk about respect for authority! I bet none of you dared to touch it 'cos you thought you wasn't s'posed to. And that's all that's kept you safe. I ain't had time to work out yet how to unwire it.'

'Why not? Where have you been? And how did you get back in?'

'Because I'm Regenerator, ain't I? Ain't nobody else here could do it, entirely. I got circuit-breakers, the lot, but this gang wouldn't have brains enough to use 'em. As to where I been, half-way to their city, that's where. That city by the sea what they showed us on the ship's disks after we woke up.'

'How far is it?'

'Over them there mountains. Not too far if there was rollways and stuff but there ain't. Jumped off afore midnight and spent most of the rest of the time running back to warn you.'

Alarm tightened Irona's chest. 'About what?'

''Bout the fact that they've got all the good land parcelled out among 'em. I seen it all from the ridge. They ain't going to let us new ones muscle in on that.'

'Why not?'

'Why should they? It's theirn, they done all the work on it. And their town's that crowded they ain't got room for no-one else. Why should they share it with a load of strangers?'

'Because . . . because . . .' Irona began, and then stopped.

'Because nothing. Just don't think they're going to, that's all.'

'Well I would, if it was me.'

'But you're all gunged up inside with citizenship and duty and all that crap. Don't mean to say they are, does it? Been away from any of Earth's Admins for – for, what, forty years? Besides, did you ever stop to think how we come here? Last I remember was that worm-room place. How about you?'

'I wondered about that but I can't keep my mind on it for more than . . . I think the Fixer must have blanked our memories to protect himself.'

'That weren't no Fixer. That were Synod,' Regenerator answered darkly. 'And what happened to the holes in our heads?'

But there was no time to pursue the idea. He jerked his chin and Irona's gaze followed his sudden movement.

Two tractors were heading out of the desert towards them.

Everyone was on their feet and buzzing with rumours by the time the tractors reached the scant greenery at the outer perimeter. Numbers of people were climbing down from the huge vehicles and deploying themselves in strange zigzag runs. Irona couldn't think why.

Twiss made his way self-importantly to the wire and went to lean on it.

'Don't!' Irona shouted. 'Don't touch it!'

'What are you on about?' But prompted by the genuine

alarm in her voice Twiss stepped back from the perimeter all the same.

The hum of electricity in the wire sounded loud to Irona now. 'It's that fence. Regenerator says it's full of live electricity.'

Twiss gave her a spare glance and then looked out again to the men and women spreading out from the tractors and lining the outer fence. 'Why would they waste electricity on a fence, then?' he asked her when he could see that the manoeuvre would take some minutes to complete yet.

'I don't know.' Irona's confession was apologetic. 'Regenerator seems to think they're not going to give us the land we were promised on the coast.'

Twiss raised an eyebrow. 'Give us? They ain't giving us nothing. It's ours for the taking. Admin said so.'

Irona watched the First Wave still darting in weird patterns to cover the fence. 'Yes, but Admin's not here, is it? It's twenty light-years away. They can do anything they want to.'

A man aboard the lead tractor swung a shining black rod at them. Even from fifty metres away he had the settlers ducking. Twiss shushed Irona fiercely.

Nobody died. It seemed the rod wasn't a weapon. And though Irona checked with all her warden's senses, there were no Arms, no Eyes, to scare them. As the skinny, dark-haired man began to speak through his voice-amplifier, the Second Wave colonists started to straighten up sheepishly.

Until they heard what he was saying.

'How did you like your night in the open?'

The First Wave leader seemed to think it was a rhetorical question but Twiss yelled across, 'It were interesting. Harith's a strange place.'

Across the outer fence, the man didn't seem best pleased at Twiss's chirpy answer. His full lips thinned momentarily under the dark moustache, then he grinned. 'Like a challenge, do you? What's your name?'

'Arcturus. But they call me Twiss.'

'Give me any trouble and they can call you through a hole

in the ground. My name is Tang, Arias Tang, and I've come to sort out your settlement.'

Twiss nodded, reassured by the absence of obvious weaponry. 'That's what we've come to do as well.'

'Don't get cocky. This is our proposition—'

Twiss interrupted. Though he was spattered with mud and his hair was uncombed, Irona would never forget the strength in him as he answered, 'Take us to our land-grants by the sea and give us our supplies back and we'll talk.' There was nothing left for Twiss to say; he turned his back and melted into the crowd, or tried to. The sleepers unconsciously drifted away from him, but whether out of respect or to dissociate themselves from him Irona didn't know. For an instant Irona saw Twiss hesitate then he walked over to his place by the dead lamp and sat down, fingering the stubble on his chin.

Irona looked at the First Wavers again. Arias Tang's thin face creased into a smile with vertical folds lining the hollows of his cheeks and disappearing into his neat black moustache. 'Very good, young Twiss. Very confident. But this is Synod's proposition. If you want to get your hands on the supplies, and borrow the converters to build your homes, and if you want fresh water to drink and to irrigate your crops, you'll have to strike a bargain with us. And the bargain is, you work what land we give you and you give us a third of your produce every season or you don't get a damn thing. You don't even get past the fence.'

Twiss didn't so much as look round. But all around her in the enclosure, Irona saw the Second Wavers looking askance at each other. A mood of distinct unease lowered over the camp, not helped at all by the fact that the men and women of the First Wave were moving back towards the balloon-tyred vehicles – and they didn't look like they were going to unload.

Arias Tang smiled at the Second Wave, superior. The tractor on which he lolled, his clean fresh clothes, the threatening posture of his followers around the outer fence, all showed him confident in his power base.

Irona looked at the taggle of sleepers around her and thought helplessly, *What have we got to answer that?*

Calmly Tang said, 'I'll be back in three weeks for your answer. Just remember, though, any time you decide to see reason, send us a message. Who knows what's out here? What diseases you'll get? What beasties will bite? How many kids will die of poisoned water?'

And he tossed the shining black amplifier casually over his shoulder into the tractor's cabin and jumped inside out of sight.

'They should have been there a couple of weeks by now, I'd have thought,' said Elditch. Outside the vast Synod chamber at the top of Camelford the planned rain was the same mournful grey as his moustache, his eyes. 'Have you heard anything yet?'

Bernardina raised her wispy brows at him. Her fingers curled round the armrests of her throne. 'Of course not. Why would I?'

Elditch shivered at the chill in her tone. If he hadn't known better, he might have suspected her of planting mood-controllers in Synod. 'No reason,' he said, and shied away from the subject.

It was an uncomfortable period, though, waiting until the rest of the councillors arrived for the Synod proper.

Waiting.

The Matriarch of Matriarchs remembered: Gundmila, seated regally at the oval table in the Synod chamber in the highest tower in Kifl. China-blue eyes, the colour of her robes, the colour of the sky behind the volcano over the bay. Gundmila with the flawless skin of youth, who had looked the same when Towy had been Matriarch of Matriarchs and Bernardina at seventeen the most junior of juniors. How Bernardina had envied Gundmila! Power, beauty – Bernardina knew she would one day get the power but the beauty was forever beyond her reach.

That image of Gundmila on Harith was the ikon of Bernardina's downfall, the years out in the cold . . .

Gundmila was a legend that Bernardina had seldom met in the flesh. Oh, Bernardina had seen too much of her on training disks – and heard even more. Towy had raved about her as she sent young Bernardina running errands that demeaned her intelligence. As Bernardina silently seethed, she formed the opinion that in Gundmila cunning replaced IQ. Especially when Gundmila used to sneer at Bernardina, calling her 'the ugly duckling'.

'Gundmila the child prodigy, why can't you be like she was, Gundmila would never have done that. Years ago and I still remember everything she ever said. She was the best junior there's ever been. You couldn't forget her.'

The way Towy's eyes slid away from her, Bernardina knew she herself was instantly forgettable.

Not like Gundmila. Not like Gundmila who was strong already in her own power-web in the matriarchy when she was a year younger than Bernardina the junior of juniors. Bernardina grew to loathe the very sound of her name.

And when Matriarch Towy made her watch Gundmila's justice, her planning, her decisions, over and over again to learn from them, Bernardina screamed inside. *The only good thing about her*, Bernardina used to think in silent rage, *is that Towy sent her away to be a plaster saint somewhere at the other end of the universe*. Slim, elegant, a face to make angels weep jealous tears, Gundmila had received the ultimate accolade: sent with the first ship to Harith, to build a Synod of her very own. *If I'd ever had to meet her*, Bernardina seethed, *I'd have rowelled out her china-blue eyes with a corkscrew*.

Bernardina, Matriarch of Matriarchs now, old and dried-up like a flower someone had dropped and forgotten behind a radiator, waited with Elditch for the Synod to begin and she filled her waiting with memories.

It had been here in this very room, standing looking respectful beside this very chair with the harridan Towy in it, that Bernardina's disgrace had begun so many years before.

Bernardina the junior had followed orders. She'd gone by stratojet to the spaceport to meet the *Starwing* on its return from the Admin's prize new colony.

The place where Gundmila had gone to queen it over a Synod of her own.

Bernardina had watched the ship land. She had taken the

image-disk of the first landing on Harith straight out of the captain's hands as soon as the *Starwing*'s docking-bay had cooled enough for the crew to emerge. She had scarcely noticed the captain, red hair and eyes as green as Ireland. She had snatched the disk and all but run with it to the Synod's private transporter.

What could it be like, that Harith place? What could be on the disk? Young Bernardina hadn't even acknowledged to herself the existence of her bitter curiosity about Gundmila.

Instead, sitting in the stratojet on the way back to Camelford, Bernardina had struggled to control her impatience.

But the disk had winked at her in the sunlight between the towering clouds around her. There was half an hour yet before the jet docked outside Camelford. *Towy'll be none the wiser.*

No.

The disk gleamed.

I can't.

Then she had.

By itself her hand skipped out and slid the disk into the reader. Even then she didn't really mean to look at the Matriarch's private communication.

She just had, though. Just a peek. Just twenty seconds. No, just ten.

The sights, the sounds, the scents, the undreamed-of beat of surf shooting at the foot of the volcano.

And Gundmila the beautiful, the same age as she, but Matriarch of her own planet already.

Trembling, aghast at her own stupidity, Bernardina ejected the disk and put it back in its clear pouch, didn't even touch it again, only the drawstring of the pouch to carry it as she hurried to hand her temptation safely to Towy, Matriarch of Matriarchs.

Nervous in her new blue robe, Bernardina had entered the chamber for – what? the second or third time? The same chamber where she now waited with Elditch. It felt as though she had been waiting all her life.

The whole Synod had hushed when she came in. She had felt the weight of their collective gaze.

Skirting the table, the most junior of Matriarchs had all but dropped the disk into the hand of the most senior.

She won't find out.

Towy, her hair the colour of caramel, had ordered the disk-reader in the table to relay the message the *Starwing* had brought back from the new colony of Harith.

And to report if it it had been tampered with.

Gundmila's china-blue eyes . . .

The disk formed the accusation with Gundmila's rosebud mouth.

Total humiliation. *Worse even than worm-death because then I wouldn't have known I was being humiliated.* Exile – exile to the warrens amongst the stupidity of the sleepers.

Bernardina had hated it. Drab colours and drabber lives. Mealy-mouthed men and pathetic knots of obedience that meant nothing. Marriage to show she conformed, but Synod! How he bored her when the lustre of sex had worn off.

Always watched. Always observed.

To bring up her daughter filled with cant and pap.

Weaving her schemes and waiting.

Waiting 'til Towy died.

Once the tractors had pulled a safe distance away into the scrublands, some of the braver Second Wave colonists ran to examine the fence. Irona called, 'Don't touch it!' At her shout clots of people backed off in a rush. Others moved towards Twiss, some merely seeking help and others tinged with hostility. The rest seemed to mill indecisively, looking to anyone else for guidance.

If Admin wants colonists here, why on Earth didn't Synod wake them up properly? Irona wondered in the beginnings of an anger of her own. But there was no time for her to explore her feeling because out at the perimeter Fessbar, trying to follow his father Sinofer's vacillations, stumbled and fell onto the wire with a shriek that drew everyone's attention.

Electricity crackled through the air and strung his little body out jerking. A thread of smoke spiralled from his hand but he couldn't seem to let go of the wire. His scream died but his body kept on dancing obscenely, a horizontal doll.

Amidst a chorus of wailing, Sinofer, big and burly, ran back to yank him free and Irona watched in horror as the electricity netted him too in ozone-scented turquoise fire and starred his limbs in a back-arching spasm. It was as though the current held him in crepitating tentacles that writhed like chains of lightning. Tebrina ran to help him but she wasn't stupid. She stood by, wringing her hands in an agony of helplessness.

Before anyone else could grab them and be seized by the blue fire, Irona yelled, 'Stop! Don't touch them!' and the sleepers obeyed the ferocity in her tone.

It was Renegerator who shouted, 'Hold on! I'm coming!'

Shoving back past Twiss, he hauled a piece of stiff padding out of a computer-case. The skinny figure barged past Twiss again, clouting him accidentally with one sharp end of the plastic. Twiss lashed out instinctively but Regenerator's speed carried him free and he brought the tough plastic down on the tortured child's hands with a mighty thwack.

'How dare you?'

'Bully!'

'Stop 'un!'

But the cries of repulsion were only half uttered when Regenerator's blow threw the child clear to lie unmoving in the dirt, Sinofer's body inert beside him. Tebrina pitched herself down on her knees beside the boy, sobbing on his motionless chest. The whole incident hadn't lasted thirty seconds from beginning to end.

'He's dead! Oh, Synod, Fessbar's dead! And my Sinofer!'

Around her the ring of watchers fell silent in a collective embarrassment that still didn't let them leave the woman to mourn her dead in privacy. One or two cast openly accusing glances at Twiss.

And though Irona looked to Twiss to solve the problem, he just scratched his ear and pretended not to notice the dark mutterings around him. Even in her shock at the deaths of two of her fellow passengers from the sleep-room, she felt a stab of sympathy for him.

Irona found Jai beside her. 'Isn't there anything we can do?'

Jai looked at her blankly. 'Of course not if they're dead.'

'Well hadn't you better take a look at them then?' Irona
said sharply. 'You've only got her word for it, haven't you?'

With the air of one humouring a lunatic, Jai pushed her cap
a little further off her forehead, shrugged, and moved closer
to the bodies, passing Regenerator.

Inside the circle of spectators, he squirmed uncomfortably.
He looked spare, left over, the plastic now hanging forgotten
from his bony hands. Sidling furtively over to Irona, Regenerator whispered, 'Bet Jai don't realise it's electrical shocks
they've got. Bet she done something about it in her nursing
course. Ask her. Resusification, ain't it called?'

'I don't know.' Irona gave it a go anyway. She knelt beside
Jai. Under cover of the mother's keening, Irona pushed a
loose knot of black curls from Jai's ear and breathed,
'Regenerator says it's called electrical shock and there's
something called resusification.'

It was miraculous. As though someone had wiped a dud
view-disk and overlaid blankness with intelligence, positivism
sparked into life in Jai's face. Irona could see it firm the slack
muscles, giving the warm brown cheeks a bright allure. 'You
have to breathe into them if it's electric shock,' Jai told her.
'Pinch the nose and breathe your breath into their mouths.
We've still got plenty of time if we start now.'

Irona was already on her knees in the mud beside the bulky
sleeper, hauling at his shoulder to turn him over, checking
that there was no mud in the man's mouth. She arched his
neck backwards and, holding the man's nose, she suppressed
her modesty and laid her lips over the man's bristles.

From behind her, somewhere in the forest of legs, Twiss
called encouragement as though it were all his idea.

Breathe in. Breathe out – and the out-breath was a strain,
like blowing up a tight balloon for carnival. Breathe in –
breathe out. Within moments Irona's head was swimming
with the effort.

'Slow down a bit,' Jai called. 'Don't want you getting dizzy
or you'll fail.'

And fear of failure dropped its weight on Irona's back.
Her thoughts came and went with the rhythm of her labours.
I can't fail, not with this man's life in my hands. Not with Twiss

*– with everyone watching me. I'm not some useless sleeper. I
was Irona Warden back there and I don't want to be nothing
here. I can do it. I can do it here on Harith. It's going to be
all right.*

Still they watched her. She could see it whenever she
looked up from her patient – so she didn't look up if she
could help it. She knew every square centimetre of his chest,
every wrinkle of his heavy, red-veined face. She felt the pricks
of his stubble on her lips, tasted the staleness of his mouth.

'Feel his pulse, Ro.' That was Jai, still working on the
toddler. 'Touch his chest above his heart.'

Nothing.

Breathe in. Breathe out.

And the weight of their gaze crushed her but she could do
nothing else.

Then, as she knelt back on her cramping feet, the dank
skin of his chest fluttered and stilled.

'His heart beat!' she shouted.

'Then see if he can breathe alone.'

Panic darkened Irona's mind: *What if he can't? What
do I do?*

But the broad ribs rose a little and for just a second she
slumped over him. It was the right thing to do. When she
pulled herself off him a scant moment later, his chest moved
higher.

Tears sprang out and stung the sore spots around Irona's
mouth but she didn't care. Lifting her raptured face, she
sought Regenerator. As their eyes met, she sobbed, 'He's
alive! Regenerator, you're wonderful! You can do anything!
Anything, Regenerator! You could even turn the weather on
and off.'

And Twiss beamed down and said, 'That's my little weather-
man. Well done.'

12

RAINSHADOW

Fessbar was sleeping now in his mother's arms. Careless of her own comfort, Tebrina was kneeling in the lumpen muddy greenery, gently rocking him back and forth, with her husband's head pillowed on her legs. She had been there so long that Irona knew her legs must be numb by now and her back aching with the chubby weight of her child held against her breast, but Tebrina wouldn't move. She cared too much to disturb them.

Irona felt moisture sting her eyes. Cross with herself, she tore her gaze away and said 'Regenerator? Come and help me sort out what we're going to do.'

'S' easy. You're hungry, ain't you? So'm I. So's they sleepers. Entirely. Let's feed our faces first but you get someone else to deal the stuff out fair and shared. And not too much of it either. Could you see to it, Twiss?'

Twiss looked across at the odd little man, the sun making him screw his eyes up against its glare. He raised his eyebrows but before he could protest, Granfer said, 'I could do with something to eat too. You tell 'em, Twiss. They listen to you.'

So Irona let herself sink back onto the heap of quilts that were steaming gently in the morning's warmth and before too long Sticker came back with a pile of reconstituted bread and canisters of coffee. The loaf was warm and carved into doorsteps spread with tangy protein and it put new heart into her. She noticed that they had finished eating long before most people had even been served. *That's something else we'll have to sort out when we've got a moment*, she thought, but there was more pressing business at hand.

Like the wire.

'So how come,' she started around her last mouthful, 'They've got this place wired? And how did you get out?'

Regenerator wiped a smear of grease from his chin with the inside of one knobby wrist. 'Easy peasy lemon and squeezy. 'S wired because they think they can keep us penned in here so's we starve ourselves into submission. They sleepers wouldn't know no different but you can get out of it by going under it. Made myself a nice little crawl-way down a little gulley-tunnel but ifn I shows everyone where it is they'll be tromping through it and smash it to bits. Entirely. Don't want any cave-ins, do we? So now I've had this nice bit o' grub I'll go and fix it in a minute.'

'Get on with it then,' said Twiss when Regenerator didn't move.

Regenerator's round cheeks rose in an expression of faint disdain. 'Well I will then – when I'm ready. But you ain't no king really, Twiss. You might have all they sleepers fooled but you don't tell me what to do. But I got to sort out you lot first or you'll be running round like headless rats.'

'Yeah?' Twiss's belligerence tightened Irona's stomach. Sticker jerked upright and Granfer reached out a calming hand.

Regenerator wasn't affected by the tension. He said, 'What we need is, what we need is a plan. This lot can't even wipe their own bums without someone's say-so and the someone who's to say it appears to be you, Twiss. But have you got it sorted what you're going to say?'

Twiss opened his mouth. He seemed surprised that no pearls of wisdom came out.

Regenerator grinned at his discomfiture. 'Thought not. Try this for size.' He hitched his crossed legs higher. 'What are the priorities then, me old son?'

Twiss ran his broad fingers through the back of his hair. 'Talk to 'em, I suppose. Negotiate, like. Which means you getting us through—'

'Can't negotiate from a position of weakness,' Regenerator said and Granfer nodded. ''Cos if you do you lose. I'll get the wires down, all right, or at least I'll fix 'em so's we're in control. Fences can keep people out as well as in.' It was obviously not a thought that had struck Twiss, and Regenerator grinned again.

Warming to his task, the little man went on, "'Nother thing. We got to get you to their city so's you can see what we're up against with no back-up from any old Admins. We need supplies and something to keep the rain off. We got to build our own shelter 'cos if they First Wavers dole power out like charity our lot's just going to sit up and beg. And we need food and water.'

Jai spoke up, quietly, shyly, but quite definite. 'And sanitation.'

Regenerator nodded encouragingly, his smile seeming to make the motley parts of his face belong to a coherent whole. 'And sanitation. You're right, Jai, entirely. Otherwise everybody and his wife'll be taking sick. So how?'

Jai's eyes sparkled a little and her cheeks flushed but she said, 'We need ditches to bury the stuff in. And a rope that people can hold onto to stop them falling in after it. And screens up around it for modesty and a picture to show which is the men's part and which the women's.'

Twiss speared his friend with a glance. 'See to it, Sticker. And once you've got it organised, come back for the next bit.' And Sticker unfolded himself without a word.

Jai added hastily, 'Make sure it's as far away from anyone as possible – and not near any water, OK?'

A brief nod – Sticker's greasy blond hair bounced – and he was gone. Irona could hear his shouted commands fading into the distance. He was Twiss's friend; the sleepers would obey him.

Granfer said, 'We ought to get the food stacked somewhere safe. They First Wavers obviously don't think what they've left is going to last us three weeks so we got to guard it and deal it out fair. And we need to find some water.'

'For the time being we can collect the rain-water in some packing-cases,' Irona said.

Jai cleared her throat. 'We'll have to boil it up before we drink it though or else we'll get sick.'

Twiss looked as though he were about to speak but Granfer

forestalled him. 'Don't you be afraid to speak up, little missy. You're doing a fine job.'

Jai ducked her head into the crook of her shoulder in embarrassment but a smile of pleasure spread across her dusky face.

Irona said, 'Then we'll need to dig the power-packs out and ration them, too. And the computers to show us how to run it all.'

Twiss had tried several times to get a word in edgewise. Now he commandeered the conversation. 'I'll put Sticker on it when he comes back.' He looked like he would have liked to say more but he had scarcely opened his mouth again when Irona added, 'I've been thinking. If they're anything like back home they'll have watchers on us, maybe psychicators' – he looked blank so she explained without saying how she knew – 'or Eyes or Ears or anything. We don't know until we get the computers fixed.'

'Can you do that?' Twiss asked in surprise.

'Course she can!' Regen said.

Irona shot him a warning glance. If Twiss ever realised she hadn't just been a warden, if he honestly believed she was the one who'd caught him . . .

Twiss looked at Regen. 'How do you know?'

'Cos she said she could. Ain't going to call her a liar, are you?' Aware of Irona, the little man changed the subject. 'Reckon you can find us that water then, boy?'

Twiss nodded. 'That's just what I were going to say.' He unfolded himself to look down on them; Irona saw how the prospect of action brightened him up. 'We'd better get a move on,' he said. 'Meeting tonight at sundown to find out what we've done and what we've got to do.'

When he had gone, Irona looked at Regen. 'The Eye'll find water a lot quicker than he will.'

'Mm-hm.' Regen's eyes twinkled. 'Keep him out of hair for a bit though, won't it? Only thing now is, what are they First Wavers going to do?'

Sunset veiled the sky; night painted it with the feather-strokes of clouds but it didn't rain. Instead a thin wind swept coldly out of the dunes. Weary to the bone, the leadership group huddled round the warmth of their power-pack. Yawning, too tired to say anything much, they felt the need of its comfort and drew closer to its ruddy glow while the wind plucked at their backs. On the western horizon lightning flared over the mountains but the thunder came to them only fitfully against the sand-laden gusts.

Regen had already curled up in a nest of boxes. Granfer fell asleep where he sat. One of their few quilts was around his shoulders, another underneath him. When Sticker, his head almost split in two with a gigantic yawn, would have dragged one of the quilts off the old man, Twiss stopped him curtly. 'Leave him be or we'll never hear the end of it.'

'But we ain't got enough else.'

'Tough. We can share, can't we?'

Sticker shot a glance at him. 'I ain't sleeping with you.'

'Didn't ask you to. Irona, come over by me.' Twiss smiled at her and held one hand out in a welcoming gesture. 'Come on. I know it ain't modest but it'll beat freezing our bu— freezing ourselves. Come on, Irona. I ain't going to hurt you.'

For a second his voice, his eyes, had been incredibly gentle. He leant forward into the lamp-glow to switch the power-pack off and sudden darkness sprang over them. Irona was glad it hid her blush. Then he said, 'Get your foot out of my ear, Sticker!' and she wondered if she had imagined Twiss's tenderness even as she obeyed him.

Shivering with more than cold, she lay stiffly beside him, facing out into the night, embarrassed when her foot accidentally touched his leg. But he pulled the covers across her and as she lay wide-eyed in the dark she felt his arm slip across her waist and pull her in to the warm curve of his stomach. 'Ssh,' he whispered into her hair. 'It's all right. You're safe.'

He tucked his knees in to the back of hers – she started – but his arm stayed unthreateningly where it was. His body-heat and the clean musky smell of him wrapped around her in a security she couldn't relax into because she was frightened that at any moment what she had longed for would be taken away from her.

'You're trembling,' he murmured in surprise, and she was mortified that he might know why. Her mind felt naked. Then Twiss's hand found hers and squeezed it reassuringly. 'You're all right, Irona. You're safe. I've got you. You're all right now.'

His thumb caressed her hand, his tender litany fanned his breath across her cheek. Irona couldn't say anything but his warmth cradled her. Little by little the dark blanket of sleep softened the edges of her nervousness.

She wasn't sure if he kissed her then she was drifting in peace and the world was very far away.

In a day or two a routine had sorted itself out. The Second Wavers rose with the sun – not that they wanted to. It was just that with so much daylight spilling in through the roofs and walls of their dugouts that they hadn't much choice. Besides, the accommodations were still so crowded that even aching in muscles that they'd never used before it was hard to stay asleep once the first person stirred.

As soon as first light began to sheathe the stars in grey, Irona crept creakily out of the dugout, her shoes in her hand. The cool air shivered her awake. Stretching in the monochrome chill, she was tempted to crawl back into Twiss's warm friendly embrace.

She spent a moment puzzling about that. In the day he was the same Twiss he had always been – or at least, since he had woken aboard the *Starwing* – friendly, teasing, accepting her ideas and then annoying her somewhat by passing them off as his own. She never said anything, though, because he was what the sleepers needed. He spoke to her if he came across her in the course of their work, but he didn't seek her out.

Sometimes she looked at him, the breeze lifting his blond-brown curls, the sunlight crinkling his eyes against its glare. It was almost as though he were some wild creature she was watching back in Camelford Park, trying to work out his secret life from the easy way he moved and the sound of his laugh. He treated her exactly the same as he treated everyone else and she was stung as often as anyone by his flashes of sarcasm when he was put out.

In the night, though, he was different. Under their quilt in the darkness, Twiss wasn't hard, but gentle. Knowing his strength, she appreciated his softness even more and she loved the way he held her all through the night. Her body trusted his.

But nothing else ever happened. He held her, he stroked her and whispered safety, and that was it. She wondered if there would ever be more, and hoped that there would. *What If I'm wrong, though? What if I make a fool of myself?*

The sun's rim crested the dunes in a fanfare of saffron and gold, bringing her back to the realities of daytime. Her computer called. It came up with solutions – witness the dugouts that mass labour had created on her and the computer's suggestions. Nothing fancy, but it gave shelter that would do until they had leisure to build something permanent.

Glancing back once, regretfully, at the snug group behind her, she closed the door made of a slab of packing-case and went to check things out. It was so early that there wasn't even anyone else at the latrines. She did her business and splashed cold water on her face, making a mental note that the stored water was running out. *Still*, she told herself as she walked quietly over to the one totally rainproof shelter where the computer was installed, *if I'm right we should get that sorted by the end of tomorrow, or at least the day after*.

And she wondered why the storms that flashed over the mountains every night hadn't brought any more rain to their lands. But the desert gleamed a skeletal yellow and the clumps of low-growing vines were hunched and dry.

A pity, really, she thought. *Now we've got shelter and we need the rain, there isn't any. It would save us so much effort . . .*

Running a race with the growing daylight, she sighed and walked in to begin her first task of the morning. With the door wide open to let in enough light to see by, she settled herself to the keyboard and coupled the machines up to the power-pack. The swirling images of the 3-D monitors glowed out over the expectant keys.

As soon as the images of the land steadied, she had the

machine make print-outs enough for a chief surveyor and the ten gangers King Twiss's group had picked. In firm colours the maps sprayed themselves onto the clear plastic sheets: pictorial maps with the optimum pathways marked out. Browns shaded from the darkness of the highest foothills to the pale beige of the chalk and clay plains where minute green dots even marked off every individual plant that the scanners had picked up only the day before. The scanner itself – Irona called it an Eye, because that was what it reminded her of, floating above their heads – had cast a tiny shadow that Irona could see under the noon light of the captured image. And there were the hummocks of bald earth that made up the settlement. She could even see the plastic doorways and ventilator pipes shining pale in the sun.

Red dots appeared, showing the relative depth of the underground stream they proposed to tap. It rose in the sepia shale of the Moon Mountains only to sink through the chalk until, in a maze of shallow caverns, the water hit the stratum of impermeable clay and spread out to form a lake that lay a scant ten metres below the moisture-starved scrub. Eventually it meandered out, a river once more, to join the sea some forty kilometres away as one of the mouths of the estuary where the First Wavers had built the township of Kifl.

Cursing at the waste of labour-hours – it would take the three hundred workers many times longer than a single one of the machines the First Wavers had stolen from them – Irona shrugged and put the maps of hope to one side.

That was the easy bit. The hard part was convincing everyone in the Second Wave that they had to stick up for themselves. No Admin here to lay everything on for every citizen, no Synod to order society out here beyond the pale. And what she and Regenerator were proposing seemed, superficially at least, to go against every principle of citizenship that the Admins of Earth had stood for. Not gratitude and acceptance and making do with what you were given, but the taking or making of what you actually wanted. *I just hope the sleepers can stick to it. But if anyone can make them, it's Twiss. And Granfer and Jai and me.*

A flicker of pleasure at her new-found self-confidence painted a smile on her face. She was developing an identity outside the lattices of the Synod.

The light in the room shifted from shades of pink to yellow. *I guess that's it, then. Time to put on the show.*

Exchanging cheery greetings, Irona walked back through the activity of the settlement. Long morning shadows were stealing from the mist-garbed ball of the sun and retreating towards the dun mountains, but overhead the sky was unroofed blue that smelt of eternity and there were threads of sound that the Eye above told her were made by living beings. According to its observations, though, they were harmless, and their strange faint piping rose and fell dizzily down the startling sky. Buoyed by the spell of Harith, Irona ducked into their dugout and spent a fond moment gazing at the innocence of Twiss's relaxed face.

He could sleep for our Admin, Irona thought to herself as she shook him awake, dodging a flailing hand. *He'd beat anyone Harith has to offer, that's for sure.* And a small proprietorial grin slid on and off her countenance as he struggled back to the world outside his head.

After the last of the reconstituted bread the First Wavers had left them Twiss called everyone together. Scratching and yawning, five hundred or so people gathered around the small knoll Twiss had taken as his own.

'Good-morning,' Twiss started, and dutifully the sleepers chorused, 'Good-morning, Twiss.'

Irona couldn't decide whether it was embarrassing or comforting, this return to the programmed behaviour of Camelford. *Still, it augurs well for today's decisions*, she thought.

Twiss waved a hand for silence. Slanting rays of gold limned his hair as if he were some haloed hero of the Admin, outlining his tall, sturdy figure. With the rising sun behind him his face was shadowed but his eyes were bright and his teeth shone in a friendly grin. Irona held her breath but she needn't have worried.

'Well, we're going to do something a little different today, folks.' Twiss's strong voice carried easily to the outliers, a warm and somehow neighbourly sound that brought them together. 'Now we've got somewhere to live, we're going to start ploughing. Because what we're going to do is, we're going to do what proper colonists do, what we came here for. We don't need nobody else because we're strong. We're going to be self-sufficient.'

Sporadic cheers that strangled in embarrassment.

'And we're not just going to start ploughing. We're going to do seeding as well.'

'It's called planting,' Sinofer hissed and Irona hid a smile.

'Whatever,' Twiss glared down in mock anger, 'we're going to start doing it today.'

'We can't, though,' a turkey-faced woman called Marjine said. 'We ain't got no tractors yet.'

'Yeah,' said a man at the back, 'nor we ain't on no decent land. This ain't my patch like they showed me on the disks.'

'For now it is.' Twiss spoke with real power that began to enthuse his listeners, especially when his voice dropped to mention the menace that had left them in this plight. 'This is our base and it's got everything we need, whatever they say. Because we don't know what the First Wavers'll let us have. But who cares about them? This time next year we'll have tractors and Synod knows what all. But for now we've got only one hundred and forty days or so of growing time at this latitude. And we're not going to roll over and die for they First Wavers, are we? We came out here to be free men.'

'And women,' Thebula said, scratching the red hair under her cap.

Twiss nodded impatiently. 'Yeah, and women. We don't need they First Wavers.' His enthusiasm caught them; it was as if his words were written in fire that burned into their hearts. 'But we got to make sure we got food for ourselves or we'll have to give in. Do you want to do that? Be some sort of slave like we used to see on they newscasts?' Now his anger torched their emotions; they swelled with a rage that began to match his and it empowered them.

'Is that what you came here to be?'

'Nah!' called Sinofer.

Twiss went on, 'Someone they can beat up or push

around or anything they like? Is that what you want? To
see your children starved and your women shared out like
in Saharistan with never a bit of decent modesty? Because
if you do, you can go right now. We'll let you out past the
fences. We ain't going to stop you. But you just crawl out
right now because we don't want you around.'

Amidst a rising tide of muttering, Marjine said, 'Hold on,
Twiss. What if they First Wavers don't like it?'

'Then they can lump it.'

'But what if they got Arms?'

A ripple of fear spread amongst the sombrely-clad
settlers.

'Arms?'

'I don't want my head tore off!'

'Nobody ain't going to throw my missus to no worms.'

Twiss called for quiet but nobody listened. He shouted
again, louder.

Regenerator said, 'Leave 'em be for a minute. They ain't
got no chance of making a decision between 'em this side of
Carnival. Wait 'til they're good and stymied and you'll be
fine. Entirely.'

And he was right. As Marjine began to work herself up into
a state of increasing desperation, Twiss yelled, 'Quiet!' This
time his air of calm worked with his commanding presence.
He stood solid against the golden freshness of sunrise and an
uneasy silence spread outwards to the back of the crowd.

'Would I let they send Arms up against you?' Twiss said.
'If you'd asked I'd have told you, there ain't no Arms on
Harith. Nor no Eyes and Ears neither, except ourn. You
don't have to take my word for it – ask that computer
Irona's got. There ain't nothing but they First Wavers and
us and a lot of good land. This ain't it, but you stick with
me and we'll be all right. I promise you that. This time next
year we'll have our fair share of that nice rich land by the sea
and all the power-goods you could want. We'll be fine, you
wait and see. I ain't going to let no harm come to a one of
you. Trust me.'

'Well I ain't staying,' said Marjine, hitching up her rolls of
fat. The slanting light worked against her, showing every line

of her flabby flesh. She must have been every bit as old as
Granfer and a lot worse preserved.

'What's your name?'

'Marjine, and you know it. Why? What's that got to do
with it?'

'Just wanted everyone to know what to put on your
death-lilies.'

Marjine's chins went as red as turkey-wattles. 'You what?'

'Oh, don't look at me like that! I ain't going to kill you. But
they might. That's assuming you make it across the mountains
to that old Kifl-town in the first place. Because you're walking
out of here with nothing but what you stand up in.'

Her face went redder still, if that were possible. 'That's
not fair!'

'Oh, ain't it? Then how come you're mad at me? It was they
First Wavers who took everything away from us, not me. I
ain't got no more than the rest of you.'

Marjine didn't reply, but she seemed to be swelling with
the resentment boiling up inside her.

'That's true enough,' Sinofer said. 'Twiss's shelter ain't no
different from what me and Tebrina and Fess got to put
up with.'

Thebula said with loud irony, 'You thick or something,
Marjine? You seen they tractors running off with our stuff,
didn't you? That weren't Twiss, were it?'

'Ain't none of the rest of you coming with me?' yelled
Marjine.

No answer.

Marjine stabbed a fierce glance at her daughter Desselie
drooping behind her. 'What about you?'

Trapped, Desselie looked around wildly for escape but
there was none. Marjine prompted her, 'Well? Well?'

But no-one stood up with the young widow to give her
strength. Finally she muttered, 'No, Mam.'

'What? Not even my own daughter?'

This time Desselie was a little more forceful. 'No, Mam.
Not if it means my poor baby'll suffer. I'm staying here where
we know we're wanted.'

That was the last of the open resistance. To make sure,

Twiss said forcefully, 'Anybody that does want to go, stand over there by the death-fence. Regen'll let you out. We ain't stopping you but we ain't helping you neither.'

Not even Marjine stirred. Long moments hung on the bright morning, slow-moving as the fluffs of cloud that flocked over the brown hills. Almost Irona thought, *He's missed his timing*, but just when the silence had thinned to a thread, it was Twiss who snapped it.

'We ain't going down. We ain't going to let them beat us, are we? This is our future and we ain't going to let them steal it from us. Together we can make it, you'll see. All of us, together. Who's with us?'

Scattered shouts of, 'I am!' 'I am!' swelled to a cheer Twiss orchestrated to a crescendo. It seized Irona and lifted her heart until she felt as big as the morning. The golden light poured into her on the exotically-scented breeze and the fuzzy piping of the air-creatures spiralled a chain of sound that wove everyone together in determination.

Children took up the cry: 'I am! I am!' shouting, so full of the tide of energy that they couldn't stay still.

People were clapping in time now, chanting, stamping their feet until the earth shook. 'I am! I am!' Irona gazed about her, so rapt in the mass emotion that swept the crowd that her eyes shone with unshed tears and she found her hands beating in rhythm. Her throat was hoarse from cheering. Love for Twiss surged through her and she looked at him, thinking, *He can do it! I never thought he could do anything but mouth off, but look at him! A king.* And her mouth kept shouting, 'I am! I am!'

Again Twiss held his timing. Just as the roar of the crowd had crested he waved his hands for silence. A respectful hush grew and he said so softly that the people at the back had to strain to hear him, 'We're all together now and we can do it. Who's for digging irrigation channels?'

And, bit by bit, he sorted out his workers who, united, set about widening the tunnel under the fence. Their tools were only chunks of salvaged plastic, roughly-shaped by the power-packs, but their faces shone.

Regen trailed Irona over to her computer-shed. Brushing

her brown hair out of her face, she said, 'How long is it going to be before the First Wavers find out, Regen?'

He couldn't answer that one so he didn't. 'Bet they old First Wavers ain't going to be too pleased, and there's a sight more of them than there is of us.'

Irona looked down at the gangling man cross-legged on the floor. 'I wonder what they've got up their sleeve?'

Again Regenerator shrugged. 'Don't know yet. But you keep yourself tuned to that Eye of yourn. Because whatever they got, it ain't going to be good.'

And it was Irona who stared seriously into his eyes and answered, 'Entirely.'

13

FIRST WAVE ATTACK

On the third day of the digging Irona let curiosity overcome her. Playing hookey from her computer she joined Twiss and Granfer as they went out to the canal-head diggings. Relaxing, she let a sense of holiday enliven her as Settlement Knoll fell away behind them. Then she discovered something she hadn't considered.

It was one thing to go out in a crowd of three hundred to the heart of the scrubland. The chalky soil puffed up around trampling feet; the strange all-but-invisible creepers whitened in the dust-clouds until the waving of their stems blurred her vision with the mere suspicion of their movement that she could never quite see. Sure, everyone kept glancing apprehensively at the threat of open space around them, but with the others around her, she could hide it.

Granfer took her hand to steady her over the rough scrub that seemed to shimmer into motion whenever she wasn't looking at it directly. In reality, though, it was because he could see she was shaking. Glad of the pressure of his gnarled fingers, she held on tightly, following after Twiss and Sticker with another copy of the map.

'Back before the Sky,' Granfer told her, 'we used to sail ships wi' nothing but a map, a compass and a sextant. Out of sight of land, an' all, on seas that reared up as tall as they mountains.'

Pretending to take him at his word, she asked slyly, 'I didn't know you were alive before they had radar.'

Granfer looked levelly at her, his seamed face expressionless but his eyes twinkling. 'You're a baggage, Irona.' And they shared a chuckle which had Twiss turning round to wonder what he had missed. After that moment of closeness, Irona didn't feel so apprehensive.

Besides, in a work-party of diggers there would always be someone to grumble ironically or to strike up a song that would leap from gang to gang. It was a relief then and a bonding until throats grew hoarse from singing above the noise of the improvised picks and shovels and the slithering crunch of rocky rubble. She felt safe in the mass of workmates and she could forget the huge sky stretching naked overhead and spun in sunlight with gossamer lizard-piping.

Later, when Twiss had laid the lines to show them where to dig that day and Granfer had sat down on a rock to take a rest from being cock o' the walk, Irona had a word with the man Twiss had put in charge of the canalisation project.

'How can you stand it?' Irona asked, knowing the question would increase Sinofer's self-confidence and that that was what he needed if he was ever to stop being just another sleeper.

Sinofer smiled down at her, his face already showing the beginnings of a sun-tan. 'I don't mind it a bit. Back on Earth I was a tractor-tender. Walked all over the croplands round Londover. The sky don't hold no terrors for me.'

Irona smiled encouragingly at him though he was twice the size of her. Then she dug until her hands blistered and the blisters bled. Unlike some, she survived the outdoors until the end of the day, but she was glad to stay in Settlement for a while after that.

It was something else again, though, to contemplate the fury of the tempests that danced on the western mountaintops each evening as night fell. There was no more rain in Settlement, though. Irona couldn't understand why not.

It was the seventh day of the canalisation project. Irona was just a little bit bored with her dawn to dusk planning. Hot spring sunshine washed the interior of the computer-shed in gold and dust-motes sparkled and danced in the breeze from the open door. She wished she could just get up and go outside into the enticement of the scented air but her conscience wouldn't let her. All the same she leant back in her makeshift seat, pushing her hands against the edge of the console to rest her shoulder muscles.

For once she acted on idle curiosity and floated her weaponless Eye out over the scrubland. She followed the images it projected, scarcely noticing the map-overlay that showed the irrigation canal following its proper course, even though she as much as anybody had radically underestimated the length of time the digging would take with so few tools and so many blisters.

Almost white now, the dried land glared so fiercely in her eyes that she dimmed the screen. Yet again the shifting movement of the creepers bothered her subliminally but after a moment or two she identified it and tuned her perception to discount it.

Where was Twiss? (Memories in sepia guilt and moonshot pleasure that she had shared without his knowing from the Watchtower.)

Oh, yes. There. Twiss was grabbing a computer-improvised pick from a boy who was taking a breather. She watched him swing the pick above his head and bring it down; she saw the way it jarred his arms when it struck and chips of stone flew up from the point of impact. Streaks of sweat dripped dark runnels through the chalk-dust on his face; his shirt showed a deeper blue under his arms and down his spine. But Twiss seemed to be bursting with energy which contrasted with the lethargic movements of most of those around him.

That was when the impulse struck her. Almost reflexively she keyed for a psychicator, not seriously thinking that such a little computer-rig could be so sophisticated. It came almost as a surprise when the visual screen faded under the amorphous colour-densities of feeling.

What was it that was going on in Twiss? Though the relays were missing so that she couldn't empathise with him, the scan showed a reckless bravado covering doubts. The irrigation was taking too long and he couldn't figure out why.

And what was the prevailing colour? A faint gloom, an air of hopeless defeat. Obviously everyone else was thinking the task was too much for them.

There, though. What was that? A pall of fear with a blazing spark at its heart? Why? What was there to be afraid of?

Another thing to file away and ask Regen about when he came back.

No, maybe not. Maybe she could track the source of the purple fear herself.

Intrigued now, Irona pinpointed its location, turning down the psychicator and sharpening the visual. The fear radiated sharpest from Sinofer.

Weirder and weirder. He was the last one she would have suspected of groundless terror. Why on earth – *No*, she thought. *Why on Harith?* – did he keep turning his head to the mountains that way? There hadn't been a sign of the First Wavers since that Arias Tang man delivered their ultimatum.

She dropped the Eye lower, homing in on Sinofer. After the thrill of the vertiginous plunge made her smile as it always had, she stared curiously at the burly farmer. He was talking with two or three of his gangers, gesturing along the path the watercourse would eventually take, but all the time he kept glancing up at the lumpen brown horizon to the west.

He shouldn't let himself get distracted that way, Irona thought, and with it came the realisation that his unease was communicating itself to the men and women working around him, who were nervous enough anyway with their lingering heritage of agoraphobia.

Then a cloud-shadow swept out from the desert, touching him.

And Sinofer flinched.

That's it! she realised. *It's the electric storms he's afraid of. The lightning. No wonder he keeps an eye out for clouds. I wish – no. I got to hate the Admin manipulating people's emotions. I'm not going to start that.*

Then Irona laughed out loud. *Of course I'm not! Even if I had the stuff it wouldn't work in the open air. The chemicals would just get blown away.*

Back to her old obsession: she stole a minute to look for Twiss but he had jumped down into one of the shallow chalk caverns they had uncovered. Feeling cheated and smiling wryly at her own childishness, she followed Sinofer's apprehensive glances.

And started.

Something had glinted at her. Just for a moment, something had glittered and then winked out almost as if it had felt her gaze. *Where is it? And what is it?*

Nervous now, Irona sent the Eye spinning high into the air, hoping that it wouldn't be noticed among the puffy noon-time clouds. She wasn't sure what she'd seen but whatever it was, it felt like a threat.

'Eye, track that to its source but keep your distance.'

Of course, the Eye didn't move. There was no voice-operation on this little computer-rig. Presumably the First Wave hadn't bothered with it because it seemed so small and primitive. Irritated, Irona flicked the keys.

This time she played no games with the Eye's point of view. Goose-flesh prickling her arms despite the sunlight trapped in the shed, Irona had the Eye relay on all frequencies at her command.

It's Regenerator, she thought, and underneath was the wordless desire *Let it be*.

There!

But it wasn't the slight, gangling figure Irona had come to value. It was a single woman, a lone scout for the enemy, and the noon sun flaring on her vision-enhancers was the only thing that gave her away. Half-hidden in a dry gully that leaped down the flank of the brown mountains, the woman pushed back her long free hair with the inside of one wrist and put the binoculars to her eyes again, batting casually at some sort of insect. She was healthy, ruddy-fleshed, and her clothing rippled as cloud-shadows stroked it in the echoes of the thermal currents circling high above. However closely Irona watched, it seemed the woman had no concept of the Eye spying on her from above.

And she was recording the progress of the canalisation. The First Wavers were beginning a data-base from which to move against them.

Why isn't Twiss here? Irona asked herself. *Or Regen? Where are they when I need them?*

And suddenly there was Regenerator, his tattered clothes

making the only movement that gave him away. His face was smeared with dried mud to protect him from the sun. He was above the woman and far to her left, so still that had the wind not tugged at the rags of his shirt Irona would never have spotted him.

Hit her! Irona prayed with uncitizenlike violence. *Knock her out!* But Regenerator's bulging brown eyes watched the woman calmly. All the long afternoon, whenever Irona looked, he was motionless, even when the hot sunlight pushed back the shadows and left him exposed to the bright heat of the day, camouflaged only by the dust on him and by his stillness.

Irona shoved herself to her feet. *I'll go and tell Twiss!* she thought.

No, that would give the game away. Who knows what might happen if the enemy knew they were being observed?

I'll jolt her with the Eye!

But Irona couldn't do that either, not with this simple unarmed scanner.

And so, leaving the Eye high up out of sight, Irona made herself leave the hut for her customary rounds, forcing herself to chat as though nothing were wrong, helping Jai wash a few clothes in the last of the stored rainwater, taking her turn at winching the heavy plough along the lines that stranded the first field from one side to the other.

But always she returned to scan the Eye's data.

The scout-woman made no overtly threatening moves. Mostly she sipped at her flask, swatted gilt- and green-flecked insects as big as her hands, shifted to keep her head in the shade. The worst she did was key in data on a handset of some sort.

Irona had to contain her anxieties until sundown. Then, in the purple desert dusk, Twiss led the diggers home. Above him a golden sunset fired the edges of the slate-grey thunderheads that chained the mountaintops. Yellow lamplight streamed from the settlement doors and rich odours of chicken casserole reached out luxuriantly on the evening breeze, bringing the scents of home to the weary throng. Sleepy children called out, stretching their arms to welcome their parents. Above the dark eastern horizon, gemmed stars hung so low you could touch them and ruby-eyed lizards piped their songs in aerobatic hieroglyphics that were so beautiful they must mean something if only you knew how to decipher them.

Jai came to the door of the computer-shed. Irona was pacing a restless pattern, three paces to one wall, four to the other, between the few crated power-packs that were left. Her eyes never left the screen.

'Hi, Ro. Have you seen those locust-lizardy things?'

Irona absently answered with a non-committal mmm. She was vibrating with tension she tried not to pass on.

Jai leant outwards, one hand on the door-jamb, watching the aerial dance. 'Beautiful, aren't they?' As a lizard swooped past in its curving flight she reached out to touch it but it veered away, chittering. 'Hey, I almost touched one! They're getting so tame, aren't they? D'you remember when we first landed here it seemed like there was nothing living out here in the wilds? Doesn't seem like only sixteen days ago, does it? Or is it seventeen?'

'Mmm?'

'Hey, c'mon, Ro. It's me. Got a problem?'

Irona shook her head. 'No, it's all right.'

'They're coming home.'

'I know.' Irona gestured with her chin at the monitor where the Eye showed the well-deserved homecoming.

'Well, aren't you going to come and have some supper?'

'I guess so.' But Irona made no move to leave, much less to switch off her computer.

Jai's friendly face puckered, her thick brows drawing together. 'Is it something I've done?' she asked quietly.

At that, Irona pulled herself out of her abstraction. 'No, of course it's not. Don't mind me.'

Jaimindi smiled faintly in relief. 'Well, I wondered. Because you never normally miss Twiss coming home, but then you didn't talk to me either so I wasn't sure . . .' Her voice trailed away in embarrassment.

Irona came over to the doorway and gave her friend a quick hug. 'No, it's not you. Come on, let's go and see

Twiss. Got a bit of news for him.' She headed on back to their dugout.

Jai followed her. 'Aren't you going to switch your computer off?'

'Not tonight, no.' And she patted the reassurance of Regen's pocket-screen hidden in her skirt.

She turned the brightness up to full power and peered into the non-reflective surface for a moment. 'Yeah, there he is, look. Still keeping watch on her.'

Twiss leant over her. 'Why doesn't he just clonk her one?'

Granfer tutted. 'Because then she'd know we're onto her, you moron. This way we've got a chance to prepare without they knowing it.'

'What are we going to do, hide a canal, three hundred diggers *and* a couple of ploughed fields?'

'No, idiot.' Granfer was equally angry and totally impervious to Twiss's irony. 'But I dare say between us we can come up with a couple of little surprises for when they come back. Because they will, Twiss. They're not watching us for fun.'

'I know that. Another week to go, though.'

'Maybe,' said Granfer with a knife-like irony of his own, 'they'll come back sooner.'

'Let 'em!' Twiss was stiff with belligerence. 'We can beat the likes of they as easy as knocking over a rabbit. Shut up, will you? I'm tired.'

Granfer shook his head. They were camped out in the computer shed. Soon Twiss was snoring, his back to the power-pack. But Jai and Irona sat far into the night, knees drawn up and hands out to the warm red glow, and at every sound they looked to the door. Neither of them mentioned Regenerator; both of them wished he were there.

It wasn't until the fifth day after that that the First Wavers attacked.

Regenerator was the first to know it, but hidden out of the way in the scorched hills as he was, there was nothing he could really do. So he did the one thing that was available to him: knock out the lone scout-woman.

She didn't stand a chance. Not that she wasn't stronger than Regen, because she was. But when he suddenly hurtled his gangling weight down onto her, coming out of the glare of the sun, he took her completely by surprise. She fell heavily, Regenerator on top of her, and he gave her no opportunity to resist. In that first breathless second when they hit ground, he twined his fingers in her mane and pounded her head, once, hard, on the stones.

Regen seized what he'd come for: her pocket-computer.

Irona was the second to see the danger.

She had grown accustomed to the presence of the scout. Though she flicked her screens every half-hour or so to display what the Eye could see, there was never anything but the long-haired woman in the drab camouflage, spying down through her vision-enhancers and from time to time wiping the sweat from her hands to play the keys of her computer. Synod alone knew what she was doing.

Now, though, Irona turned from her calculations to scan the sun-shimmered valley – and went in seconds from boredom to horror. This time, orange and angular, there were four tractors, each with a balloon-wheeled trailer. They were already bucketing down the lowest gap in the foothills not two kilometres from Twiss, dust smoking up into the blue sky behind them.

Alarm shrilled through Irona and instinctively she moved to call the Arms. But of course she couldn't, because on Harith there weren't any.

Roiling purple and green horror filled her inner vision. She banged her hands on the console in frustration. Then she flew the Eye to the work-party, sending it swooping into the collapsed chalk-cave where the lead diggers were and buzzing it low over Twiss's head.

Annoyed, he flicked a dismissive hand at the thing but it ducked him, once, twice, and hovered above him just out of reach. Irona writhed in frustration as she saw that he was going to ignore it.

On second thoughts he got someone to give him a leg-up.

Irona saw his head pop up over the crumbling white rim of the cave and slowly circle his gaze over the scrublands where she danced the Eye up and down to guide his vision.

'It's there!' she yelled. 'To your right!'

But of course Twiss couldn't hear her. She had to watch while he continued scanning past the source of the danger.

'What's the matter with you?' she raged.

And then she realised. Because the Eye, right beside him, saw what he saw.

Nothing. Only the brown knees of the mountains shimmering in the heat-haze. He was too low down to see the army from Kifl.

By the time she could have got there to warn them, it was all over. Cursing, she shot the useless Eye straight up into the sun-washed clouds and watched helplessly as the tractors split into two groups to flank the diggers, appearing so suddenly out of the broken ground that there was nothing any of them could do. When the Arias Tang man's voice thundered simultaneously from the four loudspeakers on the vehicles around them, the sleepers instinctively obeyed. Not a one of them stayed hidden in the broken rocks of the foss.

Kilometres away, Irona raged at them but they couldn't hear her. And no-one else in Settlement or on the fields that sloped to the sun could see over the swells of ground that sweltered under the harsh blue of the sky. They trusted too much in the illusory safety of the perimeter fences. They didn't even know to look.

Cowering, the diggers herded together, their lines straggling either side of the ditch, their eyes circling as from one tractor after another climbed streams of men and women who fanned out around them. Twiss's party was completely surrounded.

Then, when the scuffing of feet on rock had died, there was a long silence. Irona saw the whole thing through the faint distortion of extreme magnification. She looked on, appalled at her helplessness. It was as if the heat of the air had congealed the scene in sun-gilded fear.

Twiss recovered first, breaking the gelid tableau. He

scrambled higher up the ridge to scan the tractors. No-one else moved but Irona saw the metal clubs in the rigid hands of the First Wavers and dreaded what would come next.

Just as Twiss shook his fist and opened his mouth to shout his defiance, the lines of First Wavers parted to reveal a slim, dapper figure in coat and trousers of royal blue. She knew that smooth, dark hair, the drape of the moustache against sallow skin.

It was Arias Tang.

Gundmila glanced over her shoulder, once, and turned the grav-shaft off. Gliding through the moonshot chamber at the top of the minaret, she forbade the lights to shine. No-one must know she was there.

Below, footsteps sounded in the midnight streets of Kifl. She hurried to the window, peering through the muslin curtains that fluttered in the breeze from the sea. Whoever it was down there, though, they didn't so much as glance up at the Synod tower. Gundmila nodded to herself. Then she checked that her fellow counsellors, Tang, Less and Lal, hadn't 'accidentally' left any recorders or transmitters working.

Her monitor, disguised as a carving in the apex of the room, showed that the chamber was clear.

She spoke the five-syllable tonemes that would, at long last, operate the new ansible for the first time ever on Harith. In ten minutes she would know what Towy—

'Gundmila!' No preamble, no warming-up or static. It was instantaneous. And that voice! Flat with contained shock, it still couldn't be Towy's.

One glance at the grey face with its wispy eyebrows, the blue-green eyes. In its papery skin, behind its faded lips, there was someone she should recognise.

Gundmila swayed, straightened. She was pale as the snows on the volcano. 'Bernardina!'

The old woman smiled in what surely couldn't be satisfaction. 'You may be older than me, Gundmila, but you haven't grown. Forty years and you're still the same.'

If the Matriarch of Kifl chose to hear it as, 'You haven't

grown old,' that was her business. Her china-blue eyes gazed at her rival and gloated. 'Crow's feet, Bernardina?'

Bernardina nodded faintly. Her purple lips folded into the skeleton of a smile. 'The footprints of wisdom, but you wouldn't know about that. I take it from the fact that we're having this conversation at all that the *Starwing* delivered the ansible and the rest of the consignment with no problems?'

'None whatsoever.'

'Then the sleepers are fitting in well?'

Gundmila couldn't resist patting her hair with her slim, youthful fingers. She watched Bernardina's gnarled hands whiten at the knuckles. 'Who cares about a load of sleepers? What are you doing there? Where's Towy?'

'Ah yes, your ally in Synod. How do you like being in exile?'

Gundmila's smile was like a dagger. 'Exile? I'm not in exile. Towy chose me to rule—'

'To fester. To fester at the fringes of empire where you can't meddle. And you thought it was a promotion!'

'At least I wasn't dropped to the warrens. Captain Dainty and I had a fascinating talk. How did you sneak back into—' She broke off, shouted past the image of Bernardina, 'Arms? Arms! There's a waker in Camelford Synod!'

Bernardina clicked her tongue in reproof. 'Did you think I hadn't guarded this little chat? How silly of you.'

'Towy! What have you done with Towy?'

'Oh, you can't see her now, dear. She's asleep.'

'Bernardina! You've drugged her, you devious bitch.'

The old skin folded into an origami smile. 'I didn't need to. Her mind's asleep and her atoms have gone to join the ecosphere – much good may they do it! I'm Matriarch of Matriarchs now.'

'But only in Camelford.'

'Only in Camelford – so far. But I'm on the board of the Admin. My vote sways the resources of two hundred million people. By the way, how many are you with the new batch of sleepers I sent you?'

'*You* sent me? Hah! Two thousand.' Pride.

'Only two thousand.'

Gundmila tried to hide her feeling of deflation by showing off. 'Two thousand plus the sleepers.'

It didn't have the effect she'd desired. 'Overbreeding already? Or did you forget about that one?'

'We have a whole planet—'

'That's not what I heard.' Bernardina's lips twitched as Gundmila said, 'The *Starwing* won't get back to Earth for another twenty years! How can you have—' She stopped.

'That's right, Gundmila. Ansibles weren't practicable when you went. But you've been out of circulation for a long time. Earth hasn't stood still waiting for you, you know. Ansibles aren't just for Synods now. Do you think I don't know where you had the captain drop the sleepers? And what you took from them?'

'I took nothing of any importance. They didn't have anything—'

Bernardina smiled her Buddha smile.

'I didn't! I even left them enough food to last until—'

'Until you starve them into submission.'

'It's not like that. Bernardina, don't put words into my mouth. I even left them some poxy little computer they'd brought to make them feel grown-up. Sleepers! What are they going to do with a computer?'

'I've seen the shots the *Starwing* took for me of I—'

'Don't be coy with me, Bernardina. So you know about the weather-Eye? So what? There's nothing those deves can do about the rainshadow we've amplified. That land's worthless without water. Either they'll be proper sleepers and do what I say—'

'What *I* say? Not even a pretence at being part of a Synod? Gundmila, you're slipping.'

'No I am not.'

'Well how come,' Bernardina's parchment cheeks twitched momentarily into open malice, 'you daren't integrate the sleepers then? Aren't you in control of your own people? Better keep an eye on your junior or you'll be taking the long sleep too.'

Gundmila was so self-preoccupied she didn't even notice that betraying 'too'. She said, 'Bernardina, old hag, I don't need a junior. I'll live for ever. See my face? My hands? Yours are like claws. I'm on Harith, Bernardina. I'll live to dance on the volcano when they bring me the news that you're dead.' Pleased at having got the last word, she intoned the 'off' command.

In Camelford, the last Bernardina saw of her rival was her smirk. She thought about what Gundmila had said – and said without meaning to.

Then she summoned Elditch.

He appeared almost instantly. Static from a particle shower splayed his black hair so that it showed the pale roots where he hadn't recently dyed it.

'Husband,' Bernardina said, and enjoyed his flinch. All the same she clicked her tongue and snapped, 'Stop betraying your sleeper origins, you dolt! You're married to Synod now, the same as I am.'

'At least in the warrens you loved me.'

'At least in the warrens I pretended to. You were happy enough when I elevated you to Synod, though, weren't you?'

'Because I thought you loved me.'

She sneered. 'Love? You were never anything but a slightly more intelligent screw.'

He was shocked.

'You're still such a sleeper that vulgarity stings. Synod, what did I ever see in you?'

He loomed over her, hands on the Arms of her throne. 'Don't push me too far, Bernie-love.' The old endearment was loaded with venom. 'I can still bring you down.'

She laughed. 'Not without bringing yourself down too. But don't let's quarrel, for old time's sake.' Bernardina covered his hand with hers and squeezed. She measured out affection in ergs. 'We had our moments, didn't we?'

Elditch knew she wanted something but he let himself be mollified. 'You were the best, Bernie. Nobody else counted. And you're still the best when you let me.'

She was glad he hadn't seen Gundmila with her flawless skin, her breasts that were young and proud, that hadn't sagged over twenty years like her own. Suddenly Bernardina wanted him fiercely.

'She can't win, you know,' Bernardina said. 'She's taken their food and left them to colonise the desert for her. But she left them their computer because I made it look pathetic. And she didn't find our secret weapon.'

Elditch perched on the arm of his wife's throne to bask in the fire he felt kindling within her. 'Our weapon?' he said, and stroked her withered cheek.

Bernardina smiled. When she felt like this, superior, her juices flowed and Elditch was still a considerate lover. He took longer to get there these days but that was all to the good. 'Yes, our weapon. Haven't you understood anything?' She kissed the inside of his wrist. 'Our daughter. Our amplified daughter, Irona.'

14

A GOLDEN ROPE

'What was your name again?' drawled Tang, supercilious in his fine clothes. To the Second Wavers his short queue looked faintly ridiculous.

Twiss's face darkened. 'You know fine well what it is!'

'Ah, so I do. It can't be me that has the short memory, then. It must be you.'

Twiss was too smart to fall into the trap again. Ignoring Tang's gambit, he said, 'These are our lands. We have a right to them.' Irona could see he was itching to add something else, something cocky or threatening, but he wisely kept his mouth closed. Twiss was learning.

'But we told you,' Tang said, 'that if you wanted land on Harith you had to work it with us. I mean, look at this! Trying to dig some piddling little ditch with your bare hands. It's pathetic.'

'What choice did you give us? You're the ones who've robbed us of our rich lands by the sea.' Twiss was turning now, throwing his arms wide to appeal to his own people as much as to Tang. 'What did you expect us to do? Lie down and die?'

Tang arched his shapely brows. 'You think you have to lie down to die?' He nodded at the lines of smartly-clad troops surrounding the colonists. 'There are other ways, you know.'

Even via her computer screen Irona could see Twiss seem to expand; it was as if some aura, some presence, radiated from him with his anger, reaching out to touch his followers. It was commanding. And it wasn't benign. Some of Twiss's Second Wavers shivered – Irona saw the mauves of fear shading darker patches over the screen and they looked longingly towards the safety of the perimeter wire so far away – while not a few First Wave troops swayed as if to draw closer together for protection. But mostly the new settlers united, annealed by the intensity of Twiss's feelings, as if his anger gave them permission to feel their own. And for the first time in their lives there were no wardens to stop them.

Twiss's hard stare swivelled to touch each one of the club-wielding First Wavers. 'You touch a one of our people and you die. You hear me?' Twiss's anger stretched his voice until it was a tight, hard fist hammering at Tang.

Slowly the First Wave leader smiled. 'How could I not? They can probably hear you in the Horsehead Nebula. Did you think volume is the same as strength?' He puffed mocking laughter down his nose.

Twiss glared at him, his hazel eyes shining with wrath. Irona thought to herself, *He doesn't look safe, somehow*.

'I just wanted to show you,' Tang continued as if talking to a child, 'that resistance is futile. Our population is five or six times greater than yours – and I'm not just talking about sheep like them.' He jerked his chin contemptuously at the diggers caught indecisive round the canal. 'I mean real independent people capable of autonomous action. We have forty years and more of supplies and resources behind us. We're well past subsistence level while the only bread your retards have got is what we gave them. And you've managed to con them into sucking up to you, carrying out some half-assed plan that'll kill them before you get one drop of water to that scratched-up ground you probably tell them might be a field some day.

'What are you going to live on until your crops come in? That's months away, assuming anything grows in this alien dustbowl. And hasn't it ever occurred to you that the reason we let you have this worthless desert is that it's in a rainshadow? Come summer there won't be enough water this side of the mountains to wash a baby's dick.'

'How about yours?'

Some of the troops and quite a few of Twiss's own followers sniggered. Tang's expression didn't change. 'Oh, very droll. Been watching kiddy-disks, have we? How many have you seen since you've been here, though? What have your children got to play with? Is there milk for the babies? How many clean changes of clothes have you had? I mean proper irradiated ones, not those rags you've been dipping in poisoned mud.'

'Poison?' the Second Wavers asked each other. 'What poison? He never told us about no poison.'

'You're losing them!' Irona shouted at Twiss from the computer dug-out but the screen-leader didn't respond to her urgency. Right at that moment he stood dumb. To Irona it seemed that shreds of the old days were making him wait for someone to tell him what to say. *If only I had some chemical emoters!* she thought, and all she could do was yell, 'Come on!'

And loud as Twiss's retort was, it was completely drowned by the mechanical amplification Tang triggered for himself. Serene, the voice as loud as thunder reverberated through the ranks of Twiss's people, 'Don't listen to him. What has he got to give you? Can Twiss stop your children crying with hunger in the night? Can you give them sweets or ice-cream like they remember from before you put them in this madman's hands?'

Tang gestured, a golden ring glinting on one manicured finger, and from their pockets his troops threw a shower of gaudy paper cones. Reflexively the sleepers reached out to catch them before the Carnival sweetmeats spilled to the broken white ground. Cramming the rich goodness into their mouths, the Second Wavers revelled in the first luxury they'd known since they'd been here.

'Don't touch them!' Twiss ordered, and some of the sleepers heard his fear and obeyed, but Tang pulled out a red and green paper bag of his own and tossed a few chocolate cherries into his mouth with every evidence of enjoyment. All along the knots of people there were those who tasted the goodies and murmured in delight.

Tang chewed in exaggerated pleasure and lobbed the bag to Twiss, who made no move to catch it. Arms crossed against his chest, he let it fall into the dust at his feet.

'Pure paranoia, Twiss,' the First Wave leader said, and this time his amplified voice was shot through with a sincerity

that goaded Irona's subconscious. 'We only want to look after
you. We'll never hurt you. We'll take care of your old and
your sick if you let us. Be one with us and you'll never go
short of anything again.'

Back in the computer-shed Irona jerked as the compelling
tones rolled on and the Second Wavers began looking
askance at the man they'd let choose himself as leader,
as though they had just woken up to some awful ploy
of Twiss's. Of a sudden she recognised the technique and
clenched her fists in frustration. *Sonic emotional controllers,
bottled sincerity. Out there in the open they'll be more effective
than ever chemical ones could be. Twiss has lost.*

But suddenly that didn't seem to be such a bad thing. *Clean
clothes? Water we don't have to bleed for? And is this stuff
poisonous or what? Why shouldn't we go to Kifl and live
with the First Wavers if it means we can be comfortable at
last? Who cares whether it's Synod or this lot who lead us?
I've had enough of trying to be boss.*

Only Tang went too far. Encouraged by the rebellion
fomenting among Twiss's people, he took a step or two
forward, his black boots gleaming under a thin patina of
dust, and made a mistake. He said, 'Go on, Twiss. Take a
chocolate.'

'Take!' Twiss hurled the word. 'Take! That's what you've
done.' His hand shot out to point threateningly at Tang.
'You've taken everything, even they sweets for our children's
first Carnival here. You've taken our food, our machines, the
cloth for our clothes, our land – and then you have the gall to
offer us a couple of chocolates back as if we were kids you
could bribe! Well I ain't having no measly handouts from
you. If the water's poisoned, who poisoned it? And if you're
telling the truth, how come we ain't dead yet?'

The First Wave leader reached for his microphone again
but Twiss forestalled him. 'Scared they might hear what I've
got to say? Tang, you're full of crap. I want my share and so
do these people.' Twiss's gesture embraced the new settlers.
'We want what's ours and if you ain't going to play fair we're
going to take it from you.'

Tense as a fretsaw blade, the atmosphere hardened.

Without a word more needing to be said the First Wave troops raised their bars of iron defensively.

Twiss saw and seized on it. 'That's how you do it, then? Beat up innocent people? Cripple them? Kill them if they don't do what you want? You touch a one of my people and you lose, Tang. They'll see you for what you really are. All you need from us is slave-labour and you ain't getting it. So clear the hell off back to your city and stay there.'

'Oh, no.' (Irona noticed that even in defeat Tang wore a brave face; against her will she felt a momentary flash of respect for him.) 'We don't need you half as much as you need us, Twiss. We've got everything, right? And we're going to keep it. You?' Tang laughed. 'You can keep this place. We don't need to lift a finger to harm you. By midsummer there won't be enough of you left alive to shade the ground with your bones.'

Twiss aped a shudder to make his people laugh. It didn't quite come off but some of the Second Wave forced a chuckle out of solidarity as he said, 'Ooh, scary.' Then his voice turned glacial as he stared across at Arias Tang. 'Ah, sling your hook, you worm-brained deve. You're nothing but a bag of wind.'

Tang's troops withdrew. Hardly any of them showed the same composure their leader did as they trailed back to their dusty tractors. A vagrant breeze lifted a fog of chalk that seemed to cloak them in ignominy, besmirching their blue or yellow or umber clothing that had seemed so fine before.

Seeing their stony faces or their blushes or the way their heads dropped, the Second Wavers sneered openly while their tormentors climbed aboard. With cat-calls and shouts of 'Sling your hook, you deves!' the flame of defiance leaped along the lines of diggers, banishing fatigue and fear in the dry desert air. In seconds Irona's monitor was overlaid with flickering crimson from one end to the other, annealing Twiss's people into one firm group: together in the barren scrublands against whatever Harith might throw at them. As a token of it even Sinofer waved his fist, the first time in his entire life that he had felt and acknowledged the narcotic of violence.

Irona, watching the blood-red emotion spurting from him on her screen, felt just a twinge of the old habit and her fingers crooked, but there was nothing to connect them to. No spray of chemical tranquillisers. No call to Arms at this waking. Then the urge was gone, because she knew that this couldn't be the end of it, whatever Tang might have said.

Under the strange, rich hue of his skin, Twiss coloured. They seized him, bore him shoulder-high, chanting his name to the high blue of the sky. Heedless of their stumbling on the broken chalk they danced around the canal-head with him.

Irona brought the Eye down to circle overhead, drinking in the sight of Twiss triumphant. He was trying not to give in to the grin that might have seemed like arrogance but it kept escaping through his control. The battle-glaze had gone from his eyes, leaving them a shining hazel. One strand of hair stuck up from the back of his head and, lapped by the emotional shades of her screen, it seemed like a crown of joy and power. She wished fiercely for her emotional link to share this moment with him but a bittersweet pang of regret stopped her as efficiently as any technical lack.

Where her certainty came from, she had no idea. But she knew death was on the way.

In two more days the heartened workforce brought the canal to the lip of the fields. There was no sign of Tang's poison; everyone was healthy and raring to go.

In gala mood the whole settlement turned out to watch the first water arrive. The purple shadows of evening were stretching out from the mountains to cross the sunny landscape and in the east the first planets glowed in the promise of darkness. Children raced excitedly around, trying to catch the jewel-like lizards that piped and flittered just out of reach now, polished to brilliance by the golden evening.

Maybe the atmosphere's got to them too, Irona thought. *They were shy as anything when we first saw them*.

Many a little boy and girl wore shiny red and green party hats made out of the Carnival sweet-bags the First Wavers had tried to use as bribes. It seemed fitting, somehow, to turn them into symbols of the settlement's victory over Harith.

'Let's celebrate with a proper meal and hang the rationing,' Twiss had suggested, and despite her inner misgivings Irona had agreed. Now rich odours rose from stewpans filled with an appetising concoction of beans and other vegetables that should have been used as seeds or sets for the first crops.

The warm evening breeze wafted the scent out from the settlement, whetting everyone's appetite. Irona sniffed it and said in an undertone to Twiss, 'D'you think we should have?'

''Course we should.'

'Well, yes, but—'

'But nothing. Stop worrying and enjoy yourself, why don't you?' He tugged at his best clothes that he had been saving for a special occasion, a shirt of creamy silk under a suit of soft sepia cloth. 'All right?'

Without waiting for an answer, he waved his arms and called for silence and Irona dared not break the attention he won. For once he wasn't on his knoll but near the foot of a low rolling hill next to the field that had been so hard to plough.

All around the people jostled to stand looking down at him almost as if he were on the stage of some ancient amphitheatre, and the crowning touch was the slanting sunbeam that bathed him like a spotlight. Against the pale chalky soil with its low-slung shifting vines he seemed to glow like a statue in amber, and the clean odour of soap clung to his damp hair.

'Neighbours, see this here?' He pointed dramatically to a bank of moist broken earth parted by a plastic gate. 'Well, this be the end of our canal. You done it, you tunnelled the water from they underground caves right along to under here. You, not me. All of you. You what done the digging, Irona and Regen who plotted the water-course, the ones that ploughed the fields and put in irrigation ditches and built they little gates there so the fields don't drown, and you what looked after us and the kids so's we could get on with the job. So when I raise this gate, you give three good cheers for yourselves and for how rich we're all going to be. We're looking at next month's dinner.' Many chuckled, Twiss just grinned. 'Ready?'

They were. Not a body moved; even the wind seemed to keep itself pent so that not so much as a child's apron rustled. Irona found herself holding her breath. Twiss bent to pull up the panel.

The grey plastic skreeked a little as he worked it upwards in its supports. Muddy water trickled out beneath it, faster and faster, until Twiss lifted the gate clean out of its bed and flourished it over head.

Tumbling, splashing, the waters shot out into the sunlight like a twisted golden rope. A cheer crashed out from the crowd, and another, and another, trembling the golden beads of water that the sunshine hung on the air.

Suddenly nobody quite knew what to do next. But Irona began one of the old Carnival joy-songs, softly at first, then with greater firmness as more and more people joined in. Even the familiar thunder and lightning from the evening storm on the mountains seemed to be part of the song.

Twiss slid his arm around Irona's waist and as someone else took up the round he bussed her soundly in the amethyst twilight. The children laughed; the older women's faces seamed into scandalised masks and for a moment the song faltered under Marjine's crusty look, but Twiss grinned at Irona and took up the chorus lustily if not quite on key. He winked at her, his eyes aglow in the dying sunset. She chuckled, embarrassed but pleased at her first kiss, singing along with him. Irona didn't quite know what to do with herself but Twiss didn't let her go.

Then, his arm still holding her tightly, he whirled her into a madcap dance. First Sticker and Jai, then Sinofer and Tebrina, then couples too many to count capered past the open-mouthed Marjine along the road to home and the hope of plenty.

Arriving breathless back at the tunnel-mouth Regenerator had dug under the settlement's fence, Jai stopped and grabbed Irona's arm to pull her out of the giggling, bobbing throng streaming under it to the dugouts. Off-balance, Irona stumbled to one side. Twiss saw what was going on and though he steadied Irona, he released her waist and let himself be pushed along in the crowd. She watched him go in a moment of insecurity then pulled herself together. *This is Harith, remember? You're strong here.*

Jai gasped, 'I – I haven't got enough stimulants for – for everyone, Ro. What shall I do?'

Irona yanked her cap off so that she could cool her head. 'Listen to them – do you think they need anything else? We've done it, Jai!' She fanned herself and the cap-strings fluttered pale in their own breeze. Loosing it, she let it blow away.

In the half-light she could hardly see Jai's face but she knew well enough what the expression on it would be: fear for her own inadequacy. Irona told her, 'We're enough for ourselves. And just smell that casserole! What more could anyone want?'

'But – but—'

'But me no buts, Jai.' Irona slipped her arm through her friend's and pulled her down into the dimness of the short tunnel. 'I know it's a carnival but it's fine as it is. You're not robbing anybody, OK? You haven't failed in your duty. Come and have some dinner and enjoy yourself. Or at least stop going round looking worried or you'll bring everyone else down.'

That was the kind of blackmail Jai couldn't ignore. And, as the luxury of plenty relaxed her with its carbohydrate tranquillisers, Jai did start to calm down. The casserole was strange but rich.

In the lamplit dugout Irona felt cosy and sheltered from the vastness of the night. Possibly the outrageous compliments Twiss paid her over the second plateful had something to do with it too. At any rate, soon Jai's laugh was blending with Twiss's and Irona's, though how Sticker kept a straight face when he talked such balderdash was more than any of the rest of them could work out. Even Granfer was grinning and Irona knew that if Regenerator had been there, he would have appreciated it as well. She missed him but he was still nervous around crowds.

Off by the knoll, Irona could see the settlers beginning to drift together in the starlight, talking in voices that were fearlessly loud. They were high on achievement and when an electrolin began a rollicking tune, there were plenty of cocky young lads to start a contagious jig. Other musicians strolled across to add the sound of minisynth strings and tambourines. The noise was a joyous challenge to the stars that hung low in the velvet warmth of the night. She was dying to join in but she hadn't quite got the courage to ask Twiss to join her. Maybe his kiss and the dance had been an impulse he regretted?

I'm being paranoid, she told herself and was on the point of saying something when Twiss made it unnecessary. He could hardly wait for Granfer to finish chewing. He stood up, holding out a hand to pull Irona to her feet, and, still holding onto her, wandered across to join in the high-kicking competition the young men were having. The girls stood watching in a circle. They forgot all the rules of modesty they'd ever learned and started goading their menfolk to even greater efforts with good-humoured insults, a carnival game taken to extremes.

Marjine pokered up instantly. 'Well!' she remarked pointedly, but only one or two other oldsters took any notice of her.

The contest ended when even Twiss had fallen flat on his back, laughing as loud as any of them. Only Sticker had kept his feet, as he told anyone who would listen, but the musicians struck up another roundelay that effectively drowned out his humorous complaints and Marjine's bitter ones.

Soon everyone was having such a good time that mothers forbore to look for their sons and daughters. When Irona slipped away, dizzy with dancing, to the latrines, whispers from the darkness surrounded her with the suppressed sounds of love. Years of conditioning made her want to react with the quelling instincts of a warden. But the memory of Twiss's lips against her cheek was warm on the cool dusty breeze from the desert and she wished the lovers luck. Besides, if the settlement were to survive, they'd need a lot of babies.

Unseen in the darkness above the soil-trenches, song-lizards piped a counterpoint to the raucous music round the knoll. Just rarely their ruby eyes might catch the starlight, or a turquoise wing might flash silvered in the hurtling moonbeams. Pure happiness thrilled through her.

It was only afterwards, when she was walking back to the hub of lamplight aflicker with the movement of the saraband that she felt something sting her thigh. She brushed hastily at it but when she ducked into the shelter to look discreetly under her skirts there was nothing there. Just a scratch she hadn't noticed before.

At last, when the dance had thinned to a few stalwarts jigging to a single electrolin, Granfer creaked to his feet and said, 'Well, I'm off to my bed, Twiss. It were a good day, though, and a good night. I wish your mother could have seen it.' And, washed by the atmosphere, he kissed Irona and Jai goodnight.

After that, Twiss kept Irona by his side. For a while Jai hung around them but Sticker led her off to one side. She resisted at first, then realised suddenly that she was one too many. As he gradually pulled her to the far side of the trampled space, Sticker whispered, much to her confusion, 'Don't worry. I'll take care of you,' and the darkness smothered her nervous giggles.

It left only Twiss and Irona. To the sound of the single remaining electrolin he danced her to hilarious exhaustion. Then they clung together, barely moving, their bodies hot and close in the star-shimmered night, long after the music slept.

Finally, when even the sound of parents calling their children with the anger of guilt had died away, Twiss led Irona out towards the fringes of Settlement Knoll. Torn between modesty and recklessness, she followed him wordlessly.

The energy that had been surging through her all night focussed itself in a physical excitement that she couldn't resist, though she still somehow felt that she should. She seemed to hear the sincere penetrating tones of a shrine but Twiss still had her arm linked tightly in his and she knew where she wanted to be.

The pale hills rose around them, breathing out the stored heat of the day in an exotic perfume of alien plants. As they came laughing to a halt on a crest, they saw the wind scarf the dunes with trails of moon-silvered sand.

Twiss stopped. Irona could feel the moist warmth of his

skin reaching into her flesh. He stepped closer, his face smiling levelly, mysteriously into hers. The strange light drew his features in dark lines, shone on the width of his brow and his cheekbones. His gaze magnetised her.

Slowly he tightened his hold, moving her to face him. When their hips touched a fire shot through her body so that she was flowing like liquid in Harith's night. He kissed her: it was as if she melted, not knowing where the limits of her self began and his finished. It seemed that the cells of her skin and his commingled until they were one being and behind her closed eyelids their double essence burned.

Slowly, tenderly, he feathered his fingertips down her neck to her collar-bone. Irona learned the muscles of his back through her hands, and still he kissed her. She had never imagined anything like it.

'You're safe here,' he whispered. 'Nobody around as far as the eye can see. I've got you. You're safe with me.' And his arms slid down to her wrists, tugging her gently to lie beside him. He pillowed her head in the crook of his shoulder – she breathed in his masculine scent as if it were intoxicating – and caressed first her hair, her neck, her back. Then little by little his hands set off on a journey of discovery that made him murmur his delight. Gradually Irona felt pleasure quiver through her, more and more deeply.

This time in the rich alien night, she knew when he kissed her.

And when he took the love she gave.

15

BLOOD OF HARITH

The sun was already a handspan above the desert rim when a low groan woke Irona. Instantly she sat up to see what was wrong but a wave of dizziness spun her head and she fell back against Twiss's shoulder. His arm spasmed then he pressed his hand against her side for an instant before she felt it flop back against the powdered earth. Against her naked skin she could feel how hot his palm was but he was shaking.

'What's wrong?' she asked him, and shivered herself as she reached to pull the makeshift covers up to his chin. Her overskirts were all the blankets they had brought with them to this lonely spot, and the midnight-blue fabric was dusted with the soft sand blowing across the dunes.

Twiss swallowed, a dry sound, but he didn't answer. Besides, as wakefulness seeped through Irona's body like the long shadows across the desert, her own stomach twisted. Bile filled her arid mouth and her thoughts seemed to shimmer like the heat-haze that was already beginning to hover—

Twisting aside barely in time, she vomited. The stench of her own illness made it worse and her stomach tried to turn itself inside out. When there was nothing left inside her she wiped her face with a handful of sand, then scooped more over the remains of last night's feast.

Collapsing back against Twiss she felt him gently brush the sand away from her eyes. Then, pillowing her head again on his shoulder, he stroked her hair. His fingers barely moved to make the caress but tears came to her unbidden because she had never known such gentleness.

For a time she lay crying silently, her face straight, her chest moving only to her tight-held breathing, but the moisture leaked out anyway and rolled into the hair at her temple.

Though Twiss never knew, his tenderness melted a tiny part of the glaciers her mother and Camelford had frozen into her mind.

His hand stilled; she wondered if he was asleep.

'You know what it is,' he said eventually, when his own retching had ceased.

Irona could not bring herself to voice her suspicions.

'It's them. That Tang man and they bully-boys of hisn. He said the water was poisoned and d'you know how he knew? Because his lot had done it. He stood there and told me, and I thought I knew better.'

Irona listened to Twiss's cold tones. She could hear his voice echoing round the desert of his heart, vibrating his desolation through the contact of her cheekbones, his ribs. She sought to comfort him. 'But we'd been drinking the water for weeks and it was all right, wasn't it? A bit alkaline, maybe, but just fine.'

Twiss, locked inside his own thoughts, made no answer.

Irona pitied his pain because she felt enough of it herself. She hadn't even seen the Kiflians coming to surround the canal-head until it was almost too late. So she tried again to offer him comfort. 'It's not your fault, is it, Twiss? How were we to know they'd do that to us?'

Her torso pulled itself upright. 'To all of us! Oh, Synod, Twiss! How many more are there suffering back at the settlement?'

After that, there was no question. Neither of them could just rest there waiting for recovery under the white-hot sun. Too many people might lie helpless in the settlement; too many babies and old folks dying.

The trouble was, neither of them had paid much attention to how they had got there. And bit by bit the moonglow winds had dusted over their footprints until by the time they had strength to look round, the heat of morning couldn't show them a single shadow-marked track. And there was no indication, either, of where water might be.

'Settlement's got to be that way, though,' said Twiss. 'See

that part there where the mountains are lower? Isn't that the pass to Kifl?'

'Er – I don't know. It might be. Synod, if I'd only thought to bring the Eye-contact Regen made me!'

She had the suspicion that until that moment he hadn't even given it a thought. Now she felt his blame – or thought she did – as he said, 'Oh, wonderful. That's a great help, that is. Aren't you dying for a drink?'

Irona puffed laughter down her nose. The question didn't warrant any other reply.

Leaning on each other for support, they staggered in the direction Twiss had indicated. They slogged through the soft sand that caught their ankles and hindered them with its burning grasp, heading back to where they thought the settlement might be.

'It's got to be right, hasn't it?' Irona said, the weakness of her fever fraying her mind towards the fringe of despair. She knew if they didn't get it right the first time, they would not be strong enough for another attempt. And the land between the mountains was too big to play games with. 'I mean, look at the shadows.'

'True enough. The sun' – he squinted up at the blazing star that whitened the desert sky – 'comes up over they mountains there, don't it?' He circled to point almost straight behind them to the east. 'So all we have to do is walk the same way as the shadows. I didn't think we'd come this far, though. We must be going round in circles.'

'Anyway' – Irona strove for a brittle brightness – 'once we get over that ridge we should be able to see Settlement Knoll. It can't be that far, can it?' And in her mind was the starry splendour of the night they had scarcely noticed as it had sheltered them in their walk across the silvered landscape. Harith had been a newscast backdrop fitted to romance, its breezes caressing their skin coolly with its mysterious perfume.

So wrapt had they been in talk they had no idea how far they had come to be alone. Now, with the lambent sun leaching moisture from their already-dehydrated bodies, reality gnawed at them. Flushed with hot shivers, they dragged themselves across to the foot of a knife-creased wall of sand. It seemed to grow over them, taller and taller, as they stood there, panting. But they knew it had to be done, so without a word they began to scale the barren heights.

Gripes weighted their stomachs into lumps of clay, but step by inefficient step they bulled their way up the dry-scented dune. At each footfall the baked sand slithered backward. Here and there translucent scrub-plants rolled under their feet, lashing out to skin their ankles or tug at their shoes. All but invisible, the ghosts of their shadows wavered out and uphill from the green-ball plants, hazed by the heat of the searing day.

Irona breasted the dune first. And Twiss, hearing only her dessicated breathing and what she didn't say, knew that Settlement wasn't there.

He stood beside her and she saw his head, too heavy for him to hold, wobble on his neck like a child's. Cold sweat plastered sand to his face and drew saffron gullies on the brown of his velvet jacket. His hair was greasy with fever and she knew she looked no better. Exhaustion hollowed her.

Neither of them dared to say they might be heading deeper into the desert. When they had got their breath back she said, 'Remember the helter-skelter at Camelford fair?'

Twiss could scarcely be bothered to answer.

She took off her overskirt and sat on it, opening her legs.

'Irona!' he said in exasperation.

A blush boiled up in her face as she realised what he thought she meant.

'No, you idiot!' was what she almost said, but citizenship stopped her at the brink of a descent into anger. Hastily she said aloud, 'No. Sit on my skirt, Twiss, and hold the front end up a bit like the mat on the helter-skelter.'

He was too fevered to answer. He half-fell between her legs and she pressed her thighs shakily around his hips.

'Got the hem?' she started to ask, but his motion to grab it had started them careering downhill and they almost overbalanced. She clutched him hard. They tobogganed down into hot shadow. As they bumped faster and faster down the dune they gained equilibrium and the wind streamed past them to tang their nostrils with the odours of sun-roasted terrain.

Eyes slitted against the flying sand, Irona peeked over Twiss's shoulder. Speed thrilled through her; a hectic hilarity made her yell for the sheer pleasure of yelling. This was how she would remember the desert: a blur of crocus-bright sand streaked with ochre shadows winging towards her, tossing her around like a live thing, the reassurance of Twiss's back jumping against her breasts, dust sparked with mica swooping golden to tingle in her face under the hot blue vault of the sky.

Too soon they jerked to a halt and toppled sideways, laughing weakly. She thought of all the secret times she had stolen joy from Twiss in his night-runs through the Park and grinned to keep those moments quiet behind her teeth. This was one exhilaration that she had given him and the gift made her feel her life had a point to it that she had never suspected.

Twiss sobered. 'Wait a minute,' he said, rising to his elbows and knees. 'Have we come sideways down that slope or what?'

Irona was still lolling on one elbow, giggling unabatedly. 'Mm?'

'Come on, stop laughing. This is serious.'

'Laughing's serious!' she retorted. 'I haven't done enough of it in my life and if I'm going to die anyway, this is how I want to go. Synod, my head hurts.'

'Never mind your head.' He brushed the crusted sand from his eyes. 'Didn't those shadows use to point more that way?' He waved off to their left, along the valley between the dunes.

'D'you know, I think you're right. Hang on.'

Rolling onto her back, she squinted through the shade to follow their tracks with her gaze. The shallow trench of their sledge-ride jagged this way and that; an uprooted plant stumbled in their wake, its clear chameleon tendrils flailing as it sought for a roothold.

'I don't know, Twiss. We might be a little off-beam but overall we came down pretty straight.'

His determination made his face a fierce mask between her and the aching sky. He said, 'I still think we should follow the shadows.'

Irona didn't agree but one thing she had learned in Camelford was never to disagree directly. She skirted the argument by saying tactfully, 'Well, maybe you're right. Let's see what we can see when we get to the top of the next one and then decide.'

She had no intention of giving in, though.

Settlement wasn't visible from any of them.

She felt an unreasonable anger: *You should have noticed which way we were going*, she bawled at Twiss in her thoughts, but citizenship perjured her and when he asked in a tightly-controlled voice, 'Are you all right?' she answered, 'Fine. You?'

He essayed a nod, white salt seaming his skin where his sweat had evaporated. Unless it was more of the Synod-cursed sand.

'Hey, Twiss.'

This time he was ahead of her, the dunes lower. He turned across the slow rolling aridity and walked a few paces backwards, too tired to break his momentum and stop. Settlement Knoll still played its evil game of hide and seek and stayed maliciously out of sight in the sun-glamoured wilderness.

'You notice anything?'

A vague movement that might have been the shake of his head. He took a few more paces rearwards, the sweat darkening his shirt. He had long since knotted the sleeves of his jacket around his head the way she had kilted a petticoat to replace her lost cap but still his lips showed a strand of blood where they were cracked by dehydration. All the protuberances on his face, his neck, his collar-bones, were angry as fire and his eyes were bloodshot and red-rimmed.

Irona knew that she looked no better and that soon they might both look far worse. Striving for optimism she said, 'More plants. See them?'

Ponderous as the orbit of a star, his head turned. The plants were there and not there, hovering on the fringes of vision, their phantom shadows writing glyphs that their motion erased. In the heart of each curving penumbra was a focus of pale light that danced maddeningly over the wind-dimpled sands. Through the powdery dust that lined their nostrils and settled dryness on their tongues came the sharp astringent odour of translucent beryl fronds, yet the plants themselves took on the ever-changing camouflage of the desert's hues. Irona knew that if she knelt to touch them, the suckers would writhe firm under her hands, glaucous balls that acted as leaves rippling away from contact the same way they tried to hide from sight. En masse they washed the barren terrain with a promise of green. Up close they were all but invisible. Yet Irona was right; she had trapped the elusive vision.

They had come to the wind-torn edge of the scrublands.

'So?'

'So, Twiss, we've made it. The settlement must lie south of here.'

'Which way's south?'

A glance at the sun shattered her sight. Her head felt like it was speared on shards of light but she answered anyway. 'Left. At right-angles to the shadows.'

'Can't be.'

'Has to be. The sun moves round, right, but it's never directly overhead?' Though she tried to feel positive her statement hovered with the intonation of a question. Her insecurity annoyed her especially when she was all but sure she had it figured.

He saw it; he couldn't deny she was right about the sun. 'So the shadows don't stay still. Bastard things.'

'So now we just go south and look for a flock of lizards.'

'What?'

'You're out every day, Twiss. Don't you have flights of song-lizards over you all the time now? We do over the settlement. I'm sure we do.'

'There!' Twiss croaked. 'See 'em?'

So they came in the iron heat of the afternoon to the settlement. Lying clouds spoke of rain over the whale-backed

mountains. The sky was a harsh metallic reality beating the
heat back down on them. Spiralling wings of lizard-insects
glittered over the humpy dugouts, singing a siren song whose
melody was indecipherable. And under it hung a threnody of
wails such as Twiss had never heard before.

Irona had – and quailed. That was what it had sounded like
back in Camelford when Watchwarden Roger ordered fear
to be played into a row of rioting kids and through the Eyes
she had seen them cower terrified, prey to psychosomatic or
frequency-induced illness.

The fact was worse, because even under the sweltering
breeze it reeked. Bodies lay everywhere, too weakened
to crawl back into their dugouts. Helpless fathers were
watching their babies die; they were too scared to give them
the poisoned canal-water they had fought so hard to win. An
old man lay half across his threshhold, choking on his own
vomit. It took Twiss and Irona both to turn him onto his side
but beyond wiping him, there was nothing else they could
do. Children and other vulnerables evacuated where they lay,
too sick to reach the latrines. Everyone was affected, though
some more so than others.

The couple staggered in from the desert, the need for
liquid driving everything else from the forefront of their
minds. Once through the tunnel under the wire, though,
they stopped, appalled, as the stench solidified around
them.

Irona thought first of Jai, and Regenerator. Her limbs
were vagrant ghosts which seemed unconnected to her.
They responded jerkily, as though their articulations were
controlled by alien waldoes from some place infinitely far
away. But they did respond, however chaotically, to her need
to find her friend.

Twiss stumbled past her, blind to her existence. His
cracked lips were shaping words over and over again:
'Granfer, you'll be OK. Sticker'll be looking after you.
Granfer, you'll be OK.'

He reached their dugout first. Unconsciously the scent of
water in a half-empty container drew him and even as his
parched eyes were searching for Granfer his hands were

reaching to cradle the dipper and the cells of his gullet were rich with the anticipation of a drink at last.

Irona said urgently, 'Don't touch it!'

His reach petrified. Part of him noticed absently that Granfer wasn't there. Not Sticker, not Jai, nor Regenerator. Their sun-barred shelter was empty of life. The veins stood out dark against the sinews of his wrist, shaking with the effort of not ladling the cool water down his throat. 'They couldn't—'

She knew he meant the First Wavers with their talk of poisoned water. 'Twiss, they must have! Didn't you see everyone?'

'But – but where can we get a drink from?'

Her head rocked a little on her neck as her helplessness showed. 'I don't know, Twiss. I don't know.'

'Where is he? Where's Granfer?'

Irona said nothing. She didn't know that either.

Outside voices called weakly, 'I'm sure I saw they.'

'Nah, they bain't be coming back. They bin and run off on us. Scared, most like, for what they done.'

'Can't see old Twiss scared.'

'If I were he, I would be. We could be sitting safe on the coast up to our necks in a river if it weren't for he.'

Twiss lumbered ungainly to his feet and went to hang against the door-jamb. 'It weren't me, boy. I never poisoned nobody's water. Nor I didn't steal nobody's supplies and take away their land. You want to talk to that Arias Tang. Seen what he's done to our folk?'

Irona crawled sideways and squinted against the threshing sunlight. Silhouettes, angular with rage, ranged outside, amongst them Marjine, Desselie and a thin man whose name Irona always forgot. Thebula was there too, but she was watching impassively from behind her curtain of russet hair and Irona wasn't sure which side she was on.

The skin-and-bone man said, 'Never mind Tang. You're our problem, you and your lies. You said we'd be OK. You said we could look after ourselves. We're dying, boy!'

But once Twiss got the import of it, he didn't listen. Cutting across the complaints he asked, 'I don't give a toss. Where's my Granfer? What's happened to he?'

Too busy with their own families, they didn't reply. Instead they continued their lament but it was a dialogue of the deaf: Twiss barged past them and went in search of his kin, leaving Irona trying to placate the growing crowd of settlers, all as thirsty and fevered as she was. There must have been a dozen or more of them, all staring at her with a hostility that without the resources of the Watchtower she had no weapons to combat. She was frightened at the violence lurking below the veneer of citizenship in the ragged circle around her. Thebula still stared at her impassively.

In the end Irona grasped the nettle and said, 'Look, never mind moaning!' From the doorway she reached behind her, never taking her eyes off her persecutors. Her groping fingers found what she was looking for. 'We've got to find a way out of this now. I'm going to see what the computer can come up with.'

Half of them protested at once. 'But—'

'Bloody typical!'

'That's what got us—'

Irona too walked straight ahead, as Twiss had done. Lacking his physical force she made no attempt to shove her way through the angry mob but instead paced calmly towards the computer shed. It was obvious what she was doing. And equally obvious that short of physical restraint she would not be turned aside.

After five steps everyone knew she would collide with a teenage girl at the front whose hair straggled greasily across her pale face.

Six steps.

Irona didn't deviate so much as a second from her path.

Seven steps.

The girl, trembling against the force of her own conditioning to courtesy, faced her defiantly.

Eight steps.

Nine.

Irona still stared back at the girl, her eyes like shattered agate.

Sullenly the girl turned fractionally and Irona compromised just enough: she slipped her right shoulder back a little to edge past the girl as though she hadn't really done so. She was careful to keep her face straight and not look the girl directly in the eye any more; she didn't want to provoke a confrontation.

Skirting the clumps of inimical settlers behind the girl, Irona walked over to the dugout where she hoped sanctuary would await her. Thebula stood watching her go.

Lizard-locusts piped swooping around her. Their weird calls dopplered, doubly incomprehensible in the hot fetid air. Waves of feculence wafted from the polluted latrines and she gagged but kept her mouth closed, keeping her weakness to herself. She couldn't afford for it to show now. Under the hard focus of everyone's eyes, it was the longest walk she had ever had to make.

She slipped inside the shed with heartfelt thankfulness and shut the door behind her. It took her a few seconds, standing breathless with nerves, to realise that she was not alone. A harsh respiration like some feral creature shared the darkness with her.

Suppressing a moan of fear, she groped her way to the keyboard and pressed for light. For a moment she felt like a child waking from a nightmare, too scared to turn round, but she overcame herself and looked to the corner whence the sounds issued.

Granfer. Her relief was enormous.

'How did you get here?' she asked, rushing to the slumped and shrunken figure against the wall.

Granfer's head, loose-hung on his wasted neck, triumphed momentarily so that he could look her in the eye. 'Think I'm too old, girl?'

'Are you all right?' she asked, though she could see that he was not.

'Oh, fine and dandy.' Granfer's voice was a croak. 'You wouldn't happen to have any' – he coughed, and she could hear the gas billowing in his empty bowels – 'water fit to drink, would you?'

Helplessness swallowed her. She shook her head.

He uttered an obscenity she had never heard outside the toilets at her school.

'Well, never mind, Irona. I only came to get away from Jai, really. She was fussing round me like a flock of novice pilots. Couldn't bear it. You leave me to it and get on with whatever you're going to do.'

And there was nothing she could say that made him change.

She tapped into the computer. Her fingers trembled as she asked it, 'Where can we get some water from?'

The screen pictured the canal-head with the crimson of sunset sparking its gush.

Irona shook her head impatiently. She keyed, 'No, I didn't mean that. The water's poisoned.' The computer stored the information. 'Where are we going to get some more from that we can use?'

And the Eye rose from its sleep in a corner of the shed, lurching at first like a bird with a broken wing. She garnered self-strength and tacked the thing more accurately out into the fiery skies but she had to close her eyes to the dizzy red anger it projected onto her monitors.

As the Eye soared southwest away from Settlement Knoll, flights of symbols scrolled across the monitors too fast to register. Through half-shut lids she watched them steady and chanced a look at the visual screen.

Sundown spilt carmine over the streaked sandstone hills and shadows were gashes dark as menstrual blood in the riven rock. Pale drifts of softness riding the thermals attracted the Eye; it stooped for a closer view.

Fronting the broken cliffs were aerial plants; roots with the geometry of snowflakes stroked the power to lift from currents in the air. The plants twirled slowly around as the vanes closest to the sun warmed to the dying light, but little by little the plants were sinking down towards a bloody darkness that called to them. From all along the cliff-face floated alien snowflakes that gradually funnelled down to the mother who called out to them in a tongue that existed only between Harith and her children, crooned to them by the arrangement of geography and sunset winds to suckle them with her milk.

And the Eye plunged selfishly through the cherry-blossom drifts, sending them skirling towards abandonment. Protected by an overhang trilled a streamlet. Over the aeons it had hollowed itself a comfortable bed in the stone and in the pool's rippling embrace the snowflakes rocked at rest.

The Eye's overflight stole their home for the Second Wave.

It became a legend, Tebrina and the Waterfall. How Irona went stravaiging through the camp, trying to find someone strong enough to follow her print-out map to the Southern Hills. She looked first for Twiss but she couldn't find him anywhere. Thebula and Sticker were lying retching; Jai was harrying herself to keep on comforting the sick. Regenerator was nowhere to be found. As usual.

In the end, Irona took her map and went to find Sinofer, but he was as sick as any of them. She sagged against the doorjamb of his dugout, her last hope quenched. Panting, Irona looked at Tebrina, who was nursing both him and Fessbar; the little boy was crying querulously, his chubby fingers twined in his hair.

Irona said, 'Well, I'll have to go then. I don't know what else to do,' and her voice shook with the weakness of her earlier, fevered tramp across the desert.

Tebrina looked up at her against the doorway of her dugout and said, 'Don't be such a deve. They need you here. Anyway, you'd never make it. You look like a wrung-out dishrag.'

'Cheers, Tebrina. You really know how to make me feel good.'

The two women took a hard look at each other, smiling at the affectionate mockery between them. Irona didn't argue; she knew Tebrina was right.

With the heat of fever and her work with the sick, Tebrina had let her cap fall back on her shoulders. The roots of her hair were grey, but the rest of the mass was a dark snakepit straggling over her forehead and ears. Still Irona knew it wasn't appearance that counted; what mattered was her pragmatic attitude.

The little blond boy, Fessbar, moaned, but there was

nothing Tebrina could do. She said simply, 'Where is this place anyway?'

Irona glanced at the door, orienting the map to the actuality of the darkling land. 'Over that way. I'll send the Eye to keep an eye on you.' She sighed. 'Sorry, that sounded daft.'

'Who cares what it sounded like? I knew what you meant. Give us the print-out, will you?'

No-one, not even Regenerator (whom Irona still couldn't find), had been south. The map was more of a picture than anything, faithful to the afternoon light under which the Eye had made it. The land burned under the embers of the sun, naked and alien, wraithed with the fear of First Wavers and their malice. Anything might exist in the hidden folds of Harith, things that the Eye hadn't spotted. And it would be at least a ten kilometre trek even if nothing went wrong.

Tebrina passed a hand over Sinofer's sweat-chilled forehead and reached across to squeeze Fessbar's hand, then creaked up from her knees. 'The men have been harder hit than us women, but that's men for you, isn't it? Everything they do, they have to go one better. You should hear Sinofer when he's got a cold. You'd think he was dying.' There was a second's uncomfortable silence as Tebrina wished the words unsaid. They might be too close to reality. Then she shrugged and said practically, 'Well, I'd better get going. Fessbar needs a drink and I can't stand him whingeing any more either. Must take after his dad. Keep an eye on them for me, will you, Ro?'

'Of course I will. You didn't have to ask.'

'Ha!'

'Ha yourself. And shove off, will you? I'd kill for a drink.'

The levity was broken as Tebrina turned back, a plump silhouette framed in the doorway against the crimson sky, and said, 'It might come to that, Ro. Be ready.'

16

THE EYE AND THE STORM

Heat-lightning flared long over the mountains that cut the settlement off from the moist winds of the coast. Jagged fire split the night and limned the fat bellies of the clouds that hugged the western peaks but didn't once stray toward Settlement. Over the valley the stars were as clear and cold as ice. The drop in temperature after sunset was dramatic; a glacial wind off the desert brought the smell of dust and shirred Irona's sweat-soaked bodice on her skin.

She went down to the tunnel to say goodbye to the water-seekers. Her words were coloured with hope but woven of doubt.

Tebrina, her ruddy face shadowed in the starlight, didn't seem to mind but Irona grieved that she couldn't be more supportive. With three other women and a handful of teenagers, the stocky Tebrina set out into the fear-haunted darkness. Strings of empty plastic cans clattered from their shoulders.

Just beyond the tunnel under the wire, Tebrina stopped, because Irona had called to her again.

'What is it now?' she shouted, and already Irona could hardly see her until the lightning flashed.

'You know I'm sending the Eye with you?'

Tebrina clicked her tongue in disgust. ''Course I do, you deve! Up there, ain't it?' She pointed with her chin; above her, the shiny globe shone with faint reflections like a soap-bubble in the night. 'You've told me about seventy-eight times.'

'Well do you want me' – Irona worked up spit in her swollen throat – 'you want me to rig it so it'll light your way?'

'Mm – I don't know that that's a good idea. As good as an advert, that'd be, wouldn't it? What if they First Wavers are hanging around?'

The thought had already occurred to Irona. 'Yeah, you're right. I wouldn't want to bump into them on a dark night. But I wondered if you might want to risk it so's you can see where you're going. I mean, we don't really know what might be out there.'

'Look, do you want me to go or do you want to scare me to death?'

Irona knew that Tebrina's roughness was to mask her apprehension. She answered in the same vein. 'All right, push off, then. I've got things to do.'

'You think I'm just having a nap? See you, Ro.'

'See you.' But Irona was already talking to blackness that showed no trace of the seekers. When the next lightning flickered over the valley, they were lost in the crumpled terrain. Though Irona strained her eyes the only movement she saw was the shift of shadows where the moonglow shook black velvet between the silvery hills.

All night long Irona split herself between Sinofer's dugout and her computer shed where Granfer lay breathing stertorously in his restless sleep. From time to time she would check on her monitors. They showed the image-enhanced pictures the Eye sent back of Tebrina's group crawling unevenly across the slope of the valley. It seemed for hours that they got no nearer to the sandstone bluffs but just being able to see Tebrina was a comfort somehow, especially when sleepers kept coming to ask her to solve the insoluble.

As far as Irona knew, there wasn't a drop of drinking water left in Settlement Knoll.

Then she would check on Granfer, creeping round so as not to disturb him, but wishing all the same that she dared make a noise so he would move and she could ask him how he felt. His skin showed a dry unhealthy grey but she told herself it was just the flat light from the monitors.

Around about midnight, Irona dragged herself back to Sinofer and Fessbar. Her throat hurt, her stomach griped. She was thirsty, and lonely, and she had no idea where Twiss was. Away on the rim of the world the lightning-storm still mocked them but not a drop of rain fell to caress the wounded

Valley. She brushed away a skirl of locust-lizards that hovered in clouds before her thick as midges in the Park.

In the pale hurtling moonlight someone hailed her.

What is it now? she thought in irritation, but it wasn't another problem.

It was Jaimindi, her round face breaking into a grin.

'Where have you been?'

'What have you been doing?'

Coming together, they both spoke at once and laughed a little as they embraced.

'You first,' said Irona, but Jai told her in a scratchy voice, 'No, you. I've been so worried about you.'

'Me too. Oh, I'm so glad to see you! I thought you might be . . .'

'Well, I'm not, Ro. I'm alive, just barely. Now tell me all about it.'

So they caught up on each other's news. Jai had used up all the sterile water in the medipacks on the first people she saw when she awoke. After that she'd just been emptying chamberpots and cleaning people up as best as she could with dry scraps of clothing. She hadn't seen Twiss. Now she held a grizzling infant to her ample breast and let it suck on the knuckle of her little finger but the mewling hardly lessened. There was no water left to mix any milk. Jai said sadly, 'This is Liesl. Poor little thing. Her mother's dead.'

There was a short silence. Arm in arm they limped back through the night-shadowed camp to Sinofer's place.

After a bit Jai asked with hollow brightness, 'Have you seen Granfer? I've been looking all over for him.'

'Yes. He got fed up of people coming to moan at him when they couldn't find Twiss. He's hiding out in the computer shed. Seen Sticker?'

'He's over by the latrines. A kid fell in, so he stayed to supervise and now he's just exhausted.' Jai sounded faintly proprietorial, gentled with compassion and what might one day be love. 'He couldn't make it back and I couldn't carry him so he's asleep over that way somewhere. I haven't seen Regen, though. Have you?'

But Irona hadn't either.

At Sinofer's shelter, as the ironic lightning dried out, they both fell asleep.

That was how Regenerator found them next day, huddled together for the comfort of another human's touch. Irona's sun-bronzed hair was tangled on Jai's blackberry curls. Over on a fresh-fouled pile of clothing, Sinofer was snoring faintly, Fessbar's blond head rising and falling gently in the crook of his father's shoulder. The boy was too feeble to do more than gaze around with dry, staring eyes.

It was the dry click of Regenerator's knees as he squatted before them that woke Irona.

'Want to know why it don't rain here?' he asked without preamble.

Irona yawned and rubbed her fever-hollowed eyes against the daggers of morning light. It took her a moment to accept reality then she started. 'Regen! You're all right!'

He said 'Mmm' so laconically that she grinned. But he repeated his question as Jai snuggled her head against Irona's arm once more. 'Know why it don't rain here any more? Because they First Wavers have a weather-controller.'

'They can't have!' Irona whispered. 'Harith isn't shielded.'

'Think I don't know that? That's why I been over to Kifl. Entirely. But I been wondering about the rain so I went. They got one, though. I followed that Tang man and he took me straight to it – eventually.' He chuckled at his own humour, a sound he had made so often that it felt comfortable as an old shoe to Irona. 'Want a drink?'

She stiffened in alarm. 'Don't touch it – it's poisoned!'

He tossed his head back, his adam's apple vibrating with suppressed laughter. 'Not this ain't. Brought it from Kifl, didn't I? And it ain't no old water, neither. Take a swig.'

Irona's anxious movement had disturbed Jai. Now the chubby nurse turned to the other side, cradling her head against the earth wall of the dugout and curving her back to Irona's with a little wordless murmur.

Regen sloshed the bottle that swung from a hook on his belt and threw it over to Irona. It was apple-juice, warm from his body-heat and the rising sun of morning, but it was tart and sweet and deliciously wet.

He snatched it from her. 'Not too much, now, or you'll go and make yourself heave. Leave it a minute, OK?'

Touched by his concern, she smiled and he smiled back. The scent of apples was a homely cleanness against the squalor of Settlement. Her own unwashed odour was rank in her nostrils. She didn't even want to think about cleaning up Sinofer again just yet. Outside, except for the lizard-insects' skirling, things were ominously quiet, though a girl was weeping in the distance and someone was shouting at her.

'They First Wavers, was it?' he said, nodding to Sinofer and the boy.

She swallowed, nodded.

'Poisoned the water, by what they told me on the way in. Don't fret, Ro. We'll get the bastards.'

They sat in silence for a minute. Then Regen said bracingly, 'They old gals'll be back with the water in a bit. I seen 'em in the dawn. Want to go and give 'em a hand?'

Already her throat had stopped its dry burning though she was embarrassed about the noises her stomach was making as it welcomed the apple-juice. She nodded and the fever-thump in her head started up again, though not so fierce today.

'Good for you, Ro. Mind, it'll help you to be one of the good guys, won't it?'

'It never crossed my mind!' she said indignantly.

'Well it should of done.' He was unrepentant, his head nodding vigorously on his scrawny neck. 'Fine ruler you're going to be if you don't see things like that for yourself.'

'I don't want to be a ruler.'

'Rather have they sleepers in charge? You'd of been dead by now, all of you, if it hadn't been for you and that computer of yours, and Twiss to tell 'em what they think, and you to tell him what he thinks. And me, of course, but I ain't about to let any old sleeper get me killed. If I'm going to do it, I'll do it for myself. Ready?'

She was already stroking Jai's face to wake her. 'Give us a minute, Regen. And could you have a look at Sinofer for me? And little Fessbar? I'd better go and see what the Eye shows – and find out how Granfer is.'

*   *   *

Granfer was paralysed down one side.

Irona hurried back under the weight of sunlight to fetch Jai. Regen silently stalked beside them to the computer-shed but there was nothing any of them could do but make the old man more comfortable. The only noise he could utter was a sort of strangled croak, and that was his breathing. It frightened her even before she went in to find him leant at a crazy angle in the corner. Half of his face was slack; at rest it showed only faint wrinkles, but the left side was twisted off-centre into a mad map of distress that seemed all the worse beside the smooth part. Twiss was nowhere around; Irona began to wonder where he had been all night. *If he'd been with Granfer* . . . but he hadn't.

Shocked by Granfer's condition, Irona was loth to leave him but Jai said she'd stay.

Granfer made a weak movement with his right hand.

Jai misinterpreted it. She reached out and stroked his fingers, capturing them when he eluded her grip, but it was Regenerator who said from the computer-chair, 'That ain't what he means. He wants to be left in peace, don't you, old feller? Entirely.'

And that's how it was. Granfer told them by question and answer – one grunt for yes and two for no – and by the mute pleading in his trapped and rheumy gaze.

So after a check on what the Eye showed – no First Wavers, and Tebrina's party not a kilometer from the fence – Irona, Jai and Regen went out to meet them.

Outside the fence, the glare bounced back from every ochre rock. The sky was harsh. Before Irona had gone a hundred metres she felt the hot, unyielding air drag every particle of moisture from her aching body.

Regen pointed. Following his finger, Irona squinted against the hard yellow light. She saw Tebrina heaving her load up out of a fissure.

Scrambling over the sharp-seamed rocks, Irona ran to hug Tebrina, who said, 'Get off! You're unbalancing me.' But the smile on her sunburnt face took the sting out of her words.

Irona took the burden from her friend. She was surprised at how heavy the containers were. Without stopping to think, she blurted a rebuke. 'I thought you took more cans than that!'

Tebrina shrugged in acceptance at a debate that was old to her. 'Well, we couldn't carry all they when they was full, so we've been dumping they along the way. Not so far to carry it back then, if you get my drift.'

Irona was already unslinging the awkward cannisters from her friend's back.

Tebrina nodded her thanks, a tiny gesture that was all the strength she could spare. Her face was tan with dust, her dumpy figure bowed. 'Get a move on, will you? I want my bed.' Empty-handed now, Tebrina stumped along, her head rocking with fatigue. As the cord-slings began to cut into Irona's shoulders and hands, the older woman asked with studied indifference, 'How's Fessbar? And my old ball and chain?'

'They're fine. Well, they're all right, anyway. Still alive, though the fever's still in them. We've given them both a drink—'

'Not that water!'

'No, of course not! What sort of an idiot do you think I am?' Irona saw her friend's mouth open to make a rude reply and added hastily, 'I know, I know. How many sorts are there?'

Twiss came out of the tunnel to meet them, the sun casting his long shadow back towards Settlement in the fresh air of morning. He would have taken the weight of water from Irona but she said, 'No, it's all right. I'm still fresh. Take Desselie's. Where have you been?'

As Desselie pretended to hang onto her containers with a show of martyred heroism, Twiss answered, 'Oh, you know. Around.' He seemed completely unaffected by Desselie's flirtatiousness.

Under cover of helping him balance his load, Irona said to him quietly, 'Been to the computer-shed recently?'

He shook his head. 'Nah. Been over with Sticker by they latrines since moonrise. Some deve kid nearly drownded.'

'Well as soon as you can, get over there, will you?'

Twiss seemed determined to be obtuse. 'Why?' he asked

so baldly that Irona wondered why he couldn't see she was trying to be discreet. Couldn't he tell she was whispering?

'Your Granfer's over there. He wants to see you.'

Instantly she was aware of the shock of tension that ran through the coiling muscles of his shoulder. It sparked an answering twist in her body, though she could not have said what emotion it was made of.

'The old boy all right then, is he? I ain't seen hide nor hair of him.'

Irona made a great play of moving a fold of Twiss's shirt to pad his back against the cut of the cord. She couldn't want to tell him like this about Granfer's stroke, not when he needed to be strong in front of everybody still alive in Settlement Knoll. *Not when he wants to be a hero*. Though the words sounded in Regenerator's reedy voice inside her head, she still felt obscurely guilty. Fortunately Desselie was heaving great gusty whooshes of relief that flaunted the outline of her breasts, and fluttering her eyelashes up at him. It occupied his eyes if not his mind.

Irona looked round at the scrubland and the impersonal blue of the sky that the heat was stretching out of shape but she found no inspiration there. A gold-winged locust chirped cheekily at her, its many-jointed legs teasing painfully over her hair.

She ducked; it was only partly an excuse not to meet Twiss's eye when he turned to stare at her. 'He was asleep the last time I saw him. Regen's back. He's there too – he wants a word with you.'

Already Twiss was striding ahead, his legs pumping at moderate speed to show that although he too was weakened by poison-water fever he was still strong enough to care for his people. Plunging down through the tunnel, he reappeared inside the fence, calling, 'Water! Clean water! Come and get it.' He didn't once look behind him and he stepped over the bodies sprawled in his way.

When Irona and the women caught up with him, he was dealing out water to an admiring crowd that pushed and jostled around him. He was on his favourite mound, bathing in the grateful smiles of everyone strong enough to come and meet him. The sun haloed him in the hot forenoon. The biggest water-container was firmly in his grasp as he lifted its weight for women to drink. The men were passing round another cannister, trying to snatch it from each other. Irona couldn't help but wonder how many of the rest were dead.

Tebrina raised an ironic eyebrow as she dropped her three containers well short of the mound. Fifteen litres of water. All around Twiss people were flocking to him, elbowing each other, arguing about who got the next mouthful amid shouts of "Tain't fair!'

Irona said quietly, 'Desselie, be a good citizen and go and get a few cups, will you? Or that lot's going to kill each other in the rush.'

Tebrina nodded to herself, a faint knowing smile curving her lips. 'He do like to be the centre of attention, don't he, that Twiss of yourn? Or maybe he just don't stop to think. Give us one of they bottles, Ro. I'll take it over to my 'uns, then I'll send some over to Granfer, OK? You need to stay here.'

'How dare you!' Twiss roared at her, ignoring Jai's anxious shushing.

Irona stopped a moment, the noon sun fierce on her back, her eyes adjusting to the dense shadow inside her computer-shed. She had been busy organising a party to go and collect the rest of the water from the wasteland and making sure that all of the volunteers had had a good drink, not easy when so many others wanted to carry water back to their children or their lovers. It was hard to decide who to favour with so many people calling, 'Me!' 'No, me!'

Coming at last to the haven of the shed, Irona had wanted support, or maybe she had needed to give support and so feel wanted; the last thing she had expected was Twiss's anger. Not after their night in the dunes . . .

It ignited her own. 'How dare I what?'

'Let this happen and not even tell me!'

Neither of them were paying any heed to Jai who was getting more and more agitated. Regenerator, on the other hand, scrunched even lower into his habitual squat against

the wall and kept so still that he must have wanted everyone
to forget he was there.

Irona said forcefully, 'I didn't let this happen. What do you
think I am, Twiss? A matriarch? I couldn't have stopped it
anyway. And I couldn't tell you before—'

'That's because you knew you were wrong. You didn't even
care enough to stay with him.'

'He didn't want me to!'

'I'm not bloody surprised. Who would?' Twiss's grief sawed
his anger to sharp points. 'Synod, woman, you just stroll off
and leave him though you've told me often enough you like
the old devil.'

'I do, Twiss—'

'Ha!'

'Ha yourself.' Wounded, Irona appealed for support. 'He
didn't want anybody staying with him, did he, Regen?'

Regen shook his head and said, 'No, entirely,' but Twiss
wasn't listening and Irona's whole concentration was centred
on him. His fury sliced into her like shards of glass. She
couldn't believe that only two nights ago he had held her
so intimately in the moonsilk privacy of the desert and now
he was a light-year from her behind a spike-topped wall.

Twiss sneered, 'So how come you need someone to back
your story up then?'

The protagonists didn't even notice Granfer's right hand
fretting feebly at the air until Jai surprised herself by shouting,
'Shut up, the pair of you!'

Twiss seemed to see her for the first time. Turning his
rage-swelled face to her briefly, he said in an ugly voice,
'Get out of my hair, Jai,' then dropped her entirely from his
awareness.

Pale under the plummy sheen of her skin, Jai stood up
to him. 'No, Twiss. If you're going to argue, go and do it
somewhere else. You're upsetting Granfer.'

'Don't you tell me how to look after my own flesh and
blood!'

The confrontation printed itself in Irona's mind, the short
timid nurse glaring up at Twiss, fighting like a cornered mouse
against the man's physical and mental dominance. Twiss's

anger was tangible; a pheromonal aura that sucked reason from the room into a black hole. His brown eyes were hot and hard, sheened with aggression; his head thrust forward, every part of his body tensed to hit out.

But Jai spoke up with scarcely a tremor. 'Twiss, it's bad to upset him. I'll get him to eat something and you go and look out for your people. They need you. They need you, Twiss.'

Like an automaton Twiss jerked round upon his heel, blanking Irona from his perception. She had to step aside to let him bull out through the doorway. It was as if she had ceased to exist. Jai followed him, on her way to forage for the old man.

After the glare of the sun, the room's shadow made Irona shiver.

Granfer couldn't say anything to her. And Regenerator still huddled his gangling limbs to himself, rocking ever so slightly on his haunches and crooning his long wordless distress into the black shadows of Harith's noon. There was no help for her there.

And meantime there was the problem of the poisoned water and what the First Wavers might do next with their weather controller and their twisted jealousy, and the irrigation, and the crops that might die envenomed, and the wails of the bereaved and the stench of the dying.

And the solidity that she had thought was the foundation of her new life was a stone melting in the lava of Twiss's hostility.

Irona stared blindly at the clutter of keyboards and the cryptic colours on the monitors that her mind had forgotten how to read. She didn't know any more what direction to take with her life.

Almost she gave into despair. Then she straightened her shoulders and said aloud, 'Oh no. I'm not going down. I don't know where to start or what to do, but he's not beating me. None of it is. I'm not going down.'

But if Granfer heard her, he made no sign.

Bernardina smiled as she stood up. For hours the thought had amused her. Now, as the ion-draught repelled the water from her skin, she could contemplate the sags and wrinkles of her flesh and not be hurt. The silver-grey seams of

stretch-marks were only skin-deep, however fair Gundmila
seemed.

She was going to enjoy teasing Gundmila. Without even
asking, she knew the Kiflian matriarch wouldn't have told
the planet's Synod about the ansible. Risk letting them in on
her power? Find out things she didn't know? Gundmila would
never feel secure enough to do that. Not now. She'd probably
even had the man who installed it brain-wormed or whatever
poor substitute they might have in such a backwater.

But Bernardina knew that her rival with the china-blue eyes
and fresh-bloomed skin was worried. Had been worried for
weeks. She wouldn't call Earth – but neither had Bernardina
called her.

It wasn't weakness that made her call Gundmila now. It
was just time for another dig. Gundmila had stewed long
enough.

Because whatever Irona had faced in that desert, it wasn't
enough. Bernardina knew the girl wouldn't be hard enough,
tough enough. She'd be practical on the outside with hearts
and flowers spoiling her underneath. She didn't know.

Gundmila would teach her.

Bernardina allowed a junior matriarch to slip her silk robes
modestly over her old age. Dismissing the girl with a flick of
the fingers, Bernardina teased herself now closer and now
further from the hidden ansible. She knew that whatever
time of day or night it was on Harith, the woman with the
china-blue eyes would be waiting.

Gundmila, she thought nastily, *you may be older than
me but you're the stupid chit you look. You won't help me
willingly however many governments are on my back, but I
can wind you up like clockwork. I learned humiliation from
you as well as manipulation. A word or two about what – or
whom – you let the settlers keep and you're mine.*

The old woman nodded to herself, judging what – and what
not – to say.

Yes, Gundmila would teach the girl.

17

LIVING KNIVES

A miasma of death hung over the settlement. Just breathing it in on the hot noontide air tainted each mouthful of reconstituted protein. Twiss still blamed Granfer's illness on Irona; consequently, even though she knew it wasn't rational, she felt guilty. Trying to fight off the feeling, she immolated herself in water-carrying, which she could easily have left to someone else. A screel of locust-lizards followed her and Thebula and the others to the Snowflake Pool. The insects swooped dazzlingly around them, bold enough now to dive straight at them so that they had to keep ducking and batting them away. Two of them caught in Marjine's hair where her cap had come loose. It would have been funny to watch the fat, red-faced woman run screaming across the Southern Hills pursued by Thebula who was only trying to help her, whatever Marjine said – if the silly old woman hadn't dropped her precious buckets of water, spilling them onto the baked earth.

Back at Settlement, exhausted, Irona hid herself away in her computer shed, trying to come up with some way of making an antidote for the First Wavers' poison, but she and Jai didn't have the equipment. The trouble was, Irona couldn't kid herself that she wasn't hiding away.

Giving up with a sigh, she walked across to their dugout for the noontime meal. Her head was still full of images of Twiss making love to her – then his face contorted with rage. She couldn't handle it – but she had to face him sooner or later. Quietly she slipped inside the dugout and sat to help herself to a meagre slice of dry protein-biscuit.

When Jai said in her quiet way, 'We'll have to clear out the dead or they'll spread disease,' Twiss didn't even consult Irona as he used to. In fact ever since she'd come in he had ignored her completely, his hostility spreading out in concentric waves that compressed her into a cell of silence and rejection. The atmosphere made the others feel uncomfortable too; the conversation that usually flowed so freely between the leadership group was halting.

Granfer was back in their shelter with them. Out of habit Twiss flicked him a questioning glance at Jai's remark but the lopsided old face could return no answer.

Jai held Twiss's gaze for a moment until she was sure he had got the message, then went silently back to feeding Granfer, compressing her lips at each spoonful as if to show the old man how.

'Sticker,' Twiss said after a moment, 'me and you'll rig up some barrows or something this afto. We'll take all they dead 'uns out of Settlement and fix up an incinerator with a few of the power-packs.'

Irona would have said something then but Regen said it for her and she was grateful because she didn't want Twiss amplifying his hostility by actually noticing her. 'Can't do that, Twiss. Impossible. Entirely. Not enough energy left for what we need 'til we get some back off they old First Wavers. Have to bury they dead 'uns.' Then he added something that made Irona shoot a look of resentment at him because it took away her pretence of invisibility. 'Irona'll find the best place.'

'No, she won't, then. I will,' Twiss said flatly. 'Don't want to overload her, poor little delicate thing. She ain't got enough time as it is to look after a few simple details like keeping an eye on Granfer.'

And Irona writhed. *Why didn't you do it then if it was so important to you?* she seethed, but she knew it was only Twiss's guilt acting on hers. *What's the point in arguing?* she thought, lowering her head over the powdery soya while trying not to let the unfairness of his rejection get to her. *I won't get any sense out of him until he's stopped his little-boy sulks*. All the same, it rankled. *You should have looked out for Granfer yourself* – she shot a furtive look at Twiss through the wild mass of her hair that she hadn't had time to brush out that morning – *And anyway, what were you doing that stopped you even looking for him for so long?*

A vague uneasiness crystallised into suspicion inside her. Before, jealousy had always been something that stupid people suffered from, the girls she had met in citizenship training who giggled in corners and stopped talking when anyone came by. Or the wardens she met in the Watchtower cafeteria, their eyes resting hotly on the object of their lust and tracking everyone who spoke or even came near whomever they coveted. But now jealousy was something hot inside her.

Irona didn't know how to come to terms with the circling emotions that tatted her guts into slippery knots. Her thoughts wouldn't stay still; every time she had everything arranged in her mind a new doubt slithered all her ideas awry. *What had Twiss been doing? What could he have been doing when he'd been so close to her such a short time before?* Their idyll in the starlit desert was still vivid in her mind, the warmth of his skin on hers, the affection in his kisses that had turned her body inside out, the loving way he had respected her wishes and taken the time to give her pleasure. Then, afterwards, he had still encircled her with his arms and caressed the hair gently from her face—

Twiss stood abruptly. 'Right then, Sticker. Let's get it done.'

As Twiss stalked out without so much as a word even for Granfer, Sticker hastily followed him. At least he had the grace to say, ''Scuse me, folks,' as he half-ran to catch up with Twiss in the blinding sunshine.

Later, after she had helped Regen clear up the remains of lunch, Irona set off to the noisiest part of Settlement. You could have heard Twiss's voice bawling orders from kilometres away. The sound of him should have assuaged Irona's jealousy, but it didn't and she slated herself for being such a fool as to fall prey to her insecurities. She could feel them coiling and kinking in the pit of her stomach.

The stench of corruption lay trapped in the random paths between the shelters. It hung in the motionless air that was as hot and rancid as molten butter. Wherever she walked, clouds of locust-lizards shattered the sunlight into shards that stabbed at her eyes and she swatted them away, irritated to find part of her mind still trying to work out some pattern to the endless almost-tune of their shrillings.

I'm a fool to be doing this, she told herself, but it seemed like a greater cowardice to turn away from the burial detail than to turn away from the settlement's forward planning and she would not give in to cowardice. *I am not going to hide away any more, whatever he thinks*. All the same she was scared at the very idea of seeing Twiss. She dreaded what he might say to her – or that he would say nothing at all. And she tried not to acknowledge that somewhere underneath her surface thoughts was the muddy hope that by helping with what Twiss was doing she might win back his approval.

A horrible thud reverberated in her hearing. Irona had no idea what it was; it just sounded ominous, sickening. Muffled sobs rose.

Drawn by the cries and by her need to find validation in helping, Irona ducked under a cracked lintel set into a hillside. The rippling chameleon tendrils of a ball-leaf plant made her rub her eyes as she went in.

Tebrina was there, rocking a woman against her breast. Tebrina's face was hard; she rolled her eyes heavenwards in exasperation as the woman cried and cried, but her work-hardened hands never stopped rubbing the woman's back and stroking the snarled hair.

'I've got to help, Tebrina,' Irona said quietly. 'Where can I start?'

Tebrina met her gaze. 'No, Irona, you've got enough to do. You've got to find us some food and a way to bring the water here soon's you can.'

But Irona couldn't stop herself. She knew that she should be at her computer where peace would sink into her as she worked. Yet she left Tebrina and peered into other shelters, lizard-insects darting into her face through the pestilence of the open doorways. With the afternoon stretching light through a spectrum of yellow she looked for work alongside the death-teams.

Dugout by dugout they were going systematically through the haphazard homes that had been so painstakingly hollowed out wherever there was a suitable hillock. Once Twiss saw her and turned his back so obviously that Irona flushed. *How can he humiliate me like this?* Even knowing that he was hurt by his own dereliction of duty made it no better. It just made her determined not to kick him when he was down.

She slipped away into the nearest dugout. When she saw who was there she almost backed out again.

It was Sticker, dragging the corpse of a blubbery youth towards the doorway. Sticker had the body by the wrists and where the fat shoulders scraped along the earthen floor, they picked up a moraine of dirt that clung to the boy's once-white shirt. An equally fat cadaver that must have been the boy's mother dangled half-in and half-out of a tumble of bedclothes in a niche along one wall. Lizard-insects screeled under the low ceiling and circled over the bodies in a terrible game of tag.

When Irona came in she blocked the light for a moment. Sticker skewed his head round to see who it was. Then he looked down again in confusion. He hesitated, his pale eyes shifting rapidly as though he needed something to focus on that wasn't Irona, only he couldn't decide what.

Irona cleared her throat. 'Look, Sticker, don't you start taking it out on me too. I feel bad enough as it is and I did what I could for Granfer. Ask Regen – he'll tell you Granfer wanted to be left alone.'

Sticker dropped the pudgy arms with a complete lack of ceremony. He said nothing, his bland face closed under its sheen of perspiration. But at least he listened. Or appeared to.

Irona went on, 'I couldn't have done anything if I'd been with him, could I? And nor could Twiss. Or you. But we all had plenty to do and it looked as though the old man was OK, didn't it? Anway, it's not my fault that Twiss wasn't with him, is it? And I'm not blaming him.' Though she knew that somewhere inside her, she was. For some reason the vision of Desselie's heaving breasts and fluttering eyelashes was sharp in her mind.

Sticker didn't answer any of the questions Irona had left

hanging in the air. He stood for a minute, the breath coming hard in and out of his nostrils, before he finally said, 'Take they feet, will you?'

And Irona never knew if it was an acceptance or an avoidance on his part.

Blue-black clouds rolled deep over the Moon Mountains to the west, casting an ugly light across the valley. Stretched shadows the colour of bruises trembled under the heat of the afternoon and the mass grave – a crack tortured into the earth towards the Southern Hills – breathed an exhalation of doom. Irona knew it was no accident that Twiss had picked this place because the water-carriers would have to pass it time and time again. And the diggers who worked kilometres away. He wasn't about to let the settlers forget what the First Wave had done to them. His chiselled face wore a badge of bitterness that was made up in part of wounded pride. He took the Kiflians' wickedness as a personal affront. She watched him stare unwaveringly into the death-pit and knew he was impressing the scene on his memory lest he forget the new purpose Arias Tang had given his life.

Over a quarter of the settlers were piled at their last rest. Friends, acquaintances, people she had scarcely known but who might have come to mean the world to her – in the livid slanting sunrays the white of their collars and bodices and caps was a sick hue picked out against the darkness of the tomb. The clothes were brighter than the twisted limbs of the fallen.

Twiss insisted that everyone, man, woman and child, who could walk should be at the funeral – and not just to help bury the dead. Despite her misgivings at speaking against his wishes, Irona had protested.

'It's not fair on the children,' she had told Twiss as he stood washing in a cupful of water as soon as Settlement had been cleared of the dead. The orphaned baby, Liesl, was in her arms; Irona was looking after her while Jai got ready for the burial.

'They need to know what they're up against. They need to see. And I've already told them.' He threw the washrag down. Its flat slap against the floor was the full-stop of that conversation. He dragged his cleanest shirt over his head to cover his wire-muscled torso and stalked out beyond the perimeter.

So she stood at the grave-site in her expected position by his side and listened to the mourning of the adults and the frightened wails of the children who were old enough to understand. Liesl cried, caught up in the depressing weave of the atmosphere.

The last of the diggers straggled back, picking their way across the trampled earth of the new path. A scant three hundred waited, heads bowed, and the silence drew out like elastic, gathering tension. Only muffled weeping broke it now. Then Fessbar laughed in uncomprehending glee, reaching out to the flock of bright lizards who danced above the slain. Sinofer swept him into his arms, hushing him in embarrassment, but still Twiss did not speak. From the corner of her eye Irona saw Desselie at the front, ogling Twiss; she looked towards Regenerator squatting on a knoll some distance away. The black oblong of the computer remote he'd made stuck out of his bony fist and the Eye hovered shining above the wastes.

Only when the thunder rolled mocking from the sea-plains of Kifl did Twiss raise his head. His hazel eyes held the sheen of obsession. He stared at the settlers, all of them, until some of them had to look away.

'Hear that?'

Another peal of thunder grumbled over the valley, its echo slowly answering in confusion from the Southern Hills. And just as he spoke again – or did he time it that way? – a jag of lightning flamed across the darkening world.

'That's what they done to us. They took the rain just like they took our land. Then they poisoned what was left. They took our people, our babies, your lovers, your parents. They took our supplies, our shelter, the food out of our mouths, the clothes off of your backs. Even they little things that made you feel at home. You're cold at night?' He answered himself with a question: 'Who got our power-packs?

'Your kids are bored? Who got their teacher-puters? Your folks are sick like my Granfer?'

Irona cringed, dreading what he might say, but Twiss made no mention of her. 'If we'd been where we should be in Kifl the hospitals would have looked after they properly. But they'd only have us there as slaves.'

Now his tone grew hard as diamond. 'Look down, folks. I ain't going to say no words of comfort to you. Comfort? Out here, beyond Synod, there ain't none. Look at they bodies.' A renewed outbreak of suppressed sobs; Twiss had the sleepers now and they weren't going to miss a one of his bitter words. 'They ain't people no more. They ain't the ones you loved. They've gone for ever, stolen by they First Wavers. And they ain't going to rest and neither am I until we've settled their score for 'em.'

Fears all the more hideous for being unnamed tightened Irona's stomach. The atmosphere grew denser with tension that coiled about Twiss's hearers, sleepers almost all. Irona knew that they were directionless, clubbed into submission by disaster-shock, numbed against self-determination by the training of the Synod. They would do whatever they were told. And because of his force of will they had allowed Twiss to elect himself their leader.

He swept a gesture at the sprawl of interlocked corpses. A child lay tangled in the stiffened arms of a mother who would never be able to hold him in life; tears sprang to Irona's eyes that she had never thought would cry again, so inured had she become to tragedy.

Twiss's words cut like knives. 'I ain't resting until they First Wavers have paid. Paid with their land like we paid. Paid with their food, and their clothes, and their homes. Paid for our blood with their blood. For our lives with theirs. They want war – they got it.'

No warning, no announcement. Suddenly there was Bernardina's image in front of Gundmila in the Kiflian Synod. Bernardina had waited 'til the Matriarch of Harith was alone, but Gundmila didn't know that. She didn't know the equipment had such capabilities. Her china-blue eyes almost popped out of her skull.

'Got them all exactly where you want them, have you?' Bernardina said cheerfully.

Gundmila glowered at her tormentor.

'Don't do that, child. You'll get wrinkles and you wouldn't want that.'

'Shut up, you old hag! At least I don't look like someone that's been dug up out of their grave.'

'I'll outlast you, Gundmila. You haven't got the brains you were born with. Or are you still letting a pathetic bunch of sleepers run you ragged?'

'What's it got to do with you?' Aggression came out in every syllable.

'Oh, nothing. Just curious to see how Mistress Perfection is getting on.'

'Much better without you sticking your nose in.'

And it was Gundmila who switched the ansible off to shut out Bernardina's mocking grin.

Anger whirled Gundmila's thoughts around as she considered her options. Whatever else, she knew the old witch wouldn't have called for the fun of it.

'She's got an axe to grind,' Gundmila murmured. Reviewing her co-rulers, her first impulse was to consult Arias for his intelligence and imagination. Pacing to the window, she pushed away some of the aerial plants and looked down on her city. 'He's the only one who might be able to put the clues together,' she said to herself. 'But he'd use it as a weapon against me. No, it'll have to be Less.'

And when Less answered her summons, she assessed him dispassionately. He'd looked to be in his late forties when he arrived on Kifl, so that was how his appearance had set: black hair streaked with pale grey, face tanned now. When he was relaxed, the creases round his eyes showed white. In his dark maroon suit he looked solid, worthy, dignified – and he was.

'Still no change in the sleepers' recalcitrance, Less?' Gundmila didn't mention her rival back in Camelford.

'No. They still don't want to accept the rules of our society. You can't have the benefits without the rules.'

'Quite right, Less. But if they do manage to get away with it, where's that going to leave our sleepers? We've got to do something.'

Less sat down opposite her and steepled his fingers on the cool stone of the table. His winged eyebrows drew down as he thought. Gundmila left him in peace. The only sounds were the colourful curtains flapping in the hot, sullen air of the siesta, and her own occasional sighs.

At last he said, 'We need two things.' He spoke slowly and she prompted him. 'We need to step up the attack and we need a bunker.'

'A bunker, Less?'

'A place to hide out in case something goes wrong. A secret place in the mountains – and the fewer people who know about it the better.'

'I'm not sure that all of us want to step up the offensive,' Gundmila said delicately.

'I'm not sure Tang's on our side at all,' he said, echoing her thoughts. Less always was as subtle as a nova.

The Matriarch of Harith smiled. 'But I know you are, Less. I've always admired your loyalty.'

Flattered, he said, 'You know I'll back you up one hundred and ten percent.'

'Then I'll leave it in your capable hands.'

For a day or two the people of Settlement went round numbly, trying to get on with the business of mere survival. This time the emaciated teams of diggers didn't bother trying to shade the new water-channel from the sun. Any water at all would be enough; roofing the canal over against the evaporation of the desert sun would have to come later. And in the meantime the computer analysed the strange motile plants of the Southern Hills, directed by Irona to find out if they were edible.

They were. Unpalatable, but better than starvation. Their cell-walls and the fleshy panels of their wings were indigestible but their kernels would sustain life if only the folk of the

settlement could catch enough of them. Twiss remembered
the tales his Granfer had told him of Before the Sky and
re-invented the net. Workers they could ill afford to spare
now had the job of hunting to keep them alive.

Then the first deep-sleepers were found.

At first, when someone ran to their shelter in the ice-pink
light of dawn, Irona thought that the First Wavers had
poisoned their new source of water too. But the symptoms
weren't like that.

'She won't wake up!' the man babbled, and the fear in his
voice jerked Irona awake. 'The baby's cryin' but she won't
answer 'un. Is she poisoned?'

Regen came with them, and Jai, and Sticker. Twiss still
wasn't actually talking to Irona on any level beyond 'Pass
the salt'. He certainly wasn't sharing his quilts with her in
the lonely emptiness of the night. But he made no objection
to her coming with them. In fact the only one who had to stay
behind was the empty shell of Granfer, who watched them
with a thread of spittle drooping from his twisted mouth.

Irona didn't like to think about that.

She had to run to catch up with Twiss. Grabbing the back
hem of her skirt and kilting it up between her legs, she arrived
breathless at the man's shelter where the baby was wailing in
hunger. Almost absently she snatched the infant to her and
let it suck on her knuckle. For a few moments anyway the
babe might be fooled.

'It's they First Wavers again.' Twiss straightened from
his examination of the sleeping woman. He had called
her, slapped her, but still the pale sleeping form wouldn't
respond. He glared around and Irona could feel the violence
in him. 'Same thing all over again.'

But the cloud of lizard-insects screeling under the plastic
rafters made Irona look more closely.

'No fever,' she said, kneeling awkwardly to avoid disturb-
ing the restless child any further. 'Feel. No heat in the skin,
no sweat. And she looks peaceful. She's even smiling a bit.
And there's something else.'

Jai knelt again; she had mirrored Twiss's gesture and stood
when he had. 'You're right, Ro. And look here.'

In the hollow of the woman's neck was a thin weal, pink-puckered and faintly raised, the scab still forming. A dark bead of blood was clotting on the woman's unwashed bodice.

'What is it?' Twiss barked at her and Jai looked around in a panic.

Irona and Regenerator rescued her at the same moment. 'Locust-lizards.'

'Bollocks!' Twiss said, and Irona felt a pang of doubt, but she was turning down the collar of the woman's top and there was the same mark again and again. Irona remembered the stab of pain she had felt that night coming back from the latrines. There were more of the razor-like cuts under the woman's armpits and on her thighs near her groin.

Twiss, with a hang-over of Admin modesty, looked away, disturbed by the exposure of the woman's body. Sticker looked on in concupiscence and Regen in plain scientific curiosity.

Fat, dark-gold lizards were perched hanging from outcrops of root or flint in the dirt walls of the dugout. Irona used her free hand to pull the quilt modestly up to the woman's shoulders once more, at the same time pointing with her chin at the alien life that had invaded the shelter.

'See them?'

Twiss said, 'They're always around. So what?'

'So look at their undersides.'

He had to peer – they all did – because the locust-lizards' underbellies were hidden between the multi-segmented profusion of legs that were suspended by the clawing feet from roughnesses in the walls.

Irona was right. The razor-like projections were darkened with the cracked drying crimson of blood. Spashes of it spotted the white-gold of the underbellies, too.

Twiss was loath to admit that Irona might be right. 'Could be something else,' he said. 'They never done it before.'

'Those knife-like bits would be about the same length as the woman's cuts,' she said.

Jai was wiping the criss-cross slashes with the medi-swabs

she always carried in her pocket olfactory. Almost at the same time as Irona she asked the husband the obvious question: 'Do you know of anything else that could account for the marks on her?'

He shook his head dumbly.

Very quietly, Irona said, 'Catch one, somebody.'

The trouble was, the lizards were skittish at the best of times. Even bloated with their victims' blood they were nimble enough to avoid the men's sudden wild pursuit. In seconds they had vanished through the door, camouflaged by their swarm's darting, melodious flight.

The baby cried and Irona said, 'Yes, pet,' absently, groping in her pocket for her computer remote. While Twiss went racing out after the lizards with Sticker close on his heels, Regenerator watched her call for the Eye to track the lizards and do a spectroscopic analysis of the stains on the long flat proboscis.

By the time Twiss came limping back through the anxious crowd that had gathered, irate with himself because he'd failed and limping too because he'd twisted his ankle, she had sent Regen to the computer shed.

Meantime, the noise had drawn Tebrina and she had gone off to produce some baby-milk. The baby didn't like it and was grizzling round the teat, but at least those heart-rending wails of hunger had decreased.

Just as Twiss came back, leaning on Sticker, Regen ran lightly in on his odd-jointed legs. 'You got it, Ro,' the little man said. 'Entirely. That be human blood, ain't no doubt. Don't know if'n it's hers, but it's certainly human. Entirely.' His words still came out fast as projectiles from a tribesman's gun in a newscast but he twitched much less these days.

'What did you do with the Eye?' she asked, helping Jai to sponge the woman's forehead with cool water.

'Sent it back up on watch, Ro,' the little man said. 'Ain't no sign of attack that I can see.'

Twiss was cursing the lizard-locusts, Arias Tang and fool women, obviously displeased that he wasn't the centre of attention. Irona knew what was going on in his mind; he could not, of course, complain about the hurt to his ankle without tarnishing his self-image. *At least I'm not his only target*, she told herself.

Regen, interested in what he was doing rather than in Twiss's problems, went on in his reedy voice, 'Well, I didn't want they old First Wavers pulling no more flankers.'

'You did right.'

The little man smiled at Irona's praise and preened his thinning brown hair.

'Tell you what, Regen,' (Irona noticed how Jai went to tut over Twiss's ankle and she felt the irrational razor-wires of jealousy slicing into her confidence) 'why don't you go back to the shed and have another look-see? Then you can send the Eye over to find out what it can make of the woman's blood, OK?'

'Sure. Easy-peasy. Back in a bit, Ro.' With unintentional malice Regen said, 'Hope your ankle's OK, Twiss,' and disappeared before Twiss's curses burst around his head.

As the moons rode their race across the midnight sky, Twiss reached out his good leg from the far side of the dormant heater and gently kicked Irona's ankle. 'You awake?' he whispered, though there was no need for his attempt at keeping his voice down. Granfer was no threat to whatever secrecy Twiss had in mind and Synod only knew where Jai and Sticker were. The pendulum weight of the tension radiating from Twiss had driven Sticker to seek consolation in the arms of one of his fancies. Jai swallowed and went off to work out her grief. Nobody had seen Regen since before supper, but that was nothing unusual. Irona just wished he would tell her where he was going and how long he'd be so she didn't spend the time worrying about him being caught by a predator or worse, by some vicious trap of the First Wavers.

Twiss kicked her again, harder this time, and Irona jerked her foot away. She had only just managed to drop off to sleep, so much was on her mind. *Where are we going to get supplies? What'll happen if the thistledown plants don't grow except in spring? How can we guard against the First Wavers poisoning the new source of water too? Let alone all*

*this worry over Twiss and the way he humiliates me in front
of everybody—*

'Ro!' he hissed again. 'You awake?'

'I am now, thanks to you.' She was too close to the realms
of sleep to be tactful. 'What d'you want?'

Silver-blue blades of moonlight slid through the cracks
round the doorframe. The shifting light carved slices of
vision out of the darkness: rumpled bedclothes, tools, Jai's
big olfactory, the heater. And the frozen waves of Granfer's
features pitted by the vacant black holes of his eyes.

There was no warning warble from the Eye's remote under
her pillow. Irona's eyelids closed out her view of the dugout.
Exhaustion was dragging her back down into its embrace.

Twiss snapped the stretched silence. 'Don't you show me
up again in front of everybody, Irona. I won't let you get
away with it again.'

Still not really awake, Irona yawned and said, 'Mm? What
you talking about?'

'Don't pretend you don't know.'

Sleepy bewilderment and the residues of her anger cor-
roded the sleep from her mind. Suddenly her whole body
was wide awake – and she resented it.

'Twiss, I haven't got the faintest idea what you're talking
about.'

'You know perfectly well what I mean.'

'No.'

'Synod, woman, what are you, stupid or something?'

'Definitely something. And either tell me what you're on
about or shut up. Some of us haven't been sloping round in
bed half the day like you.'

He breathed in as if to speak – then exhaled gustily.
Another indrawn breath – Irona could feel her attention
being sucked into him like the air – and this time he managed
to get the words out. He spoke quietly, his effort to control
his anger twanging the lower tones of his voice up half an
octave. 'Back there when I'd twisted my ankle running after
they deve lizard-insects like you said and you just got Regen
to do the whole thing with the Eye and told him how brilliant
he was. You made a right fool out of me.'

'I what?' Irona was incredulous. But she could feel the anger burning outwards from him.

'I mean it, Ro. They sleepers out there, they need me. Don't you undermine my authority like that again or I'll make your life worse than worm-death ever was. You ain't putting everyone at risk again with your smart-ass—'

Regen slammed the plastic door unceremoniously open. 'Ro! Come quick! I done it!'

She rolled to her feet, alarm slamming through her.

Twiss said sharply, 'What is it, Regen?' but with his swollen ankle it took him longer to stand up and Irona was already stumbling, half-blinded by the sudden starlight, after Regen.

Twiss hobbled to the door and leant out into the translucent blue of the night, hanging by one muscular hand from the jamb. 'What is it?' he called after their fleeting figures, heedless of the settlement that slept around them.

Regen turned and ran backwards, bow-legs gangling. 'It's they lizard-locusts, Twiss. A present from Arias Tang.'

18

POINT COUNTERPOINT

Kifl. The enemy's home. And for the first time they could see it.

'Well done, Regen,' Irona breathed. 'Is the Eye holding up OK?'

'He nodded, peered at the screen over her shoulder. Irona and Regen hardly noticed the chill of the computer-shed around them. They pored over the sights and sounds of the enemy's town in the night. It had been Irona who suggested it and Regen who'd built a bigger power-pack into the Eye to get it that far.

Visuals of the wave-form streets of Kifl, the curved crests of the buildings asheen with milky moonlight as the Eye skimmed low under the eaves. Tracking by the psychicator that Regen had boosted, it passed watchers hidden in the colours of boredom or nervousness. Infra-red duplicated their position; sonar probed the shadows and drew the watchers' poses.

'There, see?' Regen pointed at the psychicator screen, scattered with the pale pulsing hues of folk safe in their beds in Kifl. His forefinger, wider at the tip where the nail flattened it out, stabbed at the lower right-hand corner of the displays.

Irona saw. A spark flared with the turquoise fires of intellectual excitement. Scars of red coruscated around it: other Kiflians, anger hardening in the private depths of the night. But only tiny scintillas of crimson flickered in that deep aqua mind-play around which the leaders stood.

And sound: the Kiflian Synod was garbled with a babble of sleepy bedroom talk or nightmares. The Eye's hearing was acute.

'. . . threat to us.'

'Home in on that one!' Regen said.

'Ssh! I'm trying to!'

But interference ran: 'Synod, I wish those deves next door would shut their racket down. I'm trying to get to . . .'

'Don't leave me again!'

'. . . the Matriarch . . .' (Irona's chest thudded.)

'There!' Regen said loudly. 'That one.'

'I know. Ssh!'

Irona homed the Eye in on the flame-shaped minaret spiring dark against the snow-capped volcano. Then she keyed a command that imprinted one set of images on another. The turquoise and crimson emotions cross-hatched over the target as the Eye closed in to touch an exotic muslin curtain.

Arias Tang. A gold-haired woman with china-blue eyes, dressed in a robe of sky blue; it wasn't exactly a matriarch's robe – it was too low-cut and far too immodest – but you couldn't help being reminded of one. And two other men, a cocky young one in self-conscious black slouched with a leg over the arm of his chair, and an older man, dark hair and winged eyebrows all streaked with white.

Irona suppressed an urge to recoil from the fierce cross-currents of feeling in the minaret. Even without the amplifier she had jigged in the Watchtower, she was much more sensitive to other people's emotions these days. Assuming it was something to do with this new planet didn't help; it still hurt. Twiss's anger scalded her . . . She tore her thoughts away from her wound and looked at the four people on the screen, grouped not at the vast table but to one side.

There was no doubt that the blonde woman and the two unknown men were the ones whose hard anger burned in the night. And Tang was the cool mine of intellectual curiosity. Irona knew they were almost certainly the Kiflian Synod – but she didn't know what roles they all played in this.

'Do you think they meant her when they said the Matriarch?' Irona nodded at the blonde woman on the screen.

Regen shushed her.

'They couldn't have known' – it was the pseudo-matriarch who was speaking – 'about the set-up before they landed. So tell me, how could you let a flock of sleepers get dug in so quickly? I thought I told you to bring them to heel straight away.'

She had addressed the hostility in her question to Tang but he wasn't phased by it. He shrugged; he toyed with the slender stem of his glass.

'Answer me!' the woman snapped.

Tang raised one eybrow in what the woman couldn't prove was mockery. Maybe the man with the dramatic black and white hair was scared by her; Tang certainly wasn't. 'Perhaps, Gundmila,' he drawled, 'all your sleepers weren't asleep.'

'Nonsense.' That was the older man. 'The Admin, the Bureaugen, the Liga Mediterranea, they're not stupid. They wouldn't have chosen people who were anything like awake.'

'If you'd bothered to check, Less,' Tang said sardonically, 'you'd have known they're all from the Admin.'

The young man swung his foot back and forth, back and forth in a parody of boredom. 'Who cares?' he said. 'The trick is to take them now while they're still reeling.'

The woman in blue bridled. 'Lal! I don't take orders from—'

In a second the youth was on his feet, his face so close to the matriarch's that she backed off until she came up against the oval table that dominated the centre of the room. Then she could retreat no more, but still she arched away from him. (Irona reeled with the blasphemy.) The youth bent over the Matriarch, threatening.

'And I don't take no orders neither,' he said, his voice distinct with menace.

Still with a faint grimace of mockery, Tang broke the tableau by saying, 'Er – are you quite sure they're reeling? They've found a second water supply, they've built shelters, they're teaching themselves to forage until their crops come through. They've even got over the shock of that illness . . . I just like to point these little facts out to you in case you've missed them. Because I don't actually think these so-called sleepers are reeling, not even with the lizardoptera, do you?'

The hard-faced youth kept his body firmly in the woman's

personal space but he half-turned his head to glare at Tang. 'So what have you got to be so superior about?' the boy snapped.

Tang smiled. 'Well, if you can't work that one out for yourself, Lal, it wouldn't be much good my bothering to tell you.'

Now the fiery-tempered boy swivelled to face Tang. Gundmila, shaken, put one hand back against the polished stone of the table to steady herself.

The youth took a couple of steps to close the gap between himself and the chair in which his tormentor relaxed. It looked for a moment, Irona thought, as though he might thrust his face into Tang's, but he seemed to think better of it. There wasn't a trace of the purples of fear around their known enemy, just a little flush of adrenalin-red, no more than Twiss used to show in his moments of wild glory in the Park.

Arias Tang smiled maddeningly at the youth, whose enraged colour glowed like a furnace. There couldn't have been more than a dozen years between them but that was a world of experience and wisdom. 'I really think, you know,' Tang said, 'that we'd be better off helping them. That way they could help us too.'

'That wasn't what you said before, Arias.' It was the mature man with the black and white hair who had spoken. Since somebody else had said it for him, the boy contented himself with a totally wasted glare at Tang.

Arias Tang sketched the slightest of shrugs. 'That was before. Now we've seen that they're not going to roll over and play dead for us, Less, not with the leadership they've got.'

Gundmila said, 'Surely that's not a problem? Just eliminate the leaders. The rest will soon give in.'

'Yeah, that's what I say too. Kill the lot of them.' The boy spat the words, his body rigid in its tight black clothing.

Tang smiled that irritating smile again. 'Well you would, wouldn't you? Perhaps we should call you Echo instead of Lal.'

'You—' The boy thrust himself closer.

Tang didn't move, but the boy's quick aggression died before the look in Tang's arctic-blue eyes. To Irona it seemed as though Gundmila were enjoying the tensions between her co-rulers of Kifl.

'Oh, for Synod's sake, Arias,' said the older man, Less, 'stop provoking the boy. Olfactory, a calmant please.'

'Who's going to kill me?' asked Twiss belligerently. Neither Irona nor Regen had noticed his arrival, so rapt had they been in their spying. By his very tone Irona could tell he was radiating an aura of vermilion wrath himself. He was panting theatrically.

'Ssh entirely.' Regenerator flapped his hands at Twiss, then gestured to a small packing-case where he could sit to take the weight off his swollen ankle.

Muttering and hamming up the agony he was in, Twiss subsided. He could see it was in his own best interest to hear what his enemies were saying.

It seemed that in those few seconds the minaret-room had sprayed some soothing essence into the air. On Irona's screen the colours of emotion had faded to pastels, though the aqua flame of Tang's curiosity burned steadily. It seemed, too, that the observers in the computer-shed had missed a vital part of the conversation.

The boy was saying, '. . . what the Matriarch wants.'

'We've got plenty of time. All this will be ancient history by the time the next ship arrives,' Tang replied nonchalantly.

'Look,' Less said, nervously running his hands through his white-winged hair, 'will you two stick to the point? I'm telling you again, I want more of those lizardoptera out there as soon as you can. We've got to take out the leaders and make the rest of them knuckle under.'

Tang slanted his head a little, another version of his shrug. 'Fine, if that's what you want. It'll just take a few days to get them ready, that's all, but I still think it's a complete waste of time.'

Gundmila shot him a poisonous look but the older man, Less, interrupted. 'Look, Tang, I'm telling you. We need sleepers out there, not wakers, or we'll never have a workforce. You've let half of them die already because you haven't hit them hard enough. If you're not up to command, then step aside and let the boy do it.'

'I'm not a boy!' said Lal, thereby proving to Irona at least that he was.

'You're too soft, Tang,' Gundmila said. 'What does it matter if we kill the leaders of these sleepers? Get on with it, man.'

Tang smoothed his sallow face into the blandest of expressions. 'If you want the boy, have him. But . . .' His unspoken question hovered in the air and Irona for one agreed. She wouldn't have put the boy in charge of a can-opener.

Irona watched Gundmila fold her arms elegantly and tap one slender foot. From the way she was looking at Arias, it was obvious that she wanted to get rid of him – or rather, to let the others do the job for her. Irona couldn't work out why she wanted to drop the most intelligent man in the Kiflian Synod, but she was too intent to ask Regen about it now. It never even crossed her mind to ask Twiss.

Quite at ease, Tang got to his feet and straightened his edge-to-edge jacket, glancing briefly at his reflection in a mirror on the wall. Less was pacing round and round the oval table, picking things up, putting them down. Lal was rigid with waiting. Gundmila, her lips slightly apart in an unknowing parody of desire, slid her gaze from one to the other.

Then, leisurely, Tang called the older man's bluff. He strolled calmly to the door. The boy, Lal, grinned—

Too soon.

'Don't be so hasty, Arias,' the older man said. He was trying to be gruff, indifferent, but his words tumbled out. He knew it was he who had been too impatient, not Tang.

'Me?' Tang said. 'I'm as slow as a glacier. But if you want me to do a job, leave me to do it my own way. I'll whip them into line.'

He said something else then, but Twiss started shouting, 'The arrogant bastard! I'll pickle him in acid.'

Irona and Regen shushed him but it was too late. Whatever Tang had said, he had gone now. Gundmila watched, smiling faintly, as the door clicked shut behind him, leaving the older man and Lal glaring at each other with recrimination before the boy, too, tried to slam out of the room. His gesture was spoilt, however, because the door-hinge wouldn't let itself be damaged that way.

Back in her refuge in Settlement Knoll, Irona said, 'Regen, you did have it on "record", didn't you?'

'I thought you did.'

They looked at each other while Twiss's anger broke over them.

Irona interrupted her lover's tirade. 'Never mind that, Twiss. If they're the ones who are making the locust-lizards, they've got genetic capabilities.' She gestured out at the moonlit desert. 'All we've got is sand.'

'You sure you got time to come and see this?' Sinofer asked, trying to keep his pride in check.

'For you, anything.' Irona smiled at him, enjoying his uncomplicated feeling. Somehow it made up for the gloom in the deep-sleepers' dug-out. There were seven of them now, two children. Jai had them all in the one place and got what sleep she could there. Not that the deep-sleepers kept her awake; it was her own fear of inadequacy that did that, however often Irona said Jai couldn't do any more than she was doing.

'You don't mind, do you, Jai?' Irona asked.

'No, you go on, Ro. I'll stay here.'

'Don't let any of those lizard-things in, will you?'

Irona heard the panic in her friend's voice and did her best to still it. ''Course not. Ready when you are, Sinofer.'

All the same, opening any door had become like running a gauntlet. It was a week now since the first deep-sleeper had been found. Now the locust-lizards were everywhere. Shoals of their glinting bodies dived at the door as Irona creaked it open on its tie-hinges. Though she only pushed it a crack, still the lizardoptera swarmed shrilling at her face, their golden wings beating, scratching at her face. Raked back for flight, the multi-jointed legs fouled the razored bellies but it was hard to be rational facing hundreds of blood-suckers the size of your hand. It was hard not to retreat to the safety inside.

Holding her mouth tight shut, screwing her eyes to slits, Irona edged out as quickly as she could. Her hand thrashed at the air, the stick that never left her now flailing at the flying bodies. The air was thick with their hot acrid scent; as the stick thudded into one or two gilded flanks the copper taint of locust-blood reeked in her nostrils.

Sinofer was on her heels, lofting a rake Irona could hardly lift in one hand. He slammed the door shut behind them. Lizardoptera chanted shrilly all around.

''S all right now, Irona. They won't attack us if we keep moving.'

She shook her head in wonderment at the man's old-fashioned courtesy. 'I know, Sinofer, I know. But thank you for trying to reassure me. I appreciate it. Think any got inside?'

'Nah, not with nets slung across the doorway. Jai'll be OK. Got more nerve than you'd think, that girl.'

But you don't see her crying over her lover's infidelities. She could leave him – but she won't.

He set off along the trampled dust of the row then stopped to let Irona catch up. Hot saffron light poured down on the arid air that trembled to the almost-melodies the lizard-insects sang. Wing-beats sounded like aural heat-haze, but Sinofer was right. As yet the lizardoptera only razored those who fell asleep.

Sinofer's long-tined rake swept the tunnel clear but the insect-lizards only drew back to re-form into a cumulonimbus that showered gilded reflections and sound beyond the exit to the settlement. Wherever anyone went, now, a pillar of golden light went with them. As Irona gathered her courage and walked towards them, the cloud frayed apart to enfold her. Sinofer didn't seem to be bothered.

'Where do you think they be coming from?' he asked.

Irona swallowed. Lied. 'Beats me. The very thought of them makes my skin crawl.'

'The wife's the same but they don't bother me.'

A metallic-winged cluster swooped past her, making her duck. 'Ugh!' Irona said, flapping her whisk in a gesture that didn't quite hide her instinctive panic. 'They're getting bolder all the time. Have you seen how the kids treat 'em now? I hate the things!'

'Don't fret yourself. You keep moving and you won't come to no harm. I'd just like to know how come there weren't none at all hardly when we landed and now they're thicker than ticks on a sheep. Maybe it's just the time of year.'

She thought of Regen's news and said nothing. Spreading panic wouldn't help at all.

'Don't they give you the creeps at all?'

'Not me. I remember back in Sussex I used to walk over the fields and put me foot in a nest of they old crane-flies. They'd burst up all over the place like a bomb but they never did me no harm. So long as we keep these little blighters out of our homes we'll be all right.'

'But these are blood-suckers!'

'Well they ain't getting my blood, nor yourn neither while you're with me.'

His certainty made her feel good – but she noticed he kept looking nervously towards the Moon Mountains and the first of the thunderheads gathering for the nightfall lightning. Instinctively she began to ask herself *How can I trust the judgment of a man who's scared of thunder?*

As they rounded a gentle swell of land the fields stretched out to the sleepy afternoon. 'See that?' Sinofer gestured expansively. 'That's what we came here for. Ain't it grand?'

And the sight uplifted Irona's heart too. A ragged haze of green ravelled over the furrows. The shoots grew in lines that were dark with irrigation. Irona threw up her hands and did a jig of sheer pleasure, revelling in the sweet smell of moist earth and growing things.

Sinofer tried unsuccessfully to hide his grin. 'It's good – for a sod-crop,' he said modestly.

'Never mind a sod-crop! It's great for anything. And next year'll be even better.'

'Next year in Kifl?' he said, and she wondered what made him sound so cynical.

Trying to renew his simple enthusiasm, Irona answered, 'Any day now we'll be self-sufficient for real.' But her confidence was hollow, built on the shaky ground of the knowledge that the Kiflians had sent the locust-lizards.

Maybe Sinofer heard the doubt in her voice. He said drily, 'Don't count your chickens.'

'Sinofer' – she raked up a laugh – 'don't you ever look on the bright side?'

'Not since I been farming. And not when they First Wavers might bring their lightning over here any time.'

19

PRE-EMPTIVE STRIKE

Deep-sleepers: another four days had passed and now there were fifteen. Sinofer was one of them. Ironic, really, when he was the one who'd been least worried about the flying plague.

Irona looked sadly down at the stringy hulk of him, kept alive only by intravenous feeding. 'You should have been more careful,' she whispered.

His eyes were open but there was no response in their clouded depths.

Irona wiped perspiration from her forehead and tried to ignore the steam that drenched her. The First Wavers had taken the shiny new autoclave Jai had been so proud of. Now a pan of instruments simmered perpetually over the lowest heat she could manage from one of the last functioning power-packs. Irona found the temperature unbearable; she pitied anyone who had to stay in here, but it was the only way they could have instruments ready for an emergency – and there had been plenty of those as folk grew weaker, hungrier.

A youth groaned with the pain of his recent appendectomy and the haggard nurse winced.

On the other side of the pallet in Jai's Hospital, Twiss clicked his tongue. Irona felt it was a derogatory comment about her, but Twiss didn't even mention her as he glanced through the open netted window. The mesh bulged and wriggled with the lizardoptera pressing against it, trying to get in at the fresh blood waiting for them.

One of the glittering insects caught a wing-tip in the weave but there were too many of them crowding in for the locust to free itself and in a second the wing tore. Translucent red ichor spurted out.

Instantly the song of the packed bodies changed to a savage chorus, so high it hurt Irona's eardrums. A dozen lizardoptera plunged onto the wounded one, lancing it with their belly-razors, sucking its life while its own plangent song drowned in a waterfall of beautiful, deathly melodies. Others fought for the privilege of blood, wing rattling on wing.

The nurse jammed her hands over her ears. 'I can't take it any more! What's got into them? They were so nice at first, so sweet, so beautiful . . . and now look at them! They're trying to kill us. They're trying to kill us and I can't stop them!'

Irona walked swiftly over to Jai and put her arms around her. The girl sobbed into Irona's shoulder as though she would never stop. In the cradle Sticker had made, baby Liesl woke and started grizzling.

'Synod, Twiss, isn't there anything else we can do?' Irona asked him over Jai's bent head.

Twiss crooked a smile at her (*Irona read it as: He thinks I've given in*). 'Oh, I'm sure we can come up with something, Ro. They bastard First Wavers ain't going to get away with this. And while you've been fannying about in here I've sent Sticker out with a couple or three teams to hunt they lizards down. I'll get it sorted, never fear. Can you think of a way of setting fire to they?'

Irona appreciated that he had forgiven her – what for, she didn't know – but she still found it a stupid question. The difficulty was putting the reply as tactfully as she could. 'Well, I can't at the moment. The plants here are too wet to burn, and there aren't enough of them anyway. We've got next to no fuel left and certainly none that can be sprayed around – Twiss, you know yourself. The computer's not come up with anything sensible and Regen's disappeared again.'

Her answer was too long for him. Twiss pushed back his shoulders to ease the tension in them, and was half-way to the door before he told her, 'I'm going to the computer-shed when we've done complaints. Coming?'

She gave Jai another perfunctory hug and disengaged herself. 'Will you be all right, Jai?'

The girl nodded, wiping her tears on her wrist.

It would have been all the same if she wasn't, Irona berated herself. And she hurried to catch up with him as he strode off through the lizard-lock, two nets strung on frames across the doorway to the dugout. It was less that she was desperate to be with him and more that she couldn't help feeling repulsed and disempowered by the aliens Kifl had sent. Somehow when she wasn't alone she felt safer.

Batting away the lizard-like locusts with their plastic fans, Twiss and Irona moved from dugout to dugout. Nobody was out tending the fields, not even to raise and lower the water-barriers. Out there the crops could be dying but nobody would risk going that far. The flying death was all about them. Even when the lizardoptera were sluggish in the cool of night nobody would risk it.

Once they had got through their morning round of hearing 'plaints and solving them if they could, Irona and Twiss managed to get beyond earshot of the settlers. Not many Second Wavers were brave enough to face the skeins of lizardoptera winding through the rows. There were fewer still who left the comparative safety of the dugouts these days to cross the open space to the computer-shed. From here and there in the camp mourning sounded on the hot winds as yet another person discovered their friends or loved ones wrapped in the lizard coma. The sound made Irona feel at once helpless and even more determined to put an end to this misery.

For the last few paces Twiss raced ahead through the syrupy heat, making a break to slip through the first lizard-screen before the skirling mass had time to realise what he was doing. 'Hurry up!' he called, but Irona didn't need his impatience to slide in beside him and slam the screen door.

Outside the darkness of the shed, the lizardoptera perched to begin their unsettling harmonies, waiting.

Irona groped her way to the power pack and turned on the minimum of light. 'We're going to run out of power soon,' she told him, but he ignored it.

'Can you make a virus? Or get Jai to make one?' he asked.

'I – I could get the computer to design one but we haven't

got the facilities to build it here. Who for – the lizards or the Kiflians?'

Twiss's only answer was, 'Mm.' His red-brown face puckered in thought, his eyes half-lidded. He began to pace around the room, picking things up and putting them down somewhere else, much to Irona's unspoken annoyance.

She sat down at her keyboards, wishing yet again that she had voice-control here as she had had back in Camelford Watchtower. Or that she had Arms to call on. But on Harith there was nothing.

Scanning the screens as quickly as manual control allowed, she saw with relief that the Eye could find no danger. At least, no more danger than the lizardoptera and their deep-sleep.

Finally Twiss sorted through the implications of her last question. 'So you mean they First Wavers could disease us?'

'Well,' she tilted her head slightly, considering, 'they could. But I don't think they have.'

'You don't? What do you call this deep-sleep then? And the lizards weren't like this when they got here. You heard what they Kiflians said.'

'OK' – she glanced around and then wished she hadn't been so pointlessly furtive – 'they could have. But I don't think so. The Eye's analysed the stuff as being some sort of natural secretion the insect-lizards make so their prey don't feel it when they get razored. That way they can keep on coming back for—'

He interrupted. 'So can you make an antidote?'

'I hadn't finished, all right? The secretion's this stuff that anaesthetises the nerve-endings on the skin and then travels back up the nerves themselves. And by that time – d'you remember me telling you there's a little parasite that lives in the lizardoptera's gut? Well it carries a virus and it's transported into humans at the same time as the analgesic. By the time the analgesic has worn off, it's too late for us to do anything about it because the virus has got a hold on the deep-sleeper and paralysed them for real.

'But Jai and I have talked about it, and we've asked

the computer, and we reckon it would be too much of a coincidence for the First Wavers to tailor anything like that in only three months or so. It's probably just part of the breeding-cycle. They just found the lizardoptera and sent them to us, that's all.'

'Have you quite finished now?' Twiss asked with frigid courtesy.

'Yes.'

'Well answer the deve question then!' he roared. 'Can you or can you not make an antidote?'

'No. We could design one, but we haven't got the facilities to build it.'

'A poison?'

'No!'

'You and that computer are entirely overrated.'

Irona compressed her lips, not demeaning herself to utter her angry retort. *How dare he think I'd do anything that wicked! What sort of low-life does he think I am?*

Instead, knowing that their leadership needed cohesion if it was to be effective, she kept her anger inside and paced silently over to what was left of the window-hole. It was stupid, she knew. The nets should have been enough, but the sparkling insects gave her the creeps, batting endlessly at the weave to get in at her, so she had cannibalised strips of plastic to fit tightly over the window.

Peering through the slits, she saw a cloud of lizardoptera rise all a-glitter, singing a mad harmonic of dismay. Human shouts, polarised around Sticker's hectoring roar, indicated that another swirl of lizards had eluded the hunters.

Twiss shook his head in disgust. 'I ain't giving in, Irona. And I ain't letting them Kiflian bastards keep killing us. Ask the computer what it suggests.'

'Do you think I haven't?'

Twiss punched the sod wall in frustration. Irona watched in horror as soil crumbled around the impact. His blow drew a shining blade of daylight, slim as a stiletto, across the dim air of her refuge. Any more of that and there would be a gap big enough for the bloodsuckers to swarm in through. Outside, the lizards' ululations climbed to a tighter shrill of frenzy.

Twiss slammed away from her, kicking the chair to cannon tumbling into the opposite wall. Irona's guts clenched.

'I don't care what you think, Ro. I'm going to beat those bastards at their own game. We can't win in a fair fight. We're outnumbered, out-teched.

'But when push comes to shove I'm more of a bastard than they'll ever be. I'll think of something. Watch me.'

Two nights later Regen came back from Kifl. 'You ain't going to like it, guys,' he told them, weary to the limits of endurance. 'We ain't curled up and died fast enough for 'em and they've run out of locusts. So Lal and that Tang they're sending us a little present. Snake-rats. And Twiss, it'll do us all in. Entirely.'

Bernardina patted her ansible. The latest model the Admin had. Lots of nice little safety-features, such as friendly little lights that would warn you if anyone who shouldn't be were trying to focus in on your conversation. And a little gizmo that would tell her if the person she were calling were alone. This ansible was special. It had only one coding: Kifl.

All the same, the Camelford Matriarch of Matriarchs hadn't let it be installed in the Synod chamber, much less in her own private apartment. No, it was tucked out of harm's way in a thickening of the wall on level Upsilon, in a skinny little chamber one of the Arms had made at her request. It was strange watching an Arm brain-wormed . . .

Somehow, when the president of the Liga Mediterranea was pressurising her through his flunkies in the Londover Admin, coming here gave Bernardina a sense of peace. Settling back in her contour-chair, she analysed the feeling.

Allowing herself to fall into a deeper meditation here where no-one could find her, Bernardina traced her emotion to its source. Behind her closed lids, her eyes found a point of space where she could imagine Harith to be. And the feeling came clear.

'I feel peace because this place empowers me. I hope Irona comes out on top up there, but whichever of them, her or Gundmila, comes out on top, they'll be strong enough for

what I want. And I can manipulate the winner. Buy her
out with – what did they use to say? A handful of beads.
A few powered tools, a bit of up-market bread and circus.
Whatever it takes. Then, whoever she is, she can back me
up against the Liga. But my money's still on Irona. She's
stronger than Gundmila and she's my daughter. When she
knows, she'll be easier for me to control.'

Twiss's plan was simple. Ruthless. Savage.

Once upon a time, Irona knew, she would have been
repelled by it. Twiss wanted to leave her at home but for
once Irona dug in her heels and confronted him openly while
most of the settlement waited uneasily outside in the chill first
light of the desert.

'You heard what Regen said!' She glared at him. 'That
Lal creature is cooking up some new plague for us. Jai and
Tebrina—'

'All the same—' began Twiss but Regenerator chuckled
mockingly at them. 'Ain't you two got nothing better to
do than have another of they pointless spats? "That Lal
creature" ain't half as slimy as what he's come up with.
They snake-rats they're messing with, they touch you once
and you're dead meat. 'Nother few days and he'll have us
et up. Entirely. Every one of us in the settlement.

'Unless we stop they 'fore they get here. So, Twiss, if
'Rona wants to come with us and bring that Eye of hern,
we'd be downright stupid to leave her at home. 'Cos they
little beasties might just get to us first if we're on the march,
mightn't they?'

Regen glanced at Granfer, drooling slack-mouthed in
the corner. The little man said not a word but his look
wasn't wasted on Twiss. In the dawn-shadowed dugout,
with everyone standing in that last-minute pause before
departure when all the tired arguments are thrashed out
again, it seemed crowded to bursting. Even Jai stood over
Granfer. She didn't seem to know where to put herself.

Twiss said, 'Sticker, you sure you got all they drained
power-packs over at the computer-shed?'

Sticker tossed his hair back and scratched at the blond

stubble on his chin. 'Twiss, you've asked me that about a
million times so far and every time I've said yes, me and Ro
plugged 'em in yesterday afto. So get it through your head
right? You ain't the only one what can get things done.'

The two men glared at each other, nerves tightened to
snapping point.

Irona twisted a fold of her skirt between her fingers
Striking while the iron was hot she said, 'If I come I can
keep an Eye above us—'

Regen interrupted unabashed. 'I've programmed it to
hot-wire anything you like.'

'Anyway,' she took a deep breath, 'I'm coming whether
you like it or not.'

Outside, in the opal mists of dawn, thirty figures bulked
and faded under the flittering silhouettes of lizardoptera who
were sluggish in the chill. Yawns and the clanks of clumsy
plastic weapons sounded eerily in the thick, damp air.

Angrily (but, Irona suspected, secretly relieved) Twiss
said, 'Oh, all right. Come if you want to but don't blame
me if you can't take it. It won't be no picnic.'

'Then I shan't share my sandwiches with you,' she replied.

Twiss ignored her sarcasm. 'But I ain't leaving no woman
in charge. Who knows what they sneaky deves might do?'
(Irona wondered who Twiss thought the sneaky deves were
– the First Wavers, or women.) 'Sticker,' Twiss jerked his
chin at his friend, 'you stay here and keep an eye on things
for me until I get back.'

Sticker stood open-mouthed. 'What, you want me to miss
all the fun?'

Twiss settled his makeshift sword more firmly between
his shoulder-blades and strode towards the door. 'And
keep a watch over Granfer for me, will you?' He all
but barged Sticker out of his way. 'I'll take Thebula to
guard the hostages. Now let's stop wasting time. It's going
to be hotter than a nuclear furnace out there before too
long.'

He did the quick double-step through the lizard-screens,
the movement that everyone had adopted since the flying
invasion, and stopped to face his embryonic army. Dew

condensed on him, armouring his dark hair with a silver helmet. Other men might be taller but there wasn't a one of them that didn't stand a little straighter when Twiss ran his gaze approvingly over them.

Irona thought he would give them some stirring speech about death and glory and the sweetness of retribution. But not Twiss. He judged the mood of stern resolve and nodded proudly.

'Ain't none of you needs the bathroom, is there?' he said, and laughter rippled through their untidy ranks. 'Right then, folks. Let's get on with it. I want a swim in that there sea I've heard so much about. You with me?'

They were. Almost, Irona pitied the Kiflians. But as the outer screen clacked shut behind her with its freight of screeling lizards, she glanced back at Granfer and at the white, frightened face of Jai.

'Right, you Kiflian deves,' she muttered to herself. 'See how you like our revenge.'

The march through early summer wasn't kind. The desert dessicated them and locusts followed to pick off stragglers. At least it gave Irona a chance to chat to people. In shaggy blonde-haired Gaeta she found someone who admired her, and in skinny Thebula a sardonic, down-to-earth counterpoint. The three women toiled along together and still found the strength to laugh.

In the Moon Mountains artificial storms crashed about them in a deluge of thunder and lightning-flared rain. Irona shivered all night in her soaked, clinging clothes and Gaeta said her thighs were sore where her things had chafed until the hot morning dried them out. Thebula wrung out her wild red hair and whistled an ironic dirge through the gap in her teeth. When at last they crested the ridge and saw the town, everyone was relieved.

There were trails in the hills around Kifl, nature walks marked with daubs of yellow paint or red arrows on artfully-grouped trees that were outposts between the lapping tide of native growths. (Irona remembered how she had felt about the outdoors when she lived inside Camelford. Obviously many of the Kiflians were still scared, and she realised to her astonishment that she was not.)

Things grew here that Irona had never seen in Rainshadow Valley, strange, semi-sentient translucencies that lensed the sun onto their competitors. Here and there threads of smoke spiralled up into the sea-tang, but the plants were too moist inside to catch fire completely.

'Smells funny, don't it?' Irona heard a woman whisper, and Irona took a lungful of the pungent, alien odour.

Overhead, the sun drew a brassy smear across the blue of the sky. Irona could just catch maddening glimpses between the trees of a cornflower sheen on the horizon. Could that be the sea at last?

Nearer at hand her eyes strained to pick out the shapes of the plants. A hot wind tumbled down the hillside, dragging at the camouflage-vines whose colours shifted continually: chalk-pale soil, green and pink of rhododendrons, sun-gilded rust of rock behind them. Every now and then a green-ball plant would burst with a pop that scattered its spores like a fountain of golden dust that seemed to come from nowhere.

At least in the hills it was cooler. The desert crossing had cost two lives.

Lying belly-down with his elbows on a thin scatter of pine-needles, Twiss said, 'Hey, Ro. See that? I always wanted to know what the ocean was like. Granfer used to try to explain it to me but I never understood what he meant, not really. Seeing it on the newscasts ain't the same, is it?'

She wriggled closer to him, peering out where he gazed through an open space. Now she had to slit her eyes against the glare from the rippling mirror of the sea. It was a shimmering brightness that made the land seem heavy and dark by contrast. Purple headlands and distant bays that might have been clouds on the horizon: it held an enchantment whose language her soul kept secret from her mind. All she found to say was, 'I know what you mean.' He still wouldn't sleep with her at night and it made her tense and awkward around him.

Exhausted, she rolled over onto her back and let the branches of the cedar cast their dark fractal patterns on her retinas. All around her she heard the low buzz of conversation as the Second Wavers rested through the heat of noon. Sleep was far from them; their first battle was at hand. At least, though, there were no ruby-eyed lizardoptera overhead, flagging their position. What the desert hadn't killed, Twiss's forces had. Irona slammed her eyes shut to cut off that picture: Twiss's sudden shout, 'Now!' and the army threw the long weighted net over their aerial tormentors, bringing them to the ground. Then they had stomped the scaled insect bodies, human screams of rage drowning out the lizards' mad harmonics as their blood drowned the dead earth of the desert. It was Sticker who had hunted down the last survivors. Irona liked to think it was because he was so nauseated by the carnage beneath the net.

All the same, the Second Wavers had had to leave three more deep-sleepers by a stream.

'They'll be all right,' Twiss had said. Nobody believed him. The trouble was, there was nothing anyone could do for the victims and so they colluded with Twiss's optimistic lie.

But the images were painted on the inside of Irona's vision: acrid, copper smell of lizard-blood, hoarse-throated yells of red rage, and the squelching thud of brutal boots. *If that's what we do to insects, what are we going to do to the Kiflians?*

Irona opened her eyes wide, drinking in the sight of Twiss skylined against the sunny hillside. It paled the nightmares in her head. 'D'you think we'll make it?' she asked him.

He was so close that she felt the muscles in his forearms move as he nodded. ''Course we will. Think we come this far to fail? We ain't going down, Ro.'

And she believed him – because she chose to. Yet underneath she felt a morass of doubts and moral quandaries and plain, old-fashioned fear.

Once more she took out the pocket-screen that Regen had made from spare parts for her. So high it was slimmer than a crescent star, the Eye sent signals down that drew pictures on the screen. He had never said where he got the spare parts from, though, and she found her Watcher's sensibilities mistrusting his anarchic behaviour. It was all very well while he was stealing from the Kiflians; the question was, would he steal from his own folk too?

Twiss broke in on her thoughts. 'It's worked out fine so far, ain't it?' She wondered if he spoke more to reassure himself than her. 'The timing's spot-on. Any time now they'll be dozing away through the heat of afternoon, lazy deves, and we'll be all nice and rested. They won't have a clue.'

She followed his gaze with her own, seeing her friends and neighbours sprawled in the leafy shade. Spiring pines grew wide-spaced, and she could look down between them to the coastal plain and to the town. It rose white and pink and turquoise and peach against the foothills of the volcano that was blued with distance. The beach was dark with volcanic sand.

'Hadn't we better be moving, then?' she said, scared but wanting to get it over with.

'Oh, stop nagging, woman. See anything on that Eye of yourn?'

She dragged it out of her breast-pocket again and squinted through the reflections in its hand-sized screen. The sleepy streets were deserted; the pastel wave-form houses looked somnolent, too, with their shutters drawn against the brazen heat. Mental and emotional activity was minimal, but when she had the Eye focus on their own forces there was the deep purple of fear.

'Come on, Twiss! This waiting is driving me mad.'

He spoke with immutable finality. 'We'll move when I'm good and ready and not before. They Kiflians won't know what's hit 'em.'

20

TANG ESCAPES

In less than three minutes he gave the order.

All along the green-frothed glades the Second Wavers rippled down the hillside, one moment breast-deep in helpful bracken and the next, betrayed by the low writhing tendrils of camouflage plants that almost instantly adopted the colours of the settlers' clothing. Irona felt she was a visual shout that must attract the attention of any Kiflian watchers. 'We're not just exposed, we're on display,' she whispered to Twiss, but he just rolled his eyes heavenwards and clicked his tongue in disgust.

'Why don't you go ahead and advertise your paranoia?' he hissed. 'There might be a few people back on Earth who didn't hear you.'

Side by side, Thebula and Gaeta grimaced at her to show their sympathy. The two young women moved in harmony with each other, a rewarding friendship. But Irona didn't have time to think about that now.

They came down to stone-walled terraces where vineyards gave out the heady perfume of their flowers. Toy-bright mini-tractors rested on their tall wheels in the hot siesta sun. All along the curving hillside Second Wavers went to climb down to the next level – and cried out, stumbling and falling.

On the point of yelling, 'Attack! Take cover!' Irona stopped. Something smooth slithered around her leg – and she realised that camouflage-plants were disguising where the stone walls actually were.

'Stupid deve plants!' she muttered, groping her way gingerly down the metre-and-a-half drop.

When the settlers finally reached the road at the bottom of the terraces, there were four with sprained ankles and one with a shattered knee. Regen came sifting through the silver-green leaves of an orange-grove to ask what all the noise was about, and together he and Irona did what they could for the wounded with their pocket olfactories.

Leaving the bunch of casualties in the shady grove, the depleted army still took all too long to get to the town. In the narrow sun-baked streets the shadows were already beginning to lengthen. Soon the siesta would be over and the streets would be thronged.

Regen, the Eye bobbing above him to peer round corners out of any pedestrian's line of sight, led them rapidly through Kifl. At any moment the First Wavers would be waking; Irona could not believe that they would be very happy to find their 'slaves' at loose in their homeland.

But the tower was elusive: they could see its minaret behind other buildings and across the tree-lined plazas, yet the random pattern of the rows kept taking them round in circles. It was even worse in the centre of town, where the awnings and arches, designed to keep off the sun, stopped vision too. Even the Eye couldn't pierce the roofed-over rows.

Once Regen said, 'See that green building over there? That's the lab. It ain't too far now.' But he couldn't find the tower.

'Stop!' Irona whispered at last, frustrated by yet another dead-end. 'This is stupid. Playing blind-man's buff like this we'll never get to the tower before they wake up.'

'What do you suggest then?' Twiss asked sarcastically. 'And as for you, Regen, I thought you said you knew this place like the back of your hand.'

'I do. It's just that I'm ambidextrous.'

Irona snapped her fingers. 'Give me the screen back, Regen. I'll send the Eye to track us by emotion and we'll have that laid over the visuals from above. How's that?'

From then on they made better time. All the same, Irona was very aware of the shuffle of twenty-four pairs of feet behind her, echoing between the concave walls. And though they made every effort not to make a sound, still their clumsy weapons kept clattering and then, even worse, there would be a chorus of shushing.

Maybe this isn't such a good plan after all, Irona thought, and the nervous rumbling of her stomach embarrassed her with its loudness.

When she couldn't take it any more, Regen rescued her. He held out his arm, blocking her before she could turn a corner. 'We done it, Ro. This is it!'

Flattening herself to the ground to peer round the corner, Irona saw the full belly-curve of a building opposite. To eyes used to the regularity of Cameford's angles, or to the unplanned jags of nature, the perspective was dizzying: onion-domes, concentric rings, reciprocal hollows and bulges around the not-quite-spherical plaza. Strange native plants glimmered in the corners of vision, translucent tendrils dancing in the vagrant breeze. Colour had gone mad: between the dead indigo flowers of morning glory, motile plants of orange and scarlet were vaning themselves along on aerial roots of yellow and ochre. Nothing stayed still; even the gemmed gravel was raked into restless designs in the shadowy roofless space.

Irona's gaze couldn't settle on any one spot. She felt queasy just looking around. And echoes of the lizardopteras' song overlapped at the fringes of her hearing.

Regen clapped a reassuring hand on her shoulder. "S all right, Ro. It's too late in the season for they lizards to bite.'

Twiss came to squat over Irona. 'Let's get to it.'

He zigzagged a run through the kaleidoscopic plaza, and others followed him. Not Regen, though. He straightened leisurely, his knees popping, and handed Irona to her feet. As if it were just a Sunday stroll, he linked arms with her and crossed to key the door-mechanism that had Twiss baffled. Gaeta smothered a laugh. Regen and Irona were the first ones inside, and the first to take the grav-shaft to the top.

Irona was scared to be riding on nothing, but too proud to say so. She held her divided skirts and was glad when Regen hopped out onto the landing and hooked her down beside him in the Synod Chamber of Kifl.

Taking a second to orient herself, she saw the Eye gleaming outside the billowing curtains. She called it in, and it scanned for her the same room that she had so often spied on.

'No sign of Lal, then.'

Twiss came up beside her. 'No, nor that bastard Tang neither.'

Neither of them mentioned the woman who might – or might not be – the Matriarch of Harith.

'Well I told you, didn't I?' Regen asked. He had hitched himself onto the polished marble of the tabletop and sat swinging his legs and crunching an apple from the bowl in its centre. 'Don't know where that Less-feller is right now. They'll be here in a bit, though, if they do what they usually do, so maybe you'd better start hiding this army of yourn.'

'Never mind about us,' Twiss told him. 'What about that lab?'

Regen chuckled. 'Oh, I can find that easy enough. Been there loads of times. How d'you think I knew about they snake-rats?'

Twiss clicked his tongue sharply. 'I ain't bothered about the geography of it. I just want to be sure you put it out of action.'

'Oh, I'll do that all right. Entirely.'

'Don't total it!' Irona called out in alarm. 'Who knows what bugs they might have that you'll set free?'

But she was talking to the empty mouth of the grav-shaft.

It was hot on the window-ledge. The bright sun hammered heat into Irona's eyes until her head was throbbing. To her right the billowing draperies tormented her sweating flesh and to her left was the most frightening drop she had ever seen. The fall seemed to lure her. It seemed inevitable that she would fall, so why not get it over with now?

Her body could feel the sensations: the vertiginous lurch of her stomach, the air rushing past her, the jewel-bright pain as her soft skin split on the hard ground—

'You all right, Ro?'

Dry-mouthed, she nodded. Twiss stood opposite her, trapping a fold of the cloth in his hand so that he could peer through its weave into the council room. He didn't seem at all perturbed by the precipice. Irona envied him. Thebula was flat under one side of the table, a youth called Marselin on the other side. Gaeta was in some sort of wardrobe.

Then Twiss ssh'd her, though it wasn't she who had been talking. His whole being stiffened, attention riveted now on whoever had come into the First Wavers' Synod.

Irona heard a yawn, the muted bursting of grapes between strong teeth. It reminded her of the drop outside—

'Oh, there you are!' (Irona peeked; it was Arias Tang, his queue neatly tied.) 'I was beginning to wonder what had happened to you.'

'Nothing's happened to me,' came a slinky female voice. 'Why, should it have?'

Tang said, 'N-no,' but there was an ambivalent slide in his tone. Watching the emotions on her pocket-screen, Irona could see the silken pleasure he took in building the woman's unease. Red anger spiked from the female councillor – the Matriarch?

The sharp strike of boots on stone. 'Have you heard anything?'

'And good day to you too, young Lal.'

'Don't you patronise me, Tang.'

'Whyever not, dear boy?'

'Oh,' Gundmila said wearily, 'don't start again.'

Is she a matriarch or not? Irona couldn't rest until she had found out. She pressed the pads as gently as she could, hoping the sound they made would not be audible, but even if it was she had to know.

And the Eye, half-hidden behind a carving in the apex of the dome, showed her the woman dressed in what could have been the celestial blue of a matriarch. If it weren't so tight and revealing.

But they don't show her much deference, do they? Maybe here the matriarchs are different. Maybe she's just some woman dressed in blue. Did they mean the real Matriarch back on Earth? Oh, Synod, what do I know?

Irona had missed the next few sentences. Now she brought her concentration back on the matter in hand. After all, it might mean her life or her death.

'. . . It was breaking up, but we've recorded it. D'you want to hear the actual words?' That was the older man, Less, speaking. Irona had been so wrapt in her puzzling that she hadn't noticed him come in. He was wearing a voluminous red robe over narrow black trousers; Irona thought him as ridiculous as Lal plainly did.

'Oh, don't waste my time on that garbage,' Lal said. 'What about the snake-rat plan? How's that coming on?'

Tang shook his head pityingly. 'Lal, you're a sadist. Haven't they got enough to contend with?'

'But you agreed!'

'Actually, I didn't.' Tang raised a mocking eyebrow at the boy. 'It seems somehow, though, that in my absence I signed a request to the lab for it to go on. I must be turning schizophrenic.'

Less leant forward, his arms on the carven rests of his chair. 'What's that, Tang?'

The woman said firmly, 'Enough of that.' She seated herself at the broader end of the ovoid table, leaning back against the peacock chair so that its stone tracery radiated from her head. Thebula's shoulder was only inches from her feet. 'This meeting of the Harith Synod will now come to order. We've got more important things to consider than a few recalcitrant sleepers. They'll come to heel soon enough. The desert will see to that. Now, about housing. This baby-boom just doesn't seem to stop . . .'

And Twiss signed to Irona. She stabbed the keypad. The Eye shot out a sizzle of lightning that lassoed the woman before spinning on to leave Lal slumped unconscious too. Then Less, whose face lay naive in tranced surprise.

Irona jabbed the key again and another bolt shot out – but it was too late. Tang had already dived through the open door of the gravity-shaft, Thebula and Marselin hurling themselves after him.

'You did that on purpose!' Twiss raged at her.

'I didn't!'

'You should have got Tang first and you knew it!'

'But I couldn't get him properly lined up from where the Eye was. I'm sorry.'

'You will be. But I ain't getting into no debate. We haven't got the time.' He turned to the grav-shaft, throwing words over his shoulder. 'Thebula, you keep this Less guy safe. Make him know we mean business before you leave. And get Lal and that cow in the blue back to the orchard.' He turned away, saying harshly, 'Let's go see if Regen's managed to screw up as well.'

Twiss and his second lab squad barged through the earliest brightly-dressed Kiflians out for their evening stroll; Irona pelted along in his wake. So far the local populace seemed to have no idea of what was going on. The people turned to stare after the racing settlers; at every moment Irona expected someone to shout, 'There they are! After them!' But the worst they did was stop and gawp. Apparently they never thought the sleepers from Settlement would have the gall to show up in Kifl.

Turn another bend in the sine-wave row – Irona's heart was thudding with their dash through the sticky heat – and they were there. A haven – or a trap. It didn't seem right, just a plain, blank door in a plain, white wall.

Twiss scarcely hesitated. Irona could have done with Thebula's support but she was taking the prisoners back. Behind the men in Twiss's second lab squad, Gaeta gave Irona a nervous grin and together they walked in through the inconspicuous door.

The Synod's lab was a smouldering ruin. Smoke coiled poisonously above shattered glass-fronted tanks and there was blood up the walls. The only reason Irona, Twiss and the ten with them got through was the Kiflians' lack of suspicion. Even as Twiss turned to slam the door behind them, savage yells were beginning to rise. Beside Irona, Gaeta shuddered.

Klaxons began to sound, deafening out any possibility of thinking, until Regen jammed a wad of dead man's shirt into the speaker.

Irona leant against a wall, panting in the acrid air. 'Now how do we get out of here?' she asked but nobody paid her any attention.

Twiss swept a hard glance around the room. 'How come the lab's still standing?' he asked harshly. 'I thought I told you to trash it.'

Regen shrugged. 'We didn't have nothing to destroy it with. But we've burnt out all the storage stuff.'

'Did you get the snake-rat bug?'

'Got the bug, but the snake-rats I ain't so sure about. Could be like the lizards, live here like, or they could be something they dreamed up. They might be half-way to Settlement by now.'

Irona threw her arms open in a gesture of dismay. 'You mean we've been through all that for nothing?'

'Well, it wouldn't have been for nothing if you hadn't let that deve Tang escape,' Twiss said.

Regen turned his mismatched face up to Twiss. His gentle brown eyes stared into his leader's with contempt. Then he turned to pat Irona clumsily on the arm. 'No, of course it weren't for nothing, Ro. We've taught these ba— deves that there ain't nothing they can get over on us. We got three quarters of their Synod, didn't we? From now on they'll leave us alone, you'll see. Entirely.'

Twiss swept one hand furiously along a counter, sending beakers and petri-dishes flying to crash against the smoke-blackened walls. 'Assuming we get out of this, of course.'

'We won't if you let loose some killer germ,' Irona said astringently. 'Will they be able to salvage any of this, Regen?'

'Dunno. I downloaded their computer into ourn – at least, I hope I did. And I kept all the disks that I could lay my hands on. Hee-hee.' Regen was jumpy; a tic jerked at his cheek. He was about as bad as Irona had ever seen him, though his eyes were sparkling with excitement. 'Plus I re-routed most of their power into our packs. But yeah – unless we blow the building into the fifth dimension, they'll have it up and running again in a few weeks.'

Twiss turned to stare down at Regen. Irona could feel it:

Twiss had laid down a glacier of self-control but underneath
smouldered a rage that could burn through at any minute.
She couldn't understand how Regen managed to stand
there so calmly as Twiss said, 'I thought I told you to
total the place.'

It took all Irona's courage to say, 'We don't want to do
that. One day we might need it.'

For a moment Irona wondered if Twiss was going to hit
her. The hard wall of his anger battered out at her; she
wondered again why she was so sensitised to it.

He mastered himself and went on, 'But we got to show
'em we ain't having them killing our folk no more. We got
to prove we mean it.'

'Won't that make us as bad as they are?' she asked.

'No. It'll keep us as alive as they are.' He jerked his chin
towards the shuttered windows. The slats were shadowed
with a dense crush of hostile people and now that Twiss had
stopped talking, Irona could hear it too.

The ugly sound of a mob.

'You can't!' Irona shouted.

'You just going to ask them to let us out?' Twiss almost
spat the words. She hardly knew him any more.

'That's why we've got hostages, isn't it?' she asked.

'But we ain't got just the one we wanted.'

Irona was trembling; her warden's empathy attuned her
to the tensions in the stinking shell of the lab. Twiss knew
it subconsciously – and used it as a weapon against her.

'But Twiss,' she said, 'you can't just fire at them. Not
when they haven't done anything to us.'

'You stupid deve! If we don't get them first, they'll do
it to us.'

Regen came back from his foray through the other rooms.
On his back was a bulging bag of things he had scavenged
besides the disks. 'Right then?' he asked.

'Yes,' said Irona.

'No,' said Twiss.

'Why, what's up then?'

'Seen outside?' Twiss tilted his head in that direction.

'Yeah. No problem, though, not if we tell 'em we got their precious baby Synod tucked up safe.'

'But we haven't, though, have we? Because Irona let Tang go. I don't know where he is and that's what worries me.'

Regen shrugged. 'In that case, let's get the hell out of here before he has a chance to get it together. Ro, why don't you find out how far the others have got with they hostages?'

All the time the mob outside was growing stronger, more vociferous. They were beating on the windows with their fists now but the triple-glazed crysteel was too tough to break that easily. The muted noise of it sounded only through the doors.

Irona keyed her pocket screen and homed it in on where the others should be: half-way back to the orange grove.

'They've made it, see?' At her triumphant shout, Twiss and Regen crowded round her to look. 'Regen, have you seen a newscaster or anything round here?'

'Something like. They got one in most of the houses what I looked in.'

Twiss said, 'D'you reckon we can get their computer to send pictures to they?' As he spoke Regen was righting the seat by the blue-faced machine while his other hand was tentatively pressing keys.

'Vox-op?' Irona suggested.

But it was too late. Even as Regen ordered the computer to relay the news about the hostages, an axe crashed through the door.

21

AXES AND ACIDS

The axe smashed the door-lock. Assailants tumbled in, stumbling over one another. Irona had a confused impression of garish clothes, and fists wielding carving-knives or hoes. The screaming mob hurtled in on them.

Twiss snatched up a jar and flung it. The glass shattered on a man's face and the mob paused. Then with an inarticulate yell Twiss hurled lab-stools and anything else he could get his hands on. The Second Wavers' shock diminished and the army of eight joined in the fray.

'Stop 'em!' called Twiss, and his followers grasped his tactics. Together three of them uprooted a bench; the others seized it and charged the door, crushing the opposition. Some of the Kiflians tried to fight back, throwing their knives, stabbing with their garden tools, but the dense plastic of the bench shielded the settlers. The diamond-sharp plastic of a spade slashed Gaeta's arm, almost severing it at the shoulder. She fell shrieking but the suddenness of the defence had caught the Kiflians unprepared and they staggered over victims in their own ranks. They were hampered by their numbers and by the narrowness of the doorway, which worked to the settlers' advantage.

All the time Regen and Irona fiddled desperately with the lab computer, ducking as missiles flashed towards them.

Twiss stooped swiftly aside as a pitchfork spun towards him. He caught it in one hand, reversed it and ran weaving over to his army's improvised shield. A noise that was barely human was issuing from his throat as he stabbed again and again over the upturned bench and into the faces of the Kiflians.

Turning her head briefly, Irona saw Twiss attack the mob. She saw how blood spurted from a man's neck, jumping to the rhythm of his heart, and the blood arced and fell like a red cascade. And just for a second she remembered how Twiss had felt when he slew the rabbit – and how she had felt with him the pleasure in its death.

A broken bottle caught Regen on the shoulder and he grunted, toppling forward momentarily. His weight on the keyboard undid everything he had accomplished and the crowd's chaotic shrieks cancelled out all possibilities of voice-operating the computer. Regen groaned as blood soaked into his shirt from a long tear in the muscles between neck and shoulder.

It ignited Irona. She stood and spun in one motion, grabbing something, anything, from the shelf behind her. In the mob of Kiflians there was a tall, greying woman who teetered, one hand upraised, still trying to regain her balance after her throw.

Irona hurled her missile, watching it fly over the ranks of her companions to burst on the Kiflian woman's temple.

Acid leaped in a crystal fountain and rivered destruction over the woman's face. The eye disappeared and the woman threw up her hands too late to save it. A dreadful steam rose stinking from her face and the sick vapour blended with the woman's animal screams. Then she took her hands away and they were smoking too. Where her eye had been there was only a hidous blood-brown hollow hung with streamers of blackening flesh.

And still her screams pierced Irona. But that was not the worst thing.

Blood still welled from Regen's neck and with each drop Irona was glad she had speared that agony into his attacker.

'Ro! Irona!' Twiss gasped between mighty sweeps of his pitchfork. 'Have you – have you done it yet?' And there sang through the air the message he dared not say aloud: *We can't hold them much longer.*

Recalled to herself, she sprayed a coagulant from her olfactory onto the slash in Regen's scrawny neck then bent to the keyboard on his unwounded side. Within minutes they had worked out their strategy.

'Ro!' Twiss yelled with the last of his strength. Irona barely heard his call through the mêlée. 'Ro! Do it now!'

She snatched a glance at him. Sweat spun from his hair and his face was contorted into a vicious smile of desperation. Yet the blue tines of his pitchfork spun and stabbed as rhythmically as ever and she could see that without him the settlers' defence would have crumbled. Not a one of them was unwounded and Gaeta was unconscious under a window at the end of a trail of her blood. Yet Twiss stood indomitable and the settlers rallied to him.

Regen was faltering, his fingers mis-keying. Irona reached down and finished the sequence for him and when her hand brushed his he grasped her forearm in gratitude.

'It's OK, Regen, it's OK,' she said soothingly.

From all over the town, from bars and houses and shops, from wave-form buildings and curl-roofed pagodas, Thebula's voice sounded. Even in the lab, over against a side wall, a large flat screen suddenly dissolved into the depths of three dimensions and there was the woman who might or might not have been the Matriarch, right at Thebula's side in the peaceful light of late afternoon. Thebula was half behind her, apparently leaning against the gnarled trunk of an olive-tree, and the fluttering silver-grey leaves barely revealed her hand on the Matriarch's arm.

'Put down your weapons,' Gundmila said. 'Wherever you are, people of Kifl, put down your weapons and go in peace in our beloved town. The Second Wave have told us of their needs and of what they believe to be our oppression. Golossen, Lal and I have agreed to join them here in the groves and we should appreciate it if you were to return peacefully to your homes until the rest of the settlers have had time to rejoin us. Kindly clear the streets and allow them to depart in peace.'

And she smiled like a death's-head, her thoughts hidden behind her china-blue eyes.

Slowly the struggling Kiflians disengaged, stunned. They backed away from the door, obviously expecting the settlers to pounce out at them at any moment.

But they did it. They cleared the streets. They went into

their houses and drew the shutters tighter, and the evening slanted an unnatural peace into Kifl on its golden rays.

And the screens faded, flattening back into two dimensions. No-one could see the knife Thebula held at Gundmila's side. But Irona knew it was there just the same and her face tightened into a fierce grin. Regen took one look at her expression and dropped the hand he had been about to hold out to her. She never even noticed.

Stiff-legged, she walked over to squat by Gaeta, wishing now that she had done something before about the half-severed arm. Gaeta was slipping in and out of consciousness, her breathing strained. Her lips were ashen.

Irona fumbled in her pockets for the olfactory just as Twiss said, 'Ro, see to the wounded, will you? I need a drink.'

She knew that he had already checked on how his task-force were. She guessed that he would be thinking ahead to how Arias Tang might try and trap them on their march back to base, for surely Tang must know where the olive-groves were.

But she still felt like a martyr as she cleaned and sprayed Gaeta's horrendous wounds as though there were any point to it and comforted the girl as best she could – because they both knew Gaeta was dying.

Gaeta's eyelids fluttered open again. The anaesthetic Irona had sprayed into her nose had already taken a hold of her. She tried to speak.

Irona bent lower.

'Why, Ro?' Gaeta mumbled. Her breath was tainted; Irona tried to close her mind to it.

'Why what, love?'

Gaeta's head sank a little and her breathing became harsh. Still she tried to peer up and Irona slipped her arm gently round her friend's shoulders. 'Why didn't you heal me before . . . before?'

Trumpets of guilt blared through Irona, yet she told the truth. 'I couldn't, love. If I had, we wouldn't have had time to get the message out to Thebula and relay it back to stop them killing the rest of us.'

Gaeta's head flopped sideways to deny it. 'No. It was just
– just that you were too scared to face them up close,' she
said, and the light of her spirit departed from the eyes that
slid away from Irona's.

Seven of them made it back through the eerily silent streets,
the sunlit croplands, to where the rest of the army waited.
Irona thought they would have followed Twiss into the
vacuum of space if he had asked it of them. The sun going
down over the sea threw their shadows long before them and
though they were weary, they felt like conquerors. And there
was no sign of Tang.

The whole western horizon lit like a backdrop of scarlet
silk as they came into the olive-grove. Irona, bringing up the
rear with her arm round Regenerator's waist, turned for a
moment to bid farewell to the fire-shimmered ocean, and
the dark silhouettes of the trees held up arms twisted by
their battle with the winds. It unnerved her, stirring things
in her subconscious that she would rather forget. Even the
salt breeze no longer lured her to the cool caress of the waters
that looked like a lake of blood.

'Well what time d'you call this then?' called Sticker
jovially.

Twiss beamed an answering grin. 'Teacher kept me in after
school.' He swayed a little but even though the army of seven
sat on logs or lay in the soft-tickling grass, he stood there,
thumbs hooked in his waistband. From his modest height he
looked down at the blue-clad figure of the Matriarch sitting
primly on a stone in front of the stolen supplies. She had
obviously made some attempt to tidy her hair but Irona
was obscurely pleased to see pale wisps blowing across the
woman's haughty face.

'Well?' Twiss asked and Gundmila stared at him. Even
though she was sitting and he towered above her, she still
managed to make it seem as though she were staring down
her nose at him.

She raised a questioning eyebrow and then smoothed her
forehead with one beringed hand.

Irona could see he was annoyed but trying not to show it.

'Well have you decided to let us have what's ours?' he asked, and there was a dangerous edge to his voice.

'I have been forced to concede a certain number of items to you, yes,' she said. 'But I have always been told that coercion cancels any contract. I don't believe your thugs will get much joy of your stupid little exhibition.'

Twiss goggled at her. Then at Thebula. Then at the still-bound figure of Lal, straining at his bonds, and finally back to Thebula. 'What you been doing to her?' he asked incredulously.

'I been telling her all what's been happening in Settlement. I told her we knew it was they what poisoned the water and she said as it weren't they at all.'

Twiss tossed his head in a quick snort of contempt. 'Well she would, wouldn't she? But we know it was they all right. Who else would it have been – you?'

Thebula laughed but Twiss obviously hadn't meant it to be a joke and the poor woman changed her mirth into an unconvincing cough.

'D'you tell her about how many died? About Granfer?'

''Course I did!' Now Thebula was on firmer ground and she stood to face Twiss more equally. 'And that we know about that there weather-controller and the rainstorms they keep from us so as nothing don't grow. And that we was entitled to some good land by the sea like they told us 'fore we set off from Earth. But she ain't having none of it, Twiss.'

'What do you mean, she ain't having none of it? It's the truth, ain't it? And we'll have what's ours over their dead bodies if we have to.' He squatted before the woman, a vicious gleam in his eye. 'Don't you see that? You've took and took from us and you ain't taking no more.'

Gundmila laughed. It was artificial, a silvery tinkling sound that had an edge like broken glass. It was calculated to irritate, and it did. But Twiss kept a rein on his temper – just.

'Ain't you learned nothing yet?' he asked her, and the force of his voice could have blown down a ninety-year-old oak. 'You hurt us and we'll hurt you twice as bad.'

The woman smiled at him in amused contempt. Above

her the branches of an olive-tree swayed and rustled in the sea-breeze. 'You? You couldn't begin to make a dent in us. Now we know what you're like, filthy barbarian savages, do you think we'd let you come within a dozen kilometers of us? You've got nothing, you deserve nothing, because you are nothing. If you'd co-operated with us in the first place, you wouldn't be in this stupid predicament now.'

'Yeah,' he roared, 'and if you hadn't robbed us and poisoned us and sent your slimy blood-sucking lizardoptera to us, you wouldn't be our hostage, Madam Matriarch!'

She laughed again. With a saccharine smile she asked, 'You can't really be so stupid that you think I'm Matriarch of Kifl, can you?' She shook her head pityingly. 'Dear dear. You can be exactly that stupid, can't you? No wonder you're not getting anywhere.'

Twiss glowered. Irona knew that part of it was his self-anger for starting this conversation in front of his men. Again the branches of the olive-tree danced sibilantly. 'And you ain't going nowhere 'til we get what we want. So you needn't bother to lie. All right then, smart-arse?'

She shrugged elegantly and fell to studying her silver-lacquered nails.

'You're the Matriarch all right. You're one of the Synod,' Twiss said in exasperation. 'And that there Lal, and old Less with the badger hairdo, he's another. So your folks ain't going to get you back 'less you give us our due.'

'Oh dear,' she said with maddening indifference, 'and I wasn't cut out for a life of savagery either. Oh well.'

Over by the tumbling stone wall, Lal was grunting behind his gag. His dark eyes shone ferally with the ruby reflection of the sun. Irona thought the whole thing was becoming surreal.

Then Twiss said, 'Well, we'll just have to show your precious citizens what it looks like when a councillor gets tortured. Wonder if Synod members have blue blood like they say?'

From above Tang said, 'I shouldn't believe all you hear, Twiss.'

Twiss rocked on his heels and almost fell over before

getting his balance. Head tossed back to stare up into the darkling branches, he said, 'Tang, you bastard! I wondered where you'd got to.' Behind him his followers got to their feet, groping in the long grass for their weapons.

Still invisible, Tang said, 'Wonder no longer. I've come to bring you a message, Twiss, and if you let us leave in peace you'll get what you want – or some of it, at any rate. I've told you, it's just not possible for you to have that coast-land all for yourselves, but we can work something out. I told them sending the lizardoptera was going too far.'

'The poisoning's what got to me.'

'Ah well, Twiss, there Gundmila's right. We never stooped to poison.'

'Yes you did.'

'This is turning into a playground debate, do you know that? But we didn't, for what it's worth. I may be a devious, manipulative bastard as you imply, but I never lie. Can I come down and talk to you or not? There's a caterpillar crawling down my neck.' So saying, he slithered limberly to the ground.

Twiss stiffened, obviously in two minds whether to kill him or not. But Tang strolled peacefully over to a wall that just happened to be backed by a solid tree. Irona's gaze wandered over to him then shifted uncomfortably away, knowing that Twiss was watching her. *Or is it him that's making me uncomfortable?* she asked herself.

But there was no more time for internal debate. Tang sat, elbows on wide-spread knees, his hands curled loosely. From the corner of her eye Ro watched him reach towards a thigh-pocket.

Twiss leaped towards him, knife at the ready—

Settlers froze in horror, tensed to throw weapons—

And Tang chuckled. 'It's only a computer-amp! No need to be alarmed.' He held the slim, pronged, gold-veined crystal aloft and it shone like a soap-bubble in the crimson of sunset.

Everyone else slumped back with relief. Except Regen, whose little pot-belly was bouncing up and down in silent mirth.

And Twiss, who stood over Tang, his very posture threatening. Anger flowed from him until Irona thought she could smell the ozone of a lightning-storm.

'What are you playing at?'

'With a dozen or so of my citizens dead and a fair number of yours down, I didn't actually think it was a game.' Irona felt Tang's own anger as a cold rapier to Twiss's volcanic aura.

Twiss wasn't phased. 'Well, let's have it then.'

Tang tossed him the computer-amp. Twiss threw it over to Irona, who leaped to catch it as it hurtled over her head out of reach, but it landed safely in Regen's lap and Irona pulled herself together, cursing Twiss inwardly for making a fool of her.

Twiss said, 'How do we know what's on here?' He stared intently at the slimmer, shorter man as though his hazel eyes could pierce Tang's mind to discover the truth.

'Well, you don't, do you? I grant you there could be anything on there, but I've told you before, I'm not a liar. There's an amplifier that will double the capacity of your system. And a power-line that won't threaten to burn your Eye out.'

Twiss never moved. Yet several of his army went rigid for a second before trying hard to act casual.

'Oh, yes, Twiss,' Tang went on. 'I don't know how many of our people noticed it but you couldn't have done all that you have without some sort of Eye. And without someone who's very good at using it. Gundmila and Lal and dear old Less may have thought you were just phenomenally lucky but you've got frighteningly good back-up. You're not going to try and tell me, Twiss, that you simply happened to come all the way over here to wreck the lab just when Lal's people were putting the finishing touches to the snake-rat plague?' He smiled, his slender drooping moustache bracketing his lips over his square teeth. 'No, I thought not. It was too much of a coincidence to be pure luck.'

'I ain't saying anything 'cept I ain't having no more of your poisons and your plagues and your endless deve thefts. We want what's ourn.'

Gundmila stood, her robes flowing hyacinthine in the warm glow of sunset. 'You have what you are entitled to, you barbarian!'

Arias Tang turned his head to look at her with eyes like shattered glass. He smiled charmingly and said in his gentle tone, 'Shut up, will you, Gundmila?'

And he turned back to Twiss, not bothering to keep a check on the maybe-Matriarch because he knew that she would obey. 'You see, Twiss, we've hit a bit of a snag. We've been here forty years and when the *Starwing* went back we didn't know.'

Twiss yawned ostentatiously and sat down further along the wall from Tang. 'D'you mind?' he said. 'Only we could do with a bit of rest so I'd like to get things settled before the colder weather. So stop fannying around and get to the point. What didn't you know?'

Tang raised an imaginary glass to toast the joke. 'You young people, you're always impatient, aren't you? And that's our problem, do you see? On Harith nobody dies – no, don't interrupt. I mean, nobody dies of old age. Accidental death, yes. But nobody who was half-way healthy when they got here has aged a day. And women can go on and on for decades until they run out of ova – it's not even a proper menopause, because with transplants they can still be having babies well into their nineties. And beyond, for all we know.'

Twiss shrugged. 'So what's that got to do with the price of fish?'

'Space. Population. Demographic pressure. Kids still grow up, you know.'

Regen shook his head, laughter puffing down his nose with the irony of it all.

Irona saw it too, and Twiss, but the rest of the sleepers hadn't caught on.

'Spell it out to them, why don't you?' Gundmila said tartly, '*Lebensraum.*'

Strapped into immobility by shock, Twiss looked at Irona. 'You tell 'em,' he mumbled through numbed lips.

'They don't grow old. They keep having babies and they

grow up and have babies of their own. There's too many of them to let us have the land that should have been ours. They're already living on it.'

Gundmila stared superciliously at Irona. 'And?'

Irona could have slapped her face. 'And they're outstripping their available power. That's why they needed ours. That's why they took just about everything we had.'

'They've got a whole planet to go at!'

'No, Twiss, not really. They've got the only habitable part.'

But that wasn't enough for Gundmila, who smiled nastily as she prepared to speak. Tang flicked a glance at Irona in which there was a spark of sympathy and said, 'You don't have to rub their noses in it, Gundmila.'

The etherial woman nodded to herself. 'Oh yes I do. D'you see them, Arias? Sleepers, every last one of 'em. Even that Twiss! Oh, he might look big and butch but all he is is a small-time poacher fired up by a crazy old man from before the Sky with tales of ships and a bit of smuggling that would make any sensible warden laugh like a drain.'

Once again the atmosphere crackled with Twiss's attempts to keep his anger under control. 'You leave my Granfer out of this. And why don't you use what power you have got to tame more of Harith?'

Gundmila tossed her head in a juvenile gesture of pride. 'Because it's one thing you barbarian sleepers grubbing away out in the wilds but my people don't want to go through that again. Putting up with broody lizardoptera eating everyone in sight, pushing the snake-rats beyond the mountains. We didn't come all the way out here just to turn into drones. And anyway, it's as your perceptive young lady said, we don't have enough power, or at least, not enough to squander on a pack of unknown sleepers. Whatever you threaten us with, there's nothing my people can do except sterilise you and keep you as workers.'

As she spoke Arias Tang had risen and gone over to Gundmila. Now he laid one hand on her arm. She tried to shake it off but the strength in his slender fingers was

more than it appeared to be. Without making an undig-
nified scene she could do nothing. 'Gundmila, Gundmila,
Gundmila,' Tang said almost flirtatiously in her ear. 'I must
introduce you to tact sometime. You appear to be a total
stranger to it.'

The Matriarch, if Matriarch she was, hissed, 'Tang, you
forget yourself. These vile deve sleepers have just killed
some of our citizens. They've robbed us of supplies and
they're threatening our children's very existence. I won't
have it, do you hear me?'

'All very edifying,' Twiss said. 'But what we come here
for is to get our due and to stop you killing our folk off like
they was bugs. There's no way you're going to sterilise us.
You going to give us our rightful land or what?'

Tang grasped Gundmila firmly by the elbows and moved
her aside. 'Twiss, you must see that you can't actually have
the land. We need it for ourselves. We didn't know when we
got here how it was going to be.

'It wasn't meant to be like this. I wanted to let the rains
come to you. I wanted you to have a home in the desert
so you'd leave us alone, but not her. Enough supplies to
look after your cataleptics – your deep-sleepers, I think you
called them.'

Bound and gagged, the wriggling figure of Lal thrashed in
renewed frenzy.

Twiss said, 'Don't give me that crap. You were the one
who took our stuff. You were the one who brought an army
to back yourself up when you tried to bribe us. And it don't
take no brains to realise you were the one who poisoned our
water.'

Arias Tang started to protest but Twiss rode roughshod
over him. 'I ain't talking to the hired help.' He faced the
Matriarch. 'You started this war. You give us what you want
or you die, Gundmila.'

'Kill me then.' The Matriarch stood straight and noble,
and the sky was a lake of blood behind her. 'Kill all of us.
And see what good it does you. Because we Kiflians will
fight you to the death.

'You're scum, do you know that? Dirty, anger-driven

misfits who would have been worm-dead at home. I would have offered you a place – not a vote in Synod, just the place sleeper-deves like you deserve – in our society. You could have had shelter, and food, all the things you had in the warrens, only you were too pig-headed to accept your station in life. But you threatened us. Your very existence here threatens us. And we won't take that lying down.' Gundmila smiled, and it was not good to see.

'You're too late with all your drama. The snake-rats are already seeded. We might not have had a chance yet to infect them, but the snake-rats will get you anyway.' She sneered. 'I give you two weeks before you come crawling to beg us to take you in. You haven't got a chance.'

22

AN X IN THE DESERT

From where he sat on the stone wall Twiss erupted in a flame of motion. He seized Gundmila's neck and dragged her head back. She would have screamed – if she could. A vein pulsed on his forehead and the tendons on his hands flexed with the urge to strangle her there and then. Or to break her neck and have done with it.

Shock paralysed the tableau for one eternal instant. Then Tang said mockingly, 'Oh, Gundmila, you are priceless. What you know about dealing with people could be summarised in a decimal point, couldn't it?'

Twiss said through vised teeth, 'Shut up. Shut up! Not one more deve word or she dies right now.'

Tang chuckled. 'You make my heart bleed, Twiss. You pierce me to the marrow.'

'Shut up, all right?'

But Tang wouldn't. Twiss's anger broke over the frozen group with all the force of a hurricane. His silent ferocity battered at Irona's psyche – and she knew she was only on the fringes of it. It washed through the olive-grove, setting the silver leaves a-tremble, reaching out to extinguish the red ball of the sun over the glimmering sea. Its force seemed to ice the stars in the mauve sky of dusk. And it tore at Twiss himself, clenching his fingers around Gundmila's slender neck. It would be so easy—

'Go on, Twiss,' Tang said. 'Save me a job.'

And Twiss flung her from him, sending her sprawling in the dewy grass. Gundmila curled in on herself like a foetus, not caring that her blue robe was hiked up about her buttocks, showing her legs like white worms in the darkness. Hands fluttering around the dark bruises at her throat, modesty was the last thing on her mind. Irona could feel her pain and her terror. And underneath it was her own fear of what Twiss was becoming.

A long silence drew out between the trees. The whisper of wind through the branches and the hush of night-creatures only served as a backdrop to Gundmila's sobs and the harsh sound of Twiss's breath. Nobody else dared make a sound.

'You don't know how lucky you are to be alive,' Twiss told the Matriarch hoarsely when he had himself a little more under control. 'You came so close to it. But you can stop it now – stop them spreading that snake-rat plague – and that's the only reason you ain't dead.'

He turned a face like a death-mask on Irona. 'Fix some sort of com-link with Kifl.'

Irona jumped a little as he spoke to her. Then she obeyed.

Tang almost said something, but one glance at Twiss's face stopped him. Though Twiss was unmoving, his eyes were hard and wild. He seemed just this side of madness; he was capable of anything.

And Irona dared not prompt Tang to let slip what he had been about to say. *I'm sure it was something we need to know. Just look at the way he's looking at Gundmila and Lal.*

She fought her trembling and finally said as the image of Less's face formed in her screen, 'OK, Twiss, you can reach their communications-sys—'

But he didn't even give her time to finish her sentence. Snatching the portable screen from her, he stared his hatred at the fourth member of Kifl's Synod. Less was ashen, a bruise purpling on his temple. Irona could see he was trembling.

Twiss didn't care. He said to Less and to the others they could see waiting behind him, 'Right, you bastard Kiflians, I know you can hear me so do what I say or you won't be doing anything else ever again. Ro.'

She swept the Eye over the trees to transmit the scene and knew from the Kiflians' shocked expressions that they had seen it.

Twiss speared the Kiflians on the screen with his berserk stare. 'Stop they snake-rats and your precious Synod might

live. Destroy your weather-Eye so we can have our rain. And
bring us a tractor out to the olive-grove now – or else.'

'And food and medicines,' Irona added. Twiss shot her a
glare but she turned away.

His threat might have sounded childish – but not the way
he said it. On the screen, Less drew breath to reply but Twiss
couldn't have cared less. Irona knew that the mood he was
in, he would just as soon kill their hostages as not.

Clicking the remote off, he flicked a glance at Irona and
received her nod to say the message had been transmitted
and received. 'Then we wait.'

Irona shivered as the dew soaked slowly through her clothes.
In the grove there was none of the earlier hilarity or sense
of triumph. The bright moment had turned sour. Regen was
dozing restlessly, breaking into odd sudden noises or words
that weren't quite words. Each of the group was isolated. Lal
was still bound and gagged, struggling fruitlessly to escape.
Tang and Gundmila merely had their elbows tied painfully
behind them, but nobody drew Twiss's wrath by speaking.

All around the camouflage plants writhed disturbingly, so
that it seemed the stone walls rippled and the trees were on
the point of walking. It did nothing to help Irona's unease
– and nor did an echo of lizardoptera song so elusive that
she wasn't sure she had really heard it or if it was inside her
mind. With Twiss so dangerous, though, now was not the
time to ask.

And time dilated.

The swift moons were swimming half-way across the sky
when a tractor hummed up the road. White light fanned out
from it, slicing through the darkness under the trees.

Even so, everyone started when a loud-speaker blared,
'Sleepers, we've done what you asked. Now give us back
the rest of our Synod.'

Twiss's shout was loud enough to shock his companions
in the grove. 'You can have 'em back one at a time.'

'But that wasn't the agreement!' Gundmila exclaimed.

Twiss skinned her with a vitriolic glance. 'There weren't
no agreement.'

'But—'

Tang said smoothly, 'Gundmila, darling' – the word was pregnant with contempt – 'what he said was they wouldn't give us back unless they got a tractor. They didn't say they would if they did.'

'That's not—'

Twiss laughed. 'Not fair? Robbing us weren't fair. Poisoning my Granfer and they others weren't fair.'

'But we—'

'You're still alive, ain't you? So shut up because that can be changed.'

She did.

One by one the Kiflians climbed down from the tractor and lay prone in the roadbed as Twiss ordered. A chunky, fair-haired man said, 'We brought you some food. Less sent it. He thought—'

Twiss looked down at him. Rage still quivered in his body as he spoke to the man. 'I don't care what he thought. You' – he nudged the figure with his toe and the man cringed away from him like a whipped dog – 'go and get a couple of they cases. I'll open one and you can eat whatever's in it. We ain't going to be poisoned twice.'

And the man worried down mouthfuls of pâté and rice and dried fruit. He didn't know what Twiss was talking about but he could feel the aggression and he wasn't going to risk – anything. Then he and his companions were wired inescapably to the vine-supports of the lowest terrace.

His adrenalin burning sleep from him, Twiss waited until dawn was a palette of greys behind the jagged mountains. He scarcely seemed to let the blond man out of his sight, yet there were no discernible symptoms.

Nothing that might have been more poison. The man was as nervous as a mouse when an owl stooped on it but that was only to be expected. His tied limbs shook – yet he had no fever, just a stomach that provoked in him visible embarrassment every time it rumbled.

Tang had long since gone to sleep. *Or*, Irona thought, *he's a very good actor*. She hadn't decided which one it was when Twiss clapped his hands.

'Up and at 'em. Don't look like they've poisoned us this time.' His voice was flat, the upper frequencies suppressed as Twiss tried to keep himself under control. The madness wasn't in him now but Irona could feel that it wasn't far away.

Yawning, stretching – and in Regen's case, humorously complaining – the settlers stumbled sleepily beneath the trees. There was a slight pause as they scattered to relieve themselves modestly.

Irona was one of the first back in the clearing. When Twiss saw she had returned, he yanked once again at the tight knots around Lal. 'He ain't going nowhere,' Twiss said under his breath. And he too ducked under the branches and was gone from sight.

A moist breeze from the sea trembled in the leaves and Irona could still hear that almost-lizardoptera song yet there were none of the wicked things flittering around. There were one or two similar-looking locust-lizards but they neither sang nor flew, as far as she could tell in the grey light of dawn. Instead they crawled peacefully along the twigs, chewing at the leaves, though that elusive song still came from somewhere, ringing inside her head. But when she dared to have a closer look, they didn't even seem to have proper wings. She relaxed – a little.

'You and you' – Twiss's command broke in on her concentration – 'load that Lal feller and Gundmila into the machine. Go on, go on, don't take all day about it! Irona, keep 'em up to the mark.'

Shoving his sleepy followers along, Twiss bundled everyone towards the tractor, staying behind himself to guard the prisoners on the terraces. Or to free them, Irona didn't know. She couldn't hear what he said to the captives in the vineyard, nor see quite what he was doing with the wires that strung them helpless to the flowering vines.

Anyway, that was none of her business. As ordered, she supervised the man and woman hauling Lal's bound figure up the vehicle's side. His black suit bulged between the tight wires that criss-crossed him. He struggled but with his legs bound together and his arms strapped to his sides there wasn't a lot he could do except make life awkward for the people carrying him.

He should have thought of that. Wriggling as they dragged his body through the hatch, his knee trapped the man's fingers. The man snatched his hands away and the woman couldn't hold the weight on her own. Lal fell heavily into the dark interior.

'Serve you right,' the man said, blowing on his stinging hands.

Irona slid down into the roomy cockpit. It was the first time for months that she had been inside a powered vehicle: the smell of ozone and mineral oil lunged out of the dimness to enfold her. For just a moment it was like being back on the ship – or worse, in Camelford. Irona couldn't think what memory it was that tugged at her but whatever it was, she didn't want to follow it.

Instead she bent and lugged Lal to one side. She could hear him trying to curse around his gag; the words weren't clear but the meaning was. Then she helped Regen grope his way to a seat at the back. She knew Twiss would want to be at the front and the way he was at the moment, she didn't want to be anywhere near him. She knew that whatever she did would be wrong.

Gundmila came next, stepping delicately, holding her long blue skirts around her so that not a glimpse of white ankle gleamed.

'Ain't no point in that, is there?' Regen chuckled weakly at his own humour. 'We already seen everything she's got.'

Irona nodded slightly at her friend. Beside the dainty Gundmila with her perfumed, flower-stranded hair, she felt huge and awkward, like a shire horse beside a circus pony. Knowing she was being catty, she tried to hide her smile, but Regen's caustic remark had made her feel better.

But where was Twiss? Irona couldn't think what could be keeping him. Unless he had had another call of nature? Her modesty made her turn away from the thought in embarrassment. If that was it, though, what were all those strange clangs and rattlings from the base of the tractor? But she didn't want him to think that she was spying on him so she tried to possess herself in patience. It didn't stop her worrying, though.

Then she saw Twiss climbing up the side of the vehicle. He swung down through the opening. Naturally he scorned the steps and dropped lightly to his feet, settling himself at the controls. As he leant back in the driver's seat, the control-panel lit up, faint blue lights glowing around the circular keys. They underlit the blond spiky growth on his chin until it looked like lightning-struck stubble in a field.

'Where's Tang?' someone asked.

The weird blue light making him seem like some warlock from a historical dramadisc, Twiss answered, 'Don't you worry about him. He's all right,' and he grinned.

It worried Irona all the more.

For long moments Twiss sat running his hands over the controls, puzzling them out. Just as Irona stood to go and help him, he shouted 'Move!' and the vehicle rocked forward. She almost fell.

'Are they following us?' she asked, ducking and peering back as though she had meant to all along. For some reason she didn't want anyone thinking badly of Twiss for being so inconsiderate. *Besides*, she told herself, *it's a legitimate question. We've killed some of the Kiflians, invaded their space, hijacked their leaders. If it had been me, I would have followed us*.

But Twiss said with only the most cursory glance in the rear-view scanners, 'Nah. We got the only brains right here. There won't be nobody coming after us. You wait and see.' And she could see by the moonstone curve of his cheek that he was smiling again.

Soon the tractor nosed its way along the dusty roadway and out of the olive-groves. All around now Irona could sense the growing light: as the vehicle edged southeast around the mountains the new sun sprang out at her. Spiked on a pine in the notch between two peaks, it looked like the symbol for some ancient religion. And the sky was as blue as a matriarch's robe.

Ducking in and out of shadowy vales, the road abandoned the coast. Irona kept turning round to gaze at the sea, as though she could hold it inside her if she could only look long enough. But the tractor whined higher into the rain-soaked foothills, and soon the copses of rhododendrons and native growth hid all sight of it.

Until, at the very crest of the pass, a vast sheet of glittering blue spread out behind her. Fringed with the roofs of the trees, misted with the early morning light, it was a magic sight that lifted her soul.

I'll see you again. I'll be back, she vowed to it. *And I promise for Gaeta's sake that the next time, it won't just be for a visit. It'll be ours as much as the Kiflians'.*

Mid-morning baked the air into wavering liquid. They had been travelling for hours now, dust pluming from the high balloon-tyres as they descended into the dry landscape behind the mountains. Out in the desert, Irona could understand why the tractor seemed to have no windows. The whole of the superstructure was a one-way window, coated on the outside with a turquoise paint that reflected back most of the heat. All the same, with so many people breathing inside it, it was stuffy. If they left the hatch open, the heat was even worse, and grit blew in to turn their clothing into sandpaper.

The only variation in the monotonous landscape of Rainshadow Valley was the change in the colour of the rocks, and with the tractor-skin fully polarised that wasn't much. Grey to brown to yellow-brown to ochre, and back again. She sighed.

'Beats walking, though, don't it?' Regen said. Blood was oozing down his neck.

She nodded, smiled, too tired to talk, too tired to sleep.

And with Twiss still riding the wave of his adrenalin-surge, that was about the full extent of the conversation inside the shadowed tractor until suddenly the vehicle lurched to a halt.

'What – what's the matter?' someone asked. 'Have we broken down?'

Twiss eased his shoulders until a muscle cracked, then swivelled round. 'We ain't, no.' He grinned. 'But I know someone as is going to.'

Something clenched inside Irona, knowing that his brittle humour boded no good for someone. But she didn't know who was going to suffer until Twiss said too brightly, 'Well, come on then! Who's going to give us a hand?' He nodded at her. 'You'll do, Ro.'

Twiss climbed out into the desert. With a backward glance at Regen for reassurance that the little man couldn't give, Irona followed him up the steps.

She saw Twiss take a few stiff paces around the tractor. She thought it was just to stretch his legs until he turned round and nodded at something that she couldn't see from the top of the vehicle. Coming to join him, she looked at what held his attention.

Something bulging, something angular. Part of it seemed to be branches that were snagged on odd projections on the tractor's nose.

What is it? she wondered, but she wouldn't ask Twiss because he obviously wanted her to find out for herself.

A figure – she couldn't quite make out what. She squinted, went closer, squatted to peer at the thing – then drew back, not wanting to believe her eyes.

Underneath opaque layers of dust the figure seemed a mockery of something not quite human. But it couldn't be, surely not. Not flattened against the mud-caked chassis like a bent X, the knees hanging under the metal of the subframe, feet angled out towards the hubs of the axle, feathered with dried grass and wilting lense-plants.

Then the ball of dessicated mud moved between the tree-limbs that had to be arms. Somewhere in the thickness an eyelid fluttered and opened to a slit. It couldn't widen any further than that because of the clods of soil clinging above it.

It spoke. A sound like the earth itself, gravelly, hoarse. It said, 'Hi, Irona. Don't ever travel like this if you can help it. It's a real pain in the ass.' He gave what might under other circumstances have been a dry laugh.

'Tang!' she exclaimed.

And Twiss strolled casually over and slapped the ball of mud several times. Hard, ringing slaps that sent the head clanging against the front of the tractor. 'Have to get the muck off of you somehow,' Twiss said by way of an apology that wasn't. 'Anyway, Tang, this is where you get off. You reckoned we could live out here – and we can. Now see how you like it.'

Twiss tried to unravel the wires holding Tang's arms and legs to the frame but so thick with filth were they that he couldn't move them. Irona climbed back aboard the tractor, leaving Twiss tutting, tossing his head a little with impatience and pulling one corner of his mouth down. 'Wonder if they got any wire-cutters on this thing?' he muttered, giving up in disgust.

Irona jumped down from the tractor with some cutters, and all but shoved Twiss aside. He shrugged, indifferent now he'd taken his revenge, and sauntered away.

Chewing away at the wires, Irona talked to the mummified figure. 'I didn't know' – she stopped, not knowing what to call him – 'I didn't know,' and the endless wind carried her repetition off into the desert.

The remnants of Arias Tang gathered his shoulders in an attempt at a shrug. Now that the tractor had stopped moving, his feet trailed downwards, and something dark oozed slowly from the wires round his dustclumped ankles. He muttered something and she had to duck her head to hear: 'What the hell.'

Once she would have punished him for such a breach of modesty. Once she had been a warden. She shook her head slowly from side to side and carried on chewing through the encrusted bonds with a pair of pliers. Twiss wandered casually back to chat merrily to his victim as though they were at some polite social gathering back on Earth. 'You really shouldn't mess with me, you know, Tang. Under other circumstances I could have liked you.'

One of Tang's arms came loose and he flopped forward, his head dangling above the desert. 'As it is, though, Tang, you touch my Granfer – or any of 'em, come to that – and you touch me. And I ain't having it.'

Another bond broke with a twang and the Kiflian leader collapsed onto his face, unable even to put a hand out to save his head from the rocky sand. His feet were caught up behind him now, his back arched in a position of fiendish torture.

Irona shifted a little to squat closer under the high-arching tyres and began to saw roughly through the bird's-nest of wires around one of Tang's legs. 'So I'll leave you a couple of mouthfuls of water or Ro'll be on at me all the way back, and then you can have a nice little stroll. Watch out for they lizard-locusts, though, or you'll have a longer sleep than you probably need. Mind, looking at you, I reckon you could sleep for about a century anyway.'

'Stop it, Twiss! Haven't you done enough?' Irona said, pushing him aside to finish the job.

The last strand of wire parted; Tang's leg fell and Irona could hear the solid thud of his shin-bone against some boulder half-hidden in the sand. Irona knew that if she could have seen any expression on Tang's face it would have been one of murderous hatred. She could feel the fierce flame of his anger but Twiss went on oblivious.

'So you tell they friends of yours on Synod that from now on you're going to leave us alone. No more screwing up our weather. No more thieving and poisoning. If we want some of that nice coastal land once we've got this harvest in, we'll have it. There's room enough for all of us if your lot stop being greedy, so we'll give you a month or two to sort it. Otherwise, next year in Kifl it won't be you that's in charge. Just remember that, Tang. It'll give you something to think about on your nice little ramble home.'

And Twiss dropped a cannister of water somewhere near one of Tang's earth-encysted hands. Not actually in reach, but at least near.

Irona scrambled across to support Tang's head as he drank. Glaring up into her lover's hard expression, she said, 'We're not going until he's OK.'

'Wrong again, Irona. He's got to take my message back so they know we ain't kidding. But I'll give you five minutes if it makes you feel any better.' And he found himself a rock to sit on.

*   *   *

Irona worked quickly to shell the mud from Tang's face and limbs. Her pocket olfactory gave him pain-killers and stimulants. Then she glanced at Twiss, feeling that the core of his anger had burnt itself out.

He jerked his head at Irona and the wild gleam had gone from his eyes to be replaced by a look of infinite fatigue. 'Come on, Ro,' he said and there was a depth of sorrow in his tone, 'take me home.'

She shinnied up the steps, skirts modestly about her legs. Twiss hauled himself up behind her. Just before he dropped the hatch shut, she heard him say, 'Remember, Tang. Next year in Kifl.'

23

THE SEA

Thebula was talking to the tractor now, piloting it. Ice-bright stars hung in the east above Rainshadow Valley, though behind the tractor Irona could see a strange sight: the rimfire of sunset over the Moon Mountains – with no flicker of lightning to bleed the rain from the valley itself.

Twiss had seen it too. He reached an arm around Irona's shoulders and hugged her and she didn't know how to react. Fear of what Twiss might be this time over-rode a sweet pang of lust and she froze. Before she could decide what to do, Twiss took his arm back in what might have been a spontaneous gesture and Irona was left wondering whether or not he still wanted her as he had before the poison robbed him of balance – or whether she just hoped he did. Side by side, they separately looked out at the landscape.

He swivelled his head, not accepting the sight of Gundmila and Lal. As his face moved the last of the sunglow laid a wash of warmth over his pallor. Twiss hadn't slept in at least forty-eight hours and Irona was no better off. 'See that, Ro?' he said. 'No lightning. It looks like they First Wavers are going to honour their agreement and leave us in peace. Who knows? Without their deve storms every night we might even get some rain in the Valley when we need it.'

What agreement? she wondered, and knew that Gundmila must be thinking the same thing. In that moment of complicity neither of the women said a word and the amethyst dusk stole out to hide their secret. Nobody mentioned Gaeta.

Here and there now she could recognise a cliff, a knife-edged gully.

'See that?' Thebula yelled excitedly. Everyone craned to drink in the sight. 'That there's our first canal!'

'And there's our second one. I dug that bit with Sinofer.'

'Look! Isn't that our wheatfield?'

'Remember ploughing that bit, Tariq? You drove me crazy!'

Laughter soaked through the tired ones in the vehicle. And the expectation of joy lent the weary army strength as Thebula piloted the tractor round the last of the hills and in its sickling beam Settlement Hill swelled like a mother's breast, waiting to nurture her travellers.

But their happiness was short-lived. As they drew closer frantic running figures blocked the rosy lights of home.

'Hey!' yelled Tariq. 'What's going on?'

'Synod!' breathed Twiss, and it wasn't so much a blasphemy as a dread.

Gundmila smiled. She wiped the expression from her face to one of blandness, but not before Irona saw.

Twiss had planned to ride into Settlement in glory, backlit by the red skies of sundown. Irona knew; he had told her as she drifted along through the heat of afternoon, but she was half asleep and it hadn't really registered.

But now night had fallen and Harith was darkly hostile.

Twiss had gone to shoulder his way to the front of the rolling tractor, where everyone else was jostling for a clearer view of the chaos inside Settlement. Peeling the sleeping Regen off her shoulder, Irona eeled through after him and tugged at the collar of his shirt. For a few seconds he ignored her, still cursing, then he turned his head the slightest fraction to ask impatiently, 'What is it?'

'Twiss, it's dark. The gates'll be shut – they don't know it's us. They can't see inside the tractor, can they?'

He smacked the side of his own head. ''Course they can't! You're right, Ro. I'm so shattered I ain't thinking straight. Stop here, Thebula.'

The tractor sank to a halt with a sigh of pneumatic brakes.

'It sounds tireder than we are,' Irona said to nobody in particular.

'I'll go,' Twiss said firmly. 'You stay here.' And he climbed out, his every movement stiff with the aches of fatigue.

Irona didn't bother to contradict him. She merely said to

everyone else, 'Keep an eye on Gundmila for us, will you? We may need her yet.' Then she went to stand by Twiss's side at a discreet distance from the barred mouth of the tunnel, holding herself tall as together they faced the people they had saved. An arrow wobbled towards them, fell short.

Twiss called, 'It's us, folks. We're back. There weren't no thunderstorm over Moon Mountains, did you notice that? We got supplies, and an antidote, and a tractor. You going to keep us out here all night or what?'

'Where's the Eye then?' a nervous voice called from inside the perimeter. It was Tebrina by the sound of it, with Sticker hushing her straight away.

'You want the Eye, Tebrina?' Ro said, hauling her keypad from her pocket. 'How's that then?' She sent the iridescent globe twirling and dancing over the speakers and laughed as Sticker – it had to be Sticker – almost fell flat on his face.

'How d'you know it's really they?' Sticker whispered loudly to someone else inside the perimeter. 'Keep your mouth shut or you might give something away.'

Tebrina gave him a hearty swipe and said in good humour, 'Keep yourn shut or I'll get Ro to send that there Eye straight into it. There'd be enough room left over for a couple of dugouts at that.' Laughing at her own joke, she shouted loudly enough for the whole settlement to hear, 'Stand down! It's our own come back.'

And Sticker said sulkily, 'I were just going to say that.'

'I wish you had of done, then. Raising my voice has about torn the linings out of my throat.'

The stocky woman with the grey streaks in her hair got a couple of lads to help her haul aside the barrier. She could hardly wait to enfold Irona in a giant hug that almost swept the younger woman in a circle. 'Why didn't you send the Eye over sooner, you moron?'

Irona laughed breathlessly. 'Get off me, Teb. You're squashing me,' but she didn't let go either. Practically wrestling, the two women giggled like children with all the euphoria of relief.

And Twiss, robbed of his moment of triumph, ordered the

plastic barriers to be shifted even further from the tunnel so the tractor could be driven inside.

Irona said, 'Sorry, Teb, I should have thought. But I told you as soon as we cleared Moon Mountains that no-one was following us.'

'And here's us been watching that there tractor all afternoon wondering if it were you or some deve decoy.'

'Deve decoy? Why, Tebrina, when did you ever learn to swear?'

'When a blue tractor comes towards us out of Kifl, that's when. They ain't brought us a lot of luck so far, have they?'

Suddenly the laughter was gone. The two women had to move swiftly aside as Thebula drove the vehicle recklessly through the tunnel.

'I'm sorry, Tebrina.' Irona linked her arm through her friend's and they walked into Settlement. 'I know what you mean, though, because I knew they weren't going to come after us but I still spent all afternoon with the Eye watching our back trail.' She shrugged. 'I should have asked before. How's Sinofer?'

'The same only thinner.' Her words hid a wealth of despair.

Irona patted her arm. 'Well, we'll see how the antidote is, OK? Less said it would take a night or so to work and I guess someone's unpacking it right now.'

She glanced round suddenly in puzzlement. There were jubilating crowds all about them in the rows, and bright-lit squares showed open windows in homes full of power. Only here and there could she see the defensive nets that everyone had had when Twiss's army went away. 'Teb, where's the lizardoptera?'

Tebrina looked round herself, as though surprised not to see any of the murderous locusts flittering between the rows. 'Don't know and that's a fact. We never had no luck hunting them; however many we killed there were always thousands more. Then yesterday morning someone said where did they go, and I couldn't tell you. There's still a few round come daylight, but not hardly any compared to how it was before.

And they don't hang round the dugouts no more waiting to
see who they can bite. They're just about all of 'em tame
as a kitten.' She shook her grey hair and pulled a couple
of curls down over her forehead coquettishly. 'Maybe that
Twiss of yourn's done everything he said.'

'Next year in Kifl?' Irona smiled and shook her head, but
whether in disbelief or wonderment she didn't know herself,
and Tebrina had no idea what she was talking about. 'Gaeta
would have liked that. She's dead, Teb, and I couldn't save
her. I didn't save her. And I killed someone too . . .' She
thought of the rainbow web of acid and tried not to. 'And
wait 'til you hear what Twiss did to Tang.'

She stopped and grabbed her friend's other hand, turning
her to look into her face. 'I tell you, Teb, if they'd done to us
what we've done to them, I wouldn't rest 'til I'd got it sorted.
I couldn't say this to Twiss because he's obsessed, but I'm
a lot more worried now than I was when we started. And
those Kiflians aren't going to rest either. Even if they had
land for us, they wouldn't give it us. Wait 'til I tell you. Now
it's not just who wants what. It's how to make the other one
pay for blood.'

Irona looked round the dugout that had come to be home
– not sanctuary like her computer-shed was, but at least a
place she could call home – and smiled. The power-pack
shed a warm glow over her friends and a night-scented
breeze played through the safety of the open window; not
a lizard was anywhere in sight. Boxed neatly together by the
water-bucket were the cannisters that had contained luxury
foods, and the biggest luxury of all was that she hadn't had
to cook because the cans had heated the soya-steaks and the
vegetables when their seals were broken. Kifl still had a lot
of technology that Irona wanted . . .

Twiss glanced across the cosy dugout. Granfer was tucked
up in Jai's Hospital, right next to Regenerator, and Marjine
had Gundmila safely locked up. A group of young men were
taking care of Lal, or rather mocking him when Irona had last
seen them, but Spinon, the biggest of the lads, wouldn't let
any real harm come to their hostage. Jai and Tebrina were

having a rest from their labours with the deep-sleepers who had all been given the antidote, so they and Sticker had joined Irona and Twiss in their celebratory feast.

Irona spooned up the last of the rich plum-juice and let its sweetness trickle slowly down her throat; a simple pleasure but one she had not thought to enjoy again for many years. And despite their tiredness, the chance to relax after the stress of the last eight days had brought a mellow companionship into every one of the group. Slow laughter drifted like smoke through the room. Irona knew that Regen would have enjoyed it had he been there, but at least he was safe and well-fed in Jai's Hospital. He had made her grin with his subtle irony when she had been to see him settled before coming back here for the night.

Irona wondered how the Kiflians were remembering their dead. But for now the juice was good, soaking comfort into her.

At last Tebrina put down her own pudding-dish, licking her fingers with a sigh of content. She winked at Irona and lay back on one elbow, looking as if she had settled in for the night. She finally gave in to Twiss's heavy hints but not before she had driven him wild by pretending not to notice how eager he was to be rid of her. And all the time she was winking at Irona and Sticker, who could hardly keep a straight face, and Jai, who was horrified.

'Well, I don't know about you, Jai,' Tebrina said at last, 'but I'm going to see how my old man is. I'm sorry, Twiss, but I really mustn't let you keep me any longer.'

He gulped in astonishment and Tebrina whisked out of the door, patting one of her grey-tinged locks.

Jai called after her, 'Wait for me,' and Sticker made an excuse moments later.

Twiss and Irona were the only ones there. Twiss said slowly, 'I don't reckon old Sticker's really going to dig a latrine at this time of night, do you?'

Irona felt her chest move in a silent chuckle. 'No, not really. He's just trying to get out of doing the clearing up,' she said drily.

Twiss didn't get it at all. 'Ro, how could you miss it? He's into Jai.'

She rolled her eyes skywards, smiling and shaking her head as she told him with gentle mockery, 'Tell me about it.'

He lay back on one elbow, enjoying the freshness of the air and the red warmth of the power-pack. As she spoke, he hitched himself round a little so that his just-washed hair brushed her forehead.

'You were good out there, you know, Irona. I mean that. You and Regen, you saved us. And you fought like an Arm.'

She was silent. The clean masculine smell of him was reaching down inside her, doing things to her feelings that she could scarcely comprehend. And she wanted to trust his words that might make her feel good about herself.

'We couldn't have done it without you, you know, Irona.' *(He's repeating himself!* she thought. *Maybe he feels awkward too?)* But Twiss was saying, 'I couldn't have done it. I need you, Ro. I do. I need you.' And his fingers brushed over the hair beside her ear so tenderly that she could have wept.

'I know you've seen things, seen me do things you never wanted to, but it's still me, Ro.'

No words came to her mind; there was so much that she wanted to say but she dared not trust anyone enough to let him in. If she trusted him to like her he might cut her off again and she would fall into a pit of infinite nothingness so deep that she would never come out again. He had no reason to, but he mistrusted her, and in that moment she was aware that she mistrusted him too and regret like a river of wine flowed around her.

And in the microseconds it took for her to perceive this infinity of doubt, he had no idea what was going on inside her head for he stroked her hair, her cheek, more gently than a mother could have done and he said, 'Don't be afraid, Ro. You don't have to be afraid. This is still the same me that danced with you and took you out into the dunes. I said I'd keep you safe and I have.'

She sat on the ground, motionless, her hands laced around one knee, paralysed. She could feel the pulse throbbing through her interlaced knuckles. But each time she breathed she pulled his essence deeper inside her and a panicky confusion strobed inside her mind.

Yet all the time his fingers were caressing her and his voice was soothing, a strand of calm that wove a steady path through the tumult surging through her. And her empathy picked up on his sincerity just as her senses absorbed his pheromones. She could feel a sweet tension in her breasts and somewhere inside she was about ten years old: too old to want to hold her father's hand when she crossed a busy row but too young not to want to sit on someone's lap and be cuddled.

'And you felt it too, Ro,' he went on, 'that savagery. I saw your face. I saw what you did, how you hated. It's not just me. It's still inside you too, isn't it?'

She said nothing.

'Isn't it?' he prompted softly.

A slow tear rolled from her eyelid. She brushed it away as casually as she could with the back of her hand and would have died rather than humiliate herself by crying but another tear leaked out and she couldn't stop it.

Twiss didn't even notice. 'Ro, you fought to save us. To save Gaeta. To make a better life for Fessbar and all they other kids. To bring back any sort of a life to Sinofer and Tebrina. And you done it as bravely as any of us. Don't hate yourself for being human. Or me. Because I need you, Ro. And tonight I need you more than ever.'

It was all she could take. This time her body betrayed her by jerking into a sob. He brushed the silent tears from her cheek and the touch of his knuckle was unbelievably gentle. 'Don't cry, Ro. I can't bear it.'

She curled into his embrace and the warm muskiness of his shoulder pillowed her with a love she recognised from her years on the watch. How many times had she seen this, felt this – and known it was not for her but for some sleeper on whom her probe intruded? It had never been for her.

Only now it was. If she could believe it. His physical need was sharp as lemon over the oboe notes of his own poignant need for comfort.

And as she wept his arms encircled her. She felt his triumph but it was blended with so many other emotions that her tears blurred her inner vision and she gave in to the currents of feelings that swept both of them far out to the sea she had dreamed of for so long.

And far away, twenty light-years away, in her refuge inside the wall of Camelford Watchtower, Bernardina watched her ansible, waiting for Gundmila to call.

But she didn't.

Then just watching for Gundmila's life-signs to be alone in the Synod room at the top of Kifl's tower.

But they weren't.

And finally looking for any sign of her at all.

24

LAL'S TEACHER

Harith turned and beyond Settlement Knoll onions spiked shafts of emerald between ranks of feather-topped carrots. Choke-cherries blossomed and the adapted wheat stroked the fields like a paint-brush with each breath of wind, now cream, now gold, now green. Soya and edible lupins brought colour to the scrubland that had never known any.

And Irona had never been so happy. In the blue-hazed mornings she would stroll through the burgeoning fields to talk to Sinofer, whole and wake now, riding the tractor with him as he told it to earth up potatoes or plough new land for quick-growing summer-crops. How she smiled to see the way he loved his tractor!

Sometimes she would walk up with Sinofer's son, Fessbar, his pudgy hand folded round one of her fingers, and she would secretly imagine he was her child. Hers and Twiss's. But she would never say that to anyone, not even Twiss, not even Fessbar who prattled about the pretty lizards that sometimes flittered warbling overhead, their locust-wings transparent and glistening in the earth-scented air, and who were no threat any more. They had mated and laid their spawn in the mountains; they no longer needed blood. True, they sometimes came to nibble at the tassels of maize or the tiny sprouting apple-trees only six leaves high, but Irona and Regen had programmed the Eye. Now that they had time to think rather than merely react, it had been simple to get the Eye to emit an ultrasonic deterrent so the lizardoptera stayed more and more on the green-balls, the lenses and the camouflage-plants outside Settlement. Without Kiflian evils, the land seemed good and Irona was happier than she had ever been before.

Then, Fessbar a cuddlesome weight in her arms, she would

walk back to organise, to plan, to be the foundations on which Twiss built Settlement. With Fessbar's curly head snuggled deliciously against her neck, she would see the contented, busy settlers going about the work they had travelled space for. Maybe this wasn't Kifl, but for now it was enough. The power, and the powered tractor, gave more leisure for all. No more digging canals by hand; they even, sometimes, had a little rain.

In the dazzle of noon, when the sun pressed the air to a weighted shimmer so hot it was almost solid, the settlers had taken to having a siesta. Irona would check that Tebrina was having no trouble from Gundmila, not so imposing now without her mock-matriarchal robes. But Gundmila was passive, flirtatious with any man who came her way, and no longer demanding angrily every morning, 'When can I go home?' Twiss rather hoped that Gundmila would fall in love with one of his people and settle here.

'I don't think it's a very good idea,' Irona would say to him when she got back from her rounds. She slipped onto the washed covers in their dugout, for now Jai and Sticker lived in a new room beside the Hospital and Jai no longer wept in corners. And Regen lived everywhere and nowhere. This was their place now, hers and Twiss's. Sleepy with the heat of noon, she threw her dress aside and lay beside him.

Twiss's arm stroked her flank and she felt safe. Wanted. And immodesty was not something that crossed her mind now their shyness had gone. His naked skin clung warm and damp to hers as though the glue between them were not perspiration but something so deep that it wanted to bind them together into one body.

He would ask, 'Why not? Don't tell me you're jealous of her?'

Irona would shake her head and he would laugh and stroke her head because otherwise her hair tickled his nose. 'No, I just think she's up to something, that's all.'

'What?'

But she couldn't say.

'Tang got back, you know, Twiss. Regen and I talked to him last night, and Less. Whatever she is, Gundmila makes

a good hostage. They said they're working on the land thing.
Next year in Kifl—'

'Never mind that, Irona. Come here . . .'

In the cool of the evening the children watched the subliminal
teacher Twiss had got in exchange for Lal. Sometimes it was
maths, or physics, or civic history that explained how the
Admins had arisen to replace the old warring governments
of Earth, but it was fun: cartoons or true-disks that punched
knowledge straight into their brains. Quite often the adults
gathered too on Twiss's Knoll, safe in the zephyrs of the
gloaming because Twiss and Ro and Regen kept them safe,
and Ro's Eye hung above them, keeping watch. They even
wheeled out Granfer to watch the shows because it was the
only pre-packaged entertainment they had, but whether any
of it got through to the brain inside Granfer's stringy husk,
nobody knew.

This time, though, it was the geography of Harith. Less's
face had appeared on the end of yesterday's teaching to tell
them about 'this special programme we've made to help
our Synod brothers and sisters in Settlement. And it's a
doozie. You'll love it: all the things about Harith they
never told you about on Earth. The kids'll love it.' Less's
badger-brows contorted as he tried to wink. 'There's even
something for the adults, too. And just wait 'til you hear
the song!'

Twiss and Irona finished their first fresh salad since they
had left Camelford. Regen had programmed the computer
earlier in the day, a lot happier now that his wound had
healed and he could get around a little more easily. He
liked helping her out and he certainly eased her burden.
For tonight's show, Regen had told her, all Irona had to do
was show up.

As the sun kissed the Moon Mountains in a passion of ruby
and gold, Twiss linked arms with her and stepped outside the
dugout. They didn't even bother to shut the door; there was
nothing to keep out.

'Isn't it great?' he said, seeing the thunderheads gilt-edged
over the shadowy desert of the interior. 'Not a single

lightning-storm on the peaks since I had that little word in Less's ear. With a bit of luck we might even get some more rain.' He took a step and Irona didn't. 'Come on, Ro,' he laughed. 'Catch up.'

She looked up into his smiling face and grinned back, pretending to walk on his toe.

'All right, all right, I give in. But aren't you dying to see the show?'

She was. But the anticipation was good too.

Word of mouth had obviously got round about the special show. Almost everybody had turned out to watch and they walked through the rows in a festival atmosphere. Everyobdy they met spoke to them.

'Evenin', Twiss. Evenin', Irona.'

'Hi, Irona. I don't like to ask but do you think you could get us some more soap-powder? There ain't hardly none left.'

'Well there isn't any left!' Irona smiled pleasantly, apologising for being so unhelpful, so un-citizenlike, even though it was hardly her fault. 'I'm glad you mentioned it, though, Heppie, because I'll have to see what sort of substitute we can come up with. I'll ask the computer tomorrow. I'm sure there must be something.'

'Thanks, Irona. Eriss said you couldn't do nothing but I said to her, I said, "Don't you go round being negative 'bout Irona. She understands about things like that being important. She'll sort it, never fear."'

And Irona smiled to hide her embarrassment. But it was the same every evening when they walked the cooling rows before the night's meeting.

'Hey, Twiss, my power-pack's gone wrong again.'

'D'you reckon this here teaching's going to be as good as they say it is tonight?'

The questions were simple, trusting, prompted by an innocent faith that their leaders would look after them no matter what: parents of the world.

It was beginning to get on their nerves but they could scarcely say that to the childlike sleepers. Instead Irona and Twiss smiled, and resolved disputes for a people only just beginning to think for themselves, smiled until their cheeks ached.

And on the crest of the Knoll with the Eye casting Twiss into silvery light against the desert darkness, he would gather all the day's information and give out tasks for the morrow.

Twiss signed, and Irona faded down the aura so he could come and sit beside her out of everyone's focus for once. 'Is Regen here?'

She felt the brush of Twiss's arm against hers and it sent a magic communication between them. 'No, I haven't seen him since just after breakfast.'

Behind, the crowd was beginning to hush into expectation. You would never have known there were three hundred people facing the Knoll, so silently were they waiting.

'You sure he's done the sublims, Ro?' Twiss whispered.

'Yes. He promised. And he never breaks a promise. Ssh! It's starting.'

The Kiflian teaching machine started, its logo whirling against notes of ineffable sweetness to capture everyone's attention. No-one else knew that today Regen and the computer had taken out all the Kiflians' behavioural sublims like she always had, first slowing them down to a speed where consciousness could censor their impact. As long as Kifl kept sending sublims, Twiss said – when she had explained to him what they were – then Settlement was safe from the Kiflians.

The moons flew like silken-winged moths across the damascene sky. Out in the Interior a shooting-star fell sparkling and from the endless unknown lands tumbled a playful breeze. Somewhere harmless lizardoptera sang bell-like and night-creatures hummed a counterpart.

Then the friendly face of Less claimed Irona's attention. Against a background of olfacts that most of the audience were too far away to perceive, Less leaned familiarly on a balcony in an opulent wave-home and looked lovingly at the flower-starred lushness of Kifl, its beach of warm sand, its glittering sea with children splashing and rowing in the white-capped breakers. The children laughed and

Less smiled – Irona winced – and he spoke avuncularly.
You couldn't see the weakness in his face, just the warm
brown eyes, the laughter-lines, the white stripes in his black
hair that spoke of strength tempered with wisdom. His voice
was mellow on the breeze that was soft with sea-tang and the
freshness of flowers.

The image jumped.

Irona closed her mind to Less's persuasive words and concentrated instead on a professional appraisal of his technique
and she had to conclude that despite the relatively primitive
technology, the teaching was almost as good as a shrine back
in Camelford. Except that clever Regen had—

'Why's it keep jumping?' Twiss whispered.

She chuckled softly. 'That's Regen – he was smart enough
to realise what Less was trying to get across and he's ruined
the effect. Good for him!'

'What d'you mean?'

If it's not working, who cares? she thought, and said softly,
'Ssh! Never mind. I'll tell you later.'

Because what Less was saying in scents and hormones,
in images and words and a beautiful pang of music was:
Come to Kifl. Live here. We want you. You can sleep and
never think again, and live beside this beautiful sea under
our beautiful volcano and farm our beautiful volcanic soil.

All you have to do is what we tell you. Be sterilised. Be
our slaves.

But there were no sublims, thanks to Regenerator, and
every now and then would come a midden-stench or the
odour of greasy hair.

A cheerful character made of flame talked in a voice that
made the little ones laugh. It flew to the heavens to show
Harith whirling round the sun. With a magic wand it coloured
Harith's one continent from the ice and fire of the volcanic
north to the drowning marshes of the southern peninsula.
It flew over the vast, arid central plains where rain had not
fallen in more than fifteen years and the stones were slicked
with a patina of chemicals oozing from the poisonous ground.
It showed the jagged basalt cliffs towering thousands of feet
above the crashing Eastern Sea.

Then, with a human shudder that set the kids laughing, the talking flame fled the inhospitable steppes back to Moon Mountains and explained that they too were volcanic – it showed the cracks on the floor of the highest crater, Heralia, the rim so high that even in summer there were snows frosting its shoulders. And it explained how the mountains cut off the moist westerly winds so that the rain didn't often penetrate beyond the coastal plains. (Pictures of a night-storm, all ozone and lightning-riven darkness and wet trees that still burst into terebinth flames.)

'So you see,' said the talking flame with a smile and an apologetic shrug, 'there's really only this little coastal strip that's habitable in this phase of colonisation. But in another forty or eighty years when the next ship comes we might be able to terraform more of Harith. Maybe even build a city on stilts over the continental shelf. Won't that be nice?'

And his smile against the palm-fringed sea blended into Less's smile. For just a moment Less was the flame, then his mature features blocked out the fire in his eyes and he was just a human again. Just good old Less. 'Well, that's all for tonight, folks. Tomorrow I'll tell you all about the Native Americans with their feathers and their teepees and how the Settlers from Europe made the West their own. See you!'

Irona wondered how many Second Wavers even without the sublims had seen the threat and counterthreat.

A couple of days later, while Tebrina was supervising the men and women washing on the banks of the New Canal, Irona happened to straighten her back for a moment. She had always said she wouldn't ask anyone else to do anything she wouldn't tackle herself, but as she ruefully regarded her pruny hands she said to her friend, 'I wish I'd never said anything about washing bedclothes for the ones who can't do it for themselves.'

Tebrina laughed and came closer, her bare feet feeling their way surely over the rounded pebbles of the stream-bed. She clapped Irona on the shoulder so hard that Irona nearly fell headlong into the shallow stream. Beside her, Sticker cursed as her mis-step sprayed water into his eyes. He might have agreed to help Jai out in the Hospital but he wasn't going to enjoy it if he could help it.

The two women exchanged a little friendly gossip. Tebrina whispered, 'By the way, I'm expecting again.'

'You're not!'

'I am!'

Maybe it was the catch-phrase, maybe it was the joy of the moment, but Irona and Tebrina swapped a splashy embrace and much delighted laughter. Sticker, who hadn't heard what they were talking about, carried on cursing over the hospital sheets.

'Looks like it's contagious,' Tebrina added. 'Jai's told me there's four or five others got pregnant about the same time as me.'

'Maybe it's something you catch from the latrines,' Irona said, her eyes sparkling with merriment. Automatically she stretched to get her keypad from the bank and checked, but the Eye showed nothing harmful anywhere about. She did it so often she hardly noticed it any more.

'Hey look, there's Regen! See him, Ro? Coming up the road behind us.'

'Hi, Regen!' Irona called, glad of any excuse to climb out of the water that swirled numbing around her ankles. 'I haven't seen you to talk to for days. Where've you been?'

His knobby cheeks rounded, shining in a grin against the mid-morning sun. He hugged her briefly. 'Eurch, you've made me all wet now. Oh, here and there, round and about. I got to get my strength back, don't I?'

She linked her arm through his. At least since he'd been in Jai's Hospital he was clean. 'Come here a minute, Regen.'

Leading him off a few paces so the rest of the work-party couldn't hear them, she said quietly, 'I wanted to thank you for putting the jumps in Less's tape the other day. And for taking out the sublims.'

'Well, I thought Less was coming it a bit strong so I soon put a spoke in his cog-wheel. But I never took out no sublims, Ro. There weren't none.'

In the hot sunlight Irona suddenly felt as cold as her shadow. 'No sublims? None at all?'

'Nary a one. I went through it two or three times, just to make sure. And the computer never found none neither. I thought you must've done it already and forgotten to tell me. It really got up my nose for a while 'til I remembered you'd never mess me about on—'

'No sublims at all, Regen?'

The implications began to hit him too.

'Then the Kiflians have had almost three days' start on us.' She ran to grab her shoes. 'We'd better tell Twiss.'

25

SOWING TEETH

Breathless, Irona pelted into their shelter and skidded to a stop.

No Twiss.

Where can he be? On the mound? In the fields?

Must go to the computer shed. I'll send the Eye to find him.

She ran out into the fierce heat, almost colliding with Regen who couldn't yet keep up. He grabbed her or they would both have fallen. Nervous sweat polished his face.

'Sorry,' she panted. 'He's not here! I'll get the Eye to find him.'

His bony fingers held her arms just above the elbow. 'Slow down, Ro. Get your breath back.'

'We haven't got time for this!'

'We ain't got time not to. They First Wavers've had plenty of time to work out their next move. A few minutes here or there ain't going to make no difference.'

She jerked her elbows free of his grasp and ran a few steps backwards. 'I've got to get to the computer-shed.'

'Then don't show your people how scared you are. Don't panic 'em, Ro. They need to believe in you. Entirely.' He had to call after her; he just hoped no-one had heard them. But this late in the morning everyone was out at work somewhere and the rows were deserted.

He was right. Irona slowed, dancing with impatience until Regen caught up with her. He touched her hand and she was glad of the contact. 'Well done, Ro. We'll make it. You'll see.'

But panic still rilled electricity along her nerves. Death could come from anywhere . . . 'I'll find Twiss,' she said quickly. 'You go and get Gundmila over there.' Already Irona was backing away, giving commands as she walked. 'She was by the New Canal a little while ago, washing. Don't let her inside the computer-shed though. I don't want her wrecking everything. And bring a couple of heavies with you to guard her. She could be our king-pin. See you there.'

Regen moved away stiffly, weakened still by his injuries. Irona went to look on the mound, praying she wouldn't see anybody on the way.

Twiss wasn't there either. The mound was bare and silent. She spun away across the open ground, heading for the shed. It took all of Irona's self-control to keep down to a brisk walk but even that looked unnatural in the height of summer.

The computer-shed seemed to retreat from her across the syrupy air. The cracks in the ground gaped to catch at her feet. A lone lizardoptera swooped almost into her face and she batted at it frenziedly but it meant no harm and chittered off into the distance, its golden locust-wings flapping so fast she could see its belly-razor through them.

The whole thing was like a nightmare where she ran and ran but she couldn't outdistance the thing that came behind her.

Then the nightmare was over. She pushed open the shed door and slammed it behind her, irrationally glad she had never got round to taking out the lattice over the window. In the chequered shade she slid into her seat and ordered the computer to find and summon Twiss.

The Eye had him in a minute. He was in Jai's Hospital. Gently, very gently, he was feeding Granfer, spooning up the drips that fell from the flaccid mouth, trying not to mind the hostility that poured from Granfer's eyes. And he nodded at the summons the Eye sent now it could transmit but he finished mopping Granfer's chin before he handed the bowl to little round Jai. Jai, who was also pregnant, though nobody knew about it yet except her and Irona.

She had to be there, didn't she? thought Irona, and wondered where that bitterness had come from. It was unworthy of her. *Of course Jai would be in her Hospital. She's a nurse, isn't she?*

Why doesn't he get on with it?

Then Twiss was standing, smiling – always smiling – telling the old feller, 'I'll be back this evening. See you then.' He was thanking Jai for looking after Granfer. He was chucking Desselie under the chin – and how Desselie loved that! He was ducking out into the hot liquid air.

Twiss was coming.

Irona brought the Eye back and sent it to search Rainshadow Valley visually.

Nothing. No tractor, no walkers. No other sources of power.

So what were the Kiflians up to? And when would it start?

She analysed the water in the Old and New Canals. A high proportion of alkali, but that was normal. Nothing else in it that shouldn't have been there.

Over in Kifl there was no-one in the Synod tower.

And the crops were safe.

So what was going on?

That's what Twiss said too, when he crossed the baked ground to find her fretting in the doorway.

'Thank Synod you're here, Twiss!' Momentarily she clung to him, wanting his strength to feed hers, but he didn't return the embrace and she felt stupid. Her hands dropped ignored to her sides.

'So what's going on?'

'I don't know.' Needing something for her body to do, she sat down on the plastic seat Regen had rigged for her. 'But you remember you said if ever the Kiflians stopped sending us subliminals in the teaching that they'd be up to something? Well they have.'

'Look, stop babbling and start again.'

So she told him. And he went still, feeling, as she did, the threat, but not knowing where to look for it.

Suddenly he strode to the door. No word, no explanation.

'Where are you going?'

He tossed the words over his shoulder. 'To find Gundmila.'

'Regen's bringing her here now.'

Twiss swung back, frustrated. And, each in their own

silence, they marked time as the sun slid its chequerboard
ever-shrinking to the window and outside the shadows
shortened towards the desert noon.

When Gundmila came there was quite a group. Flanked by
short, stocky, grey-haired Tebrina and the red-wattled Marjine
who were obviously suffering from the heat, Gundmila looked
calm and elegant by contrast. Commanding, even, in her blue
robe once more. Though her hands were work-roughened,
they still glistened with rings. And she stood straight though
the hot wind from the dunes whipped strands of her golden
hair across her face.

Regen was still worrying his way across from the rows on
the other side of the open ground. But a nineteen-year-old
lad – *What's his name again?* – stood just behind Gundmila,
an angry scowl fitting ill on his good-natured face.

'What do you want with Gundmila?' the boy said.

'Well, Spinon,' Twiss said, and he spat sand from one
corner of his mouth. Eyes slitted against the wind and the
glare, he was threatening. Irona was glad she didn't have to
stand against him. Twiss looked the boy in the face, stopping
just short of contempt. 'I don't know what it's got to do with
you, but she's one of the Kiflian Synod. Her and me, we've
got some talking to do. So if you want to wait, go right
ahead.'

'You're not to hurt her!' the boy blurted, and seemed no
more surprised than Twiss that he had had the temerity
to speak.

'Lad' – Twiss smiled, and this time it wasn't his politic
look. Irona hated it – 'this woman's a hostage. Her and her
buddies, they've – well, if you don't know what they've done
to us, how many of us they've maimed or killed, then your
head must be fuller of rocks than it looks. And now they've
got another little scheme lined up for us.'

The boy, sunlight gilding his cheeks and riding the worry-
lines around his eyes, stared at Twiss through the hard
brightness. 'What, like letting us have a tractor? And
supplies? And medicine?'

Twiss shook his head and laughed unpleasantly. 'Spinon,
lad, what has she been telling you? The only reason we

got they things was 'cause me and my army, we took
'em.'

'She's never done you any harm!' The boy stood defiant
leaning forward slightly in his urge to convince Twiss
Nobody else mattered now in this confrontation.

'Nor I ain't done her none – yet.'

'You lie, Twiss.' Fury worked the boy's features, making
him ugly. His shadow was a black pool of hate beneath him
'You've half-strangled her, humiliated her—' He stopped
incoherent with rage.

Twiss stepped in close to him until his face was only
centimetres from the boy's. 'You're right. I've only half
strangled her. And if I have any more lip from you she'll
get the second half.'

Spinon's fist whipped out but his clumsy move had tele
graphed his intent. Twiss swayed aside and sent the boy
crashing to the ground with one hard punch to the chest
The boy fell full-length, his head cracking on the sun
baked earth.

The boy wiped blood from his split lip and he looked at
it in surprise. One front tooth dangled by a thread of skin
'D'you think that makes you a big man, Twiss?'

'Well it makes me bigger than you.'

'But I love her!'

'Love?' Twiss's laughter flayed the boy worse than hi
blow had done. 'D'you really think she'd love a skinny little
sawn-off runt like you? You ain't half her age.' He saw the
doubts begin to creep into Spinon's eyes, and he followed the
chink they opened. The acid light of his reason burned away
the boy's night-sweet delusions. 'What's a kid like you got to
offer her? She's just winding you up, boy. Having you on so
she can wrap you round her little finger, make you stand up
for her. You can fall for it if you like, but it ain't going to stop
me getting the truth out of her. Now shut up and go home
And try not to make yourself any more ridiculous than you
already are.'

Twiss's gaze abandoned the boy but the look of burning
contempt still glowed in his eyes as he jerked his head at
Tebrina and Marjine. 'Take her round to the back. And Ro

– the eye away from Gundmila winked at the woman pinned by the tides of emotion to the doorway – 'bring that there truth-serum the computer cooked up from the Hospital. Gundmila don't mind putting it off for a bit, do you?'

He waited until the mock-Matriarch had begun to frame a reply then walked away from her. Spinon slunk away, forgotten.

And Ro went to fetch a drug-patch from Jai, thankful when Spinon stumbled down a side-row. She was half-way to the Hospital before the cruel currents of feeling left her. It was as though she was empty. True, she had stopped shaking. But now everyone's adrenalin had left her she was weak and the cruel sun battered at her.

It was even worse for Gundmila. When Irona got back with a patch she found that Twiss had left the captive standing in the sun while he and the others lounged at their ease in the slender shade cast by the shed. And he had ordered that her skirts be hacked off at the thigh, leaving the woman's white legs immodestly exposed. The angry sunburn reddening her skin could not have scorched her more than the humiliation.

As Irona rounded the corner to the welcome sliver of shade, she could not help but pity Gundmila. She might have been one of the Synod once but she wasn't invincible now. Brought up to be one of the exalted, the woman was trying to hold herself as still as a statue but her embarrassment breathed in every line of her, even in the sweat-stains darkening her robes beneath the arms, even in the way she wouldn't lift a hand to brush aside the hair that was plastered with perspiration to her forehead. Still, she could not help but droop a little in the killing heat though she tried to fight it. And a thread of blood was beginning to slide down her sweat-slick thighs.

Compassion twisted like hot wires in Irona's womb.

Twiss never even bothered to look at Gundmila. Unless she moved, he ignored her.

'I've brought it,' Irona said unnecessarily. The tensions between the group were already sawing into her. She wondered if she had done the right thing. Sunlight daggered a scintillating headache into her eyes.

'Well put it on, then.'

'You can't do this!' Gundmila said, trying every trick in the book to sound commanding although she knew she was helpless.

Twiss merely cocked his head. Tebrina and Marjine rose to flank the woman, holding her arms tightly while Irona sterilised the skin above her collar and slapped the patch onto the side of her neck where the drugs could get into her bloodstream. Then they held her arms down until the patch had had time to take effect.

Tebrina and Marjine moved to seats they had brought out into the shade, so close that Gudmila felt her personal space violated. They relaxed, passed round a jug of reconstituted fruit-juice with the pungent smell of orange. They drank with every evidence of enjoyment – but they didn't pass it to Gundmila.

She said, 'I wanted some of that. I did. You don't want me here and I don't want to be here. Why don't you let me go?'

'Why don't you want to be here, Gundmila?'

'Because I don't belong in this miserable pestilential hole with you filthy sleepers and your nasty barbarian tricks. I am – but I'm not going to tell you that.'

Irona leant forward, compelled to ask, 'What are you?'

Twiss said, 'Shut up, Ro.'

But Gundmila's grievance had blocked her ears anyway. 'I'm Towy's representative! I'm Matriarch of Harith and you demean me!' she said. 'You make me do manual labour as though I were some brain-numbed part of the masses. But I'm not! I'm Synod. And the only reason Synod picked you out of all the sleepers to come to Harith is that you're such mental pygmies you're only fit to be our servants. You couldn't wake up if you lived a thousand years.'

Marjine and Tebrina pokered up but Twiss smiled winsomely and said, 'Is that the only reason you don't want to be here, Gundmila? Or wasn't there something else? About snake-rats, say? Because they'll get you if you're here, won't they?'

Gundmila opened her mouth to speak and then shut it

with a snap like broken elastic. She giggled. 'Aha! You nearly tricked me into telling you. But I'm not going to. Nobody knows about the snake-rats here. Did you think we'd tell you? Did you think Less would tell you on the teaching-machine? You've never even noticed his conditioning, have you? You're so stupid you think you can survive out here in the wilderness and you haven't got a clue. You've made it to summer and you think that's it, you've won. Synod, you're such a deve!'

Gundmila laughed, rocking back and forth in the fire of noon, the palm of her hand to her mouth as though to cut off the words that fountained from her. She was laughing so hard that the words had to tumble over the awful paroxysms; Irona could barely understand her. But she had learned: the Eye was on hand to record it all.

Between her mad cacklings Gundmila said, 'You're all going to die and there's nowhere you can go. You've seen that. Synod, my head hurts. He showed you – Less showed you. And you think we're too stupid to irrigate this poxy deve valley, but we're not. We could do it. But we didn't and you don't know why. Only any day now you're going to find out. Your stupid Eye won't show you. And you were dumb enough to build your pitiful hovels in the ground. Synod, how thick can you get?'

She repeated it, her body growing boneless now, swaying on her feet. The noontide sun burnt her legs that had never known its naked rays; they crimsoned with pain and with her menstrual blood and she babbled on about how stupid they were, how stupid and barbaric and cruel. And it was all pointless. Who cared about lending them a tractor for a while? They'd not be able to use it long Nor the power. And the bit of food didn't make a dent in their stores.

'You'll never survive unless you come to us. And then we'll make you grovel. We'll make you lower than slaves. You could have had a good living before, looking after our people because there's things no machine can do, but no. Not you. You wanted it all for yourselves, our nice land, our rich land by the sea that we need for our growing families. And now you'll be corpses and it's all your fault because you're so stupid. You're going to let all your people die, Twiss, and they'll know it was you because I'll tell them since they're too dumb to work it out for themselves. You're sleepers.'

Twiss and Irona exchanged a look. 'Why will we die, Gundmila?'

'Because you're sleepers. Because you're too stupid ever to be anything else. And they'll get you.' She began to weep, keening, falling to the ground. Her delicate face was already blistered by the sun and her hands ground into the dusty earth. 'And they'll get me too. They'll come up out of the ground when their cocoons split and you won't let that little boy take me back home to be my slave. So I'll die here too.'

Incoherent between sunstroke and her own weakness, Gundmila raved.

When he could see they would get no further sense from her, Twiss rose to stand over her hunched body. He tapped her with his toe until he got her attention. 'One thing, Gundmila. We never had no truth-drug. It were only water and you told us everything.'

Twiss walked away. Irona followed him, asking, 'Why did you say that?'

He puffed laughter down his nose. 'So she can hate herself properly, that's why.'

'She never had no more information,' Twiss said when they had replayed the tape, but Irona doubted it. The woman was half-way to a matriarch, wasn't she? She wouldn't give in completely to such a simple ploy. Now she lay in a stupor in Jai's Hospital.

Days passed. Nothing happened, and the whole of Settlement grew tense, knowing something was wrong though the leaders never said. Even Marjine, who usually found something to carp about, kept her mouth shut.

Irona's eyes grew red from her endless looking at the Eye but there was never anything to see, not in Kifl or Settlement or the soil of Rainshadow Valley, however much Twiss snapped at her. Not even Regen could find anything wrong.

Dread tightened its grip on Settlement. Bickering flared in the endless dry winds that blew sand relentlessly into everything, and Twiss kept finding Spinon at the centre of little groups of people who faded away as he approached.

Then, one hot night when Irona lay sleepless in Twiss's arms, listening to him breathe and watching the two moons line up in the star-jewelled mantle of the night, she heard the patter of earth.

She thought no more about it. Now that high summer had parched Settlement except where the irrigated fields lay ripening, the walls of the dugout often slipped a little, but it was nothing to worry about. It happened all the time.

Only not as much as this. She told herself, *Don't be stupid. The roots of the green-balls hold those sods good and tight same as they ever did.*

Then earth spattered on her face. She twitched aside; Twiss didn't wake up but his arm tightened involuntarily about her and even in her apprehension she smiled for a second.

But the gliding moonlight showed the walls writhing and she jerked to sit upright. Earth showered down on them between the cracks in the plastic ceiling and a sharp stone slashed the corner of Twiss's mouth. He awoke with a start.

Twiss rolled instantly to his feet, anger blazing from him beacon-sharp in her mind. He whirled to face her. 'What did you do that for?'

'What? It wasn't me!'

Then the thing at his lip stung again. He clawed at it and something soft pulped between his fingers. Soil rattled down on the two of them as he flung the thing aside but she saw him scratch savagely at his mouth again.

'Let's get out of here!' she said, snatching up her clothes and shaking them hard before dragging them on any old how. Formless terrors rose in her, remembering Gundmila's fear. Something fell out of her boot but she didn't stop to investigate.

Twiss was outside before her, still picking at his bleeding lip. And the rows were alive with others, shadowy figures, shouting, angry.

Irona dived back inside to grab the power-pack. She turned it up to full brightness and saw four thorns sticking into Twiss's face. Twiss recoiled from the light but she said, 'Stand still a minute. There's something on your mouth.'

They weren't thorns. She picked them out with her nails – it was hard, because the things were barbed – and held the light to turn them over curiously on her palm.

They were teeth, little teeth like needles with a hollow eye, but curved. She threw them aside. Where they fell, the ground was moving like a carpet that somebody shook.

26

EARTH-BITES

Twiss wiped blood from his face. The night was alive with shrieks of fear and pain. Taking in the scene at a glance he 'snapped his fingers at the nearest men. 'Get Gundmila.' His voice was harsh, unrecognisable, and under his feet the ground crawled in the moonlight.

Irona laid a hand on his arm. It felt like rock, not living flesh. 'What are you going to do, Twiss?'

'Get over to your computer-shed. This don't concern you.'

'Twiss, listen to me. This concerns all of us. Listen!'

But it was like talking to a block of granite. And if nothing else the computer might give her some answers. She took her frustration over there, her progress barred by the people who flocked round her, panicking, their faces contorted in the red light of the power-packs, asking her for explanations she didn't have, but all she could do was help them pull out the barbed teeth and the blood streamed down like tears on the ruby flesh. Some, though, she couldn't touch: the ones where the snake-rats had left their teeth inside a child's ear, or in a girl's nose. A man ran past, screaming, his hands clasped between his legs, to throw himself against the barrier. He died in a sheath of crackling blue fire and the smell of his burnt flesh stalked the rows.

Irona stumbled past them then. Pushing through the night, dodging the dancing figures of hell, she crossed the open ground and the stars showed her the soil slimed with gorgon writhings. Moist bodies burst under her feet. She ran to her shed, her dark sanctuary, and slammed the door against the sleepers who came banging on it, demanding help.

Her skin crept over her flesh. Horrors jagged inside her eyelids, fear punched her heart into arhythmic spasms. In those few lightless steps towards the power-pack she lived a dozen lives. And the sound of earth slithering on earth flared like thunder in her ears.

She reached the power-pack as if she were a drowning woman clutching at a floating spar. Even though she was expecting it the light exploded in her vision and she reeled back. And all the time, outside, sleepers were pounding on the door, calling her name.

Knuckling the dazzle from her eyes Irona snatched up a plastic rag and dashed from corner to wall to console, steeling herself to pluck the snake-rat larvae and hurl them through the lattice on the window. Even as she did it, more were pouring from the walls, the floor.

Half the length of her finger, the larvae were pale, the colour of dead skin. Four vestigial hands helped them to excavate themselves from the soil where they had been laid. They would ooze from the walls or the ceiling to fall with a soft plop on the beaten earth. Some burst as they fell and a stench of mould and corruption rose from them but it didn't last long. In moments the flat, mindless eyes of their nest-mates would spot them and their bony jaws would clamp on the helpless bodies to suck them dry.

Irona gagged and gave up. She couldn't stem the tide of larvae so she squatted on the chair before the console, skirts kilted up around her ankles and the back draped over her head for protection from the ones that pattered onto her from above.

And still the sleepers knocked maddeningly at the door, endlessly calling her name.

Instead of Settlement the screens showed a purple sheet of fear. Keying in what data she knew, she read the list of suggestions. Most of them depended on a technology she hadn't got but she seized on two of them and dashed outside.

She barged through the clinging, weeping press outside her door and yelled, 'Get to the canals or the rocks! Tell them! Tell everyone! Get to the canals or the rocks!'

And as she quartered the rows she could hear the shouts echoing above the screams: 'Get to the rocks! Get to water!'

*   *   *

It was cold in the canal, but, they had discovered, safer than the rocks where pockets of windblown soil gave birth to larvae. Chilled to deep shudders, Irona listened to the despair all around her and wondered where Twiss was. Though she had searched for him she hadn't seen him all night long, not even with the Eye. Locked in the silence of her dread, she waited for the dawn.

The sun rose, a glory of pink and gold that washed the sky with a blue so delicate it could have been a symbol of purity. It brought a sweet nostalgia into Irona's heart, a wish for Camelford as it should have been. Far away on the seaward horizon floated a cone of white that could have been a cloud – or the tip of the volcano. A breeze sprang up in the east, seemingly born of the light for it brought long shadows from the dunes and the scent of alien dust that was the taste of Harith, and the white triangle vanished.

Welcome to reality, Irona thought, and felt a faint interior laughter that armoured her against the day to come.

Under the innocence of the new day she began the task of assessing, of coping, of cheering and encouraging despite the anxiety that sucked at her like a vacuum in her heart. Besides, there wasn't much she could do.

All around the canal the larvae looped along, their giant shadows arching. They were so thick that they crawled on each other, tumbling eastward over the lips of the canal. They fell, they drowned, their bodies afloat on the lazy current. They formed a pallid scum on the margins and more larvae bridged them to drown in their turn. As far as the eye could see the ground was alive with them. On the scrub hillocks the bright lenses clouded and died; the aqueous veil of camouflage plants was consumed; the green-ball plants writhed in a fruitless urge to escape. The only sound was the tiny crunching of their jaws, magnified by their infinite numbers into an endless drilling inside her head.

Irona watched and her heart ached: the fields of Settlement were nothing but water-striped barrens and the wind whirled their dreams away in clouds of dust.

The larvae left nothing. They died in their millions and sucked each other dry, and still they came.

She sent the Eye to check the other canal, and shouted out who was there. Jai and Tebrina for a start; a faint smile pulled at the unwilling muscles of her cheeks. Sticker had his arms around Jai and who gave who the most comfort was impossible to tell. Irona longed for Twiss as if she were a hollow only he could fill, but her mouth went on calling out name after name.

At each one there were cries of relief from around her. Sending the Eye through the deserted streets of Settlement, she found bodies, some of them unrecognisable, and that was worse than knowing. Behind her, some people began to cry, softly, very softly, as if by crying they might draw the larvae down on them.

And she found Gundmila, spread-eagled, pegged to the ground by forks of plastic. The only way Irona could recognise her was where the bloodstains had left patches of the original colour in her matriarchal robes: a blue that was as pure as the lying skies. Even her hair was dark with clotted blood. The face, the body were totally unrecognisable.

Irona's intestines clenched. The only person who would do that to her was Twiss.

Of him there was no sign. And, now she came to think of it, no sign of Granfer, either. The larvae looped on as far as the Eye could see.

A babe began to cry of hunger. Irona told its mother to give it water, and ordered anyone who wanted to relieve themselves to do it well down-stream. It wasn't as if there were anywhere they could go out of sight of the rest.

The day hotted up. Now the larval bites began to itch and swell; as the sun bleached the sky people began to complain of headaches. Just as Jai was doing in the other canal, Irona dealt out everything she possibly could from her pocket olfactory but it wasn't enough. It was never enough.

And still she couldn't find Twiss.

'Surely they've got to stop soon?' whined Desselie.

'Why? Because you want them to?' Irona stopped, appalled. There was enough bad feeling without her adding to it by snapping at brainless deves like Desselie.

By now more children were wailing. Irona couldn't stand

it any more; she had the Eye draw power and then she said, 'I want four or five volunteers. We're going to go and get some stuff for the kids. Who's with me?'

Amid shouts of incredulity and pleas – 'Don't leave us, Irona. We need you!' – two women and a man pushed through the huddled crowd. All of them were past weeping now though their eyes were red-rimmed and bloodshot. None of the three looked completely sane.

'Why do you want to go?' Irona asked apprehensively.

'What the hell,' said one of the women, and the other shrugged.

The man stared at her with burning eyes. 'My Nirika is gone. What else have we got to lose?'

So Irona had the Eye flay a path from the canal-bank with bolts of electricity. The larvae charred and crunched horribly underfoot but there were always more to take their place. It was like ploughing a furrow on the sea.

Reaching the stores, they piled cannisters of food into discarded bedclothes and sledded it back to the groups in the two canals, trying to kick the snake-rat larvae aside. The Eye was weakening now and Irona skimmed it once round, quickly.

No Twiss.

And the second night in the canal was longer than the first as people tumbled exhausted into sleep and into the wet arms of death by drowning.

For three days the larvae crawled past. Their corpses began to choke the canal; it rose round the settlers' knees, their waists, and they had to bat the floating, rotting grubs away. Even draining every power-pack in Settlement except the ones for the computer and the Hospital, Irona couldn't kill enough of them to make any difference to the snake-rats' numbers. And day and night their itching, crawling sounds skithered endlessly eastward around the men and women in the canals.

Though Irona had the Eye steal power from Kifl through the unit Tang had given, it did not have the strength to find Twiss. Irona couldn't eat; she drank only because she had to stay alive to care for the sleepers. The water sucked the heat from her bloated limbs. Her mind floated free in some blazing desert of infinity where sun and earth and sky blended in one white-hot incandescence. An orphaned toddler dragged at her arms as she held him above the swirling waters and the pain of her muscles was a part of the hard-edged gaudiness that hypnotised her brain with its dazzle.

But when the settlers called on her, she came from far away to answer.

The third day lightning gathered by the peaks of the Moon Mountains. Yellowing sky was swallowed by slatey clouds whose fat bellies ground together. Then lightning leapt downwards, and up to strike back at its cruel parents, and still the snake-rats looped past, livid now like putrefying flesh, and the scent of death was acid as rancid milk.

Fat drops of rain plummeted to the ground, bursting in a spatter of dust. The darkening sky lanced rain. It stung Irona's face, speared her eyelids, frightened baby Liesl in her arms and she bent her head to protect her. Her knuckle could not still Liesl's cries but the rolling thunder drowned them out.

In less than twenty minutes the storm swept past them and the sharp-cut sandstone buttes of the Southern Hills stabbed into the thunderheads. They bled to death, the last of the rain falling as grey tatters, and as the pelting rain diminished to leave a weak, drained-looking sky, Irona heard silence.

Silence.

No creeping of larvae.

No larvae at all except dead ones.

And the floodwaters on the ground mirrored the pale sky.

'Get out!' she shouted.

There was a stir, a ripple in the settlers around her but they were too numbed to respond physically.

'Get out!' she shrieked, a harridan. Slapping faces, screaming and cursing, she drove them from the stream-bed.

'Why?' Spinon asked her but she stared at him with such hatred that he stepped back involuntarily and scrambled ashore.

Tossing the child up to him, she urged the slow ones out, and from somewhere came the lowest of rumbles. Only three or four settlers were left in the waist-high canal: the ones deepest in disaster-shock. They stood apathetic and unaware of what was going on around them.

Then from the south reared a wall of water, spuming.

'Flash flood!' She waded desperately towards the slow ones, her arms flailing to propel her, but she couldn't reach them and someone plucked her from behind.

'Let me go!' she howled but the vice-like grip round her midriff didn't ease and she was dragged like a child from the teeth of the flash-flood.

Where the wall of water had passed there was chaos. The irrigation-barriers were washed away, the plastic splintered and hurled aside. One blade of it stood quivering in the desolation of the fields. And everywhere the drowned corpses of the snake-rat larvae floated stinking in the sunlight. The world was pale with them; the sky was pale. There was no colour anywhere, just the splashes of blood where the broken bodies of four settlers lay.

Spinon held Irona as she cried. She knelt in the ashen mud, head to her knees, and Spinon knelt behind her, one arm awkwardly across her back.

Around her sleepers said feebly, 'Don't cry, Irona.' 'We need you, don't cry,' and she wished they would all go away. Leave her alone. And she wanted to throw Spinon's arm off but there was no-one else who touched her because Twiss wasn't there.

Out in the khaki wastes nothing moved but the wind drawing ripples from the sheets of yellow water.

Then on the rocks near Settlement a dark spot showed. Irona didn't see it.

'Look!' the sleepers said, and Irona thought, *I'm not falling for that trick.*

But more and more of them said it and words grew sharp

inside Irona: *What are the Kiflians doing to us now? I can't take any more, I can't.*

But she knew she had to because the sleepers couldn't.

So she looked and hope flamed away despair, guttering, renewing itself: *It's Twiss.*

Don't be stupid. The larvae got him.

It's Twiss.

And it was. But without his clothes she would never have known him. His face was dark and mottled, swollen with the teeth of larvae still festering in him. Patches had been torn from his wavy brown hair. His arms were streaked with dried blood, and he was carrying the drained corpse of his Granfer.

He walked slowly, stiffly towards her, and Granfer's head and knees flopped at each step.

Irona stood and went towards him. She had been thinking that the pain could not get any worse but his grief flowed into her and she accepted it. *I'll help you*, she thought to him but she didn't dare say a word. *I'll help you, I'll hold you in the night when bereavement strikes you like a serpent's fangs. I'll be by your side.*

He said, 'Granfer's dead, Ro.'

She nodded gently.

'I took him to the rocks because I thought it would be safe in the caves but it weren't. They marched right in. They got him while I slept and I didn't know because he couldn't tell me. After that I held him up out of their way but he was dead, Ro, and it was my fault.

'And the Kiflians . . . But they'll pay, you wait and see. How they'll pay . . .'

'Gundmila? Gundmila!'

No answer.

In her eyrie on Camelford Mountain, Bernardina smiled. She didn't know what had happened but Gundmila could never have resisted answering.

If she were free. If she were alive.

Therefore Irona must have unmasked and conquered her first enemy. She was toughening up nicely. Now it just depended how long it took her to find the ansible, and if she were as smart as Bernardina thought, it wouldn't be too long. *Anyway,* she told herself, *if she doesn't even know it exists, it'll take a while. And I can always give her a clue when I need her.*

What did it matter that outside her window the world was locked in a programmed grey frost? It helped to kill the bugs. And if the Liga Mediterranea was being difficult? That the presidents of the Three Americas were threatening to draw everyone into their squabbles? That a dictator was arising in Saharistan?

I guess it'll be Irona, like I thought. Like I planned. Though in her subconscious mind rolled the truth that for years she hadn't thought of Irona at all.

Bernardina's empire expanded in her mind.

27

THE WEATHER-MAN

When Twiss walked over to Jai and Sticker's quarters next morning, he saw the last of the teams shovelling piles of dead grubs beyond the perimeter. Others had filtered and boiled water to drink, and some had distributed food to the survivors. Some of the dugouts had collapsed completely; now men and women were tunnelling out a shelter in the stratum of chalk over by the Old Canal. But the reconstruction was hopeless.

Settlement was quieter than usual. There was none of the usual banter. People moved briskly about their business, or drifted along like ghosts without their lovers or their sons.

Twiss noticed that not so many greeted him this morning, nor came to him with requests. Irona had commented on it earlier when she first stepped out into the haze of morning to start work on the project. Now Twiss saw that she was right, and it was another small hurt.

Jai saw him duck to come in and as soon as she could she made her way through the close-ranked pallets in the Hospital. There were so many of them that it was hard to find a place to step between them.

She came through the connecting door, Sticker just behind her. They found a place to sit and looked at him expectantly. It wasn't a proper council, not without Irona, not without Granfer's silent presence, but from the solemnity on Twiss's sweat-slicked face, they knew it was a council nevertheless.

Despite the open doors the air in the Hospital smelt of disease. As Twiss drew breath to speak Jai noticed how his swollen face wrinkled with distaste.

Twiss dispensed with preliminaries. 'I been over to the computer-shed. Irona and Regen are already doing it. They should be ready by morning. So you'll go tonight, Sticker.'

'What if it don't succeed? What if you wipe out the supplies? Why don't you at least ask that Less for food and medicine before you start?' Jai said hesitantly.

Twiss looked at her. 'We ain't asking they for nothing. We're taking it.'

Jai looked through the open door at the patients in the crowded ranks of pallets. Two to a bed, some of them were. Desselie, next to a gangway, turned over in her fever, her arm flopping against a child who began to cry feebly. Even though Jai had surgically removed all the larvae's teeth the wounds were festering. There was hardly a settler who didn't have at least a touch of fever but Jai could only fit the worst cases in her little ward. In other dugouts people mourned or burned with the poisons spreading through their bodies. The only good thing was that the storm had drowned the snake-rats.

Jai's soft, dark eyes were full of reproach but she said nothing. Twiss absently scratched at the swelling on his neck; dark streaks were spreading from it, a spider-web under the skin. He sneered a laugh. 'Don't you look at me like that, Jai. They did it, not me. Look around – what do you see? Tell me I made the snake-rats, I poisoned the water – But I didn't, did I? You wait and see what I will do.'

The bloom had gone from Jai's dark cheeks and there were black circles beneath her eyes. She reached for Sticker's hand and he squeezed it. 'Where's Ro, did you say?' she asked.

Twiss smiled harshly. 'She ain't going to turn me neither. She and Regen, they're over at the computer-shed. I've got a little something they Kiflians aren't going to like much. We've got to act fast because we ain't none of us getting any stronger.'

Sticker cleared his throat, a sure sign he was feeling awkward. 'You've told us all this. What you ain't said, what we ain't none of us talked about, is if this is the right thing to do. Maybe Jai's right. Maybe we ought to bargain with 'em.'

Twiss said it flatly. 'We ain't bargaining.'

Sticker just looked at him.

Twiss said it again, more forcefully. 'What have we got to bargain with? Gundmila told us – they don't even want all of us. So you go tonight after we done a drill or two.' He stood to close the argument.

Jai asked him, 'Twiss, d'you reckon the snake-rats are going to come back?'

'Who knows? This is obviously their spawning ground but they just marched off into the interior, Synod knows why, the ones that didn't drown. And if they are larvae, what are they going to be like if they do come back? That's why we got to get into Kifl smartish. We can't stay out here no longer.'

Sticker stood too, grabbing Twiss to stop him leaving. 'Why do you keep saying "you go"? Why not "we go"? Ain't you coming with us?'

Twiss smiled and then grimaced as his cheeks started the wound beside his mouth bleeding again. 'No, Stick, old lad, I ain't. You'll know exactly what you're doing, and believe me, I'm more needed here. So you're going to be in charge. Regen'll be with you in case.'

Sticker and Jai looked at each other. Sticker scratched beneath his greasy blond hair and finally came out with what he wanted to say to Twiss. 'Why me?'

'Because I told you to, that's why. I'm going to be needed here. You'll see. Trust me.'

But there was a manic glint in Twiss's eyes and nobody trusted him much at all.

Twiss saw the glances that Sticker and Jai exchanged. 'OK,' he said acidly, 'so don't trust me. But you seen what they Kiflians did. You going to trust them instead?'

Over in the computer-shed Irona was asking Regen, 'Are you sure it can hold enough power?'

'It don't have to hold it. They got plenty of power and we've already figured out how to transfer it through the Eye to somewhere else, yes? That's what we been running on these last few weeks, ain't it? Juice we've put into our power-packs from theirs? And they got the anti-grav shafts. With what I've cannibalised out of that there teaching-machine, the Eye'll be safe as houses. Entirely.'

Then they both looked at the crumbling walls of the computer-shed and smiled wryly.

'Come on, Ro.' Regen slapped her knee cheerfully. 'We're nearly done. And it ain't like we're going to kill them all or anything. We'll give 'em plenty of warning.'

Irona got up, arching her back to stretch the kinks out of it. She walked restlessly to the door, still not sure they were doing the right thing. Inside her something small and secret nestled in her womb and she smiled. She was almost sure now. Jai had said it was too soon to tell really, but she agreed there might be a softening, a reshaping of the cervix. But Irona knew anyway. She was just waiting for the right moment to tell Twiss.

Irona leant against the plastic frame of the doorway, enjoying the wind on her face. Regen came to join her.

'It'll be all right, Ro. They'll give us some of that nice safe land by the ocean and everything'll be fine. You'll see. Entirely.'

Outside, under wild, gusting clouds, a girl was flying a kite. She was laughing, happy. Then an updraught tugged at the plastic diamond and snatched the kite-string out of the girl's hands.

Sticker's eyes were accustomed to the dark now. He kissed Jai, holding her to him so closely that she could feel his heart-beat; Irona knew it. She wanted that closeness but she couldn't ask Twiss. Ever since his Granfer died he had been somewhere far away. Sex, yes. He took her hungrily, mechanically gave her pleasure, but when he slept he no longer held her through the night. His hand didn't bother to curl round her shoulder, to seek her if she got up to relieve herself. And talking to him – giving him a sentence, however innocent, was like handing a child a loaded gun. Who knew where it might explode?

Irona dragged her thoughts back to wish Sticker and his forty-five soldiers good luck.

Twiss told them, 'The first army was good, but you're better. You're better trained, you're better equipped. Good as Arms, you are. And you don't have to walk through no desert nor cross they old mountains. You got maps and you been shown how to read 'em. You know exactly what you're doing and you've practised doing it. You can't be beat. They Kiflians won't know what's hit 'em. Just don't be there when it arrives.'

They smiled.

It was Regen who gave Irona a hug. 'Don't you worry none, girl,' he said into her ear. 'I'll keep 'em in line and you know it ain't like you're doing your bit for real.' He patted her back awkwardly. 'Take care of yourself.'

'You too.'

He waved, and Sticker's army climbed into the tractor. Another pocket-screen sat in Sticker's hand so Irona could try it out.

'How's it going?' Twiss asked her and she nodded towards Sticker's tiny image in her own screen. 'Yes, it's fine.'

'Then the day after tomorrow we'll be in Kifl, living like kings. How's that sound?'

It sounded ominous.

Through the night she kept watch on the little tractor skimming along over the trail it had travelled before. This time – she felt disloyal for checking – there was no figure lashed to the front, contorted to an X. Twiss lay down for a while but he couldn't sleep either. About midnight he wandered over to join them. He was manic, cracking jokes, laughing. It turned into quite a party, her and Twiss. Neither mentioned Gundmila.

But the gaiety was the sharper for the tension underneath. And ever and again there would come the sound of wailing from over in the rows.

'Are you sure this'll work?' she had whispered to Regen when Twiss stepped out into the cold grey dawn.

"Course it will. Entirely. The program's all ready to run.' Regen's warm, knobbly face had looked into hers. His gentle compassion was there, shining in his eyes that gleamed like molasses. 'But we won't do it, Ro. Not really. Twiss'll just threaten 'em. It'll be all right. You'll see.'

Now Regen was far away on the seaward side of the Moon

Mountains and the first sliver of sunlight shot out from the crests of the dunes. Twiss came back in, whistling. 'Time to go to work. Where's Sticker?'

'Don't worry. He's in position, see?'

She brought his image to the screen, visual first. The little blue Settlement tractor was well under the branches of a cedar, its balloon tyres deflated a little so the vehicle could get so low under cover. Sticker had let the fledgling army·out so that they could practise their manoeuvres: the grab from behind, the knife in the ribs, the shoulder-whip that could have a man flat on his back in a second. As they watched, they saw Regen throw a woman in a cross-buttock.

The settler army formed silhouettes under the dark arbour though the sky was paling above them. Lizardoptera sang peacefully, or munched on leaves. There was no ruby fire in their eyes now their eggs were laid.

And Sticker, for all he tried to swagger, was wooden with tension.

'Deploy them!' Twiss whispered over the system, and the overlapping psychicator flickered with the purple of Sticker's fear. Fear of failure, fear of pain, fear of being afraid.

Irona knew.

Worse than that was the terror of what Twiss was threatening to release.

He won't, though. He couldn't.

Kifl stretched peacefully to the sun of morning. Its tractor engineers strolled sleepily out to talk to their machines that rested at the ragged edge of town between the newer, hastily-constructed houses dotted through the fields.

Children played in the hedgerows or climbed trees; through her adapted Eye Irona could see them chasing each other in games whose rules she would never know, putting off going to school as long as they could. No mere single session with the teaching machines for them: they were the élite.

Men and women sauntered through the bowery avenues, gathering to gossip along the way to the food depot, waiting until someone would get around to opening its doors. There was no hurry.

From her computer-shed on Settlement Knoll she could see all that on the fringes of town, among the buildings that were vying with each other for living-space before the sloping fields began. Clear as day she saw the coloured summer clothes moving in a pattern like a dance beneath the green of the almond trees. Somehow, here on Harith, bright clothes didn't seem half the sin of selfish pride they had back in the Admin.

If she'd wanted to, she could have tuned in to the voices blending in the chorus of another day, shared those lives, but it felt wrong. Somehow she dared not touch the sound levels. Not until everything was ready for her to broadcast the ultimatum Twiss was going to give: the land they had been promised so long ago back in the Admin, before they had been frozen for the flight to a new life.

'D'you think they'll give it us?' she said and didn't realise she had voiced what was on her mind.

When Twiss answered he made her jump. 'Oh, they will.'

Towards the centre of town the pastel wave-form houses were linked by arabesques of frozen rock to keep off the sun. Or to remind them of the womb-like safety of the towns of the Admin.

Even when the women and the men below left the open rows and wandered into the maze of covered alleys, Regen had told her enough before to know exactly what was happening at – she flicked the chronometer display – seven forty-five on a Tiwsday in June. And hadn't she flown her Eye between the buildings in the loveliness of summer nights? Hadn't she heard how Gundmila and Less and Lal talked? Hadn't she been there in fire and blood?

Kifl couldn't hide from Irona.

Behind her, Twiss leaned silent once more on the back of her chair. She could smell him, the hormones of his tension warm and tickling in her nose. Out of habit she flicked a glance at the corner; Granfer wasn't there. His image arose in Irona's mind: how he had been the last time she had seen him, his veins sucked of their juices by the Kiflians' snake-rats, his mind cut off from his empty body. Her lips silently formed the words: *This one's for you.*

And – she checked on him again – Sticker and Regen were sneaking to take up their positions well above sea-level. Not far now to the lovely orchard with its orange-trees and silver birch. Right on time with their team in the safety of the hills that cupped Kifl in their loving, deadly embrace.

High, high above the town she tiptoed the shell of her sight and she felt pity for the babes that wouldn't grow and the breasts that would ache with the pain of not suckling – unless the Kiflians did justice to the Second Wave.

They will, though. And anyway, this wasn't my idea. We didn't start it.

Kiting the Eye even further from the ground, out of guilt she would suppose later, she hoped all the same that no-one in Kifl could see the threat it represented, least of all the fisherfolk plying their toy-like craft in a gavotte on the bosom of the bay. *They would be so frightened if they heard it too. I couldn't do that to people trapped away from solid land.*

The First Wave's little weather-machine was still dormant on the slopes of the Moon Mountains where it had been since Twiss led the first attack on the lab in Kifl.

In her computer-shed in Settlement, Irona tried to blank her mind to compassion, but the parched babies not two dozen metres from her cried feebly as death crept towards their fevered parents, and then Irona didn't give a curse whether They saw the Eye or not. The guilt wasn't hers but Theirs. Them – the First Wavers.

Irona watched all the little people so far below, moving as though they had all the time in the world. Time to be leisurely, and that was more power than any of Twiss's folk had.

For now.

On the storm-hot wind that came through the open door of the computer-shed, she heard a man begin to cry in deep, racking sobs.

Twiss squeezed Irona's shoulder in a grip so tense it hurt and she embraced the pain. 'Now!' he said, jaws so tight they half-strangled the word. 'Sticker and Regen's there. Now!'

She keyed in the sequence to broadcast the speech she had

prepared for Twiss and her nerveless fingers rattled on the keyboard.

But the speech didn't come.

Below the threshhold of hearing trembled a groan so deep it was as if the planet were about to weep. In Kifl the townsfolk scarcely looked up from their chatter in the shade of the trees where the last of the blossom clung, browning. They thought it was just another day, and not history.

Yet Irona's trembling fingers finished the sequence. She wasn't going to go through with it but she had to show the Kiflians the threat was real.

And over the sparkling blue waters of Kifl bay the horizon stepped higher. Wave-crests skirled like dust in a draught, frothed to flying egg-white peaks. The rim of the waters humped itself, convulsed. Deep shadow raced from the western seas and in the boats that leaped like windbown leaves the sailors' mouths turned into dark o's of fear.

'Tell them, Twiss,' she whispered, and stronger, 'Tell them!'

But he said nothing. Twiss said nothing.

And the ocean floor creaked as the weight of waters leaped off it. Dense as glass rose a tower that shaded from aqua to midnight. All along the coast the waves crawled backwards, sucked up into the ziggurat of ocean. Slowly it built, ponderously. Five metres tall. Ten.

'Stop it, Twiss!' But the keys wouldn't respond now to Irona's hands.

The Eye hung incandescent in the sunlight, drawing power from the sources in Kifl. The ocean rose. And it didn't stop as it should have.

Irona asked in horror, 'What have you done, Twiss?'

But he said nothing.

The wrecks of boats broke open on the naked shingle. And still the engine of destruction ripped off the blanketing sea to send it streaming skywards.

'Twiss, tell them now! The channel's open!'

But Twiss sat silent in hate.

A sailor spilt a moan that was the sound of the red stain spreading from his broken ribcage.

Irona's hands reached once more for the keyboard to cancel the liquid death. But Twiss's hands pinned hers and still his silence carpeted the screens of Kifl. People were coming out to see, now, sticking their heads out of the curving windows of their houses.

And Twiss imprisoned her. Irona struggled.

A liquid cornice tumbled from the towering ocean down into the bay, a cascade that snaked like a giant mane white against the blue-black roots of the water-spout.

'Hold it! Hold it!' hissed Twiss, but he wasn't talking to her, nor to the Kiflians. His attention was on the rearing waters that stripped the floor of the continental shelf.

The Eye, following the program that Irona had never believed she would see complete, ingested more power. It glowed with a ferocity Irona fought to control, but Twiss controlled her.

With the gravity of a star the Eye dragged at the waters and they fell upwards into its spell, saved for destruction. The sea was a blue pyramid to rival the hills and the shadows of sudden black clouds pulsed over it in a language that spoke Harith's pain.

From the hills the Kiflians' weather-Eye rose out of its sleep. It had to be Tang ordering it. The sleepy mechanism drew curtains of rain, cast spears of lightning, but the tonnes of water had all the solidity of their mass and no mere electric storm could touch them. Kiflian lightning could not breach the power of the Eye.

'I'm not going to waste it!' Twiss yelled, and Irona could not free her hands from the fury of his grip. The betrayal of a friend; the wound of her lover.

The salt smell of ancient mud mixed with spiking ozone. An indigo monolith, the tower of water lurched. Its shadow broke. Slabs of its glassy surface fell away, crashing in a fire of whiteness that surged shorewards then rose again in an agony of vertical rain. Mist paled the wrath to come and, irony of ironies, a thousand rainbows arced in beauty around the trembling peacock turret.

'Don't make me do this,' Irona breathed. 'Tell them now.'

But Twiss said nothing. The vengeance in his heart overmastered her pain. She tried to claw at the keyboard, countermanding the order, ripping at the cables, but it was too late; she couldn't shake him off.

Even when her desperation finally let her break free of Twiss and her Eye pulled back out into the ocean, the weight of water was beyond control.

The Kiflian weather-machine shot the Eye. It burst apart like a nova – but as its death crackled through Irona's computer, the tower strode on.

Its architecture shattered into parapets that melted into buttresses and moved ever on. Rivers of hyacinth ribboned into cyan and black as the spiring waters dripped away.

Overhead the Eye was still exploding, a bright star shining in the night it had created. It burned, a bright exclamation-point of overloaded circuits above the flattening tower.

Dropped, the waters plummetted back to the rocky sea-floor but the force of their fall sent them leaping skywards, spears.

And funnelled by the embrace of the bay they crashed over Kifl, the vanguard of a mighty army. In seconds the wall of water rolled over the palms on the promenade, breaking them off like straws, flinging them like javelins into the pastel wave-form houses.

Stonework spat into the howling air. Broken shutters sliced skimming through the avenues that were floored by the racing waters. Irona saw one decapitate a woman with her child held to her breast.

'Stop it, Twiss!' she yelled, but there was nothing he could do.

And on Twiss's face was an avid look that curled through her stomach slicker than a snake-rat.

Irona couldn't watch. But the rushing waters growled hungrily, drowning out the shrieks of the dying. The air howled out of the rows in a sound that reverberated through her bones.

Irona buried her face in her lap. Her arms curved about her ears but madness roared through her brain and the tears she could not shed swallowed her vision.

28

A NEW EARTH

Irona fled through the night she had created. What matter the dancing sunbeams, the racing clouds above Settlement? In her dugout she hurled herself onto the couch of discarded clothing, trying to bury herself alive.

She should not be alive.

And Twiss came to her, hours later, or minutes. Tears wove down his face between the dark sores and fell to drown in her hair. Deep sobs racked him and against her will her arms crept out to hold his pain. Never once had he wept for Granfer, but now he wept. Her body revolted from his touch but she could not lie quiet and feel him cry alone.

Guilt was the colour of death in midnight waters.

He was the only one who could know how she felt, exactly how she felt. Because his guilt was greater than hers.

'I didn't mean to!' was no consolation for the corpses washing between the shattered pastel walls.

In the face of such horror sleep was the only place to go, and dark dreams boiled up in the cauldron of fever to torment her.

It was sunset when she awoke. Twiss's arms held her, following her movements even when he was absent from consciousness. His touch was a comfort, the warmth of him, the familiar feel of his contours, his very smell.

Here she had known joy. Here she had known the illusion of safety. His skin was smooth beneath her hands.

And she understood that everything had a price, even pleasure, even life. Everything had to be paid for.

She lay still, feeling him breathe, her arm cramping beneath his weight. If she moved she would have to do something, and what could she do? Could she call back the smothering waters? Give life back to the floating children, so peaceful as they washed up and down between the pink and turquoise walls of the town?

So she lay without moving, wishing she did not have to wake to this, seeing the naivety of his stubbly face so plain in his sleep. The sweat of fever slicked his skin and hers was just as clammy. The larva-bite on her neck throbbed. She knew that soon she would have to get up, to be decisive, to care for Settlement and that meant caring for Twiss because he was the one who could wake the sleepers to action.

And somewhere Regen was taking possession of the Kiflian tower, setting up government in the room beneath the onion dome while Sticker rounded up the survivors and herded them to work. He would be taking Tang prisoner, and Less and the boy, Lal.

Regen. She imagined the little balding man with the pot-belly, the lord of all he surveyed, gazing through the muslined window out to the majesty of the volcano with its pure cap of snow. It would be blushing now in the sunset, pink, the colour of a baby's cheeks, and the sky would be blue shading to violet. Here and there would be a star, twinkling, serene above the agony of Kifl.

How many deaths would Sticker and Regen have on their conscience?

From somewhere came the scent of pines and rhododendrons, oranges and vines, a memory of that hillside from where she had first seen the sea. She wished she could sleep and never wake up; the sun bled into the darkening sky.

Her pocket screen pinged insistently. Sticker. The sound brought Twiss awake as her unhappiness hadn't done. He held out his hand and she silently passed the monitor over.

Sticker rubbed a hand over his greasy blond hair. He was in some sort of hall, on a balcony overlooking a crowd of Kiflians smeared with mud and tears. 'Twiss, you never told me you was really going to do it,' he said. 'I've never seen so many people dead.'

'Then you should have opened your eyes when we buried

ourn.' Twiss shrugged dismissively. 'Never mind that. Have you found Tang?'

'No—'

'Find him.'

Sticker wasn't going to argue with that. He added unhappily, 'Nor I ain't found that Lal kid neither. We're still working on it.'

'Do that.'

Twiss broke contact and told Irona to get in touch with Regen. Just as Irona had thought, the little man was in the Synod tower, leaning over Less's shoulder telling Less what he wanted on the computer.

'Regen?' Irona asked, wanting forgiveness.

He nodded to her. 'I know it weren't you. You never done it, Ro.'

Knuckling the sleep from his red-rimmed eyes, Twiss said sharply, 'Never mind that. Have you found Tang and Lal?'

Regen stared past Twiss. 'I ain't finished talking to Irona. Listen, girl, we know what was meant to happen – and what did. So we got to get past that entirely. Look on the bright side – solves a lot of housing problems. Now if Twiss ain't got anything worth saying, I'll get on.'

But Twiss thought he had. He called for the only member of the Kiflian Synod who was left.

For the first time ever, Less was dishevelled. His black and white hair stood on end; the lines on his face were scored deeply in a complexion turned the colour of mud. His satin tunic was still dripping with filthy water. Wet footprints lay behind him on the marble floor. 'What do you want?' he said. His voice was the sound of defeat.

'Our land. The land we were promised before we ever left Earth. And the power we were given. Medicines. Food. Shelter. We want everything.'

Less shook his head from side to side. 'We haven't got it. We haven't even got it for ourselves any more, not since you called up the sea.'

Twiss raised his brows. 'Then we'll take what you have got. You owe us. Now tell us how to cure the snake-rat plague.'

'We didn't send the plague, Twiss—'

'Don't you lie to me! I've got your deve plague and there's people out here dying of it.'

Less spread his empty hands, beseeching. 'We never sent it, honestly. All you've got is reaction to their bite. Believe me. Gundmila wanted to send it, and so did Lal. They made it, not me. But we wouldn't let them send it, me and Tang. I didn't want you bringing a plague back here. I knew you'd be back. And Tang said the snake-rats were enough to bring you to your knees. We never sent it, Twiss—'

Settlement's leader thrust his face closer to the pocket screen. Irona could feel his anger blaring out. Synod alone knew what Less saw.

'Don't you call me Twiss and then lie to me! Twiss is what my friends call me. You call me by my given name or don't speak to me at all. You killed my – my people! You're no friend of mine.'

Less was trembling, the grey pouches beneath his eyes sagging. 'What is your given name?'

'Arcturus.' He said it again, enunciating every syllable. 'Do you think you can manage that?'

Less's striped brows drew together. 'Of course I can!' he snapped. 'What do you think I am, stupid?'

Twiss smiled, gave a faint nod. 'I know you are. Or you wouldn't have tried to rob me. Now send the tractors out. And find somewhere nice to live for my people by noon tomorrow or we'll kill the rest of you.' Then his next words brought hope leaping to Irona: 'We're coming home.'

Home: a warm place inside her. No more Synod with its plagues and destruction and walls around her spirit. No more loneliness and hunger. Twiss would no longer be driven; he would be kind and loving and give her that feeling of safety again. The past could not be changed, but it was behind them. Once again he would hold her and whisper love in the night.

Except Tang and Lal were still somewhere on the loose.

The evacuation of Settlement Knoll kept Irona busy. For minutes together she could manage not to think of the destruction she had unleashed, the pain that kept her and

Twiss apart when it should have brought them together for mutual comfort.

Tebrina organised the women to start at one end of Settlement while Marjine marshalled the children at the other. Centimetre by centimetre they combed the dugouts for anything that might be the slightest use. Irona stacked the treasure trove in the space between Jai's Hospital and the tunnel, stowing the power-packs in crates two other women were knocking up for her. She carefully wadded soft plastic around the precious machinery.

On one of Marjine's periodic trips back to the growing bales outside the Hospital a flaccid woman called Regina grabbed her arm.

'Do something, Marjine. That Irona won't let me take my mother's table-linen with me.'

'Then leave it here.' Over in one of the rows a fight broke out between two boys. 'And get out of my way, will you? They children are running riot.'

'But my mother gave it to me.'

Marjine raked her with a glance of vitriolic contempt. 'Just pack it in that crate over there for the next trip, woman, and get out of my road.'

Regina obstinately barred Marjine's way though one of the combatants was crying now, the other boy kneeling astride him and punching his nose again and again. 'She got it special. I ain't leaving it.'

'It'll still be here when we send the tractors out again.'

She said loud and shrill, 'I ain't leaving it and that's flat.'

Irona had heard the altercation. Wearily she balanced a power-pack on a crate-lid and went around the head-high pile of salvage to see what was wrong. She found Regina, her chin stuck out pugnaciously, glowering at Marjine who was dark-faced with anger.

'It's all right, Marjine.' Irona spoke softly so they would have to listen hard to hear her. 'You get back to the kids. I'll deal with this.'

Deliberately turning her back on her aggressor, Marjine stormed off. You could hear her roaring at the boy on top.

'I'm taking it.' Regina folded her arms over her flabby stomach.

'There isn't room. I've told you that already.'

Regina's teenage son, Garwin, raced over to say, 'Come on, Mum, don't make a scene.'

Regina tugged angrily at her girdle with its old-fashioned knots of modesty. 'You stay out of this! And as for you, Irona, I'm not having no chit of a girl telling me what to do with my own mother's gifts. And how do you know it'll be all right? You never saw they snake-rats coming, nor the poison neither. How do you know what this Synod-forsaken place is going to throw at us next?'

Her words stung as they were meant to. But reason wasn't working. Looking at her in exasperation, Irona saw that she was one of the few who hadn't realised how impractical the heavy clothes of modesty were out here in the oppressive heat of Harith. Regina would never change; she shook her son's hand off.

So Irona used threat. 'Synod, woman, can't you get it through your thick head? If we take every last little thing there won't be room enough for the people on the first trip. Unless you want to stay behind with Garwin while your precious linen goes in your place.'

And Irona stared her in the eye until it was Regina who dropped her gaze.

Different faces, the same argument. All through the night as the moons cast their racing blue shadows it wore Irona down more than humping the heavy power-packs into their makeshift cases.

Meantime Twiss had the men carry all the wounded to shelters close by. At times the noise was indescribable as the little ones raced around. Everyone, it seemed, was yelling orders at everyone else.

The light of the power-packs was guttering towards a fitful orange as the first grey stole across the sky. The Second Wavers who could still fight against the fever were slumped wearily against the piles of bags and boxes, too tired to do more than spill out the odd desultory word, but everything was packed.

Irona walked round the rows for one last check to make sure that nothing and nobody had been left behind. All that was left was her computer but she wouldn't pack that away until the very last moment. She felt blind without the Eye, helpless, but the computer had other functions and she wouldn't leave herself without its back-up until she had to. As she passed, she patted it.

Then she came back to sit with Jai in the open doorway of the Hospital, each leaning her aching back against a door-jamb. Twiss moved over to kneel behind her, rubbing the back of her neck where the muscles were stiff. She shifted a little to let her head rest on his shoulder and his arm crept round her, his hand finding hers and stroking it gently. Neither of them had the energy to say a word.

Not far away, crouching in the dust, the two boys who had been fighting were playing a quiet game of jacks. The pebbles clashed softly in their hands in time to their whispered chanting.

Tebrina and Sinofer were further along the wall, their shoulders close to keep warm against the pre-dawn chill. Both of them were gazing out past the glimmering barrier at the dunes lying pale under the lightening sky. Fessbar was asleep in her lap.

'Reckon they snake-rats'll be something well worth not being here for when the rest of 'em come back,' Tebrina said.

Irona felt Twiss smile.

The barrier went dark; its quiet humming faded. There was nothing between them and the Interior now. Silence hissed in their ears.

Sinofer cocked his head at the inert wire that gleamed gun-metal in the growing light. 'Regen's done it then.'

Irona yawned. 'Of course he has. He said he would.'

A courting couple came sheepishly out of the tunnel now that the barrier no longer kept them safe. The boy ducked his chin to his chest, hoping nobody would recognise him, but the girl was made of sterner stuff. She held her head high, glancing neither right nor left as she walked towards the Hospital, heading past it for the friendly, lightless rows.

Suddenly she pointed. A child, the boy with the bloody nose, whipped round to look. The jackstones fell clinking from his hands. 'What's that?' he said nervously, his piping voice reaching fear into every Settler's heart.

Sinofer leaped to his feet. 'You stay here.' He ran to the corner of the Hospital and skidded to a halt, peered round the crumbling wall.

He didn't need to tell them because they all followed. Out to the west something flashed on the slopes of Moon Mountains.

Irona reached automatically for her pocket screen and cursed. No Eye. It had exploded over the towering seas. She tapped frantically for Sticker but he didn't reply.

Sinofer came loping over. 'Two tractors, far's I can see, with a deve great trailer behind each one. The question is, are they loaded with Kiflian armies or space for the good guys?'

Twiss looked down at Irona. 'Any word yet from Sticker?'

She shook her head. 'He's not answering. Synod knows why.'

He reached behind him for the knife at his waist.

Finally the opaque tractor lurched around the edge of Settlement and slowed before the tunnel. Twiss met it outside the barrier that was useless now – but they might not know that, the ones hidden inside the blue sides of the vehicle.

Whoever they were.

While the second tractor was still some way behind, bouncing down through the New Canal and up again on its balloon tyres, Twiss waited warily. Behind him stood a group of men and women armed with spears and bows and arrows. Some had farming tools whose plastic gleamed bronze in the rising sun. Whatever else Harith had taught them, the Second Wavers knew all that the Admin had tried so long to breed out of the human race: anger, fear, aggression.

The hatch of the tractor slammed open. Someone climbed up, silhouetted against the brightening east. The knuckles of Twiss's hand tightened on the haft of his knife . . .

And Thebula called, 'Hey, Twiss! You should see the place we've got to sleep!'

29

A NEW BEGINNING

Somewhere behind the mountains the sun crept upwards, invisible as yet but paling the sky. Kifl was still in shadow but there was a blush over the snows of the volcano as Garwin swung the lead tractor into the town. He ordered it to park on the promenade, proud of his responsibility and boyishly glad he hadn't crashed the trailer. He looked round for approval and Irona sleepily nodded and smiled her praise. Most of the forty or so settlers inside the tractor were fast asleep.

As the vehicle sighed to a halt, Irona sat up to look out of the window. It was a painful sight. The houses were battered and windowless; fallen trees were tangled with chunks of masonry to block the streets. Kifl was no longer an idyll in pastels but a ruin in shades of grey-brown mud. The place was deserted.

Twiss's head was pillowed in her lap. She woke him from his doze.

'Hi!' He yawned then a grin spread over his face as he realised where they were. 'We done it, Ro! Where's Sticker?'

Irona jerked her chin at the two figures waiting by the stumps of some palm-trees. 'Over there with Regen. Coming?'

He nodded and she reminded him, 'Don't let our people off the tractors until we know what's what.'

Climbing down, they smelt rotting seaweed sharp as sewage; mud-smears steamed on the walls of the town but a salt breeze from the sea battled with the stench. Twiss and Irona looked at each other and linked arms.

Sticker and Regen trotted half-way to meet them. Sticker looked exhausted; he said next to nothing but Regen's eyes shone with a gleam between friendly and manic as he hugged Irona.

The little man's twitches were well back in evidence; his words tumbled over one another to get out of his mouth. 'Don't ask!' he told her, wrinkling his nose too at the foulness of the air. 'You wait 'til you get into the rows where the wind don't come. Hee-hee. We ain't cleared it yet entirely. Hee-hee. And I been co-ordinating damage and casualty reports. That Less feller don't like it none but he knows he's got to help me or his lot are in the – in difficulties.'

Twiss managed to override Regen's flow of words for long enough to say, 'What about you, Stick?'

But it was Regen who answered. 'Sticker's been up half the night tunnelling survivors out of what's left of the library. Some sort of breakfast party it were. One feller told me he thought the tidal wave were the climax to his poem.' Regen giggled for a second and then plunged back into speech before his hearers could say a word. 'Some places we ain't dug out of the mud yet but we're getting a fair idea of who ain't dead.'

'How many died? And where are the Kiflians?' Irona asked.

'Couple of hundred dead 'uns swimming about in the mud. Ain't swimming very far no more. We ain't finding so many still alive when we get 'em out of the wreckage. The rest, well mostly we got 'em locked up in halls and stuff. Getting on for fifteen hundred—'

Sticker said, 'More like seventeen-fifty.'

Regen scarcely paused for breath. 'OK, seventeen-fifty. Still got they locked up though. We just let work-parties out but it'll be easier now we got more of us to keep an eye on 'em. Entirely.'

Irona was horrified. 'We can't keep them locked up! That'll just breed more resentment. Regen, they're too shocked to be anything but docile, aren't they?'

He nodded vigorously. 'I said to let 'em out to do their own rescuing, but Sticker, he weren't having none of it.'

Irona turned to Twiss. 'We need as much help as we can clearing up, don't we, Twiss?'

''Course we do. But we still need to keep an eye on they.'

She squeezed his arm. 'As soon as we've all had some

breakfast. I don't know about you, but I'm starving. Where did you make our base, Regen? Their Synod tower?'

'What do you take me for? 'Course I did. Entirely. We need their computers, don't we? 'Sides which, I thought you'd like it, Ro. And I got people taking food over there right now.'

'Never mind that!' Twiss said. 'Have you found Tang and Lal?'

'Nope. But we ain't found all the bodies yet neither.'

Twiss shook his head. 'They ain't dead, not they two. They're lying in wait. Wherever we go in their cursed city, we'll have to take guards or they'll stab us in the back.'

Irona paled. *Guards? No peace? No privacy ever?*

It seemed that the queue of Second Wavers waiting to be told where they could live was endless. There seemed to be dozens standing around talking nonsense at full volume; the Synod room echoed with it until she could hardly hear herself think. It didn't help either when Marjine bellowed for silence every five minutes, and Less wasn't as helpful as he might have been though they were working to re-house the Kiflians too.

One thing, Irona told herself as she juggled data to match survivors with habitable space, *at least the mud didn't get this high up so we can breathe*.

At last Marjine peered nervously down the grav-shaft and called, 'That it, then Thebula? Nobody else waiting?'

And from the bottom of the shaft Irona's bodyguard, Thebula, said, 'That's it.'

Irona, Tebrina and Less slumped with relief or stretched their backs in the humid air. 'Well I think we've done very well,' Irona told them.

Less wasn't so sure. He said sulkily, 'You've still thrown hundreds of us out of our homes—'

'But as few as we could possibly manage. We'll all have to share,' Irona answered him, trying to be pleasant despite the heat and her fatigue. 'And as we get more houses cleared things'll be better.'

'I know. You've told me that,' he said sulkily, brushing his hand over his black and white hair. 'May I have your gracious permission to go now? I've got my own clearing up to do.'

'Sarcasm doesn't become you. Of course you can go. But mind you're back after siesta. Six o'clock, all right?'

'It'll have to be, won't it? Otherwise you'd probably send someone over to torture me.'

Irona's patience snapped. 'Look, Less, it's your people's fault in the first place or none of us would be in this mess. Now we have to cope with the situation we've got. We're all in this together. Everyone's been fed, haven't they? And Jai's got all the wounded in hospital. Not bad for one morning. We can't do any more than we have done, so let's not gripe, OK?' She smiled brittlely at Less. 'I'll see you all back here at six.'

When she had pointedly seen him out, Tebrina and Irona shared amused glances while Marjine spread her hands on her ample hips and said, 'Well! The nerve of that man!'

It broke the tension.

Thebula drifted up to join in their gossip. Normally her cheerful, extravagant personality made Irona feel better; now, having her around all the time was a constant reminder that people wanted to kill her.

'What's the news, Theb?' Irona asked, striving for lightness.

The angular red-head scratched her shoulder-blade. 'No-one ain't found they rebels yet, if that's what you mean, but if anybody can, it's Regen and Sticker. Don't worry, Ro. Tang and Lal's history. I won't let anyone get you. Just call down if you need me.'

Irona lifted her hair from her nape for coolness. It gave her a moment to balance herself. Then she chatted with her friends for a couple of minutes before floating down a level to the two rooms she would share with Twiss: a spacious bed-sitting area and a bathroom. The grav-shaft still made her nervous but there was a thrill in it too. She was smiling as she jumped onto the cool stone floor. She couldn't see Twiss but there was splashing from behind the closed door.

Irona kicked off her shoes and spun through the vast space, her arms outstretched, revelling in the peace from everyone else's problems and the rest from so much Kiflian anger.

Curtains in shades of red kept the sun's glare out but let a sea-breeze in; she loved the feel of the cool air. To live in the moment helped her not to think of the dead . . .

'Long day, isn't it?' said Twiss, wrapping a towel around his waist as he left the bathroom, and she stopped dancing. Her hands fell awkwardly to her sides.

Irona was still nervous when he spoke. She never knew how he was going to react to anything she said. Above all, though, she feared he would take something innocent amiss and push her away again.

So she kept her thoughts superficial – it was all that was holding her together – and contented herself with answering, 'Sure was. You should have heard Tebrina trying to sound sympathetic.'

He grinned. For a little while neither of them spoke. Irona wondered what would happen to the ferocious anger the usurped home-owners must feel. What had happened to Arias Tang. To Lal. Then she found herself puzzling over the safety of Regina's bed-linen and she grinned to herself.

'I definitely need a bath.'

While the water ran she lingered to enjoy the luxury of two clean rooms whose marble walls shone from the work of dust-bugs. *I'll never have to scrub again . . . or cook.*

There was a balcony, just like her home back in Camelford. There was a real bed with real plastifoil bedclothes. Where Twiss lay back on them, fresh from his shower, smiling at her simple pleasure, the heat from his body shimmered the fabric through orange silk to gold. There were pictures on the walls, mood-scenes that blossomed at the point of sunrise: the Park, a stallion, a squirrel bounding through oak trees above a badger and her frolicking cubs.

There was a disk-viewer, just like back on Earth.

Steam curled round the door from the bathtub that filled at the touch of a lever.

'But the best thing's all this space! Synod, Twiss, that dugout wasn't a patch on this.'

Twiss lay, head pillowed on one arm, watching her. She pirouetted towards the bathroom, trying not to acknowledge the tension that still hung between them making her feel as though she were on trial, but he said, 'Come here.'

And she stopped, poised like a deer for flight.

He said it again and she moved slowly to him, sitting when he patted the bed beside him.

'I know you think I've been too hard, Irona. But I had to be. Can you understand that? I couldn't watch anybody else die.'

She gathered her courage and said, 'You tricked me; that's what hurts. I'd never have gathered the waters if you hadn't told me it was just a demonstration. A bluff.'

'I know. But you're right. If I'd told you, you wouldn't have done it and we'd still be out there dying. I had to—'

'You lied to me! You manipulated me, Twiss. Killing people one to one, I can cope with that. I hate it but I can do it if I have to. You know, Twiss. You saw me. Because then it's them or us, and I won't watch my friends killed. If I could have got to Gaeta . . . But that – we didn't have to do it. Not really.' Irona buried her face in her hands, sudden sobs racking her. She tried not to let it happen, tried not to let her shoulders shake or the tears spill scalding from her eyes, and she hated her weakness. She dreaded what he might say . . .

'I'm not lying to you now, Irona. You don't know what it did to me.'

She lifted her head then, her blue-green eyes blazing. 'It made us as bad as them. Worse, even, because we knew it was wrong! How can we justify taking the lives of tiny babies? Tell me that, Twiss, and I'll tell you how bad you feel.'

Through the window drifted the perfume of wisteria – and the rank smell of drying mud.

He reached out a hand to her but one look at the anger in her face made him drop it without ever touching her. 'Don't do this to me, Ro.' His voice was a whisper in the sunlight, soft as the coloured muslin that floated on the breeze. 'Don't hate me. I need you.'

'You don't need anyone but yourself, Twiss. Regen and me, we were just tools that you used because we happened to be handy.'

'You've never been that. Not you. You were always the same, Ro, always so kind and welcoming and loving whatever I did. I went out and hurt people to stop it happening to us any more, but I needed you to take the pain away. You showed me how to care about people. You're the one who showed me that Granfer really loved me, and I never knew. I never knew until it was too late.'

Twiss reached out again, hesitantly, and she could sense that he feared rejection as much as she did. It was just that usually he didn't let her see it. And she could feel his need for tenderness.

In the bathroom the scented water touched the base of the faucet and automatically turned itself off. The room was silent but for the sleepy sounds of the afternoon. The curtains flickered, snapped gently in the breeze. Twiss's breath came fast and shallow with his urgency to convince her. Her empathy netted his emotions: need, love, desire for understanding.

And more.

All this in the fraction of a second between his reaching out to her and beginning to recoil, hurt, into himself. *How could I let him feel that bad?* She took his hand.

He sat forward, his other arm coming around her shoulders. Inside herself was the thought, *What if he knew I really can feel what he's feeling some of the time? That I used to feed off his joy to make me come alive? Would he think I'm a freak of the Admin? A spy? I can't let him find out* – but now his fingers were stroking the skin of her arm, touching the inside of her elbow. He was so gentle that she could feel a shiver of longing building up inside her. *How much I need his gentleness! Synod* (his arm tightened around her, pulling her a little so that she half-lay against him) *he doesn't know how much I need him to love me!*

Now, still holding her against the warmth of his chest, he let his other hand tingle up her arm, his fingers drawing circles on the soft skin above her breast. He bent his head to kiss the nape of her neck, her collar-bone, his lips tender with a sincerity he could not disguise.

He does love me! she thought. *I wasn't fooling myself after all. This time he means it.*

She wouldn't let herself think *For how long?*

His fingers curled through her hair. Then, lightly, but not to be denied, he turned her face towards him and kissed her mouth, his tongue gliding over the outline of her lips before plunging into her.

She responded with a passion she had not known she could feel. Irona held him to her as though she could take his body completely into her own. Her breath came hot and fast. He kissed her again and she could feel a moan of pleasure starting low inside her and building up and up.

He slid further down the bed, pressing his leg between her thighs. Heat knotted low in her abdomen. Twiss kissed her again, fingers probing for points beside her spine that made her body move of its own accord. Then, very delicately, he parted her bodice and stroked lower. The tips of his fingers teased her nipples until the weight of her breast lay in his palm.

He moved his hips against hers then, his tongue once more speaking wordless love. It breathed in the air caught warm between their faces, sang in the trembling of their bodies until she lay naked on top of him, tasting the clean salt of his chest, licking the hollow at the base of his throat. She ran one hand through the hair behind his ear, while the other crept down to the soft curls at his loins. It was he who hummed low in his throat then.

Slowly, lovingly, he gave her pleasure with all of his being until she surrounded him with her self and he encircled her with his arms, stroking her waist, supporting her. The rhythm of her movements bound them together. There was no start and no end to their being; the barriers between worlds slipped away and she arched her back, crying out, reaching for his release . . .

And afterwards he pillowed his cheek on her breasts, holding her safe while her chin nuzzled at his hair. He didn't know the comfort of her tears, the ultimate expression of her joy. Finally, finally there was someone who loved her, truly loved her. His arm lay across her, not letting her go. Delight laughed softly in her and when he stirred in puzzlement, she kissed the crown of his head.

'Let it be all right, Irona. Make it be all right.'

But she wasn't sure he had spoken. And she didn't think now was the time to tell him of the babe nestled within her.

Clad in a bright Kiflian gown of violet with daring three-quarter sleeves, Irona sang as she walked into the council three weeks later. She wasn't a very good singer at the best of times; Regen took a nectarine from the bowl on the marble table and threw it at her, saying, 'Here, put that in your cake-hole. You couldn't carry a tune in a bucket.'

She giggled and bit into the yellow and red fruit, slyly tossing a bunch of cherries at him as she breezed past to the window. 'And I love you too.'

'Thebula downstairs, is she?'

Irona smiled in a parody of archness. 'Of course she is! How could I live without my shadow? And no doubt young Garwin is basking in the sun of Twiss's indifference.'

She caught herself and let the bitterness bleed out of her voice. Leaning on the sill, she said, 'Synod, the sea is so beautiful, Regen. I never imagined! Look at it, all blue and gold in the sun. And those houses! See how pretty they've made the solar panels? I love this individuality stuff they built for, don't you? Much more fun than the Admin.'

'They don't seem to think it's that much fun, do they? Half of 'em seem to spend their lives fannying about up in that volcano crater. Hee-hee. Seen the shots from the weather-Eye?'

Irona nodded. 'I don't get it, Regen, do you? You'd think they'd put a bit of muscle into rebuilding. Synod knows there's enough to do. Some days I can hardly get out of bed and they've got the energy to drag themselves up the best part of three thousand metres to dance the night away. It really drives me wild when there's so many houses still to shore up.'

Regen came to stand beside her. He was dressed in fresh tunic and trousers of russet and amber but he still contrived to look scruffy. For once he smelt of soap and his fine hair ruffled as the wind swooped past. 'It ain't the houses that are up that you wants to be worrying about. It's all they new ones they'll have to build. We'll have to build.'

Twiss jumped lightly from the grav-shaft, startling them. 'I heard that. And we will build. We'll build a palace the likes of which ain't never been seen. It'll be all stained glass like a rainbow.'

Regen sniffed. 'And good-morning to you too. Entirely. But it ain't no palace we need, it's more land to build on and more land to grow food. They Kiflians don't exactly love us.'

Irona could see Twiss was trying to cling onto his good mood. 'Well, we got power, and we got a whole ocean to fish in, and we got plenty of people to work for us.'

Regen blew out his cheeks to spit, glanced at Irona and thought better of it. 'Maybe, but they ain't going to like it much, are they? And we ain't got that Tang feller neither. I ain't so worried about that kid, Lal or whatever his name was, but Tang, he's something else entirely.' He let a cherry-stone fall from his mouth to spin down to the strange garden below.

Twiss threw out his arms expansively. 'But we got a whole lifetime to do it in, ain't we? Several, in fact, if that there Gundmila weren't bullshitting. I looked up her records 'fore I came up here and if they're right, she was sixty-three. Spryest sixty-three-year-old I ever did see.'

Irona wasn't going to be the one to burst Twiss's bubble. But Regen said, 'Slyest, more like. And if everyone's going to live that long with all their kids and all, it'll be standing room only before you can snap your fingers. Hardly worth leaving Camelford in the first place. And just think what it'll be like when the next ship gets here.'

'Synod, you're a gloomy deve, ain't you? We got a weather-machine now when you've finished tarting it up. We can give 'em Rainshadow Valley.'

'Yeah – soon's we sort out they snake-rats and the lizardoptera and any other little thing Harith happens to throw at us.'

Irona sensed that Twiss was only hanging onto his temper

with difficulty now and she didn't like it. He slouched back in the tallest chair, swinging his legs onto the table and letting them fall with a thud. 'I told you, didn't I? We'll catch Tang and Lal and then it'll be all plain sailing.'

'You trust that Less?' The question shot from Regen and he hunched his shoulders defensively.

Twiss smiled contemptuously. ''Course I do. He knows which side his bread's buttered on. Besides, he's nothing, just a sop to they Kiflians so they think they got a voice in Synod. And he knows what'll happen if he steps out of line.' There was power in him, a supreme confidence. 'Don't let Regen get you in a tizz, Ro. We got lifetimes to sort it all out in.'

Regen spat another cherry-stone from the window. A tic jumped fast below his eye. 'Yeah. That's what I'm worried about. Entirely.'

'Well you worry too much! You're worse than ever! What's wrong with a spot of eternal life? I ain't complaining!' Twiss stretched his arms back; it didn't take an empath to see that he was glorying in the strong pull of muscles over bone. He grinned, his mouth wide in simple delight, and the corners of Irona's mouth turned up in pleasure for his pleasure.

Twiss swivelled to sit upright, cracking his knuckles then linking his fingers on the black marble of the table. 'Now where's Sticker and that Less feller? I want to make a start.'

Sunlight slanted down through the leaves of the rhododendrons that screened the entrance to the bunker. Tang leant back against the rock wall, watching the play of emerald and gold light. Somewhere above, in the towering peaks of the Moon Mountains, he knew the weather-Eye would be out looking for him. For him and for Lal, but he knew it wouldn't be looking for Gundmila. The murderer Twiss had left her for dead.

It was Gundmila who came to him now because Lal was busy at his weapon, sending his little electronic 'viruses' to heighten the tensions in Kifl. Mostly he focussed the beam on the Synod tower but sometimes he jumped it around over the rest of the town. What with that, and Less fomenting unrest, and their supporters coming up with endless pettifogging complaints to clog up the wheels of the invaders' government, Tang was quite happy with the campaign so far.

Gundmila's uneven footsteps rounded the bend in the tunnel and she limped over to him. She had adopted a new hairstyle; one that brought a wave of her hair forward to cover the scars on the left side of her face. Propping her walking-stick within reach, she allowed herself to sit beside him in the pool of sunshine, using her hands to straighten her bad leg. She groaned with the pain in her wrist and shoulder where Twiss had skewered her flesh to the ground for the snake-rat larvae to crawl over her, eating her alive—

But Twiss made a mistake. He went to save his precious Granfer and he didn't finish the job. He and that goody-goody bitch didn't even have sense enough to transmit high frequencies to clear the snake-rats.

The pain of tearing free of the spikes with which Twiss had nailed her to the ground was still vivid inside Gundmila. Throwing off her robes which were riddled with snake-rats, she had dragged herself to the computer-shed through the deserted, infested rows of Settlement Knoll, larvae boring into her with every step. At her call Arias himself had come to take her to the hospital, but it was Lal who had hauled her out of the ruins of Kifl and brought her through the flood-waters to the bunker. *My life, my body, my – my face in ruins! And all because of Twiss. I'll make him pay with every last drop of blood in his body – and hers . . .*

'How's it going?' Tang asked.

'It's better today.' The tightness of her voice belied her words. Although she sat with the good part of her profile towards him, she still would not look at Tang. 'If I could only get back to the hospital in Kifl I'd be all right, but that murderous bastard Twiss is . . .' The rest of her sentence strangled in fury.

'We'll do it, Gundmila. All three of us, eventually. New faces and new body-identities and nobody will ever know. If Less gives us the all-clear, you and I'll do it tonight.'

30

UNDERWHEELS

Late summer burned on while Irona and the rest of the council slaved away, trying to get things right. Food, clothing, water, sewage from the impromptu camps some of the angry Kiflians had to live in while they waited for housing, and there were still whole areas of the Synod computer that Irona couldn't get into despite Regen's help. Less's access wasn't much less restricted than hers and the whole system might fall apart at any minute for lack of knowledge when it was needed.

And they still didn't know where Arias Tang was.

The builders wanted the tractors so that they could clear the ground; the agrarians wanted them to plough and seed new land with winter cereals. They needed a new reservoir and new pipes extruding. And everyone wanted everything NOW. Irona worked from dawn to dusk, but so did Twiss. Only he was out and about, jollying people along with his charm. Sometimes some of the Kiflians even deigned to smile at him.

Less peered over her shoulder at the list on the screen. His perfume was flowery, cloying. She had sometimes seen him hand in hand with a boy who looked about seventeen; it was a Kiflian habit she found strange and she couldn't decide whether the boy was Less's adopted son, his lover or his friend. Regen had said over and over that things like that weren't gossip, or judgment; they were levers, but Irona said merely, 'Whatever he is or isn't, it's none of my business and why would I judge him anyway? If he's found happiness, then great. But I'm not going to manipulate him or anyone else.'

Regen had shaken his head. 'Then you're missing the point. Entirely. Hee-hee.'

It seemed that Regen grew more and more jumpy the

longer he was in Kifl; he'd been all right in Rainshadow Valley – more or less. What he did say was, 'I ain't judging him neither. You reckon you're going to help Twiss weld this rabble into a citizenry? Then you need to use every weapon you can get. Hee-hee. And friendships with anybody count as weapons. Entirely.'

Now Less pointed to Irona's computerised list and said, 'Don't forget putting back the sea-walls your tidal-wave smashed down. We're going to need them come winter.'

He walked away again. She remembered to say thank you but she resented his cutting reminder.

She went back to screening endless personnel files to see who was best suited to what job. The trouble was, half the Kiflians didn't seem to be suited to any work at all. Reluctantly she asked Less about it.

'Well,' he said patronisingly, 'it's obvious. They were born after the colony was established. They've never had to do a day's work in their lives.'

'Why not? Even in Camelford everybody had to do something.'

'This isn't Camelford. And we're not sleepers. We always had enough power to get anything done – until you and your murderers came. We'd never had to grub in the earth, or weave, or any of that peasant crap.'

The violence of his words threatened her. Irona forced a quirk to her eyebrows, hoping to provoke him into further revelations.

Less looked at her, mockery on his slab-jawed face. 'You think you're smart but you still don't get it, do you? For the last thirty-nine years we've brought food dealt out by the depot to homes that cooked and cleaned for us, and you've taken that away. We sang; we danced; we lived in comfortable homes that we've built up over the years only you've got them now. We played elegant word-games and you got filthy and sweaty for nothing, because we knew that sooner or later Harith would drive you over here and we'd have to flog our guts out for a bunch of deve sleepers. We asked the Matriarch not to send you but she wouldn't listen.'

'The Matriarch? Which matriarch? When?'

Irona could see that Less thought he'd said too much. He covered up with bravado. 'Well wouldn't you like to know? But I owe her my loyalty and I don't owe you spit. I wouldn't piss on you if you were on fire except that Twiss would burn us all. Now put emergency services on your deve list. And have you done anything about that fractured waste-pipe yet?'

'Why haven't you? Your people live in Kifl too.'

'No,' he shot back. 'We exist in nooks and crannies in Kifl now you sleepers are here.'

'At least in Camelford most of us didn't choose to be sleepers. That's what you lot have chosen. You watch the same story-cubes over and over again like children let loose with adult toys. You won't do anything constructive even to save your lives, and we're working ourselves to death for you.'

'Then hurry up and die! We didn't want you here in the first place.'

'But we are here and we're not leaving. So you'll have to get used to it, and if you're all going to survive you'll have to get it through your thick heads that you'll all have to work. What with nursing-machines and dozens of idle relatives for every child, you're all spoiled rotten. The only thing you're good at is complaining.'

Wandering over yet again to look over her shoulder, Less said, 'And by the way, in case you haven't noticed it, that little flashing light means the next delegation's here.'

At three in the morning, two figures crossed the gardens of Kifl's hospital. The taller one was walking normally but the woman's leg dragged and she leant heavily upon her companion for support. A filthy rag dripped blood onto the floor. A splinter of what might have been bone stuck through the scarlet cloth.

A trainee nurse – a Settler, of course – helped them straight up the grav-shaft and into one of the treatment rooms since there were no other urgent cases. He said, 'Wait here, and prop that leg up. I'll just get the doctor.'

The woman's oiled hair tumbled lankly over her face and

she hadn't even the strength, it seemed, to push it out of her eyes. She was white and close to fainting.

'Can't you at least give her a pain-killer?' the man asked frantically.

The nurse, Tregannon, shook his head. 'Sorry, I'm not allowed to use the olfactory yet. I haven't been here long enough.' He didn't look too well either. He gulped and sped off.

Under her chalky make-up, Gundmila smiled at the clean-shaven man with the bald patch. 'You were right, Arias. Nobody'll think of looking for us here in plain sight.'

'Squeeze a bit more of that blood out, will you? I don't want that nurse getting any closer than he has to.'

Gundmila laughed behind her hand. 'You're gilding the lily. He's just like Less said he would be.'

'No, I'm playing safe. Once we look different and we're safe to build up our power-base, it won't matter, but I don't think King Twiss would be too unhappy if we were found dead.' He ran his fingers over the stubble where his hair was growing through its tonsure. 'Do you think being blond would suit me?'

Yet again when Irona walked in through her own door, she called, 'Twiss? Are you there?' And yet again he wasn't. Leadership was taking its toll of them both.

Trying not to mind, she dialled a snack salad from the autochef and sat down to designing houses on her computer. That wasn't easy with limits on power, but at least it was peaceful. As the sky blushed to evening and the internal lights glowed brighter to compensate, she waited for Twiss to come home.

He was out and about, she knew, trying to work his charm on the older Kiflians. She trusted him to win them over sooner or later by his cheerful pragmatism and his sense of humour. She could picture him, his cream shirt billowing loose across his chest, glorying in his physical strength as he gave a hand with the reconstruction. Or he'd order everyone about until they could have strangled him, then commission some hideous monument from a Kiflian light-sculptor to commemorate the urban renewal, and make a fan for life.

Knowing the Kiflians, another sculptor would probably argue because the commission should have been hers in the first place.

Irona sighed and spent another evening at her task. On the balcony night-lilies opened their snowy trumpets to the moons and she breathed in their satin perfume, letting it soothe her. Musky aerial plants glided in and out on the breeze from the night-dark sea. If she looked behind her, she could see the white cone of the volcano floating serene above the town.

Sighing again, not willing to admit to herself that she was lonely while Twiss was away, she settled again to plotting where to build the next batch of houses so as not to waste arable land.

When at last she called Baika, the Kiflian woman in charge of building, to give her the plans, the woman didn't do her the courtesy of coming over. She merely glanced cursorily at the blueprints on the screen and laughed at her.

'Those? They won't work.'

Irona bridled. 'Why not?'

'Because you haven't designed the bricks to interlock in case of earthquakes. Didn't you even find that much out from that computer of yours? Or maybe it's just because you're so young.'

'So how old are you?'

Baika leant back on one meaty arm and raised her brows. 'What sort of question is that to ask a lady?' she asked, and Irona stared at her in surprise. The only women she knew who objected to revealing their age were the ones who were so old it showed, like Tebrina pretending she hadn't got grey hair. Baika wasn't pretty – she was squat, her head melon-shaped, her body a horizontal oval as though someone had dropped a tonne weight on her and flattened her out, but she didn't look old. Maybe it was the fat under her sweat-sheened skin that plumped out the wrinkles but she didn't look a day over thirty. There wasn't a white hair in the wiry red bush that sprang out aggressively from her head.

Irona made a mental note to call up the woman's age later in private. 'I'm sorry.'

'I should hope so too. Now think about it, will you? Here where it's hot, we don't want over-crowding. And we need either narrow houses or ones with a courtyard so the air can circulate. And we got to get a move on. This overcrowding is vile.'

'We all have to make sacrifices,' Irona said smoothly.

Baika's answer was blunt. 'We do since you lot horned in to our space. And have you thought about where we can get the power from to change this much soil into flexible stone?'

'Why flexible?'

'Why do you think? Or don't you think at all? It's for extra protection when the earthquakes come, of course.'

'Do you get many?'

Baika laughed gruffly. 'You don't need many. One'll do it if it's a good one. We've had three since we started Kifl: one just days after landing, a big tremor two years after we built the first town – it killed dozens of us. If you want to play queen to King Twiss, you'll have to do your homework rather better than that.' And Baika signed off.

The encounter left a sour taste in Irona's mouth. It wasn't as if housing were her only problem. The town was so crowded there were even Kiflians sleeping in the grain-silos and that couldn't go on much longer with the harvest coming closer by the day. The sheer mechanics of making a colony designed for fewer than a thousand feed and clothe and shelter the prolific First Wavers was bad enough, but trying to make it work for another three hundred drove her to distraction.

She threw her stylus onto the desk and said aloud, 'I give up.'

Swivelling in her chair, she wondered where Twiss was. Loneliness dragged at her for a while but she wouldn't give in to it. She told the computer to call Jai if she weren't too busy. Even as she waited for the call to go through, Irona glanced out through the window at the night sky. She was shocked to see by the stars how late it was – anxiety about Twiss roiled her again but she overrode it. But it was so late that if the lights in her screen hadn't meant that the call was already going through, she'd have cancelled it. The sky was luminous with the moonrise over the sea. It must have been almost midnight.

'Mmm?' Jai said, her voice thick with sleep. 'Who's that?'

'It's me.'

The screen showed Jai's bedroom windowless, the way she preferred it after her years on the ship. A thread of a glow from a half-open door showed only that Jai was in bed, the covers rumpled around another figure that Irona naturally assumed was Sticker. The scene was cosy, domestic – and Irona was intruding. She averted her eyes.

'Mmm?' Jai said again. 'Me who?'

'Me Irona, who do you think?'

The man yanked the bedclothes over his head. Irona put the abruptness of his action down to irritation at being woken up.

Jai jerked upright, carefully pulling the covers up even higher to hide her shoulders. 'What do you want, Ro?'

'Nothing. Sorry to have disturbed you. I didn't know you were asleep. I just called for a chat.'

'Why – why don't you drop by the hospital tomorrow?' Jai yawned.

'I will. Sorry again. You haven't seen Twiss anywhere about, have you?'

The whites of Jai's eyes flashed in the little bit of light. 'No, not for ages. He was here buttering the doctor up' – the man beside her must have touched her under the sheets, because Jai stifled a nervous giggle – 'but that was hours ago. I expect he'll be back in a bit. G'night.'

'G'night.'

Jai didn't sound herself. I wonder what it was.

Dismissing the thought, Irona went to bed to wait for Twiss. She felt so sorry for him when he finally came in and fell straight into an exhausted sleep.

Not three weeks later, Twiss looked round his council: Irona, Sticker, Regen and Jai. They were all of them jumpy and out of sorts.

'It's driving me mad, all this.' He pushed himself restlessly out of his chair and went to look down through the window. Rain was falling persistently from a grey sky, dragging down everyone's spirits. 'They won't do a damned thing to help themselves.'

Sticker didn't seem to think it concerned him. He scratched his eyebrow, yawning. Regen, as usual, was fiddling with the computer, still trying to hook up the psychicator to the weather-Eye, but at least they knew he was listening. If he had anything to say, he'd say it.

Irona and Jai exchanged a glance; Jai cleared her throat and began to speak at the same time as Irona did. Irona apologised and waved to her friend to go ahead.

Jai said to Twiss, 'Maybe we should have a party – a big banquet sort of a thing. Make them feel more like we should all hang together.'

Twiss turned to look at her. Some of the tension relaxed from his face; the chiselled lines softened. 'Could be a good idea. What were you going to say, Ro?'

'I was going to say that maybe they'd feel better if they thought they were being represented properly in the council. Give Less his place back officially, not just as a guy we use to carry out routine admin, but as someone with the same clout as any of us.'

Regen, his grubby fingers agile about the puzzle he had set himself, nodded vigorously. 'He'll be outvoted anyway.'

Twiss sighed gustily. 'OK, we'll do that then.' Twiss was all decision now. 'But you keep your eye on him, Ro. I mean it. Regen, have you finished tarting up that Kiflian Eye yet?'

The little man half-lifted the object in his lap. 'Well, it's better. Still ain't got the full range of detectors in it but I'm getting there.'

'About time too. I don't want no secret messages getting through from Lal or that deve Tang. Have you found them yet, Sticker?'

Caught in mid-yawn, Sticker could only shake his head.

'Well I'm convinced one of they sons-of-bitches is behind all these I-know-my-rights complaints we keep getting. How many more we got coming through today?'

Irona asked the computer set into the polished stone of the table. It still wasn't completely happy about accepting her voice; there were whole areas she hadn't yet managed to access, even with Regen's help. Fortunately for her self-respect, it answered this request. 'Seven so far this morning, plus the ones we didn't have time to see from yesterday afternoon.'

Twiss threw his arms up in a theatrical gesture of despair. 'How do they expect us to get anything done with all their yap-yap-yapping? Sticker, for Synod's sake find Tang and Lal. Everywhere I go I hear their names as if they were saviours or something, then everyone shuts up when I get close. It's doing my head in.'

'We're working on it. We ain't going to let you down.'

Flopping back into the high-backed leader's seat with resignation in every movement, Twiss said, 'Make sure you don't.'

He didn't seem to notice how the atmosphere chilled as the rest of them felt the arrogance of his command.

Irona said urgently, 'Ssh!'

Regenerator obliged by cutting his jerky babble as she turned up the volume on the Kiflian computer. There were only two of the Settler leaders in the Synod room. She had kept Regen company as he worked out a way of eavesdropping on the public communications links. Now she slammed on the recorder to catch the damning fragments. Three speakers, all male as it happened, talking very fast.

'Synod, I've had enough of that arrogant bastard! Arcturus bloody Rex, indeed.'

'When Lal gets back he'll gut the stupid deve!'

'And Saint Irona. Synod, she gets up my nose.'

'When do they say they're coming back?'

'I'll let you know.'

'Now get off the line so they can't trace the call.'

Abruptly contact was broken. And the psychicator still wasn't working to pinpoint the rebels.

Shocked, Irona looked at her friend. '"They" who? Who's coming back, Regen?'

'You know. "They" must be Tang and Lal. You know.'
'We'll have to warn Twiss.'

'Can I take these symbiont bandages off now?' Gundmila
asked plaintively. They were in a twin-bedded room in a
side-ward of Kifl's hospital.

The doctor, Darien, smiled at her, no mean feat when her
face was greyish-green and swollen.

Tang drawled, 'Of course you can. That's what he came up
here for, isn't it?'

'Arias!' she said crossly.

Tang lifted an eyebrow at her, though the gesture was
hardly recognisable since he too had layers of goo plastered
on his skin. 'Then stop stating the obvious.'

Indulgently the slender doctor handed her the pot of cream
and insulating gloves. Darien had always had rather a soft
spot for the Matriarch of Kifl.

Gundmila slathered the evil-smelling stuff on her face and
neck and the doctor helped her with the delicate area around
the eyes. He also treated the thickenings on her wrist and
shoulder and thigh where the scars from Twiss staking her
had also been healing under the bio-generating bandage-
paste for the last three weeks.

Tang lay back on his couch and seemed to go to sleep
while Darien worked on him, though his slightly hastened
breathing showed that he too was under stress.

'I'll be back in an hour or so,' the doctor said when he
had finished. 'It'll probably itch and burn a bit but don't
touch it whatever you do.' He whisked lithely away down
the grav-shaft as Jai called him from below.

'Have you got everything ready, Arias?' Gundmila said
some time later.

'Of course I have.'

Time passed and the two had practically to bite themselves
to keep from screaming as the symbiont-bandage neutraliser
stung and itched. Gundmila beat at the mint-blue walls to
stop herself scratching, but at last Darien came back and
washed the clotted paste from their skin. Of course he showed
Gundmila her new appearance first.

Trembling, she took the mirror he held out. Red hair now, genetically red, growing at the roots, and a complexion pale as skimmed milk. The muscles on her jaw were broader, making her chin less pointed. A dye in the iris made her eyes a greener blue, but the doctor said, 'I'm not sure how well that's taken. Your eyes may revert to their original colour in time. Your hair-colour's fixed but I've tinted the ends until the colour grows through. But I think the triumph is the eyelids, don't you? Quite Oriental, wouldn't you agree?'

'Not a scar to be seen,' she said. Gundmila wasn't listening to him but trying to come to terms with being someone different. And with the scars Twiss had left in her psyche; the only remedy for them was revenge. She wasn't sure she liked the face she had become.

Arias Tang held in his impatience while the doctor orbited Gundmila. Finally he gave a small, deprecatory cough and the doctor said, 'Oh, right, yes, sorry.'

His eyes were a slatier blue, his cheekbones heavier so that the hollow cheeks had filled out, and his hairline now had something of a widow's peak. 'I think the longer nose suits me, don't you?'

'Not bad, Arias,' Gundmila said. 'A bit ironic, though, isn't it, that your hair's now exactly the same colour as King Twiss's?'

Less arrived. The doctor turned to greet him then went straight back to examining his handiwork.

It was a mistake. Less slapped an anaesthetic skin-patch on him that knocked the doctor out in seconds. Then, between them, they summoned down a hypno-shooter from the tangle of equipment on the ceiling.

Gundmila poised the shooter over the doctor's pineal gland, then glanced round. 'Don't just stand and watch me, you two! Less, sort the records out. Injuries in the glass-factory, remember? And use the names we told that Jai woman.'

'Don't teach your granny how to suck eggs. You get on with your part. And hurry up. You've got a riot to start in a couple of hours.'

Tang said, 'But he's on our side. Why do we have to screw up his reality?'

'Save your breath, Arias. You worry too much. He's only losing part of his mind, isn't he? What's that compared with winning Kifl back?'

Irona combed the town to find Twiss. She finally tracked him down via the Eye, and while she could have sent him a message that way now, she was too restless to stay cooped up in the Synod room. Grabbing a wind-proof jacket, she collected Thebula and the two of them strode through the rows under a cloud-wracked sky.

Twiss was on the shore, supervising the installation of new winding-gear on a trawler. A stiff breeze snapped Irona's sun-streaked brown hair around her ears and weathered her lover's face to a ruddy tan. Out at sea, mussel-farmers were dragging up their lines and a smell of fish, salt and engine-oil surrounded them. High above, battling against the wind, faded bronze lizardoptera threw out poignant snatches of song before plunging exhausted into the choppy waves.

Irona pulled him aside. She could tell the Kiflian fishers were trying to hear what she had to say; they stopped work and stood around to watch. A little breathless, she explained what she and Regen had overheard.

Twiss didn't seem at all grateful for her concern. Hands in pockets, he shrugged and said, 'So what? We knew they were coming back anyway. Sooner the better, if you ask me, then we can nail the bastards.'

'But Twiss! You don't understand! Some of the Kiflians are in with them and want to kill us.'

'Well, I ain't going to let that scare me. I can take care of myself, and you got Thebula to guard you, ain't you? What more do you want? You're such a wimp, you know that, Irona? Stop fannying about! I thought you were due to go and speak to some delegation at the food depot. So get on with it. I've got work to do.'

Annoyed, but aware that for her to quarrel openly with Twiss in front of the mixed group of Settler and Kiflian workers would ultimately damage the whole of Harith, Irona said, 'I don't need you to tell me my duty, Twiss,' and left with dignity. Not that he seemed to pay any attention. He went back to the group and threw his arm round the shoulders of a plump fisherwoman, who smiled up at him adoringly.

Normally Irona found walking through Kifl no problem, but this time when she and Thebula stepped out through the maze of narrow rows and garden squares, the atmosphere was different. *You're just being paranoid*, she told herself, but Thebula seemed nervous too and they walked close together through the dance of aerial plants in the plazas.

As they walked under the shadowed arches, the rows filled behind the two Settler women. Thebula kept glancing backwards, her hand on the hilt of the plastic sword she wore at her belt. Irona's gaze darted to every angle, every doorway and window; everyone she saw looked away. She was happier when they came out into the hot sunlight of the avenue and she discovered that Regen had sent the weather-Eye bobbing along above the almond trees. It couldn't do much good as yet but it was moral support.

At last she mounted the shallow steps of the depot with Thebula at her back, and forced herself to face the delegation, a dozen or so citizens in robes of green and red and yellow. She began to ask them what their demands were.

Her voice faltered. From side-rows and clothing depots, automatic factories and homes, hundreds of hostile First Wavers thronged out to surround her.

Her heart beat faster, the tapestry of Kiflian scents clogging her nostrils as she fought to keep her breathing calm, to look as though she weren't afraid.

Irona had to work hard to project her words above the growls of the rabble. 'How can I help you when you won't tell me what you want?'

Neither Irona nor Thebula noticed the red-headed woman in a tight turquoise bodice until she started yelling, 'Settler bitch go! Settler bitch go!'

The crowd joined in enthusiastically.

Irona caught the rage. She felt it corroding her veins, swelling her with the urge to lash out, to smash the ugly faces pushing at her with their stupid chorus. Her fingers itched to key an Eye to fire. She wanted to see electricity stab writhing at them. She wanted to hurt them.

Thebula's knuckles whitened around the hilt of her sword in its scabbard. Irona knew that at her word the red-head would carve the blood from the Kiflians' flesh. Irona lusted to give that word but she reached behind her and stayed Thebula's hand. It cost her dearly but the good of all Harith had to come first or she had lived for nothing. If the worst came to the worst, she and Thebula could always slip away through the depot.

So she stood, arms folded, tapping her foot in a faint display of impatience. Deliberately curving her brows to a patronising arch, she waited. And waited, while the breeze plucking at her rose-pink robe hid the shaking of her legs.

Then she heard someone say in a gap in the chanting, 'Arias'll screw Twiss's bitch when—'

But she didn't hear 'when' was to be because the next line of the chant rasped out of the angry throats of the mob. 'Settler bitch go!'

She tried to blank the chorus from her hearing; certainly she struggled not to show how it cut her. She was certain that they were working themselves up to kill her. Inside her, though she knew Regen would be summoning help, fear clawed to get out.

31

BEADS AND BUGS

It seemed she and Thebula had been standing for hours in the sunlight and hostility. The mob had taken over individual morality; it didn't take their contorted, rage-coarsened faces to stab their hostility in at Irona's empathy. A glance at Thebula showed she was affected too: tears of some fierce emotion were glistening in her eyes and she was trembling, but whether with fear or anger Irona couldn't tell with her battered senses. The chant echoed between the innocent curves of the walls; the aerial plants had fled. The red-head dressed in the turquoise took a step closer and Irona could see she had a brick in her hand.

Then Regen finally arrived. He had a key-pad in one hand and behind him trailed a little tractor overflowing with silks and trinkets and bottles of wine.

'Thirsty work, this, ain't it?' he called cheerfully. 'Want a drink, Ro?' He tossed her a soft plastic bottle, at the same time saying, 'What about you, mate? Want a drink?' Then he was tossing bottles in various directions. He affected not to notice when each time he turned to send a red bottle arcing into the crowd, someone stole a necklace, a bolt of gaudy cloth or a jewelled mirror.

The crowd didn't quite know what to make of it, but they seemed pleased to believe they were getting one over on the Settlers.

Regen said loudly, 'Hey, Ro, do you know they never gave out loads of goodies that come with us on the *Starwing*?'

Irona heard the hush falling, and played along with it. 'What? Stuff we brought?'

'Sure. I know where it is. Let's all go and see.'

He left, talking his little tractor along with a cheerful flow of inanities. First one or two Kiflians broke away from the mob to trail after him, then everyone followed, pushing and jostling along the row and into the vast machine shop where Sticker was standing high on a mountain of crates.

'Hi!' Sticker called cheerily. 'What's this?' His arm disappeared into a crate and re-emerged flourishing a box that gleamed as it rested on his fingers. 'Kid's musicube. Who wants it?'

'Me!' 'Me!' the mob shouted greedily.

Sticker lobbed it at a pregnant woman and said, 'Not to worry, folks. There's plenty more. Who wants the next one?'

With a showman's patter, Regen helped Sticker deal out the goods. He had everyone laughing – and he dropped the information, in his humorous way, that it wasn't his people who had kept such little luxuries locked up from the Kiflians, but their own leadership.

When the last of the townsfolk had scurried out of the echoing warehouse before someone could take their goodies from them, Sticker clambered out of the nest of crates and shredded padding. Irona gave him a hand, but the first question she wanted to ask was, 'Regen! It was a miracle! But what would you have done if they'd turned on us?'

He shrugged. 'Beat hell out of 'em with the thirty soldiers on the roof.'

It was Irona who voiced their doubt: 'Synod, I'd give anything to know where Tang and Lal are now.'

After the abortive riot, things quietened down for a while. The chestnut trees yellowed, their leaves ragged under the hard blue of the sky. Factories preserved plums and raspberries and the over-sweet smell clung to everyone's skin and hair. Motile vegetative parasites clustered on the ripening grapes until, bloated with grape-juice, the insect-like plantlets fell to the ground and rooted. Rake-wheeled extensions allowed the tractors to harvest potatoes and the Kiflians walked beside their machines, giving their orders in a rhythmic sing-song that Irona annoyingly couldn't get out of her head. Woven with power-statistics it circled inside her mind as she tried to sleep. Each morning machines swept fallen almonds from the dusty trees in the rows and damped down the dust. They were what woke Irona.

She lay still, looking at Twiss's shoulder where he had thrown back the covers in the night. It rose and fell to his soft breathing. He so often seemed irascible that she still hadn't told him she was pregnant.

I'll have to tell him soon. It'll show before too long.

Her hand stroked the flesh on his hip, her belly pressed to the warmth of his back to still her aching. Jai had said it was perfectly normal, that everything was going well; the scans showed the baby fit and healthy. But Irona didn't want to think of Jai now.

And the tiny thought wormed in the recesses of her brain: *Why doesn't he hold me any more while he sleeps?* It was stupid, she knew. How could you blame anyone for how they lay in sleep?

Irona moved her hand carefully to scratch an itch on her scalp but he woke anyway and yawned prodigiously. Then he turned to her and her doubts dissolved as he draped a leg across her. His eyes closed again.

'Been awake long?' he mumbled. Irona smiled; he was only semi-conscious himself.

She shook her head, feeling his stubble rasp on her temple. 'A while.'

'So what's on your mind?'

Her words chose themselves. 'We're having a baby.'

'Mmm.'

'So what are we going to call it?'

'Call what?'

'The baby, you idiot!'

His eyes sprang open, warm, hazel, wide with surprise. 'Us? We are?'

Irona nodded. 'In spring. A boy.'

'How?'

'Wake up, Twiss! How do you think?'

'But the palace isn't ready!'

'We don't need a palace.'

Tuned to him as she was, enjoying his whirling delight, she

still felt something beneath his surface emotions. It wasn't
something pleasant. 'Oh, but we do, Ro. We do.'

'Why?'

He cloaked the dark thought, turned his mind away from
it and embraced her with all his strength, hugging her to
him, kissing her nose, her cheek, her eyebrow, smiling at
her, and she wondered if she had imagined it. But she knew
she hadn't.

'So what are we going to call him?' she asked him breathless
from the tightness of his hold around her ribs.

'Arnikon.'

'You what?'

'It was Granfer's real name.'

'But that's so old-fashioned. We want something up
to date.'

'I'm telling you, he'll be Arnikon.'

She laughed. There was time yet to dissuade him, to let him
think he had found another name that didn't bring up images
of someone old and hide-bound. 'So how come you're called
Twiss?'

He settled her against him and stared up at the sunlight
dancing on the ceiling. One of his hands rested protectively
on her belly, the other caressed her shoulder. Gentle laughter
rippled his chest and drifted up into the morning. 'Simple,
really. My mother called me Arcturus but when I were little
I couldn't say it. I always said Tuwiss. Tuwiss want kistal. So
she called me Twiss and it just sort of stuck.'

She smiled tenderly. 'So what was kistal?'

The hand on her shoulder waved, holding an imaginary
ball. 'It were this stone that Granfer found when he were
on the trawler at sea one day, off Liskard, before the Sky.
When they hauled in the net there were this weird fish with
great triangular jaws and a kind of light on a stalk sticking
up over its mouth. Granfer told me about it. He said it had
come from way down at the bottom of the Atlantic where
it's all dark, and the light was to show little fishes the way
into the big fish's mouth. Anyway, it were dead, and they all
said it weren't no good to eat, so they were going to throw
it back but Granfer wanted to see what it were like inside.

So he cut it open and there was this great big lump of crystal inside it, all shining and clear and green. He used to tell me it were magic when I were little. He told me it were a gem off an ancient crown and one day I'd be king in a world where we'd be free.'

'Have you still got it?'

'No. I left it in the cave where I buried him. But it's still there. I checked when I took the tractors back for the rest of our stuff from Settlement.'

Through the open window came the sound of Less arguing in the Synod room above. Twiss groaned. 'Not now, not now!' he said to the ceiling as if it would transmit his words to the council. 'I'm happy here. I don't ever want to move.'

Irona sighed. 'But we've got to. Who else is going to mind the shop?'

Twiss shook her gently. 'You're cruel, woman. Cruel and heartless.'

Feigning an evil laugh, she said, 'But I'm right, though, aren't I?'

'Yes, you rotten deve, you are. But take your hand from where it is or I ain't never going to get up again.'

Twiss and Irona walked across the wheatfields to where the tractor was humming over the harvested corn. They were curious as to what the tractor might be doing, rolling back and forth, back and forth, across the sea of threshed wheat.

'So how come, Arcturus' – they both smiled as she said the formal name he made the Kiflians use – 'you've dragged me away from my work?'

'Simple, Irona mother: you've had enough of fannying around with data-cubes and I've had enough of all they stupid arguments. If I hear another Kiflian telling me what's his by right I'll swing for him. Tell me what's the point of being in charge if you can't skive off on a summer's afternoon?'

'None whatsoever.'

'Then dump that load of guilt. You work too hard. Are you sure you're all right? I don't want anything happening to our sprog.'

'Sprog? Oh, you romantic, you. And stop looking at my

lump.' She grinned up at him. 'You make me feel like a carnival balloon.'

'But rather more solid.'

She pretended to trip him and he swung her round, her lavender skirt flying. Arm in arm they crossed through the stubble in harmony, seeing strange winged things rise up at their footfalls. From ahead came a pungent chemical scent with underneath it a hint of something corrupt. It reminded Irona of the worm-room; she glanced at Twiss but he didn't seem to have made the connection.

But the bright day reminded her of the promise of Harith and she put the sombre thoughts of Earth from her mind. Tiny plantlets claimed her attention. They wafted over the ground, a dance of red and yellow and orange in the chaff floating gilded in the sun. Overhead the sky was that blue which is only seen when summer turns to autumn, and to their right the ocean lay with white caps spuming in the hot, dry wind. Irona smiled.

Before they had got anywhere near the group of people standing around the tractor, a man broke away. The turquoise-clad figure dashed towards them yelling something they couldn't make out. He waved at them and Irona waved back.

As the distance between them closed Irona could see that the man was angry. He wasn't waving but gesturing them to go away.

She shrugged slightly. 'I guess we haven't quite won over the Kiflians' affections then,' she said, pretending it didn't hurt. If they had only welcomed the Second Wave as they should have, none of this violence need ever have happened. Matriarch Bernardina had lied to her. All Earth was a lie . . .

Twiss squeezed her arm. 'What the hell. Give 'em time and they'll see they need us.'

Now they could hear the man in the turquoise overalls. 'Get back! Get her away from here! Are you insane?'

Irona slowed, perplexed. Not so Twiss. He shouted back, 'She's got as much right to be here as any Kiflian!'

The man ran closer, a fringe of blond hair bouncing around

the tanned bald patch on his skull. 'What's the matter with you?' Near enough to see now, he squinted at them and stopped his wild run. 'Oh, Second Wavers. No wonder.'

'No wonder what?'

'No wonder you don't know spit. Keep that woman away from the seed-spray or she might never have a healthy child. Is she fat or pregnant? She ain't pregnant, is she?'

Twiss went rigid. 'Yes, she is. Why?'

'Then get her straight to the hospital. If she ain't breathed in none of the spray she might be all right.'

It felt to Irona as though a cloud of hail had rolled across the sun.

Bernardina refused to look at the ansible.

'Hasn't Gundmila called yet, then?' asked Elditch with subtle malice.

She shot him a look of hate.

'So, Bernie-love, if you haven't got the resources of Harith in your pocket after all, how are you going to cope with the Saharan Commune?'

'Never mind that!' she snapped.

'Oh, but I do. You've sacrificed me, and probably our daughter as well—'

'You never cared about her anyway!'

He retorted, 'I haven't seen her for twenty years. And neither have you.'

'No, because I sent her away on the *Starwing*. I saved her life! You were going to brain-worm her. You didn't even recognise her.'

'But you stopped me clearing three wakers. You, Bernardina. You're the one that rules the whole of Admin now, not just Camelford. It was your responsibility. How's that going to sound next week when you make your bid for World Council?'

'It's not, because you wouldn't dare.'

Elditch bounced a little on the balls of his feet, a habit which his wife found both pompous and irritating. 'You don't think I've got friends?' he said.

She raised an eyebrow but made no other reply.

'You want to win over Oceana?'

Bernardina didn't deign to answer. Her thoughts were of the *Starbird*, despatched not eight years after the *Starwing*. The Crown of Novaya Zemla had sent it.

But the Crown didn't know what Bernardina had put on board.

32

OMEGA

The hospital's walls were pink and pistachio green. It was just like the central hospital in Camelford: calming olfacts and subharmonics sang of forest glades carpeted with bluebells, starred with lilac. As soon as you sat in a chair it began to caress you.

Irona jumped away at that artifical touch. She hated the place. Twiss reached to catch her hand but she hugged her elbows, trying to hold herself together. Before her, Jai watched as the First Wave doctor – a silk-haired man called Darien – told the computer what he was looking for.

'Sorry,' he said to them, but he didn't sound it, 'only everyone in Kifl knows women shouldn't go near the crop-spray.'

Twiss held himself rigid as though he could armour himself against the news he dreaded. His face was harsh, his blond brows drawn forbiddingly down. Even in the soft cambric shirt she had given him only that morning, Irona could hardly recognise him. When his gaze came to rest again and again on her belly it felt like an intrusion.

Darien smiled – was it maliciously? – and his baby-face was rosy in the sunlight from the mood-pictures on the wall. Jai had told her that he was fifty-eight years old but he didn't look as if he was out of his teens. And she said that in the crater he was the most daring dancer of them all. Irona didn't trust him.

Behind Darien the computer chimed. It said, 'If you'd like to look at the hologram display now we'll give you the graphics. From the blood analysis it looks as though the woman Irona has inhaled a heavy dose of crop-spray—'

Twiss interrupted, his voice low but hard. 'What is this spray?'

The computer showed blue lines linked to red nodules in a repeating pattern. 'This is an atomic model,' said the computer, rotating it, but it meant nothing to Irona and even less to Twiss. Science hadn't come with their lessons in citizenship.

Irona trembled with the tension. Something seemed to be compressing her lungs; she breathed heavily through her mouth, fighting for air. Her lavender gown seemed to encase her like a shroud.

'So what does it do?' Twiss asked the computer.

Luckily for the computer, it was smart enough to realise he didn't mean the hologram. 'The soil of Harith is seeded with a group of symbiotic bacteria that feed on concentrated sugars such as are found in seeds of Earth-varieties of plants. The bacterium that does the damage when in contact with the others is found all over the planet so there is no point in spraying the fields; new bacteria would be blown onto the soil every day. So all seeds sown on Harith must be coated with a refined poison that will kill the toxin-producing bacterium.'

Irona said, 'All seeds? Do you mean *all* seeds?'

'Most certainly, otherwise nothing of Earth could grow here at all. This was discovered by the original probe that verified the ecosphere of Harith as viable for human habitation within limits. The defensive spray was created on Earth some forty-two years ago when the First Wave of colonisation was initially projected.'

Before Twiss could say another word, Irona asked in words that anguish squirted from her, 'What would happen to anyone eating coated seeds?'

'If eaten raw the spray would probably result in the death of any species of terrestrial origin, paralysing the gut and that part of the nervous system relating to digestion and temperature regulation.'

'What if it was cooked? Boiled?'

'Then the effects would be mitigated, except in cases where the organism had a weakened circulatory system. Such an organism would probably suffer from tachycardia to the point where death would be almost inevitable.'

Twiss had been listening bemused to the jargon. Now he said impatiently, 'Never mind about that. What about Irona's baby?'

The computer said calmly, 'Scans on all frequencies down to the cellular level show the foetus is sufficiently developed to avoid abnormalities. Obviously atomic-level scans are inadvisable. Future pregnancies, however, may be at risk. The lady's ova will need to be examined, but this child appears to be safe.'

Twiss's elation split his face into a grin that couldn't contain his emotion. He hugged her and called Jai in from the waiting-room. Even Darien was affected by the atmosphere of joy to the point where he shook everyone's hand, although they weren't native Kiflians, and slapped the computer in spontaneous friendliness.

Jai was the first to notice. 'What's wrong, Ro?'

She shook her head, forced a ghastly smile. 'Nothing. I'm just suffering from shock a bit, that's all.'

So they gave her hot sweet drinks and made her sit in the pink and green room that smelled of forests. They talked of the fun she would have with her child, and Irona's head filled with memories of settlers dying by her hand. Then Twiss said, 'Come on, love. You've had a hard day. Let's get you home to bed.'

Irona nodded, even let them call up a small vehicle to drive her home though any other citizen of Harith would have had to walk now the influx of settlers was using up so much power. She saw how their eyes followed her resentfully as Twiss talked the little machine through the pools of sunshine in the streets.

It was only when she was finally alone with Twiss that she let herself say what had been on her mind. She whirled to face him, desperation in the lines drawn on her face. Her hair tangled over her shoulders, caught on a button, but she ripped it loose. 'Don't you understand, Twiss? We poisoned ourselves. Out there in Settlement, we had a feast, don't you remember? It was your idea. To celebrate the canal. And I said to hell with it, let's use some of the seed-corn so we'd have enough to eat, and we boiled up a stew with it. The

Kiflians didn't poison your Granfer. They didn't poison any of us. We did.'

He stared at her in disbelief.

'We started this war, Twiss. You and me.'

Lal let his partners into the bunker. 'Pathetic!' was his first word. And his second. 'Synod, Gundmila, couldn't you do better than that? It took me ages to hop everyone up enough for a riot. You shouldn't have waited so long. Gave them the initiative.' He turned his back on her and savagely shoved the slider to maximum as Arias Tang folded his arms and watched.

From the transmitter at the top of the spruce tree on the hill above the bunker, nerve-jangling electric impulses wired down towards the town. The carrier-beam sprayed tiny irregular variations in frequency, pitched at the same micro-level as the electrical bursts between one brain-cell and another so that their randomness interfered with both motor-nerves and thought processes. As yet Lal's gizmo wasn't well enough developed to incapacitate, and certainly not on a wide beam, but it tightened tensions, interfered with co-ordination and clouded thinking in an area a block or two square.

With the transmitter on full power, Lal whirled back to face Gundmila. 'Call yourself a matriarch? I wouldn't put you in charge of a sweet-stall. I told you you should have let me handle it.'

'You think you could have done better?'

Lal sneered, his pencil moustache amplifying the down-curve of his thick lips. 'I know I could have done better!'

Gundmila clasped her elbows across her turquoise bodice. It looked as though she were trying to hold herself back from slapping Lal. 'Then why, petal, did you back out of having your face changed? Too scared you'd lose your identity?'

Lal half-turned to fiddle with his transmitter. 'No, of course not!' he told her, but she just nodded, her mass of titian hair bouncing around her face. 'Anyway, how come Arias did nothing? He thinks he's so smart, why doesn't he help us?'

Arias, arms still folded across his wiry chest, said, 'Because I am so smart. I told you, like I told Less, that this sabotaging of Kifl hurts us as much as them. I went to keep an eye on Gundmila, sure, because I didn't want her getting captured and giving us all away—'

'Thanks for the loyalty, pal,' Gundmila interjected.

Tang ignored her. '—but I told you it wouldn't work. I know I'm outvoted in this democratic Synod of ours, but it couldn't have worked. If you had killed Irona, Twiss would have gone ape. And, by the way, you told me you weren't going to kill her anyway.'

'I lied.'

Tang chuckled, pulled on a fresh shirt from the pile of clothing on his bed. 'Well I can't stay here listening to you children arguing all day. I don't share the same pleasure in quarrelling that you two obviously do. I've got a meeting with some kids up at Thought Pool Hollow.'

Back to back, touching only by accident, the King and Queen of Kifl lay in the bed that seemed too small now. Irona could feel the hard thoughts lashing in Twiss, waiting for a word from her to strike out. *Even if I said 'the' he'd take it out on me.* The life in her womb fluttered like a moth trapped in the bowl of a power-pack, fragile, living only tentatively. *He doesn't need to punish me. I can take it out on myself.*

Except that she knew she couldn't. Any act of immolation against herself could harm the baby. *It's not even my own life any more. Synod, why did I ever come to Harith? Why did I ever get mixed up with him? Why can't my life go right for once? I keep paying and paying and paying—*

And the darkness of isolation closed in on her just like it had in her sleepless nights in her empty flat in Camelford. It had never occurred to her that it was possible to be just as lonely with someone else as it was on your own. *The only difference now*, she thought bitterly, *is that there's two moons instead of one*.

And moonlight slid down the glassy spire of Twiss's model palace. It called to her of coolness in her blood, of icy metal slicing into her veins, luring her to forever peace . . .

It was a relief when Sticker's image chimed in the computer-tank at the end of the bed, once, twice. Irona started, keyed the remote, pulling the covers up to her chin as though she could hide from his eyes.

Sticker's lank hair slithered greasily on his collar as he turned his head away from someone off-screen. 'Oh, there you are, Twiss. You been long enough answering – I thought you weren't going to.' Anxiety sheened his flat face with sweat that glistened on his yellow stubble.

'So what's worth waking me up for? As though I been asleep in the first place.'

Sticker's adam's apple bobbed up and down as he swallowed nervously. He knew these hostile moods of his friend. He said, 'Tang's been seen.'

Twiss barked out the word: 'Where?'

'Over by that there pond on the slopes of the volcano – what do they call the place again?'

Automatically helpful, Irona murmured, 'The Thought Pool.'

'Shut up, woman!' Twiss said. Flakes of stone edged his voice. 'What do you know, Stick?'

'Not much more'n that, really. Some kids been up having another of they stupid parties in the crater. The weather-Eye overheard 'em on the way back down. Said he don't look nothing like he used to.'

'Bring they in, boy. I'm going to find 'un before I'm a day older.'

Ugly, mirthless humour rang in Irona's head: *And in this place it could be months before you are a day older.*

Sticker was gone when they pretended to each other to wake.

The first Irona knew of it was when she keyed for a breakfast she didn't want. It arrived in the sunny bedroom and she sat at the table, sipping soya milk and trying to ignore the smell of fresh bread that nauseated her. Hostility chilled the atmosphere as he sat down without so much as a word and leant across her to touch the sense-pad on the screen. There was Sticker with the wild rose and violet of dawn all around him. He had stopped for a breather on the flank of Mount Heralion and maple trees were flaming where a single shaft of sunlight came through the pass. The way he was holding the pocket-screen, it showed his round chin from underneath. There was a scab amongst his stubble.

He said, 'I've took one of they big tractors. Tang and Lal is supposed to be hiding out in Rainshadow Valley. Don't know how many's with 'em but I got a dozen with me. And I got the weather-Eye an' all. See you.'

It drove Irona wild. Impaled on the spikes of her own guilt and anger, she fought to calm herself. Wanting to seek comfort in Twiss's arms, she knew that she dared not touch him because anything might send him over the edge.

Until she could speak without her anger spewing out destruction, Irona watched Twiss crumbling his bread onto his plate. At least she had the excuse of morning sickness for not eating anything herself. Finally she managed to hold her voice down to a monotone. Concentrating on the dahlias in a vase, she said, 'Twiss, we can't afford to let Sticker's mob have the tractor just now. Get him back. The Kiflians are restless enough as things are. We need it to start laying the foundations.'

'We can't afford not to, you stupid deve!'

She recoiled, tried to cover up her hurt.

Twiss didn't care. Irona doubted he even noticed. He went on, 'We've all got to work together or Kifl ain't going to work at all.' That was his slogan; she'd penned it for him and now she was sick of hearing it. 'Anyhow, they Kiflians can just wait for their precious foundations. They got a roof over their head, ain't they? If they'd done us justice they'd have built us a place soon as they knew our ship was close to landing. Now we need to stop Tang wrecking everything. Thought I'd taught him to stop sticking his nose in my business.'

Irona hated his anger, his arrogance. *My business? What happened to our business?* On a level deeper than consciousness she thought, *Where's the man I used to laugh with?* But she couldn't absorb any more pain so she took her hurt and turned it outwards.

'What, when you wired his wrists and ankles and dragged

him through every patch of thorns in the desert? Oh yes, that's really going to make him respect your reason!'

Twiss jerked to his feet, sending the chair clattering to the floor behind him. For a moment she thought he was going to hit her. She couldn't believe the jags of fury he was pushing out towards her. But he just speared her with a look of contempt and said, 'So you'd rather him and Lal cooked up some other genocidal bug? Or built a couple of Arms maybe? Ain't enough of our people died to suit you?'

'Don't be so paranoid! Who's got the lab? We have. If Tang and Lal are out in the desert the most they're going to cook up is sunburn.'

'Synod, you just don't get it, do you? You've got the brains of a coconut.'

Which is twice as much as you have. But she didn't say it; childish insults weren't going to make things better, nor get her what she wanted. 'Look, just call Sticker, will you? The Kiflians are still simmering. If we attack their hero – '

'No, and you won't call him neither. I don't care if you have got the hots for Tang. I'm going to fix him once and for all.'

When Twiss had slammed out of the room the anger quivering in the air slowly dissipated. A bronze petal fell onto the table; it soaked up her attention for a long time then she blew it away.

She was on the point of calling down the shaft for Thebula when the door opened, Regen's head and fingers peeping round its edge. 'Coast clear, is it?' he said.

'Entirely.' Laughing at her own little joke, she waved to the coffee-pot. 'Come and talk to me, Regen. I'm going crazy.'

He helped himself to coffee then walked jerkily around the room, stopping at the window. 'They ain't as good as screens, are they? Can't change the picture.' He leant back with his elbows on the sill and the blue sky behind him had a thundery tinge. The skin on his hands was twitching. 'So what's the matter with you then?'

'Why didn't you tell me you'd adapted the weather-Eye? Was it Twiss told you to keep it a secret?'

Regen's brown eyebrows peaked in surprise. 'No – why ever did you think that? I just thought you'd realise it was the obvious thing to do. Entirely. They got lots of parts for circuits here – 'bout the only good thing in this place.'

'Why? Don't you like it here?'

He shook his head, his thin fingers massaging his neck. The cup in his other hand spilled coffee but she was determined not to embarrass him by wiping it up. 'Too many people, Ro, all bossing each other about, all at each other's throats – can't you feel it? Can't you see what it's doing to you and Twiss?'

She seized on it as though it were a rope and she were about to drown. 'D'you think that's what it is?'

He shrugged, 'What do I know? I know I'm jumpy as all get-out now. I miss the desert – I were better there. Seen what's happening out there?'

She got up to go to look outside but he said, 'I don't mean that' – he pointed with his chin to the strange avenue at the base of the tower – 'I mean every time one of us walks down the rows they look like they could kill. Hear about that kid that got beaten up last night? Remember, what's his name, the one that fancied Ludmila and Twiss gave him a bang on the snout? Spinon, wasn't it? Got three broken ribs, he has. I heard someone say it was Lol that done it but I don't reckon he sneezes without Tang's say so. We got to find them, Ro.'

'Then you'd better build me another Eye.'

'Think I ain't? There's enough crap going on here that we all got to watch our backs. I ain't overfond of Garwin, neither. Nor we ain't heard no more about this matriarch of Less's. Didn't sound to me like he meant Gundmile. It'll be ready in a couple of days.' He drew a breath and then stopped.

'Well go on, then. Tell me what you were going to say.'

Regen opened his mouth a couple of times, moistened his lips, cleared his throat. She smiled at him in encouragement, wondering what Regenerator had to be shy about when he was usually so outspoken. He looked past her, focussing at a point behind her shoulder. And quietly he said, 'Then I'll guard your back if you'll guard mine. I ain't got so many friends, Ro. 'Fact, you're it.'

She smiled at him, rubbed a hand up his neck and he started.

'Friends, Regan. For always.'

He turned his skinny back on her to hide his embarrassment. For a moment she thought he said, 'For until Twiss gets one of us killed.'

But it couldn't have been that.

33

THE ELECTRIC KISS OF DEATH

Sticker came back eight days later – without Tang or Lal. Garwin, dour as always, was in Irona and Twiss's apartment, fiddling with a story-disk by the closed door to the grav-shaft. He heard the message that Thebula sent up from the ground floor of the Synod tower and without consulting Irona said, 'Let him in.'

Twiss came out of the bathroom, rubbing his freshly-washed hair, when the door hissed open.

'Oh, they're up there all right, old Tang and Lal,' Sticker told Twiss wearily, slumping back onto the bed without so much as a by your leave.

Irona wrinkled her nose in distaste. By the smell of him Sticker hadn't washed since he left. Twiss didn't seem to mind. He picked up the jug of fruit-juice and left the table where he'd been sitting with Irona to go and perch cross-legged beside his friend. It was absurd, she knew, but she felt left out.

'How'd you know?' Twiss asked.

'Seen the sign out in the valley and on the slopes of the Moon Mountains. Like you said, footmarks an' that. And the Eye found places where they'd camped out in caves but there's about a million caves and we never actually come on 'em when they was at home. They got to have some sort of comm-link theirselves 'cause it felt like they knew just when we was coming.

'Twiss' – Sticker swigged grape-juice straight out of the jug then handed it over, not even wiping the spit off the rim – 'there ain't just the two of 'em out there. Must be about a dozen.'

Twiss turned to look at Irona. 'How come you never told me there was some of they Kiflians missing?'

Feeling as though she'd been caught out in wrong-doing though she knew she hadn't, Irona said, 'Who knows how many of them we actually – how many of them died when the tidal wave hit? I know who's left – I'll print you out a hard copy if you like. But how many of the others are dead and how many are – enemy – I haven't got a clue.'

Twiss scratched at the side of his neck, a habit he'd picked up. Irona had warned him already that he was making himself sore but Twiss had merely said, 'So? You ain't my mother.' Now, rasping his square-cut nails into his hair-line again, he said, 'Fine watch you're keeping.'

'How can I watch them all?' she retorted. 'I haven't got enough Eyes—'

'Then get some.'

'Regen's making some right now. He said he thought he saw one that wasn't ours. And,' she went on, 'I thought we came to Harith to get away from all that?'

'You ain't got a clue why I came.'

'You came,' she said icily, 'because if I'd left you, you'd have been brain-wormed.'

Sticker hunched down on the clean red covers, fiddling with a fold of the material, trying to pretend he wasn't witnessing their argument.

'What do you want me to do?' Twiss shouted. 'Bow down and kiss the ground every time you deign to look me way? Or should I just touch my forelock? Would that make you happy?'

Anger lifted her like a wave on the sea. 'You don't give a toss whether I'm happy or not! You pick me up and put me down like a doll. Half the time I daren't even talk to you. Sometimes you hold me like I really matter to you then the next minute you turn into—'

Twiss hurled the jug from him. Its plastic shattered into a thousand crystal fragments that went spinning across the floor, whirling rainbows in the pattern of the sunshine. 'You're talking shit, you know that? You are shit. You're nothing. If I stepped in something like you I'd scrape it off my shoe.'

'I saved your life because I loved you!'

'Loved? What do you mean, loved? You don't love anybody but yourself, you stupid deve. You don't want me, you want some sentimental lap-dog that'll jump for you every time you click your fingers. Synod, every time you start slobbering all over me my skin crawls. And you're talking shit anyway because we don't neither of us know why we came. We just woke up on the ship a couple of thousand light-years from Earth and then you say it was you that saved my life? Drop dead.'

Slowly, feeling as though she were held up by strings, she stood and went wordlessly to the door. His words kept exploding between her atoms, breaking her apart until her body, her limbs, right down to the capillaries and the cells of blood in them, went howling micron by micron into the universe.

Ust-Staritsa: almost three hundred kilometres north-west of Tomsk in the Siberian Plain. Nearly a thousand kilometers from the centre of Novaya Zemla.

Elditch had told Bernardina, 'What, not even to his capital? You're mad!'

'We can't have a secret meeting in his capital, now can we?'

'The trouble is, Bernie-love' – the venom in his epithet made her smile inwardly, as it always did – 'that if he wants it kept as secret as all that, nobody will have proof of where you are. This could be dangerous! If anything goes wrong—'

Bernardina's face creased in its origami smile. 'If anything goes wrong, you'll know where I am.'

'But—'

'But, my husband, I trust you.'

He recoiled, glancing anxiously around the bluebell glade in Camelford Park. 'Ssh! Don't call me that!'

She dismissed the subject of Ears with a flick of her gnarled fingers. 'That, Elditch, is why I trust you. You love your promotion. You want to stay as the head of the Camelford Synod. I've keyed various little secrets that'll pop up all over the system if I don't cancel them personally within thirty-six hours. So I know that if anything does go wrong, you'll come looking for me.'

Now, having abandoned the luxury of her stratojet, Bernardina felt less sure about this private encounter with the young Crown of Novaya Zemla. She had worked with his predecessor on several mutually profitable schemes, but a face-to-face meeting alone? So close to his borders? When she'd never even met him? She glanced around Ust-Staritsa with loathing – and something more.

As far as Bernardina could see, it consisted of endless birch forests with marshes and mare's-tails. It was also depressingly cold for a spring day, with patches of grey snow melting on yellowed grass. The Sky was a strange dark blue, and sunlight slanted pale between the stark trees. For hours the only sounds she had heard were the hum of insects and the louder hum of her electronic insect repellent. The little town of Ust-Staritsa itself was out of sight beyond low rolling hills and more of the birch swamps, and she had been left to squat in the ruins of some ancient palace for longer than was necessary to convince her of the Crown's importance.

What if the Liga finds me before he gets here?

What if one of his aides is in Oceana's pocket?

What if the Crown doesn't want to make a deal at all? What if he simply leaves me out here all night to freeze to death? Maybe Carandis is behind this.

She was beginning to wonder if she had made a mistake coming here at all.

And for the millionth time she asked herself how come Irona hadn't yet discovered the ansible. *Where are you now that I need you?*

Hours after she had walked out on Twiss, Irona found herself sitting on the black volcanic rocks washed smooth by the sea. She had no idea what she was doing there. Combers broke about her feet, drenching her with spray that shone opal in the starlight. A flight of lizardoptera flew overhead, singing as though this time it might mean something. One by one they dived exhausted into the ocean and the autumn was complete in her heart.

She hugged her cold arms around her lumpen body, wondering what sort of being it was growing inside her. What Twiss had invaded her to plant where it could cut.

I love you, she told it, *he's not going to use you to hurt me. You're part of me and we'll always be together*.

Jai came, a dark figure out of the darkness, a silhouette against the silver and ebony of the sea. 'I wondered if I'd find you here.' Jai was still soft and plump with the weight she had put on during her own pregnancy. She settled on the rock beside Irona and said, 'What are you going to wear to the party?'

Irona shook her head. She couldn't believe that Jai was talking about parties when she was battling with something real. Feeling that Jaimindi was galaxies away from her, she said over endless distance, 'What party?'

'The one Twiss has asked me to organise for when you have your baby.' Jai smiled; her own baby, Tendor, was asleep in his cot.

'What?'

'In the volcano.'

'*What?*' The idea wouldn't fit into Irona's head: *Twiss does care about me after all. This is his way of saying sorry*.

Jai said, 'Remember I told him in council one day that we ought to have a banquet so's the Kiflians think we care about them?'

Hope died, a clinker nagging its sharp weight in Irona's belly.

'Oh yes, Jai. I'd forgotten.'

Winter in Kifl: the sea sullen under the cold damp winds, or pounding against the new surf-breakers that Twiss had sulked about Irona building with Baika and Less. Now, with Heralia whitening under the snow it ripped from the grey clouds over its cone and a plume of vapour feathering endlessly from the thermal spring at Thought Pool Hollow, Twiss said, 'I should never have let they go.'

Without asking she knew what he meant. Lal and Tang.

'You need more Eyes,' he said.

'Regen's making them as fast as he can get the lab to churn

them out. I still say we'd be better off putting all our energies
into making Kifl a home for all of us. I don't want us to be
a police state. I had enough of that in Camelford. I thought
you had too.'

'And,' Twiss went on, 'you'd better train Garwin and
Thebula to use 'em.'

'I have.'

Twiss wasn't listening. ''Nother one of us – remember that
lad, Spinon? – he got hisself killed yesterday. Went up to the
volcano, high on olfacts, and got hisself sliced up by some
Kiflian deve.'

On the surface, the life of the town went on normally.
People ate, and slept, and went to joint cultural events
that somehow Irona thought would help, but there were
attacks on settlers almost daily. Of course, nobody ever saw
anything. Now Kiflians were starting to turn up dead too.

Irona waited for Twiss's child to ripen to sunshine inside
her. She felt that she no longer existed as Irona – *I'm nothing.
I'm a piece of shit* – she felt Twiss's arm around her in the
night and knew that the whole of Kifl was only waiting for
the birth so that they could party up in Heralia's crater.

Even though she couldn't talk to him above a practical
level, she still found his physical touch comforting despite
the fact that she no longer trusted it. And the tractor engines
whined through the short winter days, fed by the cold sun
and the fires below Heralia that Regen had found how to
tap. Transmuted from the pale sands at the far end of Kifl
Bay, shining walls were rising. Irona had been afraid he had
resurrected his dream of a palace called Tingalit, but he made
no mention of it these days. She assumed the pre-fabricated
sections were to rehouse the last of the First Wavers, and
that finally there would be peace.

Then, on a sleety night at the tail-end of winter, she
summoned Jai to the Synod tower.

Twiss was transfigured when Arnikon was born. His ruddy
face shone as Jai cut the cord and wrapped the boy in a
towel, but he couldn't take the baby. 'I'm scared I'll break
him,' he whispered, and backed away, but Jai showed him
the thin blond hair with one longer strand hanging down in

curls besides the boy's pointed ears and said, 'He's perfect. You won't hurt him.'

From within the transparent olfactory, Irona heard and smiled. The baby cried and it pulled at the place where he had been plugged into her flesh and that was right. *You're part of me*, she thought, and held up her arms. Soon Jai and Darien had healed her and cleaned Arnikon up; as soon as the olfactory had been peeled apart Irona held her first-born against her breast.

Twiss smiled at her, radiant. So tired she couldn't think of anything that was worth the effort of saying, she smiled back at him.

Then he called Thebula in. After she had exclaimed and cuddled the infant, though, Twiss said, 'Arnikon makes us more vulnerable than ever. Thebula, don't you let they First Wavers anywhere near him.'

The moment of wonder was broken. Outside, fireworks and lasers hurled their challenge to the night-dark stars.

'Come on,' Jai called from the cribside, 'aren't you ready yet?'

Outside, one of the few private vehicles whined in the dark row, its lights reflecting on the ceiling of the bedroom in Synod Tower. In the bathroom, Irona leant on the windowsill and saw the white beams of the tractors climbing up the flanks of Heralia on their second or third journey. The two moons were crescents in the endless sun that shone on the other side of Harith; wracks of clouds drifted silver-edged against the night sky. The weather-Eye had promised a fine night. Everything was up in the crater already: the food, the drink, the tables and chairs.

Everything was ready but her.

Nothing had been heard of Tang or Lal in weeks though two more Second Wavers had been found mutilated, and their friends took their reprisals out in blood. Still Irona had had time to make sure that the Arcturian Guard were alert and strategically placed around the town. That was why she hadn't been fully dressed when Jai arrived to take her downstairs.

'Be with you in a minute,' she said, and fixed the stasis-crown to her head. Its sensors coiled her hair, highlighted it with sapphire gems of light that contrasted with its blonde-streaked brown.

Keying for bath-bugs to suck the moisture off the mirror, Irona stood back and looked at herself. The sight of her pale face and the shadows under her eyes made her drop her gaze to the rich blue of her gown. Its soft velvet bodice clung low to the curves that birth had amplified but fell kindly around the empty sac of her belly. Arnikon was a month old and Irona was afraid she would never get her figure back.

Still, the points of her tight sleeves came nearly to her knuckles in the style of Kiflian beauties she had seen – and secretly envied. She wondered briefly what her mother would have said to such vanity. *If my mother is still alive. If she cared enough to say anything.*

Bertrecht, the life-jewel artist, had vied with the other artisans of the city to carve her a necklace and earrings that held the fires of midnight in iridium filigree. 'A gift,' he said, 'from the citizens of Kifl to their lady.' Irona wondered what poison was hidden in their links.

The jewellery made her even more uncomfortable than the dress did. She longed for her plain round robe with its knots of obedience and its squeaky-clean cap.

She swallowed. The Kiflians didn't want to see her with old Earth's knots of modesty. They wanted no reminders of wardens and Arms and worm-death. They wanted to see someone who respected their customs enough to dress as one of them. And Twiss wanted her to be a queen.

'Oh, Ro!' Jai said in exasperation.

And Irona answered, trying to keep the tiredness from her voice, 'Ready.' Labour wasn't called labour for nothing; all she really wanted right now was her bed.

Music swelled as Irona's personal tractor crawled over the lips of the snow and into the crater. Lasers struck chords of light on the mists where hot volcanic air met the ice of outside. As Thebula talked the tractor down the trail to the high table where Twiss sat in splendour with Less, a perfume of lilac and musk vied with the spicy scents of Kiflian delicacies. She knew one of Regen's aides must be somewhere about, tinkering to produce marvels of technology to give light and sound to the scene.

And she knew the Kiflians saw the waterfalls of coloured light that the Eye showered down upon her. But, as Twiss and Regen had intended, they saw more than its beauty.

They saw its threat.

Raising her brows at Thebula, she stepped down from the tractor. The Kiflians who had been standing in the loose clumps of any conversation fell silent and shifted to two lines leading from her to Twiss. Tingling notes fell like water down her spine; she suspected irony but the Kiflians seemed genuine in their desire to do her honour.

Irona wondered what was wrong.

I must work out how to access the rest of their damned computer. Synod only knows what Gundmila had in there, she thought, and wished she didn't have to waste time here when there was so little of it.

In those long fifty paces to her husband, Irona felt the weight of their expectations. More land, more power, more fish, more food, as though she could wave some wand and grant all their whims right now – if they placated her.

. But Twiss smiled encouragingly at her. The flowing lines of his shirt gleamed like opal and a crown – *Surely they don't mean that?* – rose from his brow. A dark gem – *kistal?* – glimmered above his eyes and his curls stuck out endearingly beneath it. Liquid steel, his trousers limned his hips, his legs.

Desselie was standing close behind him. She didn't seem to have any trouble wearing the immodest Kiflian robes.

Irona fastened her eyes on his smile and let it reel her in to safety.

He kissed her and she felt vindicated. *Let Desselie get over that!*

There were speeches and the youthful Kiflians performed rhyme-games for her and Twiss's delight. Even Sticker pretended he was listening, Jai beside him now, having moved slyly to her place while the Kiflians were applauding by stamping their feet.

Irona tried not to yawn.

Finally someone served her food and she ate it sparingly, hoping its richness wouldn't betray her into sleep.

'It's great, isn't it?' said Twiss, touching his fingertips to her arm, or pretending to whisper in her ear so he could brush her face with his. Irona wasn't sure what she could feel radiating from him, but she hoped it was affection. *If only I could trust it!* But ever and again in that nervous gesture she was coming to hate he scratched at his neck and she remembered things he'd said.

She wished Regen were there but she had pleaded with him to stay and keep an Eye on Kifl. It hadn't taken much pleading at that. Regen was getting jumpier by the day and crowds always made him bad. At least she had her own Eye now to keep a watch over Arnikon and Twiss. And Garwin stood behind Twiss's chair.

With the stars wheeling overhead and flagons of a drink that warmed and refreshed by its very strangeness, Irona relaxed as the party went on. The music was keyed to alpha-rhythms; sublims (she guessed) made people inhale deeply of the olfacts that opened hearts and minds to a sharing that wasn't normally possible – especially between First and Second Wave.

Then she began to notice something strange.

As group by group the Kiflians relaxed enough to dance, they moved to one angle of the crater where basalt columns formed a corner. In the warmth that rose from the ground, camouflage plants and lenses shifted over the inky towers of stone, dizzying the mind. Early starflowers danced their perfume on the air, dropping golden pollen that scented the air like roses. And, though down on the coastal plain the peaceful lizardoptera had long since vanished singing into the sea, here they lived on, eyes still ruby, wings still diaphanous gold, and their songs weren't plaintive but plaited into the music jumping in her blood. Other than the higher temperature in the already hot crater, Irona's Eye couldn't find any reason for the Kiflians to dance there.

She leant across to Twiss, but he didn't know. Then she

turned to Less and asked the same question: 'Why do they dance in that one spot?'

Less faced her, his skin copper in the light from the flaring power-packs, his eyebrows still slanting upwards. His green eyes shone dark as he said, 'Haven't you got it yet? Immortality hurts. Until your people came, nobody died. Now – look at them! – the young people dance, and the not so young, right where the crust is thinnest. It's a gamble, do you see? You've taken their way of life and made it meaningless, you Settlers. They've always had parties up here because it's so beautiful and strange, but now they do it for a purpose.'

She tried to close off but it still hurt when he said, 'Don't you understand, Irona, wife of Arcturus who thinks he is our King? And what is he? Just some sleeper! We could cope with forever when it was for our people, but now it's for you. For outsiders. You'll never belong here. So they dance with death, half-hoping they'll plunge through the crust into the fires below. That's what you've given us, you sleepers. You've made us want to kiss death.'

How much of it Twiss had heard she didn't know. But he swayed to his feet and led her, protesting and laughing, into the dance. Heat funnelled through the floor of the volcano and stung her feet through the soles of her shoes. Sweat soaked into her bodice and clung to the small of her back, to her thighs. And all the time Twiss whirled her clumsily through the knots of Kiflians, still not one of them. He tried to copy their steps and his agile body managed it, but she didn't. She was too tired to remember, too tired to keep up. He smiled at her and rubbed his lips on her cheek, seeking the soft skin beneath her jawbone.

But the fires that burnt her were the core of the magma so close underground and the pain of the words with which he had lashed her the last time she told him she loved him.

At last he felt her lagging and circled her breathlessly to her seat. He kissed her full on the lips, saying, 'You must be exhausted. Don't worry, love. You have a rest.'

Then the stranger, Arcturus, took Desselie's hand and pulled her into the dance.

Irona pulled back the Eye from him and left it gleaming above Arnikon's cradle. She wondered where Tang was, and where Tang's Eye that Regen had seen. She hoped he couldn't see her discomfiture. She didn't like the notion of Tang having an Eye.

Less winked at her and grinned.

Head on fire from the effort of keeping awake, Irona stuck it out until an ice-pink winter's dawn scrubbed gravel under her eyelids. Twice she had linked with Regen but he said the Guards were yawning at their posts; this dance was no trick spawned by Arias Tang.

'And has she shown up on the ansible?'

'No, Irona, we ain't had no visitations from no matriarch neither. Don't let yourself get paranoid. The next ship ain't due for another' – he glanced theatrically at his wrist-chrono – 'thirty-nine years.' (Irona smiled wanly.) 'You're safe yet. Enjoy it.'

In a slit sheath of shimmering gunmetal organdie, Desselie swooped past in Twiss's arms. Irona saw him talking, laughing so widely his teeth gleamed in the nascent day.

Irona couldn't believe her Eye when Thebula drove her, Twiss and Arnikon home in the morning. Where the two-storey walls of the new homes should have been there rose a palace of shimmering glass. It was set amongst full-grown trees that Twiss must have stolen from Kiflian gardens. The pale sun of winter polished its curves to garnet and zircon; flames of amber were its banners and emerald was its spire.

Emerald – like the gem in his crown, like the crystal Granfer had given him to tell him he could be king.

Twiss smiled at her. Gesturing expansively to the construction by the beach, he said, 'I promised you, didn't I? What do you think?'

'It's – it's a palace.'

'And you have the Rose Wing – see it, that corner there closest to where the hills come down to the beach? You'll have a beautiful view first thing in the morning when the sun rises over Heralia.'

You. Not we.

'What happened to the housing estate?'

He shrugged. 'I told you, Ro, they Kiflians'll have to wait. I told you, no son of mine's going to be brought up in some underground row.'

She wanted to say, *Synod Tower is hardly an underground row* but it was too late for that. The damage was already done, the wings of the palace already striding their long shadows across the pearly sea and the Kiflians' resentment.

Twiss slid his arm under her shoulders and his hand squeezed her arm. 'I always promised Granfer my son would live in a palace. It's called Tingalit. Isn't it beautiful?'

Astar with the cold fire of gems, it was.

It didn't happen that night, nor the next. Twiss spent his days in his new council chambers under the emerald spire, but he came to her every night and sat with her, playing with Arnikon, tossing the baby up into the air until Irona shrieked with fear of what might happen.

But it never did.

Until the air softened to spring and the evening stars gleamed after the day's heavy rains. They were so bright that she could see them as points of fire even through the red glass walls of the Rose Wing.

Twiss said, 'Ro?'

Her face softened as she saw Arnikon sleeping, dwarfed by his cradling hands. 'Mmm?' she said dreamily.

Twiss said, 'I'd rather sleep on my own tonight, if that's all right with you. Arnikon keeps waking me up.'

He was alien because he didn't understand the poison dart he had fired into her stomach, because that was where she felt it, a lost, falling sensation as though she'd been found guilty of some monstrous crime and were being punished for it.

'Fine,' she said. What else was there to say? If she asked him not to he'd feel trapped and resentful towards her. And that would drive him even further away.

'I'm glad you understand,' he whispered, pulling her close and kissing her hair. His hand caressed warmth into the bare skin of her arm and she was rewarded. She thought.

Then he got up, laid Arnikon on her lap and closed the door behind him. All he said was, 'Good-night.'

How did it happen? Why did it happen?

Irona pulled herself together and called Jai but all she got was the colourful shimmer of the privacy symbol. Then she keyed Tebrina's number and got no answer at all. If she had had the courage to face anyone, she might have gone out into the corridors and up to Regen in his indigo eyrie, but she couldn't. They would see her alone at this time of night. They would know her shame.

Silent, pretending she had seen nothing, Thebula sat in her corner of the Rose Wing. Night dripped down the glass walls until Thebula seemed to be drowning in blood-red light. She avoided Irona's gaze and said nothing.

The one thing Irona did not do was send her Eye to track where he went. *I trust him* she told herself. *I won't hound him.* But Arnikon felt her anxiety and began to wail.

At last she managed to soothe him to sleep. She held him, rocking gently, not wanting to put him down, and the night wore on. In her alcove Thebula was giving out little ladylike grunts that in anyone else would have been called snores. Irona wondered when her bodyguard had gone to bed.

Her arms were numbed now to the weight of Arnikon. She couldn't sleep either when he grizzled; she had almost the same amount of work to do as Twiss. How come he was so special all of a sudden? What gave him the right to change her life? And how come he had dismissed the Kiflian grandmother she'd chosen to be the boy's nurse?

King Arcturus.

She was on her own. *I've been on my own before. I can handle it. I wonder what's on the wall?*

But there was only some educational stuff whose enticing odours barely grazed the surface of her attention while her mind wondered what was wrong with her that Twiss didn't want to stay at her side.

I'm nothing. I'm shit. He told me and now he's showing me.

No – he's just tired and he needs his sleep. Who knows what might break out before he gets his hands on Lal?

And Tang. He tortured him, too.

Irona called for music and the computer read her mood. Igniting the shadow-fire, it dimmed the lights to play her a song of visual nostalgia where the man – why did it have to be a man? – strung lyrics of sepia and faded silver that drew pictures of his father from the dead habits of his childhood.

At the bottom of the cracks in her mind boiled the old pain: *Why didn't my mother take me when she left? Why didn't she even tell me she was going? My father never loved me anyway, but I thought she did.*

And long thoughts embroidered their spidercurves across her mind. *Why aren't I all right on my own? Why do I need to live my life through other people?* She thought of the vacant hours of darkness and felt like a two-legged stool ready to tumble at the slightest movement. *What's wrong with me? Does everybody feel this way?*

Then she wondered if she were being manipulated, and of course she was. Yet again she was giving in to what he wanted. But if she didn't he might lose a grain or two of his love for her, so she polished up her memories of the times he had said he loved her – and tried again to guess if he were lying. And if so, why.

To get what he wanted of her, obviously. And it wasn't what she wanted of him. She wondered if her emotional investment were worthwhile. Or if she ought to leave him, find somebody else, learn a new vocabulary of incomprehension . . .

And she thought of the good times when he had given her strength and value in the way he curved into her as they slept, or laughed at her jokes. He had made her feel safe. Irona was sure he had meant it – at the time.

The moons had sunk into the sea when Twiss burst into her room – but not out of love.

'Quick, Ro, get Arnikon out of here. Lal's coming for him.'

34

RED LAL

Twiss's sudden eruption into the room frightened Arnikon into screams. Irona rushed to her son, snatching him to her breast to still his fear but Twiss dragged at her arm. 'Come on! Get him out of here!

'Thebula? Thebula! Get your ass out here.'

Twiss skidded cursing on one of Irona's rugs as he bundled her towards the door. Kicking the thing out of the way, he hustled her into the corridor right in the path of Regen.

He was just as hopped up as Twiss was; all his twitches were well in evidence. Sparks practically flew from the pair of them. Irona could feel their panic fracturing the air around them. It was contagious.

'This way!' yelled Regen.

Twiss and Thebula at her heels, she dashed behind him, along the passageways that were dark as entrails between the islands of rosy light winking on and off.

'They've sabotaged the 'lectric!' Regen yelled. No-one had breath enough to answer but they all knew only Less could have betrayed them.

And all the time Arnikon was crying loud enough to test his lungs. But there was no-one in the lonely palace to hear. Irona tried to hush him all the same.

Regen seemed to know which way to go and Twiss let him lead until they came to a grav-shaft where the red glass met the green. Twiss went to hurl himself into it but Regen roared out with the adrenalin of fear, 'No! It's electric!' and Twiss swung round to the emergency ramp.

They slid down its sharp tight spiral. Still the baby cried, his face darkening with temper in the jade light. Even slithering down the cold glass of the emergency exit Irona managed to keep her balance well enough to protect Arnikon's head each time they careered close to the walls but she didn't have a second to spare to suckle him to silence. Arnikon's wails broke and echoed inside the ramp-well. Twiss was yelling at her but she couldn't hear what.

As the ramp flattened out at the bottom they slewed to a halt. Scrambling to their feet they charged for the door that led to the beach.

And stopped.

Red Lal was there, the glass of the door wide open to the night. In the months he'd been hiding he had dyed his pencil moustache red but he still dressed all in black. He was enjoying himself. There was a wide, ringed tube in his hand.

Twiss tensed to attack. 'Don't try it, Twiss.' Lal's tone was patronising, the name freighted with contempt. 'See, this little thing the computers remembered for me from before the Sky throws little arrows, lots of them, hard enough to punch a hole right through your thick skull. All I have to do is press this button. Just think what they'd do to your baby's head.'

He waggled the thing about, smiling at the dread he caused. Irona pulled Arnikon closer to her breast, frightened on his behalf yet willing to die for him. A towering anger was building up inside her.

Lal spoke a code that should only have been known to Tingalit's environmental systems. Brighter light sprang out sending emerald sparks jumping from the green glass, but Lal didn't just want more light.

He wanted to prove that he was in control of the Rainbow Palace.

'In case you're wondering,' he said, 'there's a few of my friends outside. We're going to your throne room now, King . . . Octopus, wasn't it?' Scorn dripped through his words like vitriol. 'And when we get there we're going to get a few things sorted out. Think of it as your final curtain after all your cheap theatrical power-plays. And what a tacky setting!'

Lal waved them past and out into the cold night. From the bulk of the lilacs dark shadows closed in on them, flanking them all the way to the portal and up the ramps to Twiss's suite. Irona could only just make out Twiss's silhouette and Regen's but even in the hint of starlight that filtered through the green or amber corridors, she could see that both of them were twitching, jumpy. She was bad enough, but the two of them were manic. It wasn't natural. She remembered all the times they had faced danger. Off-centre they might be, sometimes, but for Twiss's head to be jerking that way—

Static electricity stood her hair on end. Neon blue sparks shot from Twiss's shirt. When she glanced back at the boy holding the flechette-gun, the red hairs of his beard were crawling as if they were alive.

Irona shivered. Arnikon was wriggling so violently she thought she would drop him.

Behind them came a dozen figures, tall and powerful. Their outline reminded Irona of something evil . . .

Arms.

Silent but for their unrelenting footsteps their faceless threat drove the prisoners along.

They came in through the private ante-room and the vast empty space of Twiss's Synod Hall threw back their footsteps in a confusing tapestry of sound. In the darkness the glassy walls were mirrors of black. Above them the Round Window magnified the uncaring stars; the crystal and ebony of the epidiascope hung in the centre of its wiry web. Polished until it gleamed, the marble of the table stretched out its oval to either side and the high-backed chairs stood up like teeth around it. In its centre was the ebony and opal 3-D view of Kifl that the epidiascope cast.

The floor was cold under her feet. It seemed like forever before they came close to the seat with the highest back of all. Twiss's seat. At this angle Irona couldn't make out who was in it – but she had a very good idea. One thing she was not going to do, however, was show her fear, however oddly Twiss and Regen might be behaving. Irona transferred Arnikon to her other breast so that he wouldn't cry either; his restlessness was giving way to sleep and he tugged only spasmodically at her nipple. Behind her she could hear the rustle of Thebula's trousers. At least Thebula seemed normal.

The distance closed. In the high seat someone stirred, losing his absorption in the model of Kifl and drumming impatient fingers on the table. In front of him was Twiss's crown, the huge crystal in the iridium seeming almost black in the darkness.

A silence grew slowly.

It got to Lal. 'I've brought them,' he said unnecessarily.

The figure said, 'Well there's a surprise,' and it wasn't a man after all. Irona recognised every nuance of sarcasm in the fruity, sensual voice. It was a ghost, a female ghost.

Gundmila.

Turning her head slightly – with a shock Irona saw the structure of Gundmila's face underlying the thickened muscles – Gundmila said, 'Sit down and keep your brat quiet. And you, King Arcturus.' Her tone hardened. 'We're going to have a proper Synod for once.'

Further round the table, another chair swivelled. Another ghost.

Irona was prepared this time. Under the widow's peak, under the heavier cheekbones, even without the moustache or the tail of his queue hanging over his shoulder, it was definitely Arias Tang. He nodded pleasantly.

Groping to steady herself, Irona sat on the edge of a seat not too close to Gundmila, her own seat with her console recessed into the surface of the table. Irona held herself ready to leap up at any second. She felt the weight of Arnikon snuggling into her and rested one hand on the table, allowing it to creep little by little nearer the console.

Twiss walked pointedly round the table to sit as far from Gundmila and Tang as he could get. Then he pushed his chair back further as if to increase the distance even more. With one careless, elegant backhand Gundmila flicked her enemy's crown so that it slid across the table. It strobed black and silver through the rows of the shrunken Kifl and slithered, half off the edge of the marble, to stop in front of Twiss.

They faced each other across the narrowest point of the oval. Tang sat at one end, observing, saying nothing. Neither Gundmila nor Twiss noticed when Lal signalled with his gun for Regen and Thebula to slip into their seats by Irona. Regen leant forward, his head jerking bird-like to watch each of the protagonists.

Now that Irona's eyes were growing accustomed to the faint silver and gold light in the blackness of the hall, she could see Tang arch his brows mockingly. Her hand was close to her keyboard now. A subtle glance at Lal's Arms showed that they weren't looking at her.

'You see, Twiss, it's like this,' Gundmila said. From the very ease of her manner it was impossible not to realise that she had control of the situation. 'Kifl needs a leader, a strong one. You think you're so strong but you're not. You're stupid. You've blundered on making mistake after mistake and then crawled up people's backsides with your phony charm so they'll like you. But they don't. They only pretend.'

Twiss would have fleered an answer but Lal trained his weapon on Arnikon.

Gundmila turned her head beneath its dark, tumbling mass of hair. 'You. Irona. Settler bitch!'

Irona gasped but with Arnikon in her arms she dared say nothing. Little by little she was lowering her son until he was protected under the curving rim of the table. For the moment she let her free hand lie inert on the stone.

'Yes, Miss Innocence,' Gundmila said, 'I orchestrated that riot and you were too much of a moron to realise it. Know why I did it? I wanted to kill you. But I've got something better now. I'm going to leave you alive because that way you'll suffer more. You're besotted with that murderous bastard. You let him hammer stakes through my body in the path of the snake-rat plague. You'd let him do anything, wouldn't you? But you don't know how many times he made love to me while you thought he was off martyring himself to the cause.'

Emptied, Irona cast a look of hurt and beseeching at Twiss.

'I didn't!' Twiss yelled in fury. Blue sparks danced like fireflies from the ends of Twiss's hair. They fled like shooting stars above the dwarf township on the table. 'You lying—'

He subsided as Lal cocked the trigger. Sticker subsided back into his seat too.

Tang spoke and everyone looked at him in surprise. He had been forgotten. 'You're very vindictive, my dear,' he told Gundmila coolly. 'I never did care for your taste in sado-masochism. And if you want to stay on as Matriarch of Harith I think you'd better stick to the script we agreed.'

'Stuff your script!' she shouted. 'Did you really think Lal and I want any part of your pacifist nonsense? If you want to show these deves how much you care, you'd better shut up, Settler-lover! That baby'll be just as dead if you interfere.'

Now she faced Twiss again, her anger spiking hot in the atmosphere. 'You killed more people in Kifl in five minutes than have died here in forty years. So even if you weren't a murdering, child-killing, arrogant . . .' Spittle flew from her mouth and her words jumbled into incoherence before she got herself under control once more with a glittering smile. 'You tortured me, you bastard! You humiliated me. You scarred me. And now you die. She turned to the Arms. 'Shoot!'

Red Lal said, 'What about me?'

Irona, caught up in the drama round the table, had forgotten Lal. Now, in the cavernous hall, she heard the slither of plastic on plastic as the Arms in the shadows tensed, waitng for Lal's command.

The red-bearded boy stepped sideways, leaving his warriors a clear field of fire while allowing his own flechette gun to cover Tang now as well as the Second Wave prisoners. 'What about me?' he said again.

Tang flicked his moonsilvered eyes in a sideways glance at Irona. She gave the faintest of nods; Arnikon's sleeping form was well out of sight below the level of the table.

Gundmila skimmed her gaze over Twiss, Regen and Thebula. None of them was armed, nor close enough to Lal to be of any practicable value. And the mouth of Lal's flechette-gun waved hypnotically from one to the other.

Gundmila said, 'What about you?'

'You promised me a place at your side! You said . . . Who was it who came up with the electronic virus? Me! Who stole all the stuff you needed from the lab? Me! And it's my warriors that are standing you off. Me and my Arms built your bunker. So what's in it for me?'

'What do you want?'

'I want you to get rid of this big-headed Tang deve for a start.'

Tang laughed. 'Ah, there you have it, don't you, boy? You can't do it yourself for all your standing army! You want me to do it for you. Your ideas are bigger than you are.' He shrugged; the fabric on his chest seemed to disappear behind the spires of the miniature palace.

Gundmila yelled, 'Shut up, Arias! This is nothing to do with you.' Brittle, barely holding herself in, she said, 'Kill them now, then, Lal. And we'll talk about it.'

Lal brought his weapon up to eye-height to aim. A smile of cruel pleasure opened up under his moustache.

Irona slammed the ENTER key for the command she had little by little tapped into her console and everything happened at once.

Ebony and opal, the epidiascope dropped its 3-D image of Kifl. Tall as trees Lal's Arms leaped on the table in its place, a blur of shadow-demons thrown out by the machine. Even as the real warriors around the room reacted with webs of blue lightning, so their shadow-targets seemed to fire back, to duck, to take cover exactly as they did. It was chaos.

And the weather-Eye she had called spun humming into the hall, shooting paralysing jolts of power at the heat-sources Lal had called his army. As each one fell, so did its image in the epidiascope.

Twiss hurled his crown at Lal's head. It punched into his nose and dark liquid fountained. The crown rebounded but even before it had stopped clattering on the floor at Lal's feet Twiss had leaped the distance between them. His weight carried the staggering Lal to the ground; Twiss tore the flechette gun out of Lal's grasp and fired at the same time as Tang raced past him to snatch up the crown.

Ripping a second cannister of darts from the corpse of his fallen enemy, Twiss whirled. Irona, huddling with Arnikon wailing in her arms, couldn't tell which was Twiss's target, Arias Tang or Gundmila.

Gundmila was reaching for her own console when Tang tackled her. With mad strength she tried to throw him off, screaming impossible bloody threats. Her hand groped for the keys that would summon more Arms, or unleash the Eye again, or some other nameless threat.

Twiss fumbled to load the flechette gun.

Gundmila punched at Tang. He ducked and her fingers grazed the firing button of the Eye's control. Lightning speared down towards him but Gundmila's control was too poor.

Before she could fire again, Tang stabbed the peaks of the crown into Gundmila's face.

Twiss would have killed him then but Irona screamed, 'No, Twiss!' and Regen chopped the weapon from Twiss's grasp.

Irona brought the lights up and killed the power to the ghost-warriors. They shrank back inside the mechanism of the table. With the first grey light of dawn seeping in through the plain glass of the windows, the smell of blood came coppery on the air.

Gundmila was dead. The peak of the crown had stabbed through her eye and into her brain. A dark teardrop of blood wept itself into her hair. The Arms lay sprawled in death.

'I did it!' Twiss yelled, leaping into the air.

Irona and Tang looked at each other.

'You're next,' Twiss said. Between him and Arias Tang, the epidiascope once more cast its 3-D image of Kifl with dawn rising over the Moon Mountains. The bodies had been cleared away.

'Wrong again,' Tang said, as Regen and Irona both said, 'No!' Sticker, of course, said nothing and Irona wondered why Twiss had bothered to summon him, while Thebula dozed with Arnikon cradled against her.

Twiss shot them a wolf's-grin. 'Why not? We hold all the cards now.'

'Because—' Irona began.

'Because—' Tang started to say, then smiled. 'After you, dear lady.'

Twiss watched them sardonically. 'Happy now?'

Irona looked down at her hands where they rested by her

console, then gazed levelly at Twiss. 'Because politically it would be a mistake we might never recover from. You've killed two of their Synod, including their Matriarch, and you're hunting down the third one, Less. The Kiflians will know you've edited his brain however subtly you do it. Unless you make them out to be a conspiracy, which they were, with Tang here as the one who broke his misguided fellows, we're going to have an action replay of this us-and-them thing for the rest of eternity. Want any more of our friends to die?'

Regen nodded. Tang shrugged, his head slightly to one side and his brows quirked in self-deprecation.

'So,' Twiss said slowly, 'why did you betray them?'

'For the same reason I wouldn't let them kill you. It would have been stupid, as Irona said. Jointly we can hold Harith together. Separately we'll just be involved in unnecessary internecine war when we should be preparing for what good old Mother Earth is going to send us.'

Twiss snorted his contempt. 'Fat lot you know, then. Earth ain't going to be able to send us nothing for another forty-odd years. You're starting at shadows.' He sneered a laugh. 'You ain't got it, Tang.'

Tang raised his brows and shook his head. 'Oh, the Admin let you in on all the Matriarch's plans, did they? Including for the last twenty years that you were asleep on board ship? How considerate of them.'

'Hold on—'

'No, you hold on, Twiss.' Tang's voice cut like a dagger. 'Did all the scientists of all the Admins tell you what their research programmes were? Do you know for a fact that no ship can get here in less time than we took? That Camelford didn't send another ship out a year after you left? Or the Liga Mediterranea? Novaya Zemla? Oceana? They could all be at war and Harith one of their prizes.' The dawn light polished his eyes. Irona couldn't read them but she felt his mental strength reaching out to weave around the group at the table.

Tang gave Twiss a get-out. 'You don't know anything and neither do I.'

Twiss's hands clenched into fists; Irona saw the muscles

sliding under the smooth skin of his forearms. 'I know you killed my Granfer—'

Tang lifted a hand wearily to prop up his chin. 'Not that old thing. You know you poisoned him with crop-coating. You know he was old anyway and his arteries were about as elastic as a stalactite. You killed him, Twiss, like you killed dozens of our children when your tidal wave smashed the school.'

'Don't give me—'

'Don't flatter yourself. I wouldn't give you the time of day except that Kifl needs you. Not some so-called king who squanders resources on a palace to his ego while his people live in silos without a power-pack to keep them warm. We need someone who'll look after all our people, not just half of them.'

'What, like you, you mean?'

'No, you deve. You, because you're strong and you're ruthless and you stick up for what you think is right. And because you can talk people into anything. And Irona to temper your cruelty and find solutions for you and smooth all the feathers you've ruffled. Sticker to carry out your orders. And Regen to make your schemes work.'

Irona felt a warm, liquid flow of pride filling her as Tang gave her recognition.

Then he said, 'And me to look after your First Wavers and make them accept you.'

Irona twiddled with her computer keys. 'It could work.'

Regen said, 'It's the only thing that could work. Entirely.'

Tang yawned elaborately. 'Well, I'm going to bed.' He stood, stretching, and shuffled sleepily towards the door. Irona couldn't find any trace of fear in him. Leaning on the glass door-jamb, Tang added, 'See you later. Synod at eleven, is it?' and walked out.

Leaning forward aggressively, Twiss said, 'I don't trust 'un.'

Regen smiled, the little round knobs of his cheeks gleaming in the first rays of the sun. 'He don't trust you neither, but we ain't the ones who can build Arms. If'n he'd wanted to, he could have killed the lot of us entirely without lifting a finger. I'd say we're better off with him than with that Less.

We got enough work fighting the planet without fighting Kifl too.'

Twiss pulled a face. 'We can always kill him later if we have to.'

It was Irona who said, 'And he's right about one thing. Earth isn't done with us yet.'

35

THOUGHT POOL HOLLOW

And Harith rolled through the years. Jai smiled or cried as Sticker came and went to his lovelies but he always came back to her in the end. Irona watched her friend laugh and held her when she wept, and she saw her bear a string of golden-brown babies while Irona's own womb slept beneath its damaged ova and there was nothing Darien the doctor could do. Year by year Arnikon grew without brothers or sisters, a little boy with everything but what he needed. His father was always off being important and, however hard she tried, Irona couldn't make it up to him.

The day Arnikon started school, she couldn't go with him like the other mothers did. Baika and Tang were arguing with Twiss about the new building project; Twiss insulted them and Irona had to stop Baika walking out while Arias just sat there and grinned.

Auntie Jai took Arnikon, though. When Irona made time to drop him off a few days later, he ran in with his new friends. He didn't even wave her goodbye.

As she drew level with the hospital as she came to pick him up, she heard his childish treble grow fangs. He had no idea she was there; he was playing in the hospital garden with Jai's children. He must have hurt himself because he wailed and ran for comfort. Irona hurried along the wall to the gate because she thought he needed her. But she was too late and it was Jai who kissed him better.

Irona heard him say, 'Auntie Jai, you're the best mother I've got in the whole wide world.'

Meantime Twiss gave her duties on duties while he was out and about talking people into things, or left it to her to make decisions, so that the weight bowed her down. Especially the weight of having to leave Jai to look after Arnikon while she was in Synod.

Regen was still her friend, though, and Tang made her laugh. If she'd done something right, he said so. The only trouble was, she didn't trust him.

How can you do it, Arias? she wondered, looking at his smiling face. *How could you plan plagues and leave us to starve out in Settlement – and let Twiss torture you – and never drop your polite political beam? You talk to me but I don't know what's going on behind your face. How come you make me feel good? What are you after, Tang? When are you going to erupt?*

The rift between the Kiflians and the Second Wave scabbed over; not too often now, not more than a score of times in a dozen years, a Settler would die or a Kiflian would disappear. Then an ugly mood would smoulder and flare for a while. And the threat from Earth still hadn't come.

Elditch said slyly, 'Has she found it yet?'

'I don't want her to. I'm leaving her to ripen. Now go away.'

Elditch chuckled to annoy her as he shuffled out, his shoulders starting to hunch with age. He glanced back as he went down through the trapdoor: his wife was staring out into the night.

Beyond the windows of her personal room, Bernardina watched the snow she had ordered falling softly on Camelford Mountain. Fat white feathers tumbled lazily down to caress the countryside, to wrap the fields in a quilt that gleamed soft as the pearl smear of the moon. It had been a whim; now it was a comfort. She remembered snow from when she was a child, before the Sky. When life was simple.

Bioelectricity calmed the rhythm of her heart. Rejuvenants fought off the ageing she dreaded but the long night would claim her soon enough. The trick was, not to rush it. There was too much to do. Her body needed to float in the nutrient bath but her mind needed to remember. Thoughts drifted with the snowflakes . . .

How long has it been? Eight – no, seven years since I took the chair of the World Synod. I've suppressed the Liga, bought off the Crown – for the time being – and the president of the Three Americas pretends she's on my side. Well, she would. I put her where she is.

And it's fourteen years since my daughter woke on Harith. Does she remember yet how she got there? The old woman shook her head. No, the mindblock isn't due to decay just yet. Maybe she's found out by chance? Why hasn't she found the ansible? Maybe Gundmila had her killed before she died herself, because there's no way Gundmila could have resisted calling me for so long . . .

But they're all lying in wait for me. Saharistan still wants to bring me down. Carandis hates me for keeping her off the board of the Admin. She's not too happy that I've kept her out of this room . . . So petty! She'd sell me out to get her hands on power, and there's plenty of takers. Bernardina thought of the latest crisis. It made her feel tired. *Oceana for one. I can't hold on much longer. After me, the deluge.*

Irona, call me. I need you.

One autumn afternoon Tebrina called Irona in the Rose Wing of Tingalit.

'Tebrina, hi! I haven't heard from you for ages. How's things?'

'Oh, fine.' The way Tebrina spoke told her things were anything but, though her face wore its usual serene expression under the mop of grey-streaked hair. 'I just wondered if you fancied coming over, Ro. If you're not too busy, that is.'

'There's about a dozen things I should be doing but I don't fancy any of them. I'll be over in a bit.'

The bougainvillea was dying now and the sky was that clear blue that only comes in the fall of the year. Irona decided to make the most of the sunshine and walk. People greeted her like old friends, though some of the old-school Kiflians only gave her a sullen nod. The new houses reached half-way up the slopes of the Moon Mountains and the air that swept down through the cedars and rhododendrons carried the tang of the snowfields spreading down the skirts of Heralia.

And Thebula still walked behind Irona to guard her back.

When Irona arrived at Tebrina's house, there was the usual flock of small children playing in the dusty yard. Late roses breathed over the green-ball plants and Irona stopped to play a game with them, dusting the children with sudden clouds of pollen the way she had once done with Arnikon when he was a toddler.

Then Tebrina called her inside. Thebula stayed dozing in a hammock.

Irona loved the little wooden house Tebrina shared with Sinofer and their brood. It was cosy under the cedars. Irona drank fresh lemonade and relaxed in the afternoon light as below them Kifl slept its siesta. She wanted to ask her friend what was wrong but she knew Tebrina would tell her when she was ready.

'Heard about Arnikon trying to climb the crag?' she asked, when Tebrina ran out of superficial conversation.

Tebrina nodded.

'He's so stupid! He thinks he'll live forever.'

Tebrina put her glass on the window-seat; it rattled as she set it down. 'My Fessbar's the same. Do you remember when he broke his leg?'

'Re-inventing skis, wasn't it, just because he'd seen it on disk?'

The words burst from Tebrina. 'Now he's started dancing on the volcano!' Tears rolled down her ruddy cheeks. She said, 'Excuse me,' and rushed upstairs.

Irona had an idea where she would find him. Fessbar was sat on a bough of a tree in the wild land above the house.

'Why do you do it?' Irona asked him. 'There was a girl fell through the crust only three weeks ago. You've got everything – health, strength, you're good looking, you've got your whole life before you.'

'Because there's nothing else,' he said. 'It makes sense to me. Anyway, what about Arnikon?'

Fear seized Irona's heart. And Fessbar would say no more.

Back in the house, Tebrina pretended it had never happened. She peered closely at her friend and said, 'Irona, you're pregnant!'

'Ssh!' Irona stole to the door but her bodyguard was sleeping under a pile of children in the sunlight.

'About time too. I'm really pleased for you. What does Twiss say?'

'I daren't tell him. What if it goes wrong?'

'It won't, Ro. Everything'll be fine, you'll see.'

Still the undeclared war of Kiflians and Second Wave spread its tentacles. It didn't help that Arcturus kept Arias Tang away from Synod as often as he could.

'We need a man of your abilities out in the new Settlement in Rainshadow Valley, Tang,' Twiss would tell him. 'You know it's true. Nobody else could do it.'

But on the ever rarer nights that Twiss slept with Irona in the Rose Wing – never in his rooms – he would whisper savagely, 'And let's hope, that they snake-rats'll get him, or a pregnant lizard-locust.'

Irona didn't say, 'At least I can talk to him. At least he doesn't call me a stupid deve and let me down and not come back when he says he will. At least he doesn't flirt with other women in front of my face. At least nobody ever said he slept with Gundmila.'

But she thought it, and didn't tell him about the babe.

Twiss found out anyway. He was more than usually savage with her and Tang in Synod, accusing them of ganging up on him, and the atmosphere cut Irona hard. Her ear rang with the suppressed violence that crackled around him. It was no easier when they left.

She stood up to go, no longer expecting him to come with her, but he grabbed her arm and his fingers sank into her flesh.

'What is it?' she asked, alarmed.

'Why didn't you tell me? How can you shut me out this way?'

Irona said nervously, 'Tell you what?'

'That you're pregnant, of course. Fourteen years I've been waiting for this and then I only find out through J— through Darien!'

It was as though the ground had dropped out from beneath her. 'Me cut you off! Twiss, you hardly talk to me any more. Sure, if I had told you, might have decided to spend the odd hour or two with me, but it wouldn't have been for me. And I don't manipulate people. If you wanted to come to me, you would.'

He wasn't listening. 'Don't you know how much it hurts? I love you, Ro. And you do this to me.'

Twiss left.

He always does.

It was Regen who found her later on the balcony of the Synod room. Kifl lay in its siesta and the sun burnt her fair skin, but she sat curled on the parapet, thinking how far down the ground was with its patterns of raked gravel. The ground was reality and this was a dream.

Regen sat cross-legged on the other end of the balcony-rail. 'I have to know,' he said. 'Why else do you think I rigged all they screens up? I have to know and I do.'

Irona raised her blue-green gaze to his but she didn't speak.

'Just tell me why you don't move on?'

'Because he'd fall apart without me. And Kifl would explode without him. D'you know, I'll be thirty-seven in three days' time and the baby won't live that long. I can feel it dying inside me.'

'Don't say that, Ro.' The little man stroked her foot with his.

'I'll just do it then.' She squeezed his hand. 'Meantime, we've got to find out what the hell else is hiding in that computer. And Twiss wants you to find out what Arias is really doing.'

'What about you?'

'I know what he's doing.'

But Twiss needed her and Kifl needed Twiss. Besides, she thought, *I've got him some of the time, haven't I? And I've got Regen and Jai and Tang. Regen to look after me, Jai to love me and Tang to—*

To fence with, to sharpen my wits and make me laugh.

And even if I haven't got any other living children, I've got Arnikon. If he doesn't kill himself on the volcano.

The day after she lost her baby, she woke from nightmares in her room in the Rose Wing. It was dawn and she had had little enough sleep; the red light through the red walls made her think for a second she was inside a blood-filled womb. Arnikon had seen her for maybe ten minutes the evening before. Even Twiss hadn't stayed with her. He had said she was mad with grief and that if he stayed, they would quarrel. She was alone – except for Thebula – and she had made up her mind in the long, wakeful night. She had had enough. Her physical pain was nothing to the agony of guilt and bereavement and betrayal in her mind.

'Are you all right, Ro?' Thebula asked, bringing her a breakfast to tempt the sickliest appetite.

'Fine. Well, tired, really. I'm not going to do anything today, just wallow in bed.'

'D'you need me for anything?' Thebula said too casually.

'No, why?'

'Because I fancy going over to Ider's.'

Irona dredged up a chuckle. Ider was the latest in Thebula's long string of lovers. The first time Thebula had bedded and thrown aside a perfectly nice Kiflian boy, Irona told her she was heartless and immodest.

Thebula had said, 'Look, Harith's frozen me at the peak of my hormones. I'm not going to squander all this perfectly good lust on just one guy who's going to bore me or battle me for the next thousand years. I'm not going to hurt him. I chose him because he thinks it's just a game too, oh Matriarch, so don't look so starchy. And I'm not going to go into maternal mode. I might end up like my mother.'

This isn't Camelford. If we can live forever we need a whole new set of rules to play by. Irona was still horrified but she was wise enough not to say so. *I couldn't do it. But I'm probably turning into some dinosaur that doesn't know when it's time to lie down and be a nice quiet fossil.* Instead she had made a joke of it. 'Two Marjines? The thought's unbearable!'

Now she said, 'Ider? Isn't he the one with the big nose?'

Thebula wrinkled her face in a grin. 'Well, you know what they say about big noses!'

Full of spurious candour, the Queen of Tingalit said, 'No, tell me.'

Thebula threw a cushion at her.

'And before you ask, no, I won't let Twiss find out. It's ridiculous telling me I need a full-time bodyguard in my own palace. If I was that vile they'd have poisoned me long ago. I won't let on.'

Thebula whirled round, the silky material flying out around her. 'Great! I'll be back in time to code for dinner.'

When Thebula was safely out of the way, Irona called for a personal transport and headed through the busy, sun-drenched rows of Kifl for the slopes of Heralia. It wasn't the crater she wanted, but the thermal pool on its flank. She had heard great things of Thought Pool Hollow. Reaching the vast corrie, she sent the machine back.

The mountain heights thinned the air around her. Irona halted, breathless, but only for a few seconds. Exhaustion hung down from her like chains yet sleep was a distance too great to cross. Unless, maybe, the Thought Pool could carry her away from endless wakefulness, from the pain of being in her life. After a few seconds she noticed that she was moving again though her lungs were groping frantically for oxygen.

She couldn't stop walking. Irona knew that she couldn't leave the past behind her; it followed inside her, rubescent with pain, but her subconscious goaded her into putting distance between what she was and what had happened. Her bones watery with a weariness that went beyond fatigue, she forced herself through the trees around the Hollow.

Down in Tingalit summer still lingered but here she hung between seasons, between time. There was neither past nor future but only the forever ache of Now.

The loneliness of her womb left her hollow. Her legs trembled but inside the ballooning trance of her mind her destination called her. Drifts of seeds rose at her every step and the matted stems caught at the buckles on her shoes, tripping her. But the closer she got, the more a wordless feeling swelled in her like a black rip-tide of ocean.

They can't stop me. Nobody can. She walked faster despite the gravitic drag of her weariness. The weight of pain in her back and abdomen wanted to stop her like Twiss did – if he cared. But if he did care it was only to impose his order on her, to prove that he was right and she was wrong. It wasn't because he was concerned for her, just that people should think he was. The thought called adrenalin rivering into her tired blood.

Inside her the idea of the Thought Pool grew, not an image but the shadowed memory of tales and hope. She had no idea what it would be like but her mind was so tired that a fore-echo of disappointment ceilinged her skull and she tried not to think about what she would really find when she got there.

The wind plumed the pale cloud from the side of the mountain. Insubstantial as fallen hope, the vapour ribboned above the hanging valley. The people down below would see only the eternal steam from the hot springs condensing as the air chilled it to whiteness. They wouldn't notice her. She hoped. She wondered too if Twiss had even noticed yet that she'd gone.

What if there's someone else there?

For a few seconds the thought stopped her floundering on through the alpine meadow. Not for long, though. Her need for release was desperate and it gave her the illusion of strength to believe: *They won't come here. They're all too busy being sensible. They wouldn't risk it.*

Before she plunged below the lip of the valley, she cast one last look behind her. A flight of yellow songbirds flew over the wooded slopes, wings flashing in the light. Below them was the square-cornered patchwork of fields, each with their tractors painted toy-bright, and beyond the neat plain was the sun-silvered sea. She could see the towers of Tingalit black against it. But there was no-one following her.

Unless they're still in the forest.

Oh God, let me get there first! Let me find some relief. I don't care if I die just so long as this stops.

Fear of pursuit pushed her on against the cool caress of the wind. Irona was beginning to feel feverish again now the pain-killers had worn off but she knew that if Twiss's men (he wouldn't come himself) caught up with her they'd only say that she was irrational with grief. 'Come home,' they would say. 'We'll take you to the hospital.' *As if that were home! What do they know? Bereavement has its own logic. And that's what he's done. He's robbed me of my husband and my son.*

I'm not going back. They're not having me again. He's not. They won't stop me. Even if it kills me I'm still going to do it.

And sharper than the threat of being caught was the cold stiletto of awareness that the Thought Pool might bring her into permanent sleep, the forever blackness of death. Nor was she sure any longer that she wanted to avoid it. So, hardly seeing the ruby-scaled lizards hopping up in alarm at her every step, Irona ploughed stumbling through the white gold hay of the alp, trying to get to the Thought Pool before her courage ran out.

At last she reached it. Irona blinked, her lids sandpapering her fatigue-dry eyes in disbelief. *I've done it! Maybe I'm not useless after all. Perhaps now I can sleep.*

She sank down on the slope above the pool. Exhaustion shook her limbs; her heart-beat reverberated round the cavity of her chest. The sun's heat blinked at her through puffs of warm steam; sweat sprang out on her hot skin, a prickling counterpoint to the bruised pains in her flesh.

Irona peered down through the rowan fronds. Guardian-trees, flowers, the oval of the volcanic pool itself coyly sparkling beneath its scarves of mist. At one end a slim cataract of rainbowed snow-melt plashed into the warm water; at the other, the overflow trembled over the lip and on to become a stream Twiss had had channelled for irrigation of his fields.

But here there was no sign of anybody else. The slightest noise would have startled her but there was no noise, just the gentle hush of the wind in the leaves and the soft tinkling water with the slow bubbling spring rippling its surface into transitory mirrors. There was nothing here to frighten her (though her heart still slammed its valves inside her ribs). Even the chemical odour of the volcanic spring was woven with the kindly perfume of blossom.

It seems safe enough. Anyway, what does it matter? What does any of it matter? Nobody cares.

Sobs melted her into a lake of self-pity that shamed her, but it wouldn't go away. At the same time it seemed somehow artificial, as though she were contriving it so that there would be at least one person who cared, if only herself, for her poor dead hopes and for the martyrdom of her body.

'To hell with it,' she said, and she followed her voice down into the green sounds of the coppice. 'And to hell with me too.'

Leaf-shadows frolicked insouciantly over the warm brown mud of the path that wandered up and round and down. 'Nobody cares if I die so why the hell should I? At least I can stop being awake.

'Now I'm talking to myself. Maybe Twiss was right. I am mad after all.'

And at the lowest point of the track she came to the pool. Its edge was thick with life that clung to the thermal springs. Quickly, before her bravura could evaporate, she threw off her clothes (though her nakedness made her embarrassed. *What if somebody steals my things? – It couldn't be worse than this. I just can't handle any more.*)

But while her mind was waltzed dizzy by paranoia her trembling body had taken her to the ferns and moss rimming the pool. They felt cool and soft beneath her feet. At the corners of vision something skirled, though the trees shut the wind out of Thought Pool Hollow.

It was probably a skein of mist but she didn't stop to think about it. Feeling her way with her toes through the satiny mud she edged gingerly deeper. The shattered sun on the water lanced through her eyes and into her brain but the pool was warm as a bath with cross-currents of coolness that stroked her like silk. She half-closed her eyes against the light and folded to her knees.

Nothing hurt her.

The bronze water caressed her thighs. Irona let herself sink down and the Thought Pool embraced her stomach, cupped her breasts. Fragments of light echoed dancing in her sight yet the warmth of the water soothed the pain of her ripped womb and she let herself lie, her head pillowed on the moss. She closed her eyes to rest them and the sun bled orange peace into her through her eyelids even as her murderous womb blended death into the water.

Tiny movements crumpled against her skin, softer than a butterfly's wings. Her eyes sprang open but there was nothing to justify her nervousness. The rowans formed a screen of emerald lace against the blue of the sky; exotic blooms of crocus and saffron curtsied on the blinding copper of the pool's surface and the light sifted down shimmering on the incense of mist. Lizard-flights glittered undisturbed between the trees. Rich sweet odours of wood and sap hummed through her deep as oboes and the waters sang their lullaby as they laved her with their loving touch, massaging away the aches of her body.

What do Twiss and his gang know? They've got it all wrong. There's nothing to fear.

Finally she trusted herself to the loving liquid cradle and lay back full-length while the day circled towards golden evening.

But her thoughts grew vivid, razor-edged with guilts and insecurities.

Why me? What had my poor little baby ever done? Why should some deity punish it by killing it before ever it had had a chance to be born? What was it, some horned monster that was going to massacre mankind? In which case why let it be conceived?

There came into her mind again the gut-harrowing memory: that shapeless mound of quivering jellified flesh the bruised vermilion of offal, spiked with dragon's bones of malformed blue-grey that didn't resemble anything. The cursed bloody mass lay steaming in the cold of their careless metal bowl.

And that was the worst part: it wasn't even the shape of a proper baby. (*Twiss's scornful voice: 'You can't do anything right, can you? You're not a proper woman. You can't even make a proper baby like anyone else, can you? Synod, you're a waste of space, aren't you? It's like talking to that'* – he thumped his hand against the ice-green hospital wall – *'Why do I bother?' And he walked away without a backward glance, leaving her in the goldfish-bowl of the public ward where he'd had her put to show how democratic he was*.) At least Regen had brought her home.

Why wasn't it like a memory? It was solid as life, heavy as the brassy taste in her mouth, more real than the whisper of greenery ghosting around her. And thoughts unscrolled in her of pain and failure and hopelessness, and it was all one, all her because she should never have been born.

It's my fault. Tears dripped scalding down her temples, infusing into the molten copper of the Thought Pool. *Why didn't I just let them feed his brain to the worms?* And for the life of her she couldn't remember why.

A midnight shroud of infinite sorrow dropped on her and she wanted to slide down under the surface, inhale the water to fill the hollow ache inside her, stop the useless bellows of her lungs that took up other people's air, but the dense bloomy sulphur of the air lay on her, making her too heavy to move, and the agony of being drowned her in infinity, while her body became as insubstantial as the gulf between the stars.

And while dreams shocked with colours netted her into unconsciousness, the camouflaged weavers of dreams landed in ever thicker clumps upon her skin. Light as thistledown they came to feed on her where the ripples disguised their motion and they shivered between the waterstroked hues of her flesh, translucent ivory, quicksilver, bronze. With the lines of probosces under their abdomens they razored down through her skin to her iron-rich blood, and each proboscis was oiled with an anaesthetic anti-coagulant that swam through her system, hiding the dreamweavers' presence while it clotted her memories.

The psychotrope gathered in the olfactory centre of her brain and condensed the actions of the past. So strong was it, and so weakened the left side of the brain, that causality lost its logic.

She was back in the ward and through the hospital window she could see black oily smoke crawling up the sky to write the hieroglyphics of death. Now she could smell the meaning of that skywriting: it was her child, incinerated, that reeked of hell in burning slack coal and paprika. The air conditioning smelt square with their sharp-cornered analgesics and scorched-paper bedclothes. Her stitches were daggers of disinfectant stabbing up between her thighs. And Twiss was a casein-sweated puppet dressed in a penumbra of crimson and musk who trailed his empty aura around with him lest people forget who he was and what he had once done for them.

You're not a proper woman . . .

Deeper and denser memories unthroned the ouroboros of that recollection. Unnamed, she slid headlong into a funereal pit. Acid-green links snaked from the hollowed hub of her self-perception into dark calcified nightmares: Twiss's first 'adventure'; the lying smiles of friendship she had shared with Jaimindi who had trampled on her innocence; the diamond pain of the knife across the indigo veins in her wrist. *I shouldn't have been such a coward! I should have done it then and got it over with so my baby wouldn't ever have had to die. Twiss is right. I can't do anything right.* And the words cut like caustic. And the nightmares were true.

Irona would have woken if she could, would have crawled naked through the burning peony heart of the volcano rather than live longer in the prison of her self.

But the dreamweavers were sucking her blood and her essence to sate themselves. The char-clawed vermilion and sulphur and purple ugliness of her self-image screeched through her and the acid lightnings of fear congealed her blood deep inside her. The capillaries close to her skin shut as her insides gonged with the acid of her self-terror; there was no blood now that the dreamweavers could reach.

It was ironic: she who was indifferent to dying saved herself and she didn't even know it.

She woke to the long thoughts already rambling through her. Her eyelids fluttered. The secrets of eternity were tossed in the green dance of leaves against the sleepy sky. Topaz and zircon, ruby and amethyst, flying lizards swooped to drink from the pool. Irona's dreamy blue gaze tried to decipher the mantic calligraphy of their jewelled flight. The very rhythm of their wing-beat was a fractal of the rhythm of the world. Truth was in the deep perfume of moss, the citrus fragrance of the water-lilies and her body had no borders. It was one with the planet's lifeblood: the rain-cycle that would carry her down to the shining sea to be reborn as the snows which fell on Heralia's peak. Pain was only a pulse in the life of the world and it had an evanescent beauty of its own: it was no more than a mandala, a way of knowing you were not dead.

Then the slanting rays of the sun kissed deep into the warm bronze silk of the waters. Self-awareness slid down the shafting light, pouring into her the harsher truths of waking, filling her with the hard weight of objects.

In the splendour of evening frilled anemones were creeping up inside her belly, following the iron taint of her blood. Irona felt their slimy tentacles force themselves slithering inside her, rebirthing her into pain.

Leaping screaming to her feet she beat the gelid things off her. They fell squamous down her thighs, shivered from her buttocks. Long after she had trampled them into the pulpy mud she kept on thrashing her heels into their corpses.

Panting, she clambered from the pool and up into the horizontal amber of sunbeams. Everything was washed with gold; gilded drops of water flew when she wrung out her hair with panicky motions. Sunlight shaped the mist into aurate structures and the sapphire lizards flew on prismed wings. Somehow it seemed important.

If only I could remember the pattern of their dance-flight I'd know – But the drug had left her and she stood forlorn. *What was it I'd have known?*

But the sunlight was a cold and pallid wraith of itself and

the chill nibbled at her. Irona shook her head to clear it and started to rub herself dry with pruny fingers.

It was only then that she felt the bites sting. All along the geometry of her veins were raised cuts, some scabbing over and some still oozing blood. The empty bag of her belly was thick with the dreamweavers' wounds. Her hard breasts were ripe with them. Apprehension gripped her.

Leaning over the darkened mirror of the Thought Pool she saw herself only as a pale reflection. It wasn't until, shivering, she dragged her dress onto her damp skin that she realised her neck was swollen too.

Trembling as much from fear as from cold, she dragged herself up to the lip of Thought Pool Hollow. The sun was balanced on the sea's horizon. In the last of its rays she looked down at the towered bulk of Tingalit, then back to see her enormous, slender shadow reaching out behind her.

I'm between the past and the future, she thought. *And the past is just a shadow. I've paid and paid for the future. What I make of it is up to me.*

36

FOG-FENCING

She woke alone. Not even Thebula had come back to the Rose Wing to miss her. At her throat and in her body, aches still lay trapped but not dormant.

The cold light of pre-dawn filtered in through the cut crystal of the walls. It shaded from crimson through scarlet to a static flesh and as it so often did it reminded Irona of blood. Trying to shake off the ghosts of nightmare she knocked and went into Arnikon's room.

He wasn't there.

Irona threw open the shutters to her private garden. A sad fog crept into her rooms, dull with the light of the coming day. Somewhere beyond the fog the morning stars were paling but she couldn't see them. Hidden in the mist, lizardoptera sang their swan-song, an impossibly high counterpoint to the busy life beyond the walls.

Welcoming the chill of reality, Irona threw on the first robe that came to hand, one of the garish things Twiss had chosen for her long ago, at their first banquet. It still fitted. *What was it he said? That it brought a beautiful colour to my cheeks? And I loved him for saying it, for making me feel pretty. Did he mean I was pale and boring even then?*

No, take the honey and leave the vinegar. He did love me once. Probably still does in his own little way.

Her bare feet curled to find a grip on the damp marble. Under her toes, something crunched.

A sheet of plastic with a machine access code.

Emotionally naked, she drew her robe tighter and fumbled her way into the computer. At the same time thought, *I could try that with Gundmila's computer. Find out what's at each address. Find out if she knew anything about what's happening on Earth. Where the next threat is coming from.*

The message appeared on the screen. 'When liquid dark greets light under the shadow of the volcano.'

There's only one man who would send me a message like that. Does it mean what I think it does?

Outside, the sky was grey and empty. The voices of Kifl were deadened, remote. They had nothing to do with her now. Sea-fret pearled on her roses; their scent still reminded her of the sherbet she had had at Carnival so long ago, before her mother had been translated and abandoned her.

At the bottom of the shallow flight of steps, a skinny figure hunched against the cold. Regen. He sat close to one of the great stone bears. Smiling faintly, Irona went to him.

As she approached, he started to spring to his feet, still defensive. She waved him back and sank down beside him, knees almost up to her chin. She put her arms around her legs, hugging herself, and her arms quivered into goose-bumps.

'I don't like the autumn,' he said, his words almost as rapid now as they had been when she had first met him in the tunnels below Camelford. 'It always made me feel bad, something dying, another year gone. A part of my life dying. Entirely.'

She shook her head; she saw that the dew had beaded her hair with crystal drops. The dark blond-brown curls seemed to be trembling; she found she was rocking slightly back and forth and the motion was a comfort to her. 'No, Regen, do you know what autumn always made me think? That I could turn a corner I turned every day and normality would vanish. I'd step through a wall of cloud into an enchanted world where nobody could get at me, and I'd be happy. Somewhere inside me I still think that.'

'So are you going to meet him then or what?'

'Who?'

'I saw him come. He nodded to me when he passed.'

Irona hadn't made the connection. 'What do you think I should do?'

'It ain't up to me, Ro. It ain't my life. But I always say a person does what he wants to do. Or she. Entirely.'

'You still say that, don't you?'

Regen hunched lower as though ducking a blow. 'What? What do I still say?'

'Entirely.'

He didn't know what she was talking about. His mind circled to its obsession. 'I'm not mad, Ro, honest I'm not. But someone keeps putting things in my head and I find them there.'

'You're right, Regen. They do. And they put things in my head, and Twiss's, and we none of us know what we're going to think next.'

His knobbly face looked at hers: brown eyes, brown cheeks, brown eyebrows silvered with dew. He looked like some piskie of ancient legend that Twiss used to tell Arnikon about, from before the Sky. 'You mean that, Ro? You ain't just saying that?' Regen sounded pathetic; she hated to hear it.

'No, I'm not just saying that. I wouldn't patronise you. Have I ever?'

He thought about it. She could see the thoughts racing shadows across his face, contracting his pupils so that he was wide-eyed as a deer in the Park. Or a stallion. 'No, you never have. It's the electric, ain't it, Ro? I always said it was the electric, didn't I?'

No, she thought, *you never did. You just worried about it so much you thought naturally everybody else knew too. And I did, Regen, I did.*

But Regenerator wasn't inside her head. He went on, unknowing, 'Made me feel alive. Now it just makes me feel tired.'

'Any time you want, Regen, I'll drive you out into the country. Rainshadow Valley.'

'Ain't far enough now. It's that Tang, ain't it? The dunes.'

'It was Tang. Now I think it's Twiss. But what do I know? Even when it rains I think it's Twiss, like I used to think it was the Matriarch.' She shook herself, strove to be cheerful. 'The dunes it is. When do you want to go?'

'Dunno. Soon. When are you going to see him?'

She said dreamily, 'At sunrise. But there isn't one today, is there?'

'There's always one somewhere. If we was up in space we'd look down at Harith and there'd be this bright golden crescent of dawn always moving across somewhere.'

Irona kissed him. His fingers stole to the place on his cheek, the nails so flat and broad they flattened the ends of his fingers. And while he wondered, she stood and walked away.

In the shadow of the volcano, he'd said. Down where the sands weren't pale with the broken moons of shells, but black and primitive. *Like Harith. Like us.*

Only fog moved, though, now dense, now delicate as one of Jai's veils. It drifted in formless patterns, flattening the boom of the surf. Later it would be bright, like one of Regen's dawns, once the sun burned off the grey vapour. But for now there was only the exhalation of autumn and the poignant cries of the lizardoptera who would fly out to sea until they died.

And the mist hid the volcano, made ghostly memories of the Moon Mountains, anulled the sun. The wet sand drank her footsteps as though they had never been.

He's not coming. He only said it to mock me.

Irona tried to have faith in herself as she walked to where the basalt rocks should be, but there was only the gunmetal moistness of the air.

He's not coming. I was a fool.

Now she could see the hoary splash of the waves that crashed in thunder on the rocks. She waited and tried not to feel stupid.

He's not coming.

Salt water clung to her eyelashes. At last she turned back, hoping she could make it into Tingalit before anyone saw her, but the sky was pale as oyster now and it wouldn't be just the marketeers who were up.

If nothing else I had a morning sparked with hope.

She saw a lizardoptera fall exhausted to the sea, the golden flame of its life extinguished in the dark, creamed waters.

Others lay crunching under her feet, so many of them she couldn't step between their broken bodies, their drowned wings feathering in the wind from the surf. Their belly-razors were sodden, pulping to slime between her toes.

Leaving the water's edge she held her head high. A stronger wind gusted, hobbling her scarlet silk around her legs. She saw a fishing-boat bobbing at anchor, one last lizardoptera clinging to it with golden claws, its eyes a memory of the ruby fire they had held, and its poignant trill of defiance straightened her back.

Then a wraith of fog hardened, vanished, solidified once more.

Twiss! The shame of her readiness for betrayal cut like acid on iron.

But the shadow was taller than Twiss, more slender. Arnikon. No words came to her lips and she waited for her nemesis.

From a thousand parsecs away Tang said, 'Irona?'

She couldn't believe that he sounded hesitant, unsure.

He came to her, stopped paces away as though there were an unseen barrier between them. His face was as he had changed it, the cheeks rounded by inserts of lipids, the moustache gone. The irises of his eyes were dyed to a colour so blue it was almost violet. But his hands were still the same, fingers slim and nervous, knuckles too big, and his essence was still Tang.

He peered through a scarf of mist that was opal in the growing light. 'Irona? Is that you?'

She wanted to shout, 'Of course it is.' But as she had done for so long she waited, keeping her self tight-furled inside her. If she let words out they would break down the barriers and her soul would flood out. She would give herself away and then she would have nothing left. Irona contented herself with a nod.

He said, 'I thought you weren't coming. I've been here for hours,' and she dared not believe it. She couldn't speak.

Tang came a step closer, turning to walk beside her. There were hints of colour now, the waves dreaming of turquoise, mica sparkling like diamonds in the sand as the mists whitened, thinned. Their steps matched. Something vibrated between them.

Her tongue said, 'I can't betray him.'

'I know. But you're more like me than you think. You'd do anything to hold this place together, and you don't know when the threat will come. But it will come, Irona. It could be five years, or ten, or tomorrow, but another ship will come and what will she demand of you then?'

She. Her mother – Bernardina.

Irona couldn't answer.

'Irona' – she had always loved the sound of her name the way he said it – 'you know you have to pay for everything in this life.' The words sang through her. Like a resonant frequency striking glass they shivered her being apart and recognition was the gravity that held her atoms in one orbit. She was not the only one.

He walked at her side and the electricity of his closeness reached some hidden recess inside her. 'But you don't have to pay and pay and get nothing back. You don't deserve that.'

'I can't betray him, Arias.' It was the first time she had ever called him by his given name – to his face. 'He might need Jai's body but he needs me to think for him. And he's all that holds Harith together. If he crumbles, the whole place will fall apart.'

'I know that. You and I, we've been fencing for years, but the people won't follow me. I can out-think him and put ideas in his head the same as you can, but I can't out-charisma him. Kifl needs him. And he needs you.'

She stopped, looking down at her feet. Soft sand clung to her insteps, pale and golden. 'What then?' Irona hardly recognised her own voice.

'So long as Harith wins it doesn't matter that I lose.'

A scent of him, musk and citrus, surrounded her. Irona whispered, 'So?'

'So I can't ask you to live with me and be my love.'

'Do you want to?' Her question trembled and she was glad that the salt wind whipped her hair over to cover the heat in her face.

'Don't you know I want to?'

She shook her head. Only fear of her cowardice pushed the words past the barriers in her psyche. 'If I ask you something, how do I know you'll tell me the truth? Win or lose?'

His touch delicate, he cupped her chin to make her look at him. His eyes were open, blue on blue. 'Because you know me, Irona.'

She laughed in gentle bitterness, shook her head again. 'I do know you, and that's why I ask. Do you want me for me or because you want to be the power behind the throne?'

'I want you for you. Your wit, your humour, your companionship, your strength. And yes, I want to feel your body. I look at you sometimes in Synod and I can't think of what you're saying. I only know that I want to touch your skin, hold you against me. I want to make love to you and I'm gambling everything I am on the fact that you want to have me too. I know you'd be as generous of yourself in bed as you are out of it. Don't you think I haven't dreamed of that? Because I have, Irona, I have.'

A silence grew between them and spindrift fountained from the iridescent sea.

'I'm not asking for it all, Irona. A few hours when you can spare the time. I don't want to take your life from you, or your honesty. I'll take what you can give me and make do with that. The rest belongs to Harith.'

Her gaze was fastened on his lips but she dragged it up to search for truth in his face. 'And the rest of the time?'

'And the rest of the time I'll pay. And you'll pay. But it'll be worth it. Trust me, Irona. I don't want to hurt you any more than you have been already. I'll fill the emptiness inside you. I'll give you something back for what you've paid so long. After all, hasn't he done it to you?'

Tenderly, Tang's hand slid to the nape of her neck, cradling her head.

Oh yes, I'll pay, she thought. *I'll pay because I might never know if he's lying. He's a statesman, isn't he?*

But sunlight lanced from the crest of the autumn-flamed mountains and gilded the lizardoptera as they sang to their death in the sapphire sea. Who knew what dangers lay like reefs in the future? What cause of war might be burning through the cosmos above?

Irona kissed him.

And the crown of snow on the volcano glittered in a white eternity against the aching blue of the sky.